UNDERCOVER
SAINT

UNDERCOVER
SAINT

a novel

FRANK
HOLDAWAY

Covenant Communications, Inc.

Cover image: *Nightwalk* © GerMan101, courtesy of iStockphoto.com.

Cover design copyright © 2012 by Covenant Communications, Inc.

Published by Covenant Communications, Inc.
American Fork, Utah

Printed in the United States of America
First Printing: September 2012

18 17 16 15 14 13 12 10 9 8 7 6 5 4 3 2 1

ISBN-13: 978-1-62108-044-2

To Sue, Shauna, and Cory,
who make it all worthwhile

CHAPTER 1

The Girl with the Dark Brown Eyes

SHE SPOTTED ME FROM THE second I stepped through the cabin door of the airplane. I chided myself inwardly. Agency protocol dictated that I should have been one of the first people on the plane. Instead I was among the last. This was in part due to so many parents on this particular flight traveling with small children and taking advantage of a preboarding invitation. But mostly it was due to my own stubbornness and stupidity. I didn't want to be on this mission. I wanted to be back home celebrating my birthday with friends. When the courier came to the door, I'd resisted. I'd arrived at the airport late, and now here I was. On the mission less than five minutes, and already my cover appeared to be blown.

As I moved down the aisle I felt like a deer in the sights of a hunting rifle. Her eyes locked on me and would not let go. They were the largest, darkest, most penetrating eyes I had ever beheld, and I knew immediately that I was way out of my league. She had chosen her location well. The seat that matched my ticket number was one row directly behind her—which had allowed her to board first. Had I boarded first, she might not have even noticed me. I could have hidden behind a book or a paper and pulled my ball cap over my eyes to sleep. Too late for that now. I thought about dipping into another empty seat, but the flight was mostly full and there was still a line of people behind me. Her eyes continued to draw me in like a tractor beam to the mother ship, and there was nowhere to go but toward them. As I drew closer, I saw the object she had partially concealed with her hand and knew that I was in real trouble.

I tried to act like there was no danger. I made my way to my seat, threw my carry-on into the overhead bin, sat down, and began to fiddle with the books in my laptop backpack. I could hear shuffling from the seat in front of me and, without looking, I could feel the eyes peering at me over the seat back. Out of my peripheral vision I could see the hand holding the object rise and come level with my forehead. I continued to stare down intently into my bag.

"It won't work," said a voice coming from ahead and to the right. "You can't ignore her. She marked you from the time you walked through the door."

Reluctantly, I looked up. The brown eyes were still staring at me. They were large, beautiful, and completely enchanting. They were also determined. The object was still pointed at my head. Somewhere close by, a baby began to cry, then another.

"Excuse me," said the same voice from before. "Her name is Megan, and she's three. It's time for me to breastfeed the twins, and that's an almost impossible task at home, let alone on an airplane." The dark purple crayon continued to point at my forehead. "She just needs someone to sit with her and color. Do you think you could help us out, Mr. . . . uh . . . I'm sorry. I didn't get your name." A second set of eyes now turned and peered at me through the gap in the seats.

"Manson," I said. "Charles Manson." I held out my hand and put on my best psychotic grin. If this mother were cautious, maybe she would look elsewhere for help. I wasn't trying to be rude, but I had important work to do. I hadn't yet had a chance to go through my briefing packet, and I needed to be ready when I hit the ground in Utah. Surely there was someone else who could do a much better job of helping little Megan than I could.

"Nice try," she said, lifting Megan over the seat rather than taking my outstretched hand. "But I'm the Salt Lake County prosecutor. I deal with lowlifes every day. Sorry to disappoint you, sir, but you are no Charles Manson." Megan settled herself in my lap and opened her coloring book. "I don't mean to be presumptuous, but my two older boys are already being guarded by the people in the row in front of me, and if I don't get some milk into these babies soon, we might be in for a four-hour scream fest." The crying was growing louder.

"Megan's father is a stay-at-home dad, and she frankly does a lot better with men than she does with women—me included. Megan, say hello to Charlie; he's going to color with you until we get home."

Megan opened her coloring book, snuggled against my shoulder, and handed me a pink crayon. "Princess," she said pointing to her book. "Color."

I thought I had better obey.

"You're lucky you didn't get the boys," the mother said, throwing a blanket over her shoulder and quieting one of the hungry twins. "Megan will color for a while and get sleepy. At which point I will take her back. The boys will be lucky if they aren't in the custody of the air marshall before the flight is over." She paused as she adjusted the other twin under the blanket and then mumbled, "Although a couple of hours in handcuffs would probably do them some good."

"How many kids do you have?" I asked through a mouthful of brown hair that smelled like green-apple Jolly Ranchers.

"Five," she said over sucking noises that I was trying very hard to ignore. "And I know what you're probably thinking: *What is it about these Mormon women who think they all need ten kids to fulfill their measure of creation?* Just so you know up front, that doesn't describe me."

"But I wasn't—" I began before she interrupted again.

"When I married Ben, we made a deal. I wanted a career, and he wanted kids. He told me that all I needed to take care of was the birthing and he would do the rest. So far he's kept up his end of the bargain, and I've been pretty good about pumping them out. And I must admit, the most sympathetic juries I've ever faced are when I'm eight months pregnant and in a serious waddle. Nobody wants to mess with a pregnant woman."

"I don't think I'd want to mess with you, pregnant or not."

"Sorry if I've been a little abrupt," she said. "After a week chasing kids at my parents' house, I'm at the end of my rope. I really do appreciate the help. By the way, I'm Missy Brentwood. You've already got the core of my life story. I'd put out a hand, but they're both occupied right now."

"No problem," I said. "I'm Matthew Knight." My hands were also busy adjusting the tray table so Megan had something solid to rest her book on.

"Not Charles Manson?" Missy Brentwood said. "What a shock."

"Charlie," said Megan, scolding her mother.

"Sorry, Charlie, but I think the name is going to stick."

"I'm curious," I said. "Aren't you worried about handing your daughter off to a stranger that you've barely met? I might not be Charles Manson, but I could still be a creep."

"If there is one thing that I've learned from years of working with creeps," Missy Brentwood said, "it's that you can't hide who you are. Sooner or later the creepiness will slip out and you'll be exposed. For me, it usually takes three or four hours of questioning to make an authoritative call. But Megan seems to have an instantaneous filter built in. I've actually shown her pictures of people I've prosecuted and asked her to point out the good guys versus the bad guys. She's never made a bad call. If you were a creep she wouldn't have chosen you."

"So, you trust a three-year-old's intuition?"

"Not completely," Missy said. "That's why we're about to begin the interrogation. So pony up. Let's hear about Matthew Knight."

Once again I had made a mistake. I had started to relax and let my guard down. On any undercover assignment constant vigilance was a necessity.

Maintaining a cover story required a lot of effort—which was why it was always best to stick as close to the truth as possible. I agreed with what Missy said about not being able to hide who you are. The more intricate your cover story, the more likely you are to blow it. Falsehood is just too hard to sustain. Sooner or later you will slip and your real self will come out. In my business, if you're trying to be someone you're not, you won't last very long.

I decided to face the interrogation head on. "Okay," I said, "I confess. I'm a secret agent for the United States government, and I'm on a mission to save the world." I wasn't really sure yet what my mission was, but I was pretty sure it had something to do with stopping terrorists. It's what I did.

"Right," said Missy. "We've already established that you're a smart aleck. I'm really looking for some more basic information like where you're from and why you're traveling to Salt Lake City—other than to save the world, that is."

I hesitated with my answer, and she forged right ahead like a trial lawyer—which made a lot of sense because she *was* a trial lawyer.

"C'mon, Knight, these are basic questions. They shouldn't be that hard."

"Sorry," I said. "When someone asks me where I'm from, I really don't know how to answer. I was born in California, but don't remember it much. My mother didn't like to stay in one place for very long. When she died I went to live with my grandparents in Iowa. As soon as I turned eighteen, I got out of there as fast as I could. Since then I've lived in New York, Boston, Miami, and for a while in London. I'm not sure I know what I want to do with my life so I've been a perennial student. I'm going to the University of Utah for a semester to work on my master's thesis."

"Have you ever been to Utah before?"

I hesitated and thought about lying. "Once," I said carefully and truthfully. "As a little boy. It wasn't a good time for me."

She must have heard the echo of a chill in my voice and moved away from exploring my childhood.

"So why come to Utah to work on your thesis? Surely there are lots of universities you could have chosen."

Good question. *Why was I being sent to Utah?*

"Not really my choice," I said, once again opting to stick mostly to the truth. "I was actually 'assigned' to go to Utah by my thesis adviser. He's got some connections at the University of Utah and thought some of the historical accounts of the early Mormon settlers would be a nice complement to my studies."

"And what exactly are you studying?"

"Social psychology. My thesis explores the social context that leads seemingly peaceful people to commit violent acts." I actually did have a pretty solid cover story, and I was glad I had at least taken the time to glance through my briefing documents on the way to the airport.

Missy was quiet for a moment then said, "So you're studying the Mountain Meadows Massacre."

She *was* perceptive. "How did you know?"

"It's about the only incident I can think of that fits with your thesis. Are you going to take the Mormon or the anti position?"

Since I really didn't know how to answer this question, I said, "I'm not sure what you mean."

"The Mountain Meadows Massacre is a lightning rod. Frankly, I cringe every time the subject is brought up in the press. It's one of the saddest events in Mormon history, but any discussion about it seems to have a polarizing effect—the apologists trying to justify why it happened and the anti-Mormon groups looking for any excuse to point the finger of blame. I was just wondering what side you were on."

"I guess if those are my choices, then I'm not on either side," I said. "I'm just working on a thesis that looks at these types of events and tries to explain how they could happen—basically good people turning to violence. It's a more common phenomenon than you'd think."

"So what's your answer? Why do seemingly good people commit violent acts?"

I was more prepared to answer this question than my short perusal of my briefing papers would suggest. Actually, I had been using the grad student cover for several missions, and the heart of my thesis had remained the same. After all, I was in the business of studying terrorists, and the more I came to understand their motivations, the better I was at my job.

"I don't have it all worked out yet," I said. "But at the heart I think it's pretty simple. It starts with a high dose of fear, which leads to creating an external evil villain we must destroy before it destroys us. Mix this with a few leaders that are strong in rhetoric and low in compassion, and you get some pretty horrible stuff."

Missy seemed to think on this for a while. "I guess what you say makes sense with groups," she said. "But I work mainly with individuals. People who could be—who should be—decent but end up committing terrible crimes. I don't think your explanation necessarily fits for them."

"So what's your theory?" I asked, relieved not to be the one answering questions for a few seconds.

Missy didn't take long to answer. "Drugs and addictions are the most obvious culprits," she said. "Good people who are addicted can do all sorts of bad stuff. But at a deeper level I think it's something more. When a lowlife enters my courtroom, I can't help but think that 99 percent of the time they could have turned out differently if they'd had a good mother or father to teach them right from wrong."

"It must feel good taking the bad guys off the streets," I said.

I saw her shrug in the seat in front of me. "Sometimes," she said. "But in some ways it is just unbelievably sad." She began to say more and then caught herself. "I believe I'm the one conducting this interrogation, though, Mr. Knight."

"You can call me Charlie."

"Okay, Matthew," she said, once again taking control of the conversation. "You said you'd been to Utah before. You don't happen to be a Mormon, do you?"

I started to say "no" and then caught myself. "Actually," I said, "I'm not really sure."

"How can you not be sure? Being a member of a church is like being pregnant—you either are or you're not. And I can tell you from experience that when I'm pregnant, I know it. I can also tell you with about as much surety that I am a member of the Mormon Church. It really isn't that complicated. Are you or aren't you?"

"I guess I'm not sure how it all works," I said. "My mother and I were baptized into the LDS Church when I was eight. Shortly after that, she passed away and I went to live with my grandparents, who weren't too thrilled with our choice of religion. I probably went to church a total of five or six times. My grandparents were adamant that I was definitely *not* a Mormon. So you tell me, Missy Brentwood, am I pregnant or not?"

"Did you have your name officially removed from the records of the Church?"

"Not that I know of."

"Then, you, my friend, are definitely pregnant. I'm surprised your records haven't caught up with you in your travels. Mormons are usually pretty good at tracking down their lost sheep."

"Stop talking," said Megan. "Color!" She handed me a red crayon.

Missy sighed. "I guess you pass the interrogation. If I were you I would listen to the little lady and stop talking."

For the next hour I tried to fill in the lines and pondered what Missy had said. *You can't hide who you are.* It seemed like a simple statement of truth. In fact, it was one of the basic principles that made me successful in my job. Hang around the bad guys long enough, and they will eventually reveal themselves. But I wasn't thinking about the bad guys now. I was thinking about myself. Who was I really? A man without a mother, without a father, and without a real place to call home. All I had were a few close friends with whom I had planned on spending my birthday when this assignment had come along and messed everything up. A few friends and a driving sense of purpose deep in my gut that I really had no way to explain: I wanted—I needed—to make the world a safer place. It was why I did what I did. Above all else, that was who I was. And being sent to the heart of the Rocky Mountains felt like moving away from my purpose, not toward it.

There was something else in my gut. It was three-year-old Megan Brentwood. She had finished a juice box, closed her coloring book, and nestled her head against my chest. I could feel her little frame become heavier as her breathing slowed and she seemed to melt into my heart.

Maybe I was wrong about this job. Maybe there was real danger in Salt Lake City and my services were needed. The mystical force that drove my actions suddenly seemed to crystalize. My motivations had just received a face. It was the face of a little girl with dark brown hair and fathomless eyes.

I found myself doing something I hadn't done in a long, long time.

I said a silent prayer to God that Megan Brentwood would be safe.

CHAPTER 2
Zack the Hammer

THE TAXI DROPPED ME AT a used car lot just east of the airport. A lanky man with rolled-up sleeves, a spindly mustache, and sunglasses walked quickly out of the glass lobby to meet me.

"What would it take to get you into a car today?" he said, not realizing he had perhaps just run into the easiest sale of his life.

"I'm coming to town as a student for about six months," I said. "I need something cheap to get me around."

"I've got some great deals on SUVs," he said. "If you want to get up into the mountains, that's the way to go."

I looked toward the mountains. They did indeed look impressive, and I really wouldn't have minded doing some exploring, but that's not why I was here.

"I was thinking something with a little better gas mileage," I said. "Maybe a compact or midsized Toyota or Honda."

"Sure," he said. "With gas prices the way they are, I can't blame you."

"How much for that one over there?" I said, pointing to an older light blue Toyota Camry with a seeming case of rust acne on the hood. "I really don't want to spend very much."

He grimaced, and his mustache tipped down like a teeter-totter. "Not much to look at," he said and then hurriedly added, "but I can tell you that it's been thoroughly checked out and that the engine is sound."

He was lying, and I knew it. This particular light-blue-with-rust little number had been traded in this morning prior to my arrival. The dealership wouldn't have had time to check it out. I wasn't sure why Mr. Seesaw-stache felt it necessary to lie. I guessed it had something to do with what Missy Brentwood said about not being able to hide who you were. I was pretty much convinced this guy was born to be a used-car salesman. Every word he spoke and every movement he made reeked of it.

Despite his dishonesty, I was confident this would be a good buy. The engine would be sound, not because of what the salesman said but because I knew that our boys did good work. They were also pretty good with disguise. When they wanted a car to look and sound like one owned by a starving student, they covered all their bases. I could see the ripped upholstery through the window. And I was almost sure there would be an odor. *Thanks a lot, guys.*

"Can I start it up?" I said. His mouth twitched.

"Sure," he said. "The keys are inside."

On ignition, a dark blue cloud of smoke blew out of the exhaust and floated in the air.

"Hmm," I said, craning my head out the window and looking back at it. "It looks like it burns some oil."

"I can make you a swingin' deal," the salesman said.

And he did not lie.

* * *

I drove east toward the mountains and the University of Utah, reviewing the instructions I had been given. Other than the documents about my cover, I hadn't really been briefed yet. This wasn't exactly according to protocol. When they yanked me from my birthday celebration, I was told the mission was urgent and that I had to leave right away. In the envelope I'd been handed was the name of the used car lot, the make and model of the car I was to look for, a few thousand dollars in cash, a brief cover story, and directions to an office where I would receive more instructions.

Maybe they thought if they caught me by surprise, it would be harder for me to say no. They were wrong. It took me less than half a second to refuse the invitation when they knocked on my best friend Robbie's door and told me there was a car waiting outside. I slammed the door and went back to finish my birthday dinner. It was only after some coaxing from Robbie—also an agent—that I was saved from disciplinary action. He convinced the waiting agents that he would get me to the airport in time for my plane—if they allowed me to stay and finish dinner. I grudgingly agreed to the compromise—temporarily. What they didn't realize was that I had no problem getting right back on a plane if this mission ended up being what I thought it might.

I was hungry, but I didn't stop. I wanted to get to the briefing and get it over with. I could be on a plane back to Washington this evening if I was lucky. I had some unfinished business to attend to—there was probably still some birthday cake left.

I was sure the person doing the briefing would outrank me, but I was determined to be the aggressor in the interview and quickly get to the heart of the matter. It's what I was good at—digging for the truth. It was ironic that sometimes it was easier to get the truth from lowlifes and terrorists than it was from the people that I worked for.

I looked at the sheet of paper lying on the passenger seat next to me. There was an address and a description. The address seemed pretty straightforward since the streets of Salt Lake were organized in a grid system. But the description was curious. *Tenth Ward Chapel Bishop's Office.* I had only a vague notion of chapels and bishops, but this sounded a lot like I would be meeting in a church. I *seemed* to remember something about "wards" from my brief stint as an eight-year-old Mormon—although, if prosecutor Missy Brentwood was correct, my affiliation with Utah's dominant religion had never really ended.

I slowed as I got close and pulled off to the side of the road, puzzled. I was definitely in the right vicinity, but I had a problem—there was not one but two church buildings on the block. Both of them looked nearly identical in design, although one was older with red brick and the other was newer and a light sand color. Both of them had signs that said *The Church of Jesus Christ of Latter-day Saints*, but there was no other indication of building number or ward designation that I could discern. I was also puzzled as to why two large church buildings of the same denomination would be located so close to each other.

One parking lot was empty, and the other held a beat-up minivan with a dent in the door. If you believed what you saw on television, all government agents drove around in brand-new black SUVs with tinted windows and an arsenal of weapons in the trunk. Knowing what I knew about my agency, I was guessing the minivan belonged to my contact. I pulled up next to it, walked up to the outside door of the building, wondered if I should ring the buzzer high on the wall, decided against it, and walked into an air-conditioned hallway. Two doors ahead on my right, a sign said *Bishop's Office*. I knocked and the door opened.

"Tenth Ward bishop's office?" I asked the man who stood smiling at me.

"No, no," he said laughing. "That would be Bishop Shepherd—he's in the other building. Is he expecting you?"

I looked at my watch. "I guess I'm about twenty minutes early," I said. "I'll go over there and wait."

"Are you one of the new villagers?" he asked.

Since I didn't quite know how to respond to this question, I said, "I'm not sure yet."

"Ah," he said. "The tenant screening interview. Just remember that even though Bishop Shepherd may look somewhat . . . ah . . . imposing, he's really nothing more than a big teddy bear." He chuckled to himself. Apparently this was funny.

I left him laughing, drove about a hundred yards to the building next door, and got out of my car. As I did, a black Ford Explorer with tinted windows pulled up beside me. So much for my powers of deduction.

A man stepped out of the vehicle and looked at me through mirrored sunglasses. He wore a white short-sleeved shirt and a tie. His skin color was nearly as black as his vehicle, and I guessed he stood about six-foot-five. When he moved toward me I felt like I was being stalked by a large cat. He didn't look like a teddy bear.

He stuck out his hand, and the cords in his forearms defined themselves as he crushed my knuckles in his grip.

"Mr. Knight," he said. "Good to see you again."

I peered harder at the man's features and my whole body tensed. If not for the booming voice, I might not have recognized him. The last time I had seen this man he'd weighed more than four hundred pounds. And the last time I had seen him, I'd been doing my best to break through his defenses and kill him. For more than eighteen months, my sole purpose in life had been to find a way to end his life.

"Are you all right, Mr. Knight? You look like you've seen a ghost." He still held my hand in his grip.

"I didn't recognize you without your body armor," I said, extracting my hand and unconsciously scanning his body for vulnerable targets. "I thought you retired."

"I did," he said. "Let's go into my office and talk about it."

The name plate on his office door said *Bishop Shepherd*. At Quantico, we called him "Colonel Shepherd" to his face and "Zack the Hammer" behind his back. His job was to teach us how to quickly dispatch a physical threat by rendering the attacker defenseless. In other words, he taught us to maim and to kill.

He wore a unique set of body armor with beeping sensors placed above key nervous-system targets. When we hit a target, we received a point. Gain enough points consistently, and we graduated. The problem was, to hit the targets we had to go through Zack, and though he never literally tried to kill us, he was not above inflicting significant pain. And he used his tremendous bulk to his advantage.

We moved into his office, and he asked me to be seated. On the wall behind him hung a picture of Christ. It was one of those Uncle Sam–type pictures where the eyes seemed to follow you no matter where you were in the room. For some reason this made me uncomfortable. I decided to focus on Bishop Zachary Shepherd. He took off his sunglasses, revealing eyes that were just as piercing. I looked around the room.

On the adjoining wall there was a large whiteboard with what looked like a building diagram stenciled on it. Magnetic names on small square tags were attached to the face. The other wall held another painting, this one of a young boy in a grove of trees, blinded by the light of two heavenly beings.

Joseph Smith . . . I thought.

I hadn't forgotten everything I learned when I was eight. Just most things.

"This is some cover," I said, sweeping my eyes around the office.

"It's not a cover," he said. "I am retired, and I am the bishop of the Salt Lake LDS Tenth Ward. I used my retirement funds to finance an apartment complex next door called the Village. You'll be staying there if you decide to remain on this assignment. I make a fine living and am very content being a businessman and serving in my church. I've agreed to be involved in this case on a temporary basis because I have a personal interest."

"That explains you," I said. "But it doesn't explain why I'm here."

"Why do you think you're here, Mr. Knight?"

That was a good question. After several successful missions, I'd earned a place at the top of the line. I'd been given my choice of assignments, and they'd been those of the most strategic importance. Until now. I'd been given no choice, and Salt Lake City wasn't exactly a strategic target for terrorists.

"Well?" Zack said, his fingers tapping on his desk. He had never been a patient instructor.

"I think I liked the other bishop better," I said. "Can I put in for a transfer?"

Zack grimaced. I don't think he ever really appreciated my humor.

"To tell you the truth," I said, "I think it's a burnout assignment. I think the psychologist reported that I've been under a sustained amount of stress and that I needed a break. I think they knew that I wouldn't take a vacation, so they gave me an innocuous assignment to investigate some midlevel terrorist threat in the mountains with the real purpose of giving me some mental R & R."

"You *were* under a bit of stress in Miami."

"Nothing I couldn't handle," I said.

"Your cover was compromised, and you were placed in a basement in front of a video camera, waiting to get your head cut off."

"It wasn't that bad," I said. "The basement was carpeted. Besides, I knew the guys would be coming for me when I didn't check in."

"That's not the point," he said. "Your head could have been chopped in half and your body thrown to the gators. The Agency doesn't care, though. Do you know why they read the psychologists' reports? It's not because they're worried about you burning out. They worry that you might have flipped a switch and could go on a shooting spree. They worry that you might decide to sell government secrets to the other side or, worse, to one of the tabloids. But aside from that, they're not concerned with your level of stress. The Agency doesn't care about your mental health, Mr. Knight. They only care that you can help them stop the terrorists." He paused. "This is not a burnout assignment. This is not a leisurely vacation in the mountains. But I will make you a deal, Mr. Knight. You listen to what I have to say, and if you still think that the threat here is bogus or not up to your usual standards of 'priority,' I'll put you on a plane back to Washington myself and pay for your ticket."

I hesitated. I wanted nothing more than to get back to Washington tonight. I had plans that were important to me, and I really needed to be away from this place. Maybe there *was* a real threat here, but there were at least a dozen other threats around the country that had to be just as critical—probably more so. Bishop Shepherd may have thought he was reeling me in, but he was also leaving me an option to get off the hook.

"All right," I said. "Then why am I here?"

"You are here, Mr. Knight, because I asked for you."

"You asked for me?" I said. "The last time I saw you, you had my spine wrapped around your knee. Why would you ask for me?"

"I believe that was after you gave me a solid shot to the throat and groin," he said. "You may not have been the most physically gifted student I ever had, but you were certainly the most persistent. I asked for you because you are one of the best field agents we have," he said.

"There are dozens of good field agents," I said. "Some of them might even want this assignment."

"You're right," he said. "And I considered every one of them. But no matter how hard I tried to consider someone else, my mind kept returning to you."

"I think you've taken too many blows to the head," I said. "I guarantee you, I'm not the right person for this mission."

"Still fighting?" he said. "That's what I always liked about you, Mr. Knight. You never knew when to quit. Other men were bigger, stronger, and had better hand-to-hand combat skills, but I could always count on you to continue fighting long past the point when you should have given up."

Zack was mistaking persistence with obsession. He was right about me fighting him until I prevailed, but I had a personal reason. A monster haunted me from my past. A monster without a face. I made Zack a surrogate and reasoned that if I could beat him, I would be ready for my monster. When I finally did beat

Zack it scared me. I didn't like the way I felt. I decided I needed to stay as far away from my monster as I could—which was why I could not take this mission.

"I watched the tapes from Miami, you know," Zack said. "I could have told them they were wasting their time with you."

"The tapes?" I asked, my mouth suddenly feeling dry.

"You know. The ones that the terrorists never aired because you were unwilling to cooperate."

"Ah, those tapes," I said. "How was I?"

"As a singer, terrible. I thought your rendition of 'I Feel Good' was simply embarrassing—not only to Mr. James Brown but to the Agency and your family."

"That's better than I thought," I said.

"You accomplished what I'm sure you wanted to accomplish. There was no way they were going to let the world see you making fools out them. But although they might not have aired the tapes, they certainly could have killed you. I know I would have."

"You know me," I said. "Sometimes I just feel the need to sing." Zack really hated it when he thought he had knocked the wind out of you in a submission hold and you started to belt out a tune. I cleared my throat.

"Don't even think about it, Mr. Knight. When I was an instructor, I was under specific directions not to break any bones. Those rules don't apply now."

"Not even as my bishop?" I asked.

"You haven't accepted the assignment yet," he said. "Right now we're just two guys in a room."

"With Jesus watching," I reminded him, pointing at the painting. Just in case he got any ideas.

He shook his head. "I can't understand why they let you live so long, Mr. Knight. How *did* you survive?"

"Luckily, people noticed when I didn't show up where I was supposed to be," I said. "I don't know how they found me, but when Robbie came through the door with the cavalry, that was the happiest moment of my life."

"I understand they beat you up pretty bad."

"Nothing a month in rehab couldn't fix," I said. "In fact, I'd just gotten released and was spending a pleasant birthday evening with Robbie and Becca when a courier showed up at their apartment and interrupted us. He wasn't even going to let me finish my dinner and blow out the candles on my cake."

"That wasn't my intention," Zack said. "I understand there was a bit of a confrontation."

"I told the courier to take the orders back where they came from," I said. "He didn't accept this very well. He told me I could either come with him to the airport or go straight to a detention cell to await disciplinary review."

"So you put him on the ground," Zack said. "Does your job mean so little to you?"

"I like my job," I said. "I'm good at it. But one of the things that kept me from turning into a blubbering idiot in Miami was the image of a birthday dinner with my two best friends. It was the one thing at the time I could think of that was worth living for. I'd nearly given my life for my job and my country. I figured my country could wait for a couple of hours until I finished dinner."

"Agents have been dismissed for less."

"He made the first move," I said. "Your training kicked in."

"Not my training," Zack said.

He didn't say any more, but I knew what he meant. Zack was clear that he was not training us to fight—he was training us to kill. And the only time we could legitimately use his training was if our life was in danger.

"I'm surprised the courier didn't press charges," he said.

"You can thank Becca for that," I said. "She made a plate for the courier to take home with him and promised that Robbie would drive me to the airport for the next flight out. Becca can be very convincing when she wants to be."

"She's a beautiful girl," Zack said, eyeing me curiously. "Robbie's a lucky man."

Robbie *was* a lucky man. I could feel my ears burning, and I decided I wanted to change the subject. I really didn't want to talk with Zack about Becca. What I really wanted to do was to launch myself across the desk and stop those dark, penetrating eyes from searching out my secrets.

But I had beaten Zack before, and it hadn't solved anything. I had vowed that I would not be that person again, that I would not let my demons consume me.

Yet here I was. Back in the same city I had promised I would avoid at all costs.

Coming back here—this place of all places—and seeing Zack once again, face-to-face, felt like the opening of a long-sealed tomb. I couldn't help but feel that the demons I had locked away were pounding on the crypt, howling to be released. Nothing good could come of my being here. Of that much I was sure.

I needed to leave town, and I needed to do it fast. Unfortunately, I didn't think Zack was going to let me go—at least not until I had heard his story. So I would be a good boy. I would listen. And then I would take the return plane ticket he offered and get away from this place as fast as I could.

"So what about it?" Zack said. "Are you willing to hear me out?"

"Do I have a choice?"

"You always have a choice, Mr. Knight." I heard the words but looking at Zack's eyes, I didn't believe them.

CHAPTER 3
The Lottery

"Okay," I said, anxious to get this over with. "Let's start with why. Why me? Why now?" *And why here of all places?*

Zack seemed to be searching with his tongue behind his lips for something in his teeth. "Let's start with the 'why now,'" he said. "There has been a clear pattern of chatter emerging, indicating that a major terrorist act is being planned somewhere in the western United States and that it will rival 9/11 in its destructiveness. The majority of the chatter also indicated an attack on a major water supply. Of course, this had everyone looking at large metropolitan centers like Los Angeles, San Francisco, Seattle, or Las Vegas. And then something happened that placed the exact location as somewhere in the vicinity of Salt Lake City."

"What happened?" I asked.

Zack smiled. "We won the lottery."

"Then I guess I should congratulate you," I said. "I hope this means you will be retiring soon—again."

"Actually, it's what brought me out of retirement. And it wasn't just me who won the lottery. Lots of people did. You see, it was the Nigerian lottery."

I wondered if the headgear Zack had worn in training was defective.

"Everyone wins the Nigerian lottery," I said. "I win it at least a few times a week." I sat up in my chair. "Please tell me you're sending me on a search and destroy mission to Nigerian spammers."

"Tell me, Mr. Knight, how much attention do you pay to spam when it arrives in your e-mail inbox?"

"As much attention as it takes to hit the delete button," I said.

"That's exactly what the terrorists figured out. Most spam becomes invisible over time. People look at the title or read the first sentence and then automatically delete the message. You might say that it's a way to communicate in plain sight while remaining invisible. This, coupled with the Al Qaeda cells in Africa, makes e-mail messages from Nigeria the ideal way for terrorists to communicate without being discovered."

"So the messages are encoded?"

"Using a different code every time," Zack affirmed.

"So between the millions of recipients and the ever-changing codes, the messages are not only invisible, but impossible to translate and trace."

"Nearly impossible," he said. "Unless you catch the sender in the act with the code key in his lap."

"You caught someone?"

"A young businessman in Nigeria who appeared on our radar after he suddenly began buying things that he should not have been able to afford. Our agents burst into his new apartment just as he was composing an e-mail. With the code key in his lap, it was easy to decipher."

"What did it say?"

Zack pulled out a piece of paper and slid it across the desk. I read the words in front of me.

Peace be upon you, my friend, and the mercy of Allah and His blessings. You have infiltrated to the very heart of the infidels, and the time will soon be at hand when they shall drink to find refreshment and taste only death. Millions shall mourn, even tens of millions. With this act you will reserve a place for yourself among the mighty of our fathers. May Allah keep your heart firm until all is finished. His blessing be upon you.

"Sounds ominous," I said. "But what makes you think the attack will happen in Salt Lake City?"

"That's the best part," Zack said. "When the agent looked at the e-mail recipients list, he expected to see millions of addresses. Instead he saw only one. The perpetrator had not yet attached the spam distribution list, which would have added another six hundred thousand names." He let the information sink in.

"So we know who the message was being sent to," I said. "Good. Let's pick him up, send him to Gitmo or whatever place we're using these days, and lock him up for a few years until the danger passes."

"Not so easy, Mr. Knight. We do have the message, and we do know the e-mail address of the recipient, but we don't yet know who he is. Apparently this person was tipped off after we arrested the Nigerian, and the e-mail address has not been used since."

"Can't we track the location of the computer where the e-mail was being used?" I asked.

"Oh yes," he said. "Our agents were able to track down the computer. They even attempted to make an arrest."

"Attempted?"

"The man apparently didn't appreciate agents busting into his house in the middle of the night without warning," Zack said. "He ended up disarming the agents and bruising a few egos."

"He escaped?" I asked incredulously. I had seen our recovery teams in action. I could not imagine them being disarmed without a serious firefight.

"Not exactly," Zachary Shepherd said, smiling. "After the fight, the man made a few phone calls and turned himself in. When he told the authorities his story, they decided they had the wrong guy."

"But I thought you said the message was being sent to this man's computer."

"It was."

"Then why should we believe him? Who is this guy?"

Zack Shepherd unwound his fingers, spread out his palms, and chuckled deeply. I really hated that laugh. "You're looking at him," he said.

I was speechless. This made him chuckle even more. I looked behind him at the picture of Jesus. I swear He cracked a smile.

"I told you before that I own an apartment complex. Most of the tenants are students. As one of my amenities, I provide a computer room with a couple of machines for people to do their schoolwork and stay in touch with their families. The person with this e-mail address had sent several messages from these computers."

"So it's one of your tenants?" I asked.

"Apparently," he said. "Or one of their friends." The smile disappeared from his face, and his eyes looked pained. "The people in these apartments make up what we call an LDS single adult ward. A ward is like a family—a singles ward doubly so. I am their bishop, and they are my children. I don't much like it that one of my kids might be a terrorist."

"So you want me to become one of your tenants and discover who the terrorist is."

"Not just a tenant," he said. "A ward member. Someone who is LDS, single, and over thirty."

"But I just turned thirty yesterday."

"Congratulations. You made the cut."

"You can't tell me there aren't other single field agents over thirty who wouldn't be just as qualified for this mission. And I'll bet you even have some who are LDS and actually know something about the Church."

"I've considered others," he said. "I chose you."

"I haven't been to church since I was eight years old," I said. "I don't know anything about it. I'd stick out like a sore thumb."

"Not really," he said. "This assignment won't require you to know anything about the Church that you don't already know. Like any other undercover assignment you've taken on, you are mainly going to rely on the truth. In this case you are a novice in the Church. You've decided to revisit some of your spiritual roots. Since your studies were bringing you to Utah anyway, you wanted to join a ward, do some investigating of the Church, and find out if it might be for you."

"Is that what I've decided?"

"I don't know, Mr. Knight. Have you?" He reminded me of a cross between Missy Brentwood and Clint Eastwood. *Well, are you pregnant, punk?*

I sat in my seat and thought it over. In some ways Zack had me convinced. The threat was real—and a terrorist, or someone who knew a terrorist, was living in Zack's apartment complex. An agent like me—someone whose job it was to blend with the crowd, to get to know the people, and to spot the terrorists—was exactly the ticket in this situation. And I was confident I could get the job done—except I couldn't. There was too much history for me here. Too much danger of me getting sucked in by my past. Too much chance that my personal agenda could jump to the forefront and mess up everything. Zack really needed to find someone else. I couldn't be here. It wasn't good for me. It wasn't good for the mission.

"I'm sorry," I said. "It does sound like a serious situation, and I know you need a good agent on this case, but I still don't think I'm your guy."

Zack didn't look surprised, but he didn't look acquiescent either. He studied me for a long time and then seemed to come to a decision. "I had someone else picked out for this mission," he said. "A fine young man, nearly as talented as you, and with a lot fewer authority issues."

I started to defend myself and then thought better of it. Why help Zack prove his point?

"But for some reason, every time I started to make the call, your name came into my mind. This happened at least three times. Mr. Knight, I've learned to listen to promptings in my life. I don't know why you are the right person for this job. Frankly, I would have gone in a different direction. But I believe there is a reason for you to be here."

"And what if I still say no?" All this talk about promptings was making me a little uncomfortable. Especially coming from the guy who used to routinely use me as a punching bag.

"I believe in the concept of agency, Mr. Knight. The choice is yours. All I ask is that you give it a week before deciding."

"And if I want to leave now?"

"Then I'll have to break your neck."

He smiled. I thought he was joking, but you never knew with Zack. I appreciated that he was following his gut. I'd done the same thing many times in the field. But I questioned the source of his inspiration. I really didn't think God would send me back to this place.

I fidgeted in my seat as I mulled it over. Something else was bothering me. I started to speak a couple of times and then stopped myself.

"Spit it out, Mr. Knight."

"There's something a little strange about this situation," I said, finally. "Busting in on that guy in Nigeria just as he was sending that message was a one in a million chance. Thirty seconds sooner or later and we'd have had nothing." I cleared my throat. "And then there's the matter of the e-mail recipient's computer just happening to belong to an ex-Agency employee."

"Another million-to-one shot," he said, finishing my thought for me. "Do these coincidences trouble you?"

"I'm not troubled by coincidences. I just don't believe in them," I said. "That's how I've been trained."

"So what's your explanation for these events?" he asked, making it sound like a challenge. "If it's not coincidence, what is it?"

"I don't know," I said. "Maybe we were set up. Maybe we were supposed to find that guy in Nigeria. Maybe the terrorists knew that we would pay special attention to a threat right under the nose of Zack Shepherd and spend a lot of energy on it while the real plot was being hatched elsewhere."

"Is that what you really believe?" he asked. "It would be a pretty elaborate red herring."

"I don't know," I said. "But I still can't believe it was just a coincidence."

"Neither can I," he said. "I don't believe in coincidences either." He tapped the desk and seemed to glance behind him at the painting. "On the other hand, I do believe in miracles."

It was a nice sentiment. I was touched. I really was. I was tempted to agree with old Zack, although I also thought he was a bit touched himself. Instead I said, "Maybe you've been out of the Agency too long. Maybe you're letting your ecclesiastical duties cloud your judgment. Maybe you just can't get enough of making my life miserable."

Zack stared hard at me, and I could see the disappointment in his eyes. To be honest, I was a little disappointed that he was disappointed. Maybe we never quite get over wanting to please our teachers. Maybe I knew I didn't really believe what I was accusing him of.

He opened his drawer and pulled out a plane ticket.

"Happy birthday, Mr. Knight," he said, tossing me the ticket. "I hope you have a nice trip back to Washington."

I looked at the ticket, met his eyes, and sighed. "I'll give you a week," I said. "Maybe I can uncover something by then. After that, I'm out of here."

I looked at the ticket again. "Besides, this ticket is to Denver, not Washington. And it's already been used."

"Huh," Zack said. "Imagine that."

CHAPTER 4

Meet the Roommates

"OKAY," I SAID. "SINCE I'M giving this the old college try, tell me who your main suspects are. You are the bishop; you must have some ideas."

"I do," he said. "But I'm not going to tell you right now. I want you to get to know these people without having any preformed prejudices. Your first encounters need to be genuine, and if you know too much it may affect how you view people. We can talk about individuals later, once you've gained first impressions."

"So where do you want me to start?"

"With your roommates."

"My roommates?"

He reached into his drawer again and pulled out a sheet of paper. "Do you know what this is, Mr. Knight?" The paper had my full name on it, along with some other dates and information. "This is your Church membership record. It certifies that you are a member of The Church of Jesus Christ of Latter-day Saints. My having your record means that you are now an official member of the Salt Lake City Tenth Ward."

I looked down at my stomach. Missy Brentwood was right. I was pregnant.

"It also means that I am your bishop," he continued. "And as such I need to ask you a few questions to establish your state of worthiness. I want you to know that these questions have nothing to do with me being your boss and everything to do with me being your bishop. They may also make you a bit uncomfortable."

His eyes were already making me uncomfortable. They seemed to transform in front of me. Gone was the hammerlike "you're-going-to-have-to-go-through-me" look, and in its place was something else. It almost looked like genuine concern. I stole a quick peek at the portrait behind him. Yup. A perfect match. I began to squirm a little in my seat, wishing Zack would suddenly throw me a sucker punch and come out with his maniacal laugh.

"These are some of the questions used to establish worthiness to enter the temple," he said. "I use them with every new member of my ward to establish a spiritual baseline. Please answer with the truth and not what you think I want to hear. Based on the results, we'll set up a plan for spiritual progression. Does that sound okay to you, Brother Knight?"

Had Zack just called me *brother*? Before I could answer, he continued.

"When you joined the Church at eight years old, did you believe it was true?"

The question caught me a little off guard, and I had to think back. I remembered being embarrassed when I opened the door and realized that the two young men in white shirts and ties could see behind me to the mess that was our apartment. It was morning, and I hadn't cleaned up yet. The floor was scattered with beer cans and ashes—remnants of the evening before. My mom and her friends. There also would have been a number of partially smoked joints and maybe even some needles buried in the rubble. I remember thinking there was no way I was letting these guys into this apartment. They just looked too young and innocent. This was me at eight years old, worried about the innocence of someone more than twice my age.

My mom stumbled out of the bedroom, strung out and holding a cigarette. "Who is it?" she said, shielding her eyes from the light coming through the door. They introduced themselves, and curiously they both had the same first name. I remember watching my mother's eyes go from these two young men to me and then back again. She seemed to be thinking hard about something. Finally, she placed the cigarette down in an ashtray and said, "Let's go talk on the grass."

"I believe the Church was good for my mother," I said to Zack. "Those missionaries were the best thing that ever happened to us. She went through a lot of rehab programs, but she never really got clean until we joined the Church. So I guess you could say I believed in it—or at least what it could do for people. My mom was at the end of her rope. I don't know what would have happened if the missionaries hadn't found us that day."

"What a wonderful coincidence," he said with a slight smile. "What about now? Are you still a believer?"

I didn't have to think about this one. "I don't know. I don't really know much about the Church."

"Well, that gives us a place to start." He pulled out his drawer and handed me a book with a dark blue cover. I'd seen it before. The Book of Mormon. "Read this and then we'll talk about it."

I took the book from him. "Right now?" I asked, thumbing through the pages. "It might take a while."

"No," he said with a sigh. "Not right now. Right now we need to talk about your worthiness." I wondered if Zack was enjoying this. I knew that I wasn't.

"We have something in the Church called the Word of Wisdom," he said. "It designates certain substances as forbidden."

"I remember it," I said. "From the missionaries. No alcohol, coffee, tea, or drugs. Am I right?"

"You're right. I need to know if you have an issue with any of these."

I paused for a minute. This was getting kind of personal. "I have no issue with any of them," I said. "I enjoy them all equally."

I thought I saw a slight twitch in Zack's eyelid.

"Actually," I said, "I cleaned up enough of my mother's messes to give me a lifelong aversion to drugs, cigarettes, and alcohol. I've had a beer on occasion with friends, though, and I do enjoy Starbucks once in a while."

"Thank you for your honesty," he said. "Do you think you can stay away from the beer and coffee on this assignment?"

"Not a problem." I realized when I said it that I was already starting to crave a mocha latte. It was only a week, I reminded myself.

"What about women?" he asked. Now he was really getting personal. "We have a standard in the Church that intimate physical relations are reserved for marriage."

"Those are some pretty big words," I said.

"You know exactly what I mean, Mr. Knight. So tell me how you are doing in living up to this standard." All of a sudden I was no longer "Brother." Was it something I said? As I thought about his question, I almost had to laugh. I'd never really been comfortable in my relations with women—physical or otherwise. I had spent most of my late teens trying to avoid just this type of conversation because I didn't have to want to admit that there was nothing going on. The only woman in my life was currently untouchable, and considering my line of work it was probably just as well.

"I'm clean," I said.

"How clean?"

"Sir-Galahad-the-Chaste clean," I said, feeling my cheeks redden. "Can we change the subject?"

"Not yet," he said. "Two-thirds of my ward are women. I want you to know that I consider every one of them a daughter."

"I just told you I'm a monk," I said. "I get the point."

"I'm not talking about the physical anymore, Mr. Knight. I'm talking about their emotions. The Church preaches marriage so strongly that many of our young women who haven't wed by the age of thirty think something is wrong with them. They think they are somehow broken."

"Are they?"

He thought about this. "Yes," he said. "But no more broken than any of the rest of us. We are all broken, Mr. Knight. You. Me. Every single one of us. That's why we need a Savior."

"Okay," I said. I wasn't going to argue about me being broken. I'd figured this out a long time ago.

"You're a good-looking man," he said. "You are going to be investigating the people in this ward and will need to get to know them. Since most of them are women, this might involve some dating."

"Wait a minute," I said. "I've been on plenty of assignments, but dating has never been part of the equation."

"You are undercover in an LDS singles ward, Mr. Knight. Dating is what these people do. If you can think of another way to gain information, I'm all for it. What I don't need is to be working cleanup on broken hearts after you leave. Am I clear?"

"Crystal," I said. "But what if, just hypothetically, someone does somehow get attached?" Believe me. I was as worried about this as Bishop Zack was.

He placed a hand under his chin and tapped a finger on his cheek. "If that happens," he said, "start carrying around a Starbucks cup."

"But I thought you said that was against the rules."

"I didn't tell you to drink the coffee."

"What good would carrying around a coffee cup do?"

"There's an old joke in the Church," Zack said. "A young woman, obviously pregnant, comes to confess to her bishop. The bishop asks her, 'Well, are you going to marry this young man?' The young woman gasps in horror. 'I can't do that,' she says. 'He has a Word of Wisdom problem.'" He paused and then said, "I think the cup might do the trick."

He ended the interview with a few more questions and some brief instructions. I was to check in at my apartment, meet my roommates, and generally act like the somewhat lost newbie to the ward that I was. We would have similar interviews once a week—I hoped without all of the personal questions—and hopefully identify the terrorist before September 11, which happened to be one month from today. Terrorists loved anniversaries. If something was going to happen, this was a likely date.

I had my own timeline. I'd told Zack I would give him a week—and I would. But then I was out of here.

I stepped out the door with my marching orders and my Book of Mormon and wondered what I had just gotten myself into.

I had the directions to the Village—the apartment complex where I would be living—that just happened to be located across the road from the church building. But I needed to do something first. I drove to the nearest 7-Eleven and found a pay phone. I could have used my cell, but I was trying to hide something. The call I was about to make would not only be frowned on by Zachary Shepherd, but it could probably get me fired. I was making it anyway. It was a birthday gift to myself.

I waited as the phone on the other end rang and someone picked up.

"Hello." The voice was cheerful, as if emerging from a shared laugh. It was her voice. My heart began to beat faster.

"It's me."

She nearly said my name but then caught herself. She said something to someone in the background and then came back on the line.

"Tell me you're coming back," she said.

"I can't. Have to work."

"That's not fair," she said. "There's still more than half your cake left."

"Eat it for me," I said. "All of it."

She giggled. "I'd get sick."

"Then you'd know how I feel not being there." I must have sounded pitiful. I was definitely feeling pitiful.

"Wow," she said. "Did you just express a human emotion without making a wisecrack? That's some progress you're making. Did you meet someone?"

"Just my bishop," I said. "Who probably wouldn't be too thrilled that I'm having a private conversation with a married woman."

"Who said your conversation was private?" a male voice interrupted.

My heart skipped a beat. He was listening in on the other line. Her husband. My best friend. Robbie.

"Have you been on the line the whole time?" I asked. "What if I'd said something stupid, or romantic, or romantic *and* stupid?"

"Stupid, I would believe," he said. "But romantic—that would be a first. So I'll bail you out. Happy birthday, hotshot. We miss you and wish you were here. And one other thing." He paused. "We love you."

I tried to think of something witty to say, but nothing came. These were the two people I cared about most in the world. I'd barely spent an hour with them in months, and I wouldn't see them again until this assignment was over. I told myself that it would only be a week. In truth, I was a little choked up.

"Say it back," she said. "I want to hear you. And no jokes."

"I love you too," I said, meaning it with all my heart. "I love you both."

* * *

The Village was unlike any student apartments I had ever seen, and I had seen a lot. It was definitely new, but it had an older feel to it. The buildings were made of brick, only two stories high, and the grounds were filled with grass, trees, and small streams running throughout. People waved as if they knew me when I drove past. Beautiful women in bathing suits stopped their game of sand volleyball and rushed over to greet me. Okay, I made this last part up. But in truth, I was pretty impressed by the place. For singles housing, it had a strange feeling of permanence.

I found my building, put my laptop bag over my shoulder, and pulled my carry-on up the steps. It was time to meet my roommates. In truth, I was a little nervous. The first meeting of any suspect was always a little dicey. For some reason, terrorists were always suspicious of strangers—as if they might be undercover government agents or something. How paranoid can you be? I had to remind myself that these people might not be the terrorists at all, but Zachary had said he'd put me in this apartment for a reason.

I rang the doorbell and my car exploded. Just kidding. A thin Caucasian man with wire-rimmed glasses and a receding hairline opened the door. "He's here," he said to someone over his shoulder. Then he held out his hand. "I'm Roger Livingston," he said. "You must be Matthew Knight. Bishop Shepherd told us all about you."

Like that I'm working undercover to find out which of you is the terrorist, I wanted to say. Instead, I said, "Nice to meet you, Roger." He opened the door wider to let me in.

The living area was quite impressive. Not that it was fancy or anything; it was just, well—clean. Maybe I had spent too much time living with terrorists, but the male students I had been associated with were, shall we say, a little on the short side of sanitary. There were a couple of couches, a coffee table with some neatly stacked copies of running magazines, a fairly large aquarium with some sort of medium-sized striped fish, and no television anywhere in sight. Oh yeah, there was also an Arabic-looking guy sitting on one of the couches with headphones in his ears and a laptop open. He didn't look too thrilled to see me. A framed poster occupied the space on the wall above his head. The picture showed a pair of running shoes melting into the hot pavement on a lonely highway with desert sand on either side. The highway disappeared into a big orange sun on the horizon. Large letters spelled out "BADWATER: The baddest race on earth."

Maybe it was just me, but this seemed like a sign. I mean, here was a guy who looked like a terrorist, sitting under a poster that said *Badwater*.

How much more obvious could it get? He might as well have had a neon flashing arrow pointing at his head and a nametag stating, "Hello. My name is Osama bin Laden. I'm here to poison your water."

"Why are you here?" he asked, pulling out his earphones but not looking up from the laptop. All of a sudden the Village didn't seem quite so inviting.

As I tried to figure out what might be an appropriate answer to this question, Roger Livingston bailed me out.

"You'll have to excuse Joseph," he said. "He doesn't bother much with social niceties."

I figured I could overlook the social niceties. Of course, I would have a tougher time overlooking his wanting to kill millions of innocent people. But then, I wasn't sure of this last part yet.

"It's a simple question," Joseph said, looking up and addressing Roger. "And don't go high and mighty on me. You want to know the answer as badly as I do."

Roger shrugged. "You can't just ask it like that. He won't know what you mean. You need to give him some context."

Roger turned to me. "We had a less than stellar experience with our last roommate. He came in with a box full of video games and a determination to find a wife. When he found out that Joseph and I were not really the gaming sort, he began inviting other people over. Our apartment got the reputation as the gaming capital of the Village. So we had to get rid of him." Roger didn't look much like a hit man. He looked like a nerd. But looks could be deceiving.

I glanced from one roommate to the other. "Is he buried under the floorboards, or did you feed him to the fish?" I asked.

Roger stared at me, and Joseph actually suppressed a laugh. As he did, his face was transformed, and I had the nagging suspicion that I had seen him before.

"We merely suggested he move on when an opening appeared in another apartment," Roger explained. "He was more than happy to do so. But that didn't last long either. He's getting married next week."

"Which means there will be another apartment open if there is a better fit for you there," Joseph added. "So now that you have some context, I'll ask you again. Why are you here?"

"To play Dungeons and Dragons," I ventured.

Joseph frowned.

"To meet my future wives," I tried again.

He tried to frown more deeply, but I could see he was struggling. *Where had I seen that smile before?*

"How about to spend long quiet hours finishing up my master's thesis while seriously pondering the advantages of life in a monastery?"

"A monastery is a little extreme," Joseph said. "A library atmosphere will suffice."

"Suits me fine," I whispered in my best library tones. "I'm here to study, and I'm really not interested in finding a wife. But I do have a little problem."

They both looked at me with raised eyebrows.

"I've been given an assignment by Bishop Shepherd to meet as many people as possible, male and female." This was the truth. Zack said he would announce to everyone that since I was new to the area, he had assigned me to personally get to know each person in the complex. Despite the obvious candidate for terrorist of the year sitting in front of me, I really didn't have any clue as to where the threat was based. Quick exposure to as many suspects as possible would help me to narrow it down.

"And the bishop suggested that the normal way to get to know people in a singles ward is to go out on dates." They looked at me. "With women," I added.

"We don't have a problem if you date," said Joseph. "Especially if you date women. Just don't bring your dates to the apartment."

"I get that part," I said. "That's not my problem. My problem is that I don't want to go on dates. Frankly, I've never been very good at dating, and I really have no interest at this point in my life." Both statements were absolutely true. Considering the status of women in Islamic extremist groups, I hadn't had to deal much with the opposite sex in my undercover work—a detail that suited me just fine. Women made me nervous, and there was nothing more dangerous than a nervous undercover agent. "I was wondering if you guys might have some ideas on how to meet everyone without going through the whole dating thing."

Roger laughed.

Joseph kept with the poker face, but his body language suggested that he agreed with Roger. "I think you're going to fit right in," he said.

"How's that?" I asked.

"Roger here has *philophobia*. He is terrified of relationships and dating. He's much more at home with his nanobots and fish than with women."

"Nasty divorce," Roger explained. "I wasn't a very good husband, and I'm not really up for round two. I find plenty of emotional fulfillment in my studies—without all of the drama."

"Nanobots and fish?" I asked.

"Long story," said Roger. "It's kind of a mad scientist thing. I work with nanotechnology—constructing devices at a molecular scale. They aren't really robots, but I guess you could look at them that way. It won't be long before engineered molecules replace many of the functions performed by today's machines—but on a much smaller scale."

"Like what?" I asked.

"See those fish?" He pointed to the aquarium. "Do you notice anything about them?"

I studied the fish. "They're swimming?" I ventured after careful study.

"Exactly!" Roger exclaimed. "They are swimming. They are healthy and thriving and swimming." I was pleased to have gotten the correct answer, but there was something a little weird about Roger's enthusiasm.

"They're not robots, are they?" I asked, backing away a little bit from the aquarium—just in case.

"No," Roger said. "They're bluegills—a common freshwater fish. But it is somewhat of a miracle that they are able to swim—at least in this water. The water in the aquarium is salt water—taken directly from the Great Salt Lake. With the help of nanobots, as Joseph calls them, this veritable Dead Sea in my aquarium has been turned into a kind of freshwater eco-oasis. Just think of the possibilities."

I *was* thinking of the possibilities. Not only did I have a surly Arab as a roommate, but I was also sharing a roof with a genius who seemed to be able to manipulate the very nature of water. My list of potential terrorists was getting longer, and I had only been there about ten minutes.

Roger looked at me and bowed as if he were expecting applause.

"I should have been more careful about bringing up the nanobots," Joseph said. "Roger gets a little excited."

"What about you?" I asked Joseph. "What gets you excited?"

"Joseph is only interested in two things," Roger said. I loved how these guys answered for each other. "Getting accepted to a top-five medical school and completing an ultramarathon. In other words he is a masochist."

"Are you really going to run Badwater?" I asked, looking at the poster behind him. I knew the race—135 miles through Death Valley in the middle of the summer. One hundred and thirty degrees and uphill. Not exactly a stroll in the park. If Joseph was a terrorist, his choice of a cover was curious. Planning an attack took a lot of focus and effort. Not something you would want to squeeze in between premed studies and ultradistance training.

"Eventually," Joseph said. "First I have to qualify, which means I need to complete a qualifying race with a good enough time. I'm trying to get into the Uinta 100, but I'm on a waiting list. My six marathons don't seem to count."

"Of course," I said. "Marathons are for sissies." I wanted to tell him that I'd completed seven marathons, just to put him in his place. But it wasn't the time.

"Exactly," he said. "So you see, Roger and I don't have much use for dating. I'm afraid you are on your own."

"There are other ways to get to know people though," Roger said. "I've met almost everyone, and I haven't been on one date. There's church, family home evening groups, dances if you're into that kind of thing, and there are always people mulling about through the grounds. There are some regional single adult activities where people hike, do river trips, that type of thing. There's a six-month calendar posted in the commons area. But I haven't taken a look at it lately—Joseph and I aren't big attenders."

There it was again. Joseph smiled, or half smiled, and I could swear that I knew him from somewhere.

I didn't tell Roger that I didn't have six months. I was only planning on staying for the week. So I said to Joseph, "Do I know you from somewhere? Every time you almost smile I get this strange *déjà vu.*" Confronting him like this was a risk. Maybe I recognized him from a terrorist file and I would be blowing my cover. But I didn't think so. In all of the terrorist photos that I had looked at, I'd never seen anyone smile.

Roger laughed. "Twenty bucks," he said, holding out his hand to Joseph.

"He hasn't guessed it yet," said Joseph.

"He's close. Give us one more smile and I'm sure he'll get it."

"If he fails then I get the twenty," said Joseph.

"Deal."

Joseph's smile was more like a grimace, but it was enough.

"Hadadi?" I asked. "You're Joseph Hadadi? Abraham Hadadi's son?"

"Yes!" Roger said, pumping an arm in a seesaw motion. And I thought he got excited about the fish. "The Hadadi smile strikes again."

I was stunned. How could I have missed it? The Hadadi smile was not only world famous; it belonged to one of my all-time heroes. Abraham Hadadi had been the preeminent voice in the Muslim community for a policy of peace. His smile was known throughout the world as a symbol of optimism for a higher way—the Hadadi way. While most world leaders proclaimed self-righteously that "we don't negotiate with terrorists," Abraham Hadadi was traveling into the heart of the beast trying to convince the Islamic extremists that what they were doing was contrary to the teachings of the Koran and the religion of Islam. "We do negotiate with terrorists," he said. "We meet with them, reason with them, show them respect and love, and when we are through, they are terrorists no more." While Al-Qaeda was enlisting the disenfranchised youth of Islam in a military jihad, Hadadi proclaimed his own jihad and went to places like Egypt, Syria, Iran, and Afghanistan, holding meetings and enrolling recruits. He won the Nobel Peace

Prize for his efforts. While I was working my butt off to prevent an attack, Abraham Hadadi was laboring to remove the enmity at the root of the problem and to eliminate the cause.

It was on one of his "Jihad for Peace" trips that Abraham Hadadi was captured by terrorists. They starved and beat him for several months while publicly displaying the video footage for the world to see. The news media, in a surprising show of decency, refused to broadcast the footage of the actual beheading. But they did show the moments right before as the hooded figures hoisted Hadadi's now-frail body onto scaffolding and placed his neck across a beam of wood. As his flowing hair was pulled up so his face would meet the camera, Hadadi dealt his final blow against his enemies. His eyes were calm and his face relaxed. As the sword came down he flashed his now famous smile, which was recorded for the world to see. The Hadadi smile. *Time* magazine featured the picture on the cover with the caption, "The new face of peace." World leaders issued a statement saying that Abraham Hadadi had done more for peace in our time than any other single individual. His martyrdom caused enrollment by young Muslims in the "Jihad for Peace" to quadruple in matter of days. Some speculated that Abraham had been smiling because he anticipated this reaction to his death.

On a personal note, while I was lying in a basement in Miami dealing with my own group of terrorists, it had been the face of Abraham Hadadi that gave me hope—along with Becca's chocolate cake. In a way, he saved my life.

"Your father was a great man," I said to Joseph. What I really wanted to do was to go over and embrace him. I had heard that Abraham Hadadi had married a Mormon woman and that he had an only son named Joseph. I never imagined that I would become his roommate.

"Thank you," Joseph said in a tone that suggested he wouldn't really react favorably to an embrace. "And this is the last we will speak of my father. I refuse to be defined by anyone other than myself, and I will not be weakened by constant waves of pity." He pointed to another poster on the wall leading into the hallway. It showed a rock climber hanging onto the edge of a cliff with one hand. Italicized words stated, *Self-fulfillment begins where self-pity ends.*

"That's apartment rule number one," said Roger. "No talk about the Hadadi family."

"Okay," I said. "I can respect that." This would be a little hard since I really wanted to know more about the man I admired. "Are there any other apartment rules I should know about?"

"Don't touch the vitamins or supplements," Joseph said, pointing to a kitchen counter with several large containers. "They are for my training, and they are mine."

"He counts the vitamins every day and measures the supplements," Roger said. "I know. I tested him. He really doesn't like it when you mess with his vitamins."

"All right," I said. "No family talk, no apartment parties, and no messing with the vitamins. I think I can live with those rules. Did I miss anything?"

"That's good for now," Joseph said. "But of course we reserve the right to add more."

"Of course."

A low rumbling echoed through the apartment.

"Is that your stomach?" asked Roger.

"I think it was an earthquake," I said. "Or maybe a thunderstorm."

The sound erupted again. It was my stomach after all, and it was definitely trying to get my attention. "Is there a Wendy's or something close by?" I asked. "I think I could use some food."

Roger looked at Joseph. "Time for Section 89?"

Joseph looked at his watch. "Close enough."

"What's Section 89?" I asked.

"One of the fringe benefits of living in the Village," explained Roger. "I'm not sure if you know, but Bishop Shepherd used to work for the FBI."

"Or some other government agency," Joseph said.

"Or some other government agency," Roger repeated. "He's pretty clear about the fact that he was in the government, less so on exactly which branch."

Of course, I knew this part already. I even knew which branch, or more accurately, branch*es* that he worked in. When you're working as a covert agent for the government it's not always very clear. There are the FBI, the CIA, and the NSA. But there are also intelligence divisions in each of the branches of the military. The Army has its own, the Navy has its own, and so on. So does the State Department. On top of this you have the Department of Homeland Security and several terrorism task forces. Most agents rise up through one of the military branches but are then assigned—sometimes temporarily, sometimes permanently—to a particular group. I believe Zack came up through the Navy but was later assigned to a joint terrorism task force; ultimately, he became a trainer for agents assigned to joint terrorism task forces.

The structure of our intelligence community was one reason foreign spies had a hard time infiltrating our government. It was too hard to understand. I didn't even understand it and I worked there.

"Anyway," Roger continued, "did you know that Bishop Shepherd used to weigh more than four hundred pounds?"

Oh, I know, I wanted to say. *I've still got the aching bones and mental trauma to prove it.* Instead I raised my eyebrows as if in surprise. They taught us these advanced techniques in agent training.

"As he drafted the plans for the Village, he initially wanted to have a pizza parlor on site," Roger said. "But it never quite felt right. He was reading in the Doctrine and Covenants when—"

"Which is a book of scripture," Joseph interrupted.

Roger looked at him and then continued. "He came across section 89, which talks about the Word of Wisdom. Do you know what the Word of Wisdom is? Bishop Shepherd said that even though you were baptized as a kid, you didn't know much about the Church."

"Absolutely," I said. "No alcohol, tobacco, tea, or Starbucks." I stuck my chin out with pride. My time in the bishop's office had not gone to waste.

"That's not all," Joseph said, once again seeming to take satisfaction in correcting me. "It also gives direction on what to eat and not to eat. Basically, it says to eat lots of grains, vegetables, and fruits, and eat meat sparingly or not at all."

"Bishop Shepherd decided that rather than opening a pizza parlor he would install an eatery that followed the guidelines given in the Word of Wisdom," Roger said. "Including the part about meat. He started eating that way himself, and the pounds began to drop. When people ask him if he's a vegetarian, he adamantly denies it, saying that he is a 'worditarian,' and then he invites them to Section 89—the name of the cafeteria here—to see how Mormons were meant to eat."

"No meat, huh?" I asked, suddenly beginning to crave a nice juicy steak.

They both shook their heads.

"No pizza?"

"Sure," said Roger. "There's pizza."

"Whole-wheat crust, organic sauce, veggies, and no cheese," Joseph added.

"So *is* there a Wendy's around here?" I asked again. I'd been in dangerous situations before, but these people were starting to scare me.

"C'mon," said Joseph, closing up his laptop and getting up off the couch. "It's actually quite good."

"It's better than good," Roger said. "It's free."

CHAPTER 5
Permelia

ROGER WAS RIGHT. THE FOOD in Section 89 was better than good—and not only because it was free. I loaded up on fat-free mashed potatoes, spinach salad, and steamed broccoli. The place reminded me of some of the better buffets at hotels in Las Vegas—a mix between cafeteria style and chef stations. In place of posters of scantily clad showgirls and white tigers, there were tiles attached to the walls with quotes stenciled on them. Roger informed me that these came from the scriptural reference—section 89 of the Doctrine and Covenants—from which the café got its name. After going through the serving line I felt like I had pretty much read the whole section. I felt a sudden urge to go and find some tobacco leaves to use on bruises and sick cows. I didn't see anything in the quotes denouncing Dr. Pepper, so I was a little disappointed when we got to the beverage station. All that was offered were fresh juices and water.

"Mormons don't drink soft drinks?" I asked.

Roger laughed. "Depends on who you ask," he said. "If you walked around town, you'd think that drinking Diet Coke was a commandment. But Bishop Shepherd takes seriously the counsel not to partake of addictive substances, and that includes caffeine."

"What about a caffeine-free Dr. Pepper?" I asked.

"Not in Section 89," Joseph said. "Nothing but nutrition here. No empty calories. No nutritionally bankrupt fake foods or drinks. Which suits me just fine."

"Yeah, but your idea of fun is running one hundred miles through Death Valley," I said. "I'm not sure we share the same tastes."

"I'm sure we don't," Joseph replied, his nose tilting slightly in the air.

I was trying to like my new roommate, but he wasn't making it particularly easy.

"What about an athlete needing to load up on lean meats and protein?" I asked. "Aren't you afraid you're going to end up looking like an Ethiopian?"

"Ethiopians are some of the best runners in the world," Joseph said. "And Scott Jurek, the best ultrarunner of all time, doesn't eat meat. The Tarahumara Indians—the people who are defined by running long distances—live mainly off of corn and beans. Roman soldiers used to ask to be fed grains to prepare them for battle, and when they dug up the bones of gladiators, do you know what they found?" He didn't give me time to think of a witty answer.

"The analysis of their bones showed they were vegan," he said, "subsisting mainly on a high-carbohydrate diet. I think there is sufficient evidence that an athlete can do well with this style of eating."

"Wow," I said to Roger. "I thought he was the strong, silent type."

"He's got a few hot buttons," Roger said. "Healthy eating is one of them. The good stuff is up ahead." Roger pointed to a station with a sign above it that said *Fresh Fruit Smoothies*. "Try the un-shake. You'll thank me later."

"The un-shake?"

"All of the taste of a milkshake with none of the guilt. None of the milk either, as a matter of fact."

"A milkshake without milk? What about building strong bones and teeth? What about the cowboy with the white hat walking into the saloon and ordering milk instead of whiskey to *prove* he is a good guy? You're telling me Mormons don't believe in drinking milk either?"

"Mormons do," Joseph said. "Bishop Shepherd doesn't. He calls it liquid meat. His cafeteria. His rules."

"Try the shake," said Roger. "Believe me, you won't miss the milk."

In silent protest I grabbed a glass and filled it with apple juice. Zachary Shepherd had done his best to make my life miserable once before. It looked like he was trying to do it again.

We sat down at a large round table with ten chairs.

"No table for three?" I asked.

"Bishop Shepherd wants people to mix," Roger explained. "If he could have one big table that held one hundred and fifty, I think he would do it."

"Is that how many people are in the ward?"

"When it's full," Roger said. "Fifty apartments, three people each. More women than men. Ages ranging from thirty to seventy-five."

I looked around the cafeteria. It was late afternoon—between lunchtime and dinner. There were about twenty other people around. Some of them stopped by to introduce themselves to the new guy, but none of them seemed like they wanted to stay and sit with us. I sniffed at my underarms. I hadn't had a chance to reapply deodorant after my flight. Maybe that was it. Then I looked at Joseph's scowl and realized that I was not the problem.

Most of the people seemed to be in their thirties. Most of them seemed very friendly. None of them looked particularly like terrorists. Of course, this didn't mean that they weren't. I really needed a way to get to know all of them—and quickly.

A woman walked through the door, and Roger gasped.

"Permelia alert," he said. "Three o'clock." He dropped his napkin on the floor and tried to hide behind Joseph. "She'll be looking for a Saturday-night date," he mumbled from under the table.

"I'm safe," Joseph said. "I don't think she likes me."

"It's not you I'm worried about," Roger said, still bending down. "I think she has a crush on me."

"Why are you hiding?" I asked Roger. "She seems quite charming."

"She's seventy-five years old," he hissed. "And she says she joined the ward to find her soul mate. She's also crazy as a loon."

"Sounds like a match made in heaven," said Joseph. He could be witty when he wanted to be. "You might as well stop hiding. I think she spotted you. She's coming this way."

Permelia flipped her shawl around her shoulders and walked directly toward our table.

"Brother Joseph," she said with a formal nod. Joseph nodded back.

"Roger," she said, her voice becoming warmer as he sat up. She smiled and held out her hand to him. Roger took it but didn't seem to know if he should kiss it or shake it. He held it limply.

"Miss Permelia," he said. She batted her eyes at him and smiled. She continued to let him hold her hand until he finally faltered and let go. Then she turned her crystalline blue eyes to me.

"Who's your friend, Roger? I don't think we have been properly introduced."

Roger seemed relieved. It was my turn to worry.

"This is Matthew Knight," Roger said, letting the words spill out of his mouth. "He's our new roommate. New to the ward and new in the Church. Matt, this is Permelia Chapman."

"Fresh meat," she said, and I felt uncomfortably like a pork chop about to be consumed. She held out her hand. I took it and, much like Roger, didn't quite know what to do.

"Matthew Knight," she said as if tasting how the name felt on her tongue. "I hope that is Knight with a *K*."

"With a *K*," I confirmed.

"Well," she said. "Then you shall be my knight in shining armor and accompany me to the ball tonight. It's not really a ball. More of a youth choir rehearsal. But all the same, I will let you take me."

"But I really can't—" I began to say.

"No excuses," Permelia said. "I dub you Sir Lancelot, and I will be your Guinevere for the evening." She pulled her hands up to her mouth, and her eyes widened. "How scandalous," she said. "What will Arthur think?" She took a sidelong glance at Roger. Arthur seemed just fine with the arrangement.

"You may pick me up at seven. Apartment 14B," she said. "Bring your chariot and wear a suit. We will be traveling to the Tabernacle."

Then she turned on her heels and waltzed toward the door. Before exiting she announced loudly to the entire room, "Hands off, girls. The new guy is mine." And with that she left.

"Not bad," said Roger with a smirk. "Here less than an hour and you already have a date."

"Thanks a lot," I said. It was clear that Roger was enjoying the fact that he was at least temporarily out of Permelia's sights.

"I'm sure you will have a wonderful time," he replied and dug into his broccoli.

I was sure I wouldn't. Not that Permelia wasn't charming enough—in a 1920s black-and-white movie kind of way—but I had work to do. I was here to find a terrorist, not to escort amorous not-so-young ladies to a choir recital. I tried to tell myself that maybe it would work out okay. Maybe we would be going with a bunch of people and I would get to meet some of the other villagers.

When the time came for me to pick up Permelia, my fears were confirmed. No double date—we were going alone. I didn't own a suit, so I threw on a sports coat, some khakis, and borrowed a tie from Roger. Permelia bounced out of her apartment like a high school cheerleader. If not for her gray hair—pulled back into a pony tail—and a few wrinkles that pulled playfully at the corners of her eyes, I would never guess she was seventy-five. She was slim, spunky, and athletic. And then there was her dress. I think Permelia must have bought it at the Disney store. It looked suspiciously like the one worn by Cinderella at the ball.

We drove in my beat-up chariot to Temple Square and witnessed a high school chorus performance that lasted five hours. Okay, so maybe it was only an hour and a half, but it seemed like five to me. Not that I don't appreciate fine choral music—I just can't stand it. This, coupled with the fact that I was continually distracted by Permelia's hand clamping tightly on my knee, made for a very long and unproductive evening. I was pretty tired and tried to doze a few times, but each time, Permelia's sharp elbows somehow accidentally found their way between my ribs.

In *my* mind, my first date in Salt Lake City wasn't going that well, but Permelia must have had different ideas because on the way home she proposed. Marriage, that is.

"I think we make a fine couple," she said. "Let's set a date. I really want to marry in the temple, but since you're a newbie, that could take a year. So I'm fine with going civil at first if you are."

I nearly drove off the road. I decided to pull over and stop. I looked at Permelia. She had a wild look in her eyes, like a vulture sizing up a carcass. I was a little afraid she was going to go in for a kiss.

"Slow down, Permelia," I said. "I enjoy your company, but I don't think marriage is in the cards for us." Her lower lip jutted out in a pout, and she slumped back in her seat.

"Is it my age?" she asked in a hurt voice. "Is it that I'm old enough to be your mother?"

I almost laughed but stopped myself. "Permelia," I said. "My mother had me when she was sixteen. Had she lived she would be in her late forties now. You, my dear, are old enough to be my grandmother."

"But I'm a young seventy-five," she said.

This time I did laugh. "You are the youngest seventy-five I've ever met. And very lovely. I have to admit that despite finding choir recitals about as much fun as going to the dentist, I still had a wonderful time with you." I think Permelia actually blushed a little. "But marriage is out of the question."

"Is there someone else?" she asked.

I thought for a minute. "Sort of," I said. "It's complicated. Let's just say I'm not ready for any relationship at the present time."

Permelia sighed. "You sound a lot like I used to," she said. The frenetic energy in her voice shifted, and she sounded less like a crazy dowager and more like a wise counselor. "Don't put if off, Matthew Knight." She looked at me intently as she spoke. "When the right one comes along you need to stop everything and jump in with both feet. Otherwise you end up seventy-five with no grandchildren to show for it." She smiled. "Except, of course, those you can trick into going on a date with you." She put her hand on my arm. "Don't make the same mistake I did."

"Permelia," I said. "I think you've been putting on an act this whole evening. You're not really a batty old woman at all, are you?"

"Well, I am quite old," she said, pulling at the wrinkles in her neck. "No matter how much I wish this was just a mask. But I am a good actress, don't you think? It's easy to do with young people these days. They mistake a sense of humor for senility. Sometimes it's just easier to let them think the way they want to. Besides, I find out quite a lot about people when they think they are dealing with someone a few cards short of a full deck."

"Like what?" I asked.

"Like if they are decent human beings or not. People with a dark heart don't treat senile old women very well. At least not when there's nobody watching."

I examined my own behavior throughout the evening and began to worry. Had I treated Permelia all right?

"Don't worry," she said as if reading my mind. "You passed the test with flying colors. I can now recommend you without any reservations."

"Recommend me for what?"

"For my roommate, of course. You didn't think I really wanted you for myself, did you? I was doing reconnaissance work. I think you call it being a 'wingman'?"

"I call it sneaky," I said, although considering my circumstances this was a little like the pot calling the kettle black. "And I was serious about what I said earlier, Permelia. I really can't be in a relationship right now."

"Because of the other woman?" she asked.

"I don't think I said anything about another woman," I said.

"Not directly," Permelia stated. "But you hinted at it." Permelia was definitely not senile. She was sharp as a tack.

I thought about how to respond and decided on the truth. "To tell you the truth, Permelia, I *have* met the perfect woman. She just happens to be taken, and I accept that. But I really don't think there is room in my heart for someone else."

"Poppycock," she said. "I come from a long line of polygamists. The one-woman, one-man theory is an old myth. It's what turned me into a spinster, and I don't want to see it happen to someone else."

"You were in love with a married man?" I asked.

"I thought I was," she said. "But it was nothing more than girlish infatuation. I thought he was my soul mate and that God would eventually provide a way for us to be together. He was married to his wife for fifty-five years and died a happy man with dozens of children and grandchildren." I thought I saw moisture creeping into Permelia's eyes. She dabbed at them with a ruffled sleeve. "And here I am biding my time in a singles ward and going out with kids who are still wet behind the ears. So don't be an idiot, Mr. Knight. Don't let a foolish romantic idea blow your chance at real happiness." To emphasize me blowing my chance, Permelia pulled out a handkerchief and blew her nose.

"Don't you dare tell Roger that I have all my faculties," she said. "My main enjoyment in life these days is watching him squirm."

I nodded then paused. I really *didn't* want to talk about my social life anymore, but I really *did* want to pick Permelia's deceivingly perceptive brain. She'd been running a covert operation here much longer than I had, and she must have picked up on some things.

"What do you think about my roommates?" I asked her.

Permelia put her handkerchief away and put on a thoughtful look. "Roger is a good soul," she said. "But his act is about as ridiculous as mine."

"You mean he's not a mad scientist?" I asked.

"That part is no act," she said. "He's about as mad a scientist as you can be. But he's hiding something. He might come off as carefree, but I think inside he is one hurt puppy. He's got secrets. And I don't think he's sharing them with anyone."

This was interesting. When secrets and inner pain are mixed, they often become the recipe for something more sinister. I would have to keep my eye on Roger.

"What about Joseph?" I asked.

Permelia thought for a minute. "I haven't been able to figure that one out," she said. "I cut him some slack because of his father, but he really is a hard young man to get to like. I get the sense that there is more to his attitude than just the pain of losing a parent."

"As an accomplished wingman," I said, "would you set either Roger or Joseph up with your roommate?"

"She'd eat Roger alive," Permelia said. "If you think he's nervous around me, you should see him around her."

"And Joseph?"

Not in a million years," said Permelia. "There's just something about him I don't trust. He's too driven by his own obsessions. I don't think there's room in his heart for a woman."

"What's she like?" I asked before I could stop myself. "Your roommate?"

"She's like you," Permelia said.

"You mean attractive, intelligent, and extremely witty?"

Permelia looked at me and shook her head. "Not exactly."

"When you say, 'not exactly,' what do you mean—um—exactly?" I wasn't sure if Permelia had me or her roommate in mind, but apparently one of us was lacking in attractiveness, intelligence, or wit. I really hoped it wasn't my wit.

"Oh, you're both attractive and intelligent enough," she said, "but that's not what I meant."

"What *did* you mean?"

Permelia tapped her cheek. "There's more to both of you than meets the eye," she said. "I get the sense that both of you have experienced your share of pain but you haven't let the pain define you. Rather you've used it to help you to grow. Not that you let anybody see it. You both seem to be very good at erecting walls to keep people out, which is a shame because I believe that behind those walls is a pair of precious gems."

"You got all that about me from a first date?" I asked.

"I'm very perceptive," she said, giving me a wink. "I have a talent for reading people, and I've had seventy-five years to practice."

I pulled the car back onto the road, and we drove for a while in silence.

"There's one more thing," she finally said. "One more way that the two of you are alike."

"What's that?" I asked, not sure I really wanted or needed to hear anything more that did not pertain to my mission.

"You both believe with all your hearts that you are not ready for a relationship. That you are 'off the market,' as they say."

"Maybe we really are," I said. "Maybe that's just the way it is right now."

I didn't know Permelia's roommate, but I knew it was that way for me.

"Maybe," said Permelia. She didn't sound convinced.

CHAPTER 6
The Night Runner

WHEN I GOT TO THE apartment, I headed straight for my room. There was a light coming from under Roger's door, but Joseph's room was dark. Dark sounded good. I was exhausted, more mentally than physically. I hated this part of an assignment—too many new pieces of information that needed to be sorted and categorized. I liked it more when the patterns started to emerge. I was hoping for some patterns very soon.

I brushed my teeth, got into bed, and hoped for sleep. Instead I was assaulted with a flurry of thoughts that seemed to bounce around in no apparent sense of order. I thought about Joseph. Of all the people I had met so far, he acted most like a terrorist. He also had at least some link to potential Islamic extremists, if only through his ancestry. But there were several problems. Besides being Abraham Hadadi's son—my hero and one of the world's biggest opponents of terrorism—there were other pieces that didn't add up. Most of them were small.

First, Joseph Hadadi had a laptop. If the original e-mail was being sent to him, why would he be using a computer in the commons area? The laptop would have been just as untraceable if the message had been sent to the intended spam list. Second, other than partial nationality, Joseph didn't fit the profile. Most terrorists weren't dedicated medical students, and most terrorists were not ultradistance runners. Most terrorists focused on being terrorists. They might do well enough in school to not get kicked out, but they didn't excel.

I thought about Roger. I had to admit I kind of liked the guy. This made him perhaps more dangerous than Joseph. In my business we always looked for motive and means. Roger had no apparent motive, although he could have a hidden one. But he seemed to have the means. I didn't know if poisoning a large body of water was possible with nanotechnology, but Roger's fish were alive and swimming in our living room. If he could take bad water and make it good, what's to say that he couldn't do the opposite?

I thought about Permelia. What she'd said to me about losing out on my chance for a relationship still stung for some reason. It was true that I was in love with a woman who was off limits. Becca had chosen Robbie over me, and it was the right choice for everyone involved. Becca knew it, and I knew it. I still loved her, but I didn't want a future with her. I wanted Becca and Robbie to be happy. Did this mean I would never love anyone else? According to Permelia, this was "poppycock." Maybe she was right. Maybe I was using my forbidden love as a convenient excuse not to get close to anyone. Between my excuses and my job it seemed to be working pretty well. I tried to imagine where I would be at seventy-five, and it wasn't a pretty picture. There weren't a lot of field agents working undercover in nursing homes.

After a while, my thoughts settled down and I was able to drift off into an uneasy sleep.

* * *

The noise coming from the hallway was slight, but I was instantly awake. Something, or more properly someone, was moving—trying to be quiet. It was probably Roger or Joseph getting up to go to the bathroom, but in my line of work you didn't take any chances. The noises seemed to stop just outside my door. I waited for several seconds and then eased myself out of bed. If someone was coming for me, I didn't want to be caught lying down. I looked at the clock: 3:13 A.M. Not a likely time for visitors—at least not friendly ones.

I moved as silently as I could toward the door and put my ear against it. There were soft rustling sounds, low and near the floor. *Did these guys have a cat?* I didn't remember hearing any mention of one. The rustling sounds stopped, and steps began moving away from my door. I opened it and looked out. Joseph was walking away from me, dressed in sweats and running shoes. He must have been tying his shoes in the hallway. I followed him as he entered the living room.

"What are you doing up?" he said without looking at me.

"I thought you might be a prowler," I said.

"No." He reached into the coat closet by the door and grabbed a sweat-shirt. "Just a night runner."

"Do you want some company?" I said. "I really can't sleep." If Joseph was slinking around in the middle of the night, I thought it might be good to find out where he was going.

"Not particularly," he replied.

"I won't slow you down," I said. "If I can't keep up, you can just leave me."

"I don't go fast," he said. "Just long."

"How long?" I asked.

"Thirty miles tonight," he said. "Maybe thirty-five, depending on how I feel."

"How about I tag along for the first seven."

"I'm leaving now," he said. "And I don't talk when I run." He headed for the door, and I scrambled to find my shorts and running shoes. I looked out the door to see which way he was heading, then I put on my shoes. I caught up with him after about five minutes.

He said he didn't want to talk, so I didn't attempt it. He wore earbuds connected to a small MP3 player strapped to his arm. On his wrist was a portable GPS device that looked like an oversized watch. It would track his miles, his pace, his heart rate, and other various and sundry things only interesting to runners. I knew all about it because I had one just like it, although I wasn't wearing it now because I had rushed out the door. Of course, the one I had contained a few slight modifications that allowed me to use it to communicate with my handlers. In Miami, I'd been under strict orders to check in every day, and my early morning run and special GPS communicator allowed me to do this without making a call. When I hadn't checked in for twenty-four hours, they knew something was wrong. I wondered if Joseph's GPS was similarly equipped and if his running was also a cover for other activities. If he was indeed faking the whole ultramarathon thing, I should know by tonight. I was going to run far enough with him to see if he was all talk.

We settled into an easy pace, at least easy for Joseph. He said he didn't run fast, but I estimated we were doing seven-and-a-half-minute miles. Not blazing speed by any means, but faster than most recreational runners. His eyes appeared half-closed, and his lips were moving silently, like he was repeating a mantra. At seven miles out he stopped to stretch.

"That's seven," he said, not breathing hard at all. "If you turn back now you'll get fourteen in."

"I guess we're not doing a loop?" I asked, irritated that my breathing seemed a lot more labored than his.

"Out and back," he said. "It prevents cheating."

"I think I'm okay for a couple more," I said, knowing that he might be committed to running the whole way back, but I had my credit card in my sock and my cell phone in my pocket. I could call a cab if I had to. I wanted to stick with him for as long as I could to see if I might learn something.

At the ten-mile mark, I finally learned something—I was out of shape. Especially at this altitude. I was used to running at sea level. Joseph still seemed to be barely exerting himself. Okay, he really was an ultrarunner. I signaled to him that I was done and stopped to stretch and catch my breath. He continued on as if I were not there. Nice guy.

I watched for a while as Joseph disappeared into the distance, and then I began to shuffle back the way I had come. There was a little twenty-four-hour convenience store and gas station we had passed about two miles back where I could load up on some breakfast items and get the number for a cab. A sign in the window had advertised fresh-baked cinnamon rolls, and the smell in the air confirmed it. I was sure Zack would not approve.

I had the store in my sights and the smell of baking pastries in my nostrils when I heard a car approaching from behind. There were few vehicles on the road at this time of the morning, and their headlights cast eerie shadows of a phantom runner as they passed by in the moonlight. But this vehicle cast no shadows, which meant no headlights. I turned just in time to see a dark mass of metal veering straight for me.

I was running along the left-hand shoulder, and my options were limited. I could stay where I was and try to time a stuntman roll into the windshield; I could try to outrun the car; or I could get off the road as fast as I could, with the goal of reaching someplace a car couldn't follow.

I got off the road and ran straight into a brick wall. Well, almost. The cinderblock partition ran for several hundred yards along the sidewalk. It was at least nine feet tall, and I didn't think I could scale it in time. I was trapped between a car and a hard place, and the car was coming right at me. I hoped the wall would be a deterrent. The driver would need to begin braking soon or risk killing himself. Then again, if he was a terrorist, killing himself was often part of the bargain. I prepared to launch into a shoulder roll, aiming for the windshield, and hoped I wouldn't break my spine.

Tires screeched as the brakes locked up and the car began to turn sideways. I saw a hand coming up through the window. It was holding a semiautomatic machine gun. I wasn't going to get squashed like a bug after all. Instead, I was going to get shot full of holes. Lucky me.

Light from a street lamp shone on the extended arm, and time seemed to stop. *I had seen that arm before.* I'd seen it many times. Mostly in my dreams. Mostly right before I woke up screaming. Logic told me it was not the same arm—not the same man. It couldn't be. But the tattoos were the same—the swastika, the eagle, the letters *AB*. This arm did not belong to an Islamic terrorist. This arm came from another dark place. It held the marks of the Aryan Brotherhood. An arm like this had ended the life of my mother. My muscles seized, and I could not move. The features of the man's face blurred in front of me. Just like in my nightmares, I could not make him out. My monster had finally caught up to me.

Something snapped inside my skull, and I stopped looking for a place to run. The arm had not yet steadied itself to fire. Maneuvering a car into a ninety-degree slide while firing a weapon was more difficult than it looked on television. My vision remained blurred as a fire built up inside of me and exploded into my limbs. I yelled in rage and launched myself at the driver's window. I hit the gun arm with my shoulder just as it was taking aim. My momentum drove the arm—and the gun—into the metal door frame. I heard a loud crack, and the gun rattled to the asphalt. I bounced off the car and onto the pavement. The gun lay next to me.

I heard the car speeding away, the driver cursing and screaming. The impact of my shoulder had broken something in his arm, I was sure of it. But the rage inside me was not quenched. I moved to the gun, picked it up, and ran after the car, leveling the weapon in front of me. I wanted to empty the clip and watch the car roll down the pavement and burst into flames. I wanted to hear the screams as the fire consumed the occupant. I wanted them to replace my own screams and the screams of my mother in my nightmares. Lucky for the driver and for me, the car swerved around a corner before I could get a clean shot. I raced after it for a few hundred yards, but it had disappeared into the night, leaving me enveloped in a cold sweat. Just like in my dreams.

I began to shake all over. My face was wet, and I realized I had been crying as well as sweating. Crying and running. Just like that night when I was eight years old. I threw the gun hard against the cement wall, crouched down on my haunches, and lowered my face into my hands. The shame enveloped me like a cold, wet blanket. Shame for running when I was eight years old; shame for allowing the fear of a monster to remove his face from my brain; shame for forgetting my training and instead letting my fear mutate into rage. I thought I was past it. I was wrong. All the years of preparation. Everything I had worked to become. All of it gone in a matter of a few seconds. I was fear. I was rage. I was shame. I was an eight-year-old boy running in the night once again.

I leaned against the wall as the blood began to slowly work its way back into my brain. *You have a mission,* I reminded myself. *A mission that is bigger than you.* I pulled myself out of my emotion and forced myself to think about what had happened and not just my reaction to it.

It didn't make any sense. Someone had just tried to kill me. *Was the Aryan Brotherhood in league with Islamic extremists?* Not likely. The AB gangs weren't very fond of foreigners who didn't have blonde hair, blue eyes, and tattoos. Maybe it was purely a business transaction. One party paying another for a hit on a federal agent.

I thought of another explanation, but it was even more puzzling. Could this have something to do with my past? Did they think after all these years that I could identify the man who killed my mother? But I'd been gone for decades and had only been back in Salt Lake City for a day. How would they know who I was and that I was even here? After the incident the police had protected my identity. My name had not made it into any of the papers. I was whisked away to my grandparents. I told myself and the police that I wanted to help find my mother's killer—that I would be willing to return and point him out and even look into his eyes. But for all my talk, I didn't want to face anyone. The police knew it, and deep down, I knew it. There was a reason why I could remember every detail of that night except the face of the killer. I was scared. I had run away crying and had kept running. I should have done more. I should have gone back. If not as a boy, then as an adult. I should have faced my monsters and stood up to them as calmly as my mother had done.

Maybe it wasn't possible to run from your past. Maybe the past always caught up to you.

As I caught my breath, I considered a third option. Maybe this incident had nothing to do with my current assignment or with my past. Maybe it was all just a coincidence.

I gave up on this thought almost as soon as it occurred. I didn't believe in coincidences. But if this was not a coincidence, then I was no longer playing an undercover game. If someone wanted to kill me, they knew who I was. This could change everything.

I reached into my shorts and pulled out my cell phone. Funny. I didn't remember it being in three pieces before.

The lights of the convenience store in the distance were still calling my name, and I limped toward them. When I got close, I ditched the gun behind a bush. I didn't think the police would be very understanding when they saw the security cameras and noticed a man hobbling into the store with bleeding knees and semiautomatic machine gun. I didn't really want to spend the night in jail. I would get Zack to have someone come and pick up the gun before the neighborhood kids found it.

I went through the door and approached the attendant, a skinny teen with his hair tied back in a ponytail and a face full of bright red pimples that looked like they'd just been buffed with sandpaper.

"Whoa, dude," he said, looking at my legs. "What happened to you?"

I looked down. And I thought *he* looked bad. "Took a tumble," I said. "In the road."

"Anything to do with those squealing tires I heard a few minutes ago?"

"A bit," I admitted.

"Are you okay? Do you need me to call 911?"

"Just a few bumps and scrapes," I said. "I could use a first aid kit if you've got one and a phone to call a cab. I don't think I'm going to finish my run."

"No problem," he said, pulling out a white box with a red cross on it from under the desk. "You know, you really shouldn't run in the dark. It's dangerous."

"No kidding," I said. "Kind of like working the night shift at a convenience store?"

He grinned. "Touché, dude. But we haven't been robbed in months, and if anyone asks I'm supposed to hand over all the cash in the till with a big smile. They just use the cameras to catch 'em later. The phone's over there. Help yourself. If you want the cash from my register, it's all yours too. I'm here to please."

"I don't think I'm up for a robbery tonight," I said. I really needed to call Zack, not only to pick up the gun, but to get people out looking for the car. However, I didn't want to blow my cover, not even for this kid. I used the phone to call a cab. The dispatcher said the cab would pick me up in fifteen minutes. I spent a few minutes putting antibiotic cream on my scrapes and picking small pieces of gravel out of the flesh on my knees. This out of the way, I focused on more important matters.

"Is it true what they say?" I asked the kid.

"What? That snowboarders get all the prettiest chicks?" He snorted when he laughed, and I think something came out of his nose. It wasn't a pretty sight.

"No," I said, pointing to a sign. "That your store has the best fresh-baked cinnamon rolls in town."

He shook his head. "Normally they're so stale you can break a tooth on them." He must have seen the disappointment in my face because he hurried to say, "Hey, don't worry, dude. You're in luck. The bakery just made a delivery thirty minutes ago. When they're fresh, these are some seriously sick pastries."

I smiled and pulled my credit card out of my sock, hoping I was correctly interpreting his use of the term *sick* and trying hard not to look at his nose.

"I'll take half a dozen," I said.

* * *

When I got back to the apartment it was pushing 6:00 A.M. I'd already called Zack from a pay phone outside the convenience store and given him the details. The attendant had asked me why I didn't just use the free phone inside. I told him I needed to make a long-distance call to my girlfriend. Personal stuff. I hit up the ATM, and he gave me some quarters.

I had to knock on the apartment door to wake Roger up because I'd neglected to bring my key. He looked at me through bleary eyes.

"What happened to you?" he asked.

"I went running with Joseph."

"Oh," he said, as if this explained my condition. Then he turned to go back to his room.

"I brought breakfast," I said, holding up the box of cinnamon rolls and a gallon of chocolate milk.

Roger groaned. "Get thee behind me, Satan."

"You don't like cinnamon rolls?"

"I love them," he said. "But it's fast Sunday. That smell is going to torture me for the rest of the morning." With that, he stomped toward his room. "Church starts at nine," he said over his shoulder.

I hurried into the kitchen. I didn't know what fast Sunday was, but if it had something to do with me not getting my cinnamon rolls, I was going to eat them while I had the chance. If I ate quickly, I also might be able to catch a couple of hours of sleep before it was time to get ready for church. I needed sleep—about two days' worth—but I needed to be at church even more, and not for my own spirituality.

I needed to meet the rest of the suspects.

CHAPTER 7
Church

CHURCH PROBABLY WOULD HAVE BEEN a lot more interesting if I wasn't so tired and if my body didn't feel like it had been run through a meat grinder. Emotionally I was a bit of a mess too, considering my encounter with a demon from my past.

"Can we sit in the back?" I asked Roger. "I'm afraid that after my run last night, I might nod off."

"I always sit in the back," he said. "Permelia sits up front."

"Where does Joseph sit?"

"He doesn't," Roger said. "He's not very regular." We found a seat in not-too-comfortable metal chairs in an overflow area. I looked up and swore I saw a basketball hoop retracted toward the ceiling.

"Can't he take something for that?" I asked.

Roger looked sideways at me. He seemed pretty sure I was just messing with him but not certain. Sometimes it took a while for my sense of humor to grow on people. Sometimes it never did.

I was getting ready to make another witty comment when I saw Roger stiffen. Permelia was walking through the door. She seemed to be looking for something when her eyes rested on Roger. She waved enthusiastically, and Roger began to fiddle under his chair with a hymnbook. While his head was down, Permelia winked at me. I smiled. At seventy-five she looked a lot more energetic than I felt. She made her way to a row near the front and sat down on a bench that looked like it had s soft, padded seat. Maybe sitting in the back wasn't such a great idea. Turning around, Permelia looked at me and tapped on her watch. I shrugged, not knowing what she meant. She pointed to the empty seat next to her and flashed both five-fingered hands at me twice. I understood that her roommate—the one she wanted to set me up with—was either a twenty on a scale from one to ten or would be arriving in about twenty minutes. Permelia seemed determined to introduce us. She didn't recognize a lost cause when she saw one.

I scanned the rest of the room, hoping to see a group of suspicious-looking men in turbans assembling a bomb in a corner. No such luck. Mostly I saw the backs of people's heads; most of them were women; and most of the women were Caucasian. However, there was more of a mixture of various races than I would have expected in Utah—several Asians, a few Indians, and a smattering of African-Americans. With Joseph absent, there wasn't an Arab-looking individual in sight. Not that only Arabs could be terrorists, but this particular threat was coming directly from Islamic extremists, and most of these folks came out of the Middle East.

Maybe because of the incidents from the night before, my eyes locked on a well-muscled forearm with a brightly decorated tattoo propped on the bench about ten rows in front of me. I recognized the design at once. Not the Aryan markings of my assailant but rather the eagle, globe, and anchor of the U.S. Marine Corps. The man attached to the forearm sported the customary Marine crew cut, but something in his manner bothered me. Most Marines that I knew held themselves with a quiet confidence—back straight and eyes forward. This guy was talking loudly, poking other guys in the arm, and placing his hands on the shoulders of women in front of him—something they seemed to not appreciate. He reminded me of a lot of guys I had known. Guys who told everybody how tough they were and then arrived at basic training and suddenly developed an injury that sent them home; guys who were always trying to prove something when others were watching; guys you wouldn't want standing by your side in a life-or-death situation. This was definitely someone I wanted to keep an eye on.

The meeting itself was interesting. There was a song and a prayer, a few announcements by Bishop Zack, the passing of bread and water to the congregation, and then what was referred to as "testimony meeting." This last part kind of reminded me of open mic night at the comedy club—but without the alcohol and not as funny. There were also a lot more tears. People who felt the urge marched up to the microphone and bared their souls and their testimonies of the Church. The intensity of their feelings was impressive. They loved the Church, they loved the ward, they loved the prophet, and they especially loved Bishop Shepherd. Ah, if they only knew him like I knew him.

About halfway through the meeting a woman walked in and sat down next to Permelia. Permelia turned to me and gave me the thumbs-up. She nudged the woman next to her, presumably to get her to turn around and look at me, but the woman brushed her off and shushed her.

I stared in amazement. "What kind of hair is that?" I whispered to Roger. The woman was short and slender, but it looked like a volcano of curly locks had erupted out of the top of her head.

"That," Roger whispered back, "is the most magnificent mane to ever grace itself upon womankind." I looked at him. He seemed completely serious and utterly enthralled. *Womankind?* I'd thought Roger was a mad scientist, not a poet.

"I thought you had sworn off women."

"Every man in the ward has a crush on her." Roger sighed. "That is a given. She is a force of nature. But it doesn't matter. She's completely untouchable."

"Stuck-up, huh?" I asked.

Roger reacted as if I had blasphemed. "She's an angel," he said.

"If she's an angel, then why does she have that hair?" I asked. "Seems like she's begging for attention." I lowered my voice to a whisper. We were starting to get some dirty looks from people who apparently were trying to listen to the meeting.

"I don't know the reason for the hair," Roger said. "And I don't care. I just hope she never changes it."

I was a little dumbfounded. *This was the person Permelia was trying to line me up with?* Miss Betsy Big-Hair? *This was the woman Permelia said was a lot like me?* Maybe Permelia was a little senile after all. I was actually relieved. The woman was beautiful, at least the parts of her that I could see, but she was also definitely not my type. I could tell that from a mile away. The hair alone told me that we were as un-alike as you can get.

"Completely un-alike," I said under my breath and then immediately started thinking of Roger's un-shake from the day before. Have I mentioned that I sometimes get distracted by food? What was it that Roger had said about the shake? "All of the flavor but none of the guilt," or something like that.

Suddenly my mind was filled with what felt like a flash of pure light. "I've got it," I said, jabbing Roger in the leg.

"Ouch," he said. "Cut that out. What?"

"The answer to the problem," I said. I felt like rushing up to the microphone and bearing my own form of testimony. "You are brilliant, Roger."

"I'm quite aware of that," he said. "But what problem are you talking about?"

"The dating problem," I said, watching with awe as the pieces fell together in my mind. "The problem of getting to know everyone in the ward without going on a dating spree."

"That's not my problem," Roger said. "It's yours."

"You're right," I said. "But you *are* going to be part of the solution."

"Can we just listen?" Roger asked, his eyes focused on Permelia's roommate and not on the pulpit.

"All right," I replied. I didn't care about interrupting his follicle worship, but I wanted to share my flash of inspiration now. However, people were starting to stare. "I'll explain it all to you after church."

* * *

When sacrament meeting ended, I told Roger I was ready to go home, explain my plan, and then take a nap.

"This is just the first meeting," he said. "We've still got Sunday School and priesthood."

"I think I want to defect to the Church of Saint Mattress," I grumbled. My flash of inspiration had given me an adrenaline rush, but the last twenty-four hours were beginning to catch up to me. Still, I needed to meet and observe more people—no matter how tired and sore I was.

"So what's your brilliant idea?" Roger asked as we moved down the hallway.

"Un-dating," I said. "You gave me the idea with your un-shake. Remember, 'all of the good and none of the bad'? I'm going to do the same thing with dating."

"I didn't realize there were any good parts," Roger said.

"What I'm proposing," I said, attempting to be civil as several people, mostly women, smiled and nodded to me in the hallway, "eliminates all the emotional baggage and stress that typically comes with dating. Let me ask you this: What makes dating so stressful?"

Roger thought for a minute. "It's all a big, exhausting lie," he finally said. "You're trying to impress the girl, so you attempt to be something you're not. She's trying to impress you, so you have no idea what you're really dealing with. By the time you really get to know each other, you're married." His eyes had a faraway look. "Believe me, I know."

"Exactly," I said. "So what if we took away the need to impress? What if we eliminated all of the 'finding a potential mate' nonsense? What if the only purpose of getting together was to get to know each other as human beings?"

"It'll never happen," he said. "Finding a mate is programmed into our DNA. Dating equals faking, and faking equals stress. It's a dance that's been going on for thousands of years, and it's not going to change."

"That's why we aren't going to date," I said. "We are going to un-date. We are going to set up meetings with each apartment in the Village—male or female, it doesn't matter. We can meet at one of the round tables in Section 89. We'll announce our purpose, provide some thought-provoking questions to stimulate conversation, and when we get through, we'll know our neighbors better than they know themselves. And we won't ever bring up the word *date*."

"It sounds like hanging out," Roger said, the skepticism showing on his face. "Bishop Shepherd has counseled us against it. You're new here. You don't understand. This is the Mormon Church. They *want* us to pair off. Eternal marriage is the ultimate endgame."

"Look, I don't understand everything," I said. "But what I do understand is that Za . . . uh . . . Bishop Shepherd has assigned me to get to know everyone in the ward, male and female. And I certainly can't ask the men out on dates."

"I guess I see where you're coming from," Roger said, sounding hesitant.

"So you'll help me?"

"Let's just say I'm curious about your methods," he said as he shuffled me toward the back row of another meeting room.

I managed to stay awake through the next two meetings. Several people came up afterward to welcome me to Salt Lake City and to the ward. None of them looked like terrorists, except maybe the guy with the tattoos. He hit me on my sore shoulder, invaded my personal space, and in general spoke several decibels louder than he needed to. His name was Colt Mangum. A macho name. Big surprise.

After church, a man who introduced himself as the "ward executive secretary" told me that Bishop Shepherd would like me to meet him in his office. I had wondered how I was going to arrange meetings with my handler. This was way too easy.

I related the events of the night before in more detail, and Zack listened. When I was done, he said, "You were chasing a car down the street with a submachine gun. What would you have done if he had not turned the corner?" Zack must have picked something up from my tone.

"I would have tried to get his license plate number," I said, avoiding the real question.

"You know what I mean, Mr. Knight. I know your history. I don't need a vigilante on my hands."

"I'm happy to go back to Washington," I said. "When someone sticks an arm out of his car to shoot you, he should expect a broken wrist."

"It's not the broken wrist I'm worried about."

"That's all that happened."

Zack studied me for a long time. "I think I'm inclined to grant your request, Mr. Knight. I'm sending you back to Washington."

I should have been ecstatic at this news. But for some reason, the events of the past night had changed something. "Look," I said, searching my own inner motivations. "I'm not going after the Aryan Brotherhood, if that's what you're worried about." This was true. If I had learned nothing else from last night—it was that I was nowhere near ready to face my monsters. What I saw in myself scared me more than what I saw in my dreams. So why, then, was I arguing with Zack about sending me back to Washington?

"That's not the only reason," Zack said. "Someone put a hit out on you, which means someone knows who you are. Your cover is blown. You are officially done."

I sat back in my chair and let this sink in. I could be on a plane tomorrow, back to my friends. Back to eating Becca's chocolate cake. I should just keep my mouth shut and get out while I could.

I heard someone talking and was surprised to find that it was me. "If my cover is blown, then that is exactly why you need me to stay," I said. "Other than my two roommates, and possibly Mr. Colt Mangum, you have no obvious suspects. We don't even know if we're barking up the right tree."

"It's Mangum," he said. "Not Magnum. And why is Colt a potential suspect?"

"I don't know," I said. "Ex-military, probably schooled in firearms and maybe explosives. Flaunts his tattoos as if they were Purple Hearts. Seems like the kind of guy that might want to go out in a blaze of glory just to get attention. Besides, he punched me in the arm as a greeting. I hate guys like that."

"Did you punch him back?" Zack asked. "Or just try to shoot him?" I ignored the comment.

"The point is," I said, "we don't have much to go on. If they know who I am, then they know we're on to them. Sending me home won't change that. If you bring in a new agent, he'll stand out like a sore thumb. You might as well stick with me." *What was I saying? Couldn't somebody make this guy shut up?* I had told Zack I would give him a week. Now I was begging him not to send me home.

"They'll probably try again," Zack said. "Next time you might not be so lucky."

"Let's hope they do," I said. "Not that I'm crazy about getting shot at, but at this point I may be more valuable as a target than as an undercover agent. It's a quick way to narrow down suspects. We just find out who's behind the gun."

"Unless he's a hired gun. Then all we're left with is a dead body and no answers."

"Hired guns leave a trail," I said. "If we follow it, we may find the source."

"Maybe," he said. "But the fact that they used the Aryan Brotherhood worries me. Either the trail is well disguised, or the terrorists know a lot more about your past than I'm comfortable with."

"What do you mean?" I asked, knowing full well what he meant.

"You were supposed to be a witness to a murder, correct? You were supposed to be able to identify the face of the man who killed your mother."

"You've read my file. You know that my brain has blocked out anything useful."

"You still can't recall the face? Even after all of your training?" His words dug into me and twisted like a jagged knife, cutting me open to reveal my shame. I should have been able to remember that face. But no matter how hard I tried, my memory would only provide the unimportant details. I could see the street. I could see the cane that had been used as a weapon. I could clearly see my mother lying on the ground and bleeding. But the face of her killer would not come to me. The truth was that I had been so focused on defeating Zack in my training that he had become a surrogate for my mother's killer. When I thought of a face, I saw his.

"I still see a blurred image," I said. "I've tried hypnosis; I've met with the shrinks." I shrugged my shoulders. "Nothing."

"Let it go, Mr. Knight. You were eight years old. The point is that someone who knows your history could use it. All it would take is a phone call to the Aryan Brotherhood saying that a particular federal agent is in town who can identify a member of the AB in a murder case. No money would have to change hands. No trail would be left. Maybe there was just a phone call and then a hope that nature would take its course."

"That's a theory," I said. "But it assumes a lot. It's been more than twenty years. The man who killed my mother is probably dead or in prison somewhere. A more logical theory is that my photo was taken in Miami and then sent out through a network to other terrorist cells warning them of an agent who likes to work undercover. One of terrorists here recognized me from the picture, and they went to the AB with cash, hoping for a quick hit and an end to the problem. But they failed. I saw the perpetrator, and maybe, just maybe, he left a trail. Find the perp and we could be one step closer to finding the terrorists."

"We don't need you to find the perp," Zack said. "Once you identify his photo, you're done."

"But you do need me to draw them out again," I said. "Maybe next time they'll decide not to farm out the work."

Zack thought for a long time, and then I saw the muscles in his forearms relax. "All right," he said. "But you're not flying unattached like you did last night. I want to be able to trace you and know your whereabouts at all times. We've got the technology. Let's use it. We will have agents less than a minute away at all times."

"That's fine with me," I said. Having someone watch my back was not an unappealing prospect. Not only might they save my life, but they might save me from myself. "Do we have anything on the shooter from last night?"

"We found the car abandoned a few blocks from the convenience store," he said. "It was stolen a few hours earlier from a parking lot at a bar. We're dusting for prints, but it looks like it's been wiped. Our best chance is the gun since you say the man was not wearing gloves. But for some reason all of the clear prints we found belong to a certain Matthew Knight. Missy

Brentwood from the county prosecutor's office is putting together a book with photos of likelies from the brotherhood. It should be ready tonight or tomorrow. You think you can identify him from a picture?"

"If his picture is there, I can identify him," I said. The face that had originally been blurred had come into focus. I didn't mention that I had met Missy Brentwood.

"Good." Zack looked at me with those penetrating eyes. I thought he might be questioning how I was going to recognize a man in a moving car whom I'd seen briefly in the middle of the night when I couldn't identify the murderer of my own mother, even though I had seen him at point-blank range. "Have you made any progress on your investigation?" he finally asked.

"Nothing that you probably don't already know," I said. "Joseph is a difficult person, but between medical studies and ultrarunning, he probably doesn't have time to be a terrorist. Roger probably has the technological expertise to poison large bodies of water with nanobots, but what his motive might be, I can't figure out. We already talked about Colt Magnum . . ."

"Mangum," he corrected.

"Right. Colt Mangum. He seems like he's got the personality to blow something up, just to get attention, but I'm not sure why he would be aligned with Islamic extremists. And, to be honest, I don't know why they would want a guy like that. He doesn't exactly fly under the radar." I stopped, thinking about the other people I'd recently met.

"There's always Permelia," I said.

"You think she's a suspect?"

"No, but I think she would make a great agent. She's been flying under-cover for years."

"That she has," he said, chuckling. "That she has. By the way, speaking of Permelia, do you have any more dates lined up?"

"Nope," I said, smiling. "I don't plan on dating."

Zack wrinkled his nose. I don't think he liked being second-guessed.

"I've come up with a better idea," I said before he could question me. "Don't worry. Within two weeks I will be able to tell you who in the ward is authentic and who has something to hide."

"If you live that long," he said.

CHAPTER 8
The Monster's Face

ROGER WAS RELUCTANT ABOUT MY idea—at first. But the more I explained, the more his scientific curiosity took hold.

"So you really think this will work?" he asked, using oven mitts to pull a pork roast out of the oven. Apparently, the fasting part of fast Sunday was over, and since Section 89 was not open on the Sabbath, Roger had decided to use his eat-meat-sparingly card. My stomach immediately reacted to the aroma.

"I told you," I said. "I had a class on interviewing techniques. This method has been proven to get to the root of someone's personality faster than any other." I didn't tell him that my class on interviewing just happened to be taught at Quantico and that the instructor was a former CIA interrogator. "By the way, that roast smells divine."

Roger tasted it and nodded. "Your method of interviewing seems simplistic."

"Simple," I said. "Not simplistic. As in simply elegant. There's a difference."

"I know all about the simple and elegant," he said. "At least in the world of molecules and organisms, the simple theory is usually the best. But we're talking about people here. My limited experience working with people has taught me that the usual rules don't apply. Could you grab some plates from the cupboard and set the table?"

"Don't think of them as people," I said, grabbing three plates. "Just think of them as very large amoeboids." I hoped I had picked a legitimate term to describe plural amoeba.

"I do think of them as amoeboids," he said. "Believe me, I always have. But these are unpredictable amoeboids with emotions. Most of them female. As I told you before, I'm not into drama."

"That's why we're only going to focus on the positive," I said. "Only the high points. Each person will pick three peak experiences to talk about: one in their first ten years of life, one in their second, and one from the time they turned thirty. The times in their life when they felt the most accomplished, the most satisfied, or the most alive. Then other people get to ask them follow-up questions. Ten minutes total per person, including the questions. Nine people in less than ninety minutes. They won't have time to descend into drama. The structure won't allow it."

"Have you ever done this before?" Roger asked.

"Sort of."

"Sort of?"

"Not exactly like this. Not with such a big group of people. But, yes, I've seen it work in other situations." What I had in fact seen was a library of film and piles of case studies outlining the effectiveness of interrogation techniques. But Roger didn't need to know that.

"Do you really think people will open up?" Roger asked, his fogging glasses sliding slightly down toward the tip of his nose as he sliced the roast.

I started to tell him that I was sure, but then I stopped myself. "Just think of it as an experiment," I said. "If it doesn't work after three or four times we can assess and either try something else or scrap the whole thing." By the look in his eyes I could see that I had him as soon as I said the word *experiment*.

"I still see a problem," Roger said after a moment.

"What's that?"

"You and I are going to be at all of these meetings, right?"

"That's the idea," I said. "Our apartment will be hosting. You, me, and Joseph."

"You can forget about Joseph," he said. "He hasn't attended a social function since I've been his roommate. But if it's just you and me, doesn't that mean we're going to have to think up a whole lot of peak experiences?"

"That's the beauty," I said, eyeing loaves of what looked to be homemade bread that Roger was putting into the now-empty oven. "Since it will be a new group of people each time, we don't have to be original. We can use the same three stories, and we can prepare them beforehand."

"All right," Roger said, gently closing the oven door on the loaves of bread. "I'm in."

* * *

Roger was right about Joseph. He showed up for dinner long enough to scowl at the mere notion of attending a social function. He made it clear that there was no way he was going to participate in our un-dating plans. This was really too bad since I was very interested to see if Joseph's high points included training in Al-Qaeda cells in Afghanistan or making car bombs in kindergarten. But on the upside, I didn't think Joseph would have been the life of the party anyway.

During dinner, however, he did surprise me by inviting me to continue to run with him. Well, maybe "invite" was a little strong. I think his exact words were, "I run alone. If you happen to be on the same street at the same time, that is your business." Actually, monitoring his activities *was* my business, but I just smiled and nodded.

Despite Roger's initial reluctance, he was a great help in setting up our appointments. Before the evening was over, we had un-date meetings set up with all apartments except one.

"Why are you afraid to call Permelia?" I asked. "She's one of the nicest people I've met."

"I'm not afraid," Roger said. "I'm petrified. There's a difference."

"Just tell her she's too old for you," I said. "That's what I did when she proposed."

"She proposed to you?" Roger asked.

"You sound a little disappointed."

"What disappoints me is that you didn't accept," he said. "I could have been eternally off the hook."

"Why don't you just call and ask for her roommate," I said. "What did you say her name was? Hair Winslett?"

"It's Hope Winslow," he said, his face seeming to color. "And if calling Permelia is petrifying, calling Hope is petrifying to the tenth power."

"Hand me the phone," I said in a show of machismo. "What's the number?"

Roger told me. As the phone rang I felt a slight fluttering in my gut. I wasn't calling anyone for a real date, but for some reason it sure felt like I was. I hoped it would be Permelia who answered. I hoped it wouldn't be Hope. On the third ring someone picked up, and I breathed a sigh of relief as I recognized Permelia's voice.

Instead of answering with a traditional hello, Permelia said, "It's about time you called. We were beginning to feel like watermelons in a pumpkin patch. You've got dates with everyone else in the ward."

"Good evening, Permelia."

"Oh, it's you," she said, sounding disappointed. "I heard that Roger was making the calls."

"You know he's a little shy," I said. "It's always toughest to call that special person. You remember how that is." Roger punched me in the arm. At least I think it was a punch. It felt more like a gentle slap. If Roger was a covert terrorist trained in hand-to-hand combat, he was doing a good job of hiding it. He really needed to work out.

"Actually, I *don't* remember," Permelia said. "It's been too long. But I hope you've got Roger somewhere nearby listening to you."

"He's right here," I said. "He just hit me in the arm."

"You don't say," Permelia said. "Tell him I like that in a man." I had found the speaker button and Roger heard this last part. His cheeks turned an interesting rosy-purple color.

"I think I can see the hair growing on his manly chest even as we speak," I said. "By the way, you are now on speaker, Permelia." Roger's chest was anything but manly. *Concave* might have been the appropriate word for it. But this was starting to get fun.

"Hello, Roger," Permelia said playfully. "What night should Hope and I be ready for our double date?"

"It's not actually a date," I corrected. It was my turn to sweat. "It's an un-date, and there will be several people there."

"Whatever," said Permelia. "We're free on Friday." I looked at Roger, who shrugged.

"Friday is great," I said. "We'll meet at Section 89 at six-thirty. You and Hope should come prepared to talk about some of the peak experiences from the first four decades of your life."

"That's not fair," Permelia said. "For most people that wasn't so long ago. For me, it seems like an eternity."

"Then I give you permission to choose whatever decades you want," I said. "But I do want to hear about your childhood and your teens. I bet you've got some interesting stories."

"You mean like pulling handcarts across the plains? That was mostly boring."

"C'mon, Permelia, we all know that you're not *that* old."

"Tell that to my bowels," she said.

The call ended and I went back to my room to take a nap. Just as I lay down I heard the phone ring. Roger knocked on the door and brought the cordless into the room. "It's the bishop," he said, handing me the phone. "For you." I raised my eyebrows and Roger shrugged.

"Bishop?" I asked, taking the phone. I almost called him "Zack" but caught myself.

"I need to see you in my office," Zack said. "Missy Brentwood is here with the photos. Bring your Book of Mormon. If anyone asks, I'm checking up with you on some reading assignments."

* * *

Missy Brentwood gave a start when I walked into Bishop Shepherd's office. She looked at the blue Book of Mormon clasped in my hand and said, "Agent Knight, I presume. It appears that you are pregnant after all."

I looked down at the book. "I haven't read any of it yet," I said. "Just part of my cover."

"Not a very good one if you don't read it," said Zack, looking back and forth between me and Missy. "Am I missing something here, or do you two know each other?"

"We met a few days ago on a plane," Missy said. And then, turning to me, "Meggy hasn't stopped talking about her new friend 'Charlie.'"

"Make sure to tell her hello for me," I said.

"Charlie?" asked Zack.

"He introduced himself as Charles Manson," Missy said. "Is this how you train your agents to be discreet?"

Zack looked at me. Before he could answer her question, I sat down in a chair next to Missy and held out the Book of Mormon. "You want to trade?" I asked, nodding at the black binder in her lap.

"You keep your book, Mr. Knight," Zack said. "Mrs. Brentwood doesn't have all day."

I set my reading assignment on the desk and took the black binder from Missy then opened the cover and flipped through the plastic sleeves. "There are some strange-looking characters in here," I said.

"You're holding the book upside down," Zack said. "Stop messing around." I was finding that I enjoyed irritating Zack even more now that he was my bishop and not my combat instructor and probably wouldn't hit me or dislocate one of my joints. Missy covered her mouth in what sounded like a cough. Did I mention I was even more dangerous if I had an audience?

I turned the book over and started through the pages one by one. Each held mug shots of four scary Aryan-looking guys, along with their names, aliases, arrests, convictions, and last-known address. I studied each face carefully. Zack's phone rang, and he turned in his chair to have a conversation with whoever was on the other end. He mentioned he was in a meeting and that it would be best to set an appointment. The person on the other end seemed to dismiss this suggestion and continued to talk. The pleasant tone in Zack's voice as he patiently explained that he could not meet at the moment was distracting me, and I had to look up a couple of times to see if someone had sneaked in and taken his place. Then I turned the page and almost fell out of my chair.

The face of the man in the picture in front of me was a familiar one, but it was not my attacker from the night before. The face that looked out at me from the plastic sleeve was the one I had blocked out of my memory more than twenty years ago. It was the face of the faceless monster that haunted me in my dreams. The monster I ran from but could never escape. I had been shown pictures at the time of the murder. Maybe I had even seen this man's picture before, but for some reason my brain had not been ready to see it. But now, the damaged fragment of memory that I had spent years trying to recover had suddenly reinserted itself into my hard drive and was restored in its entirety. I was temporarily paralyzed. I looked into the eyes of my monster and shuddered.

"Are you all right?" asked Missy. Luckily Zack was turned the other way and didn't see my reaction.

"Yeah," I said, forcing myself to come back into the present. "I was just thinking about something else." I quickly memorized the information associated with the monster's picture and turned the page.

Zack's conversation ended, and he turned back to face us and asked, "Anything yet?"

I began to shake my head and then stopped as another familiar face looked out at me from the page. "Wait a second," I said. "That's him. That's the guy who tried to shoot me."

His name was Walter Jackson, his alias was "Grip," and his rap sheet was a mile long. He'd been arrested on theft, battery, and suspicion of murder a couple of different times. I put the book on the desk so Missy and Zack could see.

"It doesn't list a last-known address," I said. "Do you think you can find him?"

Missy Brentwood took the book and looked carefully at the picture, pursing her lips. "Finding him won't be a problem," she said. "But questioning him might be a little tricky."

"Why's that?" I asked.

"Because Walter Jackson is currently lying on a slab with a tag around his big toe at the county morgue."

CHAPTER 9
The Un-Date

I LEFT ZACK'S OFFICE AND tried to wrap my brain around what I had learned. Walter Jackson appeared to be a literal dead end. His body was found washed up in the Jordan River—a broken wrist, a bump on his head, and water in his lungs. Official cause of death—drowning. No witnesses, no suspects, and no real proof that he didn't just fall off his bicycle along the river trail. Except that most AB hit men didn't ride bicycles, and it seemed clear that whoever had done this didn't want us to use good old Walter to track him down. The shooter was dead, and so was the trail.

But these facts occupied only a small part of my brain. I was focused on another face from the gang book. Another tattooed bald man with bushy eyebrows and a goatee that was so long it looked like it had been borrowed from ZZ Top. The face was older, but it was definitely him. The dark eyes had glared out from the picture just as they had glared at me that night. And those eyebrows. They were so bushy that a family of squirrels could comfortably live in them. How was it that I couldn't remember that face when I was questioned by the police? Just telling them about the eyebrows and the beard would have had the perpetrator picked up and behind bars within fifteen minutes. Yet, because of my fear, my mother's murderer had walked free for years. Not anymore.

His rap sheet showed that he had eventually been arrested and convicted for murder. Not my mother's. Mr. Eyebrows had been busy. His name was Zelphinus Cork. With a name like that, no wonder he turned to violence. He had served fifteen years in a federal penitentiary for killing a man in a bar fight. His sheet included mention of several other arrests and convictions, which ranged from drugs, gang activity, several cases of assault, and domestic violence. Zelphinus was one bad dude. But I knew that without looking at his sheet. Nightmares about this guy had me shaking so bad that in my teens I had sometimes opted not to sleep for days at a time.

The last entry under his picture was the one that interested me the most—his current residence. It showed Delancey Street Rehabilitation Center in San Francisco. He had lived there for three years. I didn't know a lot about criminal rehabilitation, but I knew that for most bad guys the justice system was a revolving door. They got put away, they got out, and then they got put away again. From what little I knew of Zelphinus Cork, I didn't have a lot of faith in a successful rehabilitation.

So I had finally found him. What next? I knew what I *should* do. I should go to Missy Brentwood, tell her I had information that would wrap up a cold case, and extend Mr. Cork's day in the big house. But I didn't want to do that.

What I wanted to do was to drop everything, fly to San Francisco, and demonstrate to Mr. Cork what Zack the Hammer had taught me. "I'm not teaching you how to fight," Zack was fond of saying. "I'm teaching you how to kill. Don't you ever forget it." Strange words to be coming from a bishop. I had never wanted to kill anyone. Even when I was beaten senseless and had a sword held over my head. But right now I wanted to use every piece of training Zack had given me. Zelphinus Cork deserved it. Another of Zack's sayings came back to me, one that I really didn't want to hear. "There's only one legitimate reason to use what I teach you," he said. "And that is to save your own life or the life of someone else. Use it in any other way and you have moved to the other side and are no better than those we fight."

I shook my head as if to get Zack's voice out of my ears. Between what I should do and what I wanted to do lay what I *needed* to do. And what I needed to do right now was to put Zelphinus Cork out of my head and focus on the mission. If I didn't solve it and solve it quickly, lots of people could die. Including me. I would deal with Zelphinus Cork when I was done.

I also needed to worry about something else. Despite reassuring Roger, I really had no idea how the un-date meetings would go. I was trained to deal with physical attacks, ticking bombs, and men with guns. Social gatherings were a whole new ball game.

* * *

We were meeting with two apartments at Section 89 this evening—one male and one female. The good news was that everyone showed up. This was also the bad news. When Colt Mangum arrived—late and loud—I knew we weren't going to get along.

"I'm here," he announced as he plunked down his tray of food and sat down at the table where the rest of us had already gathered. "The party can officially start." I had already handed out sheets of paper and was explaining the process to everyone. Roger passed one of the papers over to Colt, who had wedged a chair into a nonexistent spot between two of the women. His chair and his ball cap were both turned backward. In fact, everything about Colt was backward, including his respect for personal space.

"Now don't move away," he said to the women. "We're supposed to get to know each other."

The women ignored him and continued to move as far away from Colt as they could. Apparently, they were already acquainted.

I began to explain the exercise one more time from the beginning. "As I was saying, you write down one peak experience from each decade of your life. These could be achievements, significant emotional experiences, or just times where you felt extremely happy. They can be small things or big things. The purpose is just to get to know each other better. Any questions?"

Most of the people shook their heads and began writing. Mr. Colt Mangum, on the other hand, looked not at the paper but at me. The typical alpha-dog intimidation stare. I really wanted to stare back—I was good at these kinds of contests—but I took my cue from the others and just ignored him.

After about a minute, he crumpled up the paper and threw it on the floor.

"This is about the lamest thing I've ever heard of," he said. "Who wants to go see a movie?" Everyone kept their heads down and their pencils on the paper, even Colt's two roommates.

He pulled a paper out of the hands of a redhead sitting next to him and began to read what she had written. "When I was eight years old, I was at a dance recital. My father was supposed to be out of town, but . . ."

I interrupted him. "Leave if you want to, but give the lady back her paper and stop acting out your infantile need for attention. You do understand the meaning of the word *infantile,* don't you, Mr. Mangum?"

Colt's smile froze on his face. It took a minute for his neck and forehead to fully turn a deep crimson. He really did have some impressive veins on the side of his temple, and they began to throb.

Colt stood up and pushed back his chair. His fists were clenched, and I could see that his defined vascularity extended into his biceps. My guess was that he'd been juicing, and I didn't mean the type that comes from vegetables.

"You and me, Bubba. Outside, right now," Colt said.

I looked at Roger. "I think he's pointing at you," I said. Roger looked scared.

"Not him. You," he said, pointing his finger at me and then calling me a name that was really not appropriate for someone in your ward family.

This was not going so well. My first ever un-date was on the verge of disaster. I needed these meetings to gather information. If a fistfight broke out in the first one, I could be assured they were over.

"I don't want to fight you," I said, trying not to let my urge to take Colt Mangum down overpower my common sense. "You're probably right. This probably is a lame exercise. Why don't you just leave, and we'll play our boring little game without you." Besides the fact that I didn't want to jeopardize the un-date project, Colt Mangum was a large guy. He'd obviously been lifting weights. And no matter what his military record, he had probably had some training in hand-to-hand combat. I was in a no-win situation. If we fought and I beat him, I would draw undue attention to myself. If we fought and I lost, it was going to hurt really bad.

"You can either come outside and settle this like a man," he said, "or we can do this right here—but these fine ladies might get blood on their clothes."

I looked at the women and could see in their eyes which choice they preferred. "All right," I said. "But I get to choose the weapon."

He smiled. "Whatever you got, I'll match."

I didn't really know what he meant by that, but I nodded in affirmation. "Let's go," I said, putting my fist in my hand. "Rock, paper, scissors."

Colt looked confused. "If you're trying to get out of this by—"

"Relax," I said. "We're just choosing weapons. On the count of three." I began hammering my fist into my palm. On the third beat, we looked at each other's choice.

"I win," he said, staring down at his two extended fingers. "Do we fight with scissors?"

"Actually, since you initiated the duel, I get to choose the weapon," I said. "I choose paper."

I could see the wheels trying to turn behind Colt's Neanderthal forehead, but he couldn't guess where I was going with this.

"Then why the game?" he said. "If you were just going to choose anyway?"

"Duel protocol," I said. "There are certain traditions that must be upheld." I couldn't tell if his look of confusion came from my answer or from my use of the word *protocol,* but I couldn't judge him too harshly. I didn't really know what I meant either. I was just trying to keep him off balance and stall for time.

"Let's go," I said. "Bring your paper." He dutifully picked his paper up off the floor and followed me toward the door. "You first," I said in show of decorum. (I didn't actually say the word *decorum* because I was afraid his brain might explode.) He walked out the front door, and I shut it and locked it behind him. I stayed inside.

"Hey," he said, his muffled shouts rumbling through the glass. "Get out here. I'm going to kill you."

"No thanks," I said. "Maybe some other time. You've been banned from the un-date for bad behavior." I thought he might put his fist through the glass so I added, "If you don't leave right now, I will be forced to call the police." When this didn't seem to faze him, I added, "Or maybe Bishop Shepherd." This last comment must have finally penetrated the layers of bone in his cranium because he turned and shuffled away. All the same, I really didn't want to unlock the door in case he decided to come back.

The woman behind the counter seemed to read my mind. "Leave it locked for fifteen minutes," she said. "That's usually long enough."

"This has happened before?" I asked.

"He makes a scene about once a month. Bishop Shepherd gave us permission to lock him out if we need to. He's a hothead, but he flames out pretty quickly."

"What about your other customers?"

"I'll put a sign on the door that says we'll open back up in fifteen. People are cool about it." She pulled a sign with a clock on it from under the counter and attached it to the glass with a suction cup.

"Can we join you for a few minutes while we're closed?" she said. "We're not scheduled until Thursday, but I'm curious."

"Sure," I said.

"Marv, come on out for a few minutes," she yelled to someone in the back. "I'm Dena," she said, taking off a plastic glove and holding out her hand. "We met at church."

"Right," I said. "I didn't recognize you with the hairnet."

She reached up and touched her head with her fingers. Then she pursed her lips and knit her eyebrows. "But I was wearing it on Sunday."

I stumbled for an apology until she said, "Gotcha. Lunch-lady humor."

Just then her companion emerged from the kitchen, and I had to stop myself from staring. Talk about lunch ladies. This woman was dressed as if she were going to a lunch-lady costume party. Not only did she have the hairnet, the plastic gloves, and booties, but the pattern of her blouse screamed either lunch-lady chic or grandma's pajamas. I looked carefully for a mole and was relieved not to find one.

"This is Marva," Dena said. "My roommate."

At least the name fit the outfit.

"Nice to meet you, Marva," I said. Marva mumbled something but looked at the floor and wouldn't meet my eyes. Which was probably just as well—the glasses she wore were huge and might have melted me with a magnifying beam if they caught the wrong kind of light.

We moved back to the table and were greeted with applause.

"Sorry about that," I said.

"Maybe we should reconsider this," Roger said, nervously adjusting his glasses.

"Nonsense," said the redhead whose personal space Colt had been invading. "This is the most excitement that's happened in Section 89 all year. Besides, my sheet is all filled out. I'm not letting it go to waste."

"We should be the ones apologizing," said one of Colt's roommates. "He's really not a bad guy, but once in a while he acts up. It's usually when he cuts out the carbs."

"Dena, can I have some potatoes and bread to take with me?" I said. "Just in case he jumps out from a bush on the way home." Everyone laughed except Colt's roommates. They eyed each other like Colt jumping out from the bushes could be a very real possibility. Roger looked like he needed to visit the men's room. Maybe he wouldn't want to walk home with me after the meeting. I had, after all, trounced Mr. Mangum's manhood—and in public. I couldn't expect that I had seen the last of him. Although something still troubled me about his behavior. Being that much of a jerk had to take a lot of effort. Why was he trying so hard?

"Well," I said, "should we get started?"

* * *

The meeting itself went even better than I had hoped for—at least for a while. People seemed to enjoy talking about their high points, and the biggest problem we had was staying within the time limits. I also was getting what I needed from the meeting, which was finding out who was hiding something. The answer in this case was nobody. Everyone seemed very genuine and sincere. I was eliminating suspects, and this was important. If I could focus my efforts on a few people rather than the whole apartment complex, my job would become much easier.

I took my turn and tried to stick with genuine high points as much as possible. I talked about winning a swimming competition in high school—the competition was real, but it had really occurred much later in the company of several Navy SEALs. For my childhood high point, I used the day when the missionaries had knocked on our apartment door and the first ray of hope I felt that my mother could overcome her drug addiction. For my third experience, I used completing my first marathon. I didn't talk about my highest of high points from several weeks ago when I thought I was going to lose my head but my best friend Robbie burst in with the cavalry and gave me a second chance at life.

Roger went next. He talked about blowing up his first chemistry set, building his first nanobot, and meeting his wife. "She left me after a few months," he said. "She found out I was married to science, and she wasn't that fond of being in a polygamous relationship." I was definitely going to need to coach Roger on focusing only on the upbeat. But I also sensed something behind his words. Permelia said Roger was hiding something, and the way he delivered the line about the reason for his breakup just didn't ring true. His first two examples seemed spontaneous, but the last one sounded rehearsed. I made a note to dig a little deeper with my new roommate. He didn't act like a terrorist, but he was definitely hiding something.

I thought we were through when Dena and Marva returned from the kitchen. They had listened in on the first part of the meeting but had gone back to their work when the coast seemed clear of Colt. When their shift was over, they decided to join us and asked if they could share their experiences tonight rather than waiting for Thursday. At least Dena asked if she could share. Marva fidgeted in her chair.

When Dena's turn was over, she nudged Marva.

Marva squirmed and looked at her paper. From my chair I could see that she hadn't written anything.

"I don't think I can do this," she mumbled. "I'm not good at this kind of stuff." She pushed her glasses against the bridge of her nose and looked at the floor.

"Forget the paper," I said, trying to rescue us all from the awkwardness of the situation. "Just tell us one thing that you do really well."

Marva acted like she was going to say something and then just shook her head.

"She makes a killer vegetarian French toast," said Dena, attempting to help her out. "It was Marva's own invention, and everyone raves about it. She makes the batter by feel, and every time it's just a little bit different— but always good. None of the other cooks can come close to replicating it."

Several people nodded. Marva blushed.

"And she's not just an artist in the kitchen," Dena continued. "You should see her drawings. I think she could go professional if she wanted to. She works on them when it's slow back in the kitchen."

"Can we see them?" I asked. "C'mon, Marva. We'd all love to take a look."

"No," Marva said, slamming her hands down onto the table and finally making eye contact with me. "No one sees them." She turned to Dena. "I never should have shown you." She got up to leave.

"Wait," I said, not understanding what had set her off. "That's a pretty strong reaction. What do you think would happen if we looked at your drawings?"

Marva seemed to search for words. "I know exactly what would happen," she finally said. "It's the same thing that always happens. Everyone would say how nice the drawings are, and then they would leave." She paused. "And laugh."

"You think we would say nice things just to be polite?" I asked.

"It's what everybody does," she said. "Been that way my whole life." She had a slight twitch in her shoulder as she said this. I had the feeling that if she kept talking she might literally come apart at the seams. This one was not just broken; she had "handle with care" written all over her. I had a sudden wave of empathy for Zack. Being the bishop could not be an easy job.

"Can I ask you something?" I said to Marva as she began to shuffle off.

She stopped but didn't say anything. So I forged ahead.

"Your glasses," I said. "What do people say about them?"

She shrugged. "Why would anyone say anything about my glasses?"

"Because they are hideous," I said. "In fact, they are probably the ugliest pair of glasses that I have ever seen in my life." I thought I heard a collective gasp from the rest of the room. I almost gasped myself. Had I really just said that to poor little broken Marva?

"I'd really like to see your drawings," I said quickly. "And I promise you I won't tell you lies just to be polite. If your drawings are hideous, I'll tell you. Just like I told you about your glasses." I held my breath. I was treading on dangerous ground. But Marva finally nodded and walked toward the kitchen.

"What are you doing?" Dena hissed. "If you hurt her, I'll . . ."

"Just wait," I said, hoping I had read Marva correctly. In a few seconds she returned from the kitchen carrying something. It wasn't a knife, which was a good thing. She came up to the table, put down a portfolio folder, and began loosening the leather latch. I really hoped that the drawings would at least be decent. I had promised Marva I would give her the truth, and I would. She deserved my honesty. But it might be painful.

She pulled out the drawings, and I heard a second gasp. Dena was right. The drawings were good. Really good. The people at the table began to gather around to get a better look.

Marva's style was distinctive. The drawings depicted angels in different scenes from biblical history, but these were like no angels I had ever seen before. They were not the pious, dressed-in-white, serious-as-death angels that you normally see. They wore brightly colored robes, and their faces shone with a rapturous glow that was both earthy and celestial at the same time.

"Well?" Marva said, looking at me. "You said you'd be honest."

"Marva," I said, fumbling on my words. "My reaction is hard to describe." Her brow began to furrow, and I hurriedly continued.

"These are some of the weirdest angels I have ever seen," I said. "They remind me of a Grateful Dead concert I once attended. Like the flower children have taken over heaven." Everyone laughed. I could tell I had put into words what others were thinking. I stepped back from the table and watched the buzz of reaction. Marva stepped back with me.

"You hear that?" I said.

"They're laughing," she said.

"Yes they are," I said. "But why?"

"Because the angels are weird?" Marva ventured hesitantly.

"Weird, yes," I said. "Wonderfully weird. But more than weird, they are joyous. You can't help but smile when you see them. Most art angels are just plain boring. But not *your* angels. I've heard of the joy of angels before, but I don't think I have ever before seen it depicted like this. These are truly amazing."

Marva sat down hard in a chair. She spoke softly, almost to herself. "That's what I was trying to show," she said. "But I didn't really think . . ."

I studied Marva as the others enthusiastically riffled through her drawings.

"There is a problem here," I said after a while.

"What?" Marva said, squirming in her seat.

"I think you are hiding," I said, "behind those glasses."

She looked hard at the tile floor and said, "I need them to read."

I ignored her response and continued. "The persona you put on doesn't match what's coming out in those drawings. And I think the drawings are a lot more accurate representation of who you are than what you see in the mirror."

"Not everyone can be attractive," she said.

"You're wrong," I said, pulling up a chair and sitting next to her. "Not everyone can be a supermodel, but anyone can be attractive—there's a difference. Physical beauty is about the features you were born with, but attractiveness is about being who you are."

From her quizzical look, I wasn't sure she understood me.

"Do you remember *Gilligan's Island*?" I asked.

"I guess," she said.

"Who was more beautiful, Ginger or Mary Ann?"

"I don't know. Ginger?"

"That's right. Ginger was more beautiful. But who was more attractive? In other words, who did more boys fall in love with, and who would more women want as a friend? It wasn't Ginger. You know why?"

She shrugged her shoulders.

"Because Ginger was fake," I said. "Nobody really knew who she was on the inside. All you had was the Hollywood glitz. But Mary Ann was authentic. She was herself. And that was attractive."

Marva finally nodded. "You're saying that everyone doesn't need to be Daphne, that it's okay to be Velma." Marva had switched from Gilligan to Scooby-Doo, but I was following her. I looked again at the glasses.

"What I'm saying," I said, "is that whoever you are, you need to be yourself. And from these drawings—which I think represent something deep inside of you—you may not be Daphne, but I don't think that you're Velma either, no matter how hard you try."

The words seemed to hit her like a slap in the face. She quickly got up and began walking toward the door. Tears streamed down her face. On the way out she pulled off her glasses and threw them into the trash. You could hear the lenses breaking as they hit the bottom of the empty can.

All eyes turned accusingly to me. No one else had been following the conversation. They had been too engrossed by the pictures.

"What did you say to her?" demanded Dena.

"Nothing," I said. "I just told her she wasn't Velma."

"You idiot," was all Dena could say. She gathered up the drawings, and everyone made excuses and wandered off. Roger and I were left sitting alone at the table. Roger also eventually got up and left. The look he gave me was even more scathing than Dena's.

Apparently, the un-date experiment was over.

CHAPTER 10
Summit and Cliff

I MADE IT HOME WITHOUT running into Colt Mangum, which may have been the only real highlight of the evening. When I got into bed, I tossed and turned, wondering what I should have done differently with Marva. The answer that came was pretty obvious. Sometimes I just needed to learn when to shut up.

At about 3:00 A.M. I heard Joseph moving in the hallway and decided that I might as well get up and go for a run with him. When I entered the living room, I got the sense he had been waiting for me. This didn't seem like Joseph.

"I almost came in to wake you," he said.

"You wanted company?" Wonder of wonders. Maybe Joseph was finally warming up to me.

"Not particularly," he said. "But my car is broken and I wanted to run in the mountains today. Can I borrow yours?" So much for warming up.

"Tell you what," I said. "If you take me with you, I'll drive."

"This is not a run for amateurs," Joseph said. "You could fall and hurt yourself."

"The car and I are a package deal."

He looked at me in my light shorts and T-shirt and scowled.

"You'll want tights and a windbreaker," he said. "It's going to be cold up there. And you'd better bring a CamelBak, a headlamp, and maybe a stocking cap and some gloves. I'll wait for you outside."

Joseph wasn't the friendliest of guys, but he could have let me find out about the weather after we had arrived in the mountains. At least he wasn't going to let me freeze. I did my best to gather what stuff I had and found Joseph doing some dynamic stretches in the parking lot. We drove along the edge of the hills until a canyon opened up and signs indicated we were headed toward Snowbird and Alta ski resorts.

"Getting in a little late-season skiing?" I asked cheerfully.

Joseph ignored me. He seemed to be barely tolerating my presence. Was this the real Joseph, or was it all an act? Maybe his car wasn't really broken. I remembered what had happened the last time we went running together. Even though I was wearing my GPS watch, which also beamed my location to those who were assigned to follow and protect me, I wasn't sure they were going to be able to keep up once we got out of the car and onto the trail. My bodyguards probably weren't wearing the stereotypical FBI suits and ties, but they also probably weren't prepared for a run in the mountains. If Joseph wanted me dead, he was leading me to a good spot. For some reason, this made me smile. Maybe I would find out tonight who the terrorist was. The smile died on my face. Knowledge came with consequences.

We drove by both ski resorts, passed a ranger station, and parked in a parking lot next to a restroom. I stepped out of the car and took a deep breath to draw in the mountain air. I choked. Maybe I should have moved further away from the restroom before breathing.

Joseph was right. The mountain air was chilly, and I was glad for the extra layers of clothing he'd suggested. I didn't have a headlamp, but I did carry a small flashlight.

"How far are we going?" I asked.

Joseph shrugged. "Not how far," he said. "How long. This is a timed run."

I waited for him to finish, but when he didn't I finally had to ask, "How long, then?"

"Two hours up, two hours back. Maybe more."

"Right." The last time I had run for four hours had been on a flat surface during a marathon. And I had barely been able to walk for a week afterward. Maybe Joseph was intent on killing me, but he was going to use the slow, painful technique.

As we moved off, I noticed that Joseph's pace was much slower this time than on the road a few days earlier. I was sure part of it was the darkness and part of it was the terrain, but still it seemed like we were moving at a snail's pace. I wondered if he was doing this for my benefit, then quickly dismissed the thought. This *was* Joseph after all. I asked him about it, which was easy to do since we really weren't breathing very hard, despite the altitude.

"Aerobic base training," he said. "Agonizingly slow but necessary. You can go ahead if you like."

"I'm not complaining," I said.

We traveled through alpine meadows, around lakes, and across ridgelines. Mostly what I could see though was the trail in front of me where the beam of my flashlight was focused. Joseph had put his iPod earbuds in, so there really wasn't any conversation. I pretended to listen to my iPod as well, but I kept the sound off. If someone or something decided to come at me from behind, I wanted to hear it first.

I did hear something after about an hour and a half, but it wasn't a bad guy or a furry creature—it was the sound of nature calling. Okay, it was more of a feeling than a sound, but nature was definitely telling me I needed to stop. I tapped Joseph on the shoulder.

"Gotta go," I said, my frantic hopping making it obvious what I meant.

Joseph made a face. "Most ultrarunners manage to do it while still running," he said over his shoulder, pulling an earbud from one ear.

I briefly contemplated how this could be accomplished and hoped Joseph wasn't going to demonstrate since I was downwind. I stepped off the trail.

"I'll wait for you up ahead," he said and nodded up the trail. From the tone of his voice I couldn't tell if he was being courteous or if he was going to be hiding behind a rock waiting to bash my brains in when I rounded a corner. I watched the light of his headlamp bob in the waning darkness until it disappeared in the trees.

I'd had a corporate executive once tell me that the secret to his success was bladder control. He would arrange the room with lots of salty snacks and water and then wait to close his negotiations until the opposing side was starting to squirm with discomfort. I'd also talked to Marine snipers who seemed to be able to use their minds to turn off the urge so they could remain concealed in their nests for days on end. I guess I wasn't cut out to be an executive or a sniper because even though my life might depend on not letting Joseph out of my sight, I really had to go.

I finished my task and then set out on the trail after Joseph. Dawn was fast approaching, and my flashlight didn't work as well in the gray as it did in the pitch black. Nevertheless, there was only one trail and it led up.

I passed through a meadow and jogged up a hill through some trees. If Joseph was preparing an ambush, this would be an ideal place. At least that's what I thought until I emerged from the trees and watched the trail stretch in front of me along a ridgeline with a precarious drop-off along one side. It was a long way down with lots and lots of sharp-looking rocks. I could see several hundred yards ahead, but there was no sign of Joseph's headlamp. Maybe he had decided not to wait for me. Or maybe he was waiting but not wanting to be seen.

At one point the trail narrowed so much that I had to constantly watch my step. This made it difficult to look ahead for Joseph but after a few near-tumbles I decided I had better keep my eyes on the trail. I had turned off my flashlight and was just getting by in the gray light. It was then that I caught something moving from the corner of my eye.

A hand shot out of the darkness, and I felt my feet slipping out from under me. I was going down, and I saw nothing below me except jagged rocks. Then, for some reason, I stopped sliding. I realized the hand that I thought was giving me a final push had a firm grip on my windbreaker.

"Easy," Joseph said. "It's a little precarious here."

"No kidding," I said, scrambling to get my feet back onto solid ground.

"I didn't hear you," he said, pointing to the earbuds in his ear. "And I didn't see your light."

"I turned it off," I said. Joseph indicated that I should sit on the rock next to him. I was happy to let the adrenaline drain from my shaking limbs.

"We're going to stop here for a while," he said, offering me part of a Clif bar.

I accepted it gratefully and said, still shaking a bit, "Why stop? And why here?"

"Wait," he said. "You'll see."

I waited, and I saw. In the course of our run, we had crossed from the west side of the ridgeline and were now facing east across a deep, dark valley toward some distant peaks that were beginning to be touched by the light. The sky behind the peaks was fading from a fiery red as the sun arose out of its slumber to blanket the waiting world with its warmth. As the valley below us was illuminated, I could see that what had looked like a dark chasm was actually a lake lying in repose, waiting for the morning sun to reveal its many shades of blue. I watched in wonder as the awakening unfolded in front me and I silently chided myself for making fun of John Denver songs in my youth.

Joseph pointed toward one end of the lake as two gigantic bull moose emerged from the trees and cantered awkwardly toward the water as if they were running on stilts. When they reached the edge they slowed but kept moving into the lake until the water licked at their shoulders. Each of them dipped their gigantic velvet-covered antlers under the water and then pulled up again, chewing mouthfuls of long, wet, green grass.

I was seized by two conflicting emotions. The first was a sense of overwhelming gratitude at being allowed to witness this perfect scene of God's creation. I felt a bit like one of Marva's angels from her drawings. I wanted to shout for joy but felt that the sacredness of the moment allowed for no verbal communication beyond a whisper. For the first time in my life, I think I understood the meaning of the word *holy*.

The other emotion hit me lower in my gut. Like a song that takes you back to a time in the past that you can never recreate; like a loss that can never be made up or repaired; like a night when a monster takes away your mother and leaves you orphaned and alone in the world. The loneliness swept over me like a gaping black hole that cried out to be filled. This was a moment that was meant to be shared—with my mother, with Robbie or Becca, with someone special. But I had no one. No one except Joseph, and although I was grateful to him for bringing me here and for not pushing me over a cliff, I didn't think he would respond well to a spontaneous show of affection. Joseph didn't seem like much of a hugger, and we were very close to the edge of a cliff.

We sat there for a long time as I alternated between waves of rapture and longing; Joseph finally stood up and we turned around to make our way back down the trail. Apparently this had been our objective all along—sunrise over Moose Lake.

Despite the blisters that were beginning to form on my toes on the downhill trek, I was deeply grateful that Joseph had brought me along. I was also grateful that he had pulled me back from the edge. He didn't talk to me at all on the way back down the trail or even on the drive back in the car. He didn't have to. I felt a connection with him that had not been there before. I really hoped he was not a terrorist. I was beginning to like Joseph.

* * *

When we got back to the apartment, Roger was up and looking a bit deflated. "Bishop Shepherd called," he said. "He wants to meet first thing."

"I wonder what he wants to talk to us about?" I said.

"Not us," Roger replied. "Just you." Roger didn't look at me when he spoke. I guess he was still peeved at how things had turned out with our un-date. "I can call and cancel our meetings later," he said.

I started to argue with him but he was right. I had messed up royally, and it didn't seem like there was any way to salvage this particular experiment. I did manage to say halfheartedly, "Wait until after I talk to the bishop. Maybe it's good news."

Roger did look at me then, and his eyes told me that he thought I should give it a rest.

* * *

I showered and headed over to Zack's office. This was becoming a pattern—me getting lectured by Zack. He gestured to my usual chair, and I sat. I looked at the picture of Christ behind him for support but for some reason this morning the eyes reminded me more of the "Righteous Judge" than the "Merciful Mediator."

Zack looked at me for a long time as if trying to solve a puzzle. Finally he said, "Tell me about the meeting at Section 89 last night."

I knew this was coming. My short career as an un-dater was over.

"Sorry about that," I said.

"Just tell me what you were trying to accomplish." His words were measured and cool. I had experienced the wrath of Zack in both extremes, and I, like Robert Frost, preferred the fire to the ice.

"I thought if I could get people to talk about themselves, I could find out who was hiding something," I said. "Then I could narrow down our terrorist candidates from hundreds to a handful."

"So you are playing on their emotions to accomplish your task." It was a statement, not a question, but I still felt the need to answer.

"I'm not playing anyone," I said. "I'm just getting to know people. It's what I do. It's what I'm good at. It's why you brought me here. The conversations are real, not contrived. I'm not trying to hurt anyone."

"What about Marva?" he said. "What were you trying to do with her?"

"I'm sorry," I said. "I was just trying to help her to let her real self out and not hide behind those glasses."

"So you've known Marva for a long time and know what's best for her?" he asked. I figured the question was rhetorical, so I didn't say anything.

"Are you a trained therapist, Mr. Knight?"

"No, sir."

"Do you perhaps have ecclesiastical experience or training?"

I shook my head.

"Did you know that I've been counseling with Marva about her esteem issues for more than two years now?" he said.

Once again, I thought it better that I not respond.

"I thought I was finally starting to see some ever-so-slight progress," Zack said. He looked at me with a quizzical expression as if he were trying to figure out what insensitive galaxy I had come from.

"And then last night—some several hours after my bedtime I might add—I got a call from a young lady who sounded almost hysterical. Do you know what she said to me through her sobs, Mr. Knight?"

I thought about making a joke but now was really not the time.

"She said, 'I'm not Velma, Bishop. I'm not Velma. It's been right in front of me all these years, and I just couldn't see it through those stupid glasses. I'm not Velma. I never have been.'"

I started to apologize again, but he cut me off.

"Do you know what else she said to me?" I shook my head.

"She told me about your little peak-experience exercise. She told me how she struggled to think of *anything* in her life that could be classified as a high point. She told me she was tired of living a life with no high points."

I leaned forward in alarm. "She didn't hurt herself, did she?"

"That was my worry too," Zack said. "But no, she didn't hurt herself. However, what she said next shocked me down to my boots. She told me, 'The funny thing is, Bishop, I now know what I would write down for my high point. It was tonight. This night has been the best night of my life. Thank you, Bishop. For everything.'" Zack sat back and studied me.

"Here's the deal, Mr. Knight. Marva thanked me, but I didn't do anything. It was all you."

I was stunned and nearly speechless. "But she left in tears," I said. "And I thought . . ."

Zack interrupted me. "Apparently, Marva's mother told her repeatedly when she was a kid that she was no Daphne and she would have to be content being Velma. So that's what she became. When you challenged that identity, it sent her over the edge. But it also helped her to find herself." Zack continued to look at me.

"I can't figure you out, Mr. Knight. You have a gift that allowed you to gain the trust of a young woman within minutes and change her feelings about her worth. You met the county prosecutor on an airplane and within minutes she trusted you to babysit the most precious thing in her life. No wonder you're so good at your job. People naturally trust you. Be careful how you use that trust. It's a gift, but it is also a grave responsibility."

I was speechless once again. I was pretty sure that Zack had nearly given me a compliment. Just as I began to relax a bit, his countenance seemed to change.

"While we're on the subject of trust," he said, "could you kindly tell me where you were at three o'clock this morning?"

I decided once again that honesty was the best approach. "Watching the sunrise over the mountains with Joseph," I said. "You should have been there. It was magnificent."

"I *was* there," he replied. "Or at least in the general vicinity. Your watchdogs called me at about six this morning worried that the man they were tailing by satellite had suddenly stopped, apparently in the vicinity of a large cliff, and had not moved in twenty minutes. You've given me a busy night."

I explained to Zack what had happened and told him about Joseph pulling me back from the edge of the cliff. He looked thoughtful.

"Does this mean that you've taken Joseph off the suspect list?" he asked.

I thought about it. "No," I answered. "He's still near the top. But I don't think he wants to kill me. At least not right now."

"Too bad," Zack said. "It would make things a lot easier."

I thought he was joking but you could never tell with Zack.

"I hope you're not planning any more predawn runs in the mountains," Zack said, yawning. "I need my beauty sleep."

"Actually," I said, "tell your boys to get used to it. If I'm going to get to know Joseph, this may be the only way."

"Your protection detail is not going to be happy," he said. "And neither am I if I find you at the bottom of a cliff."

"Does that mean you'd miss me?" I asked. By the look he gave me I could tell that the interview was over.

* * *

I walked back to the apartment, ready to grab a bite of breakfast and catch up on a few hours of sleep. It looked like our un-dates might not be cancelled after all. I needed to let Roger know before he called and cancelled all of our appointments.

I should have been paying more attention. I stepped through the door of the apartment and immediately saw the dismay on Roger's face. He stared at me vacantly, and I saw that there was a red mark on the side of his face. I turned too late as a blur slammed into me from behind.

CHAPTER 11

Hope

BEFORE I KNEW WHAT WAS happening, my arms were pinned to my side and I was under attack. Well, maybe not under attack. Maybe more kissed and hugged and smothered. I really hoped it wasn't Joseph behind me. I mean, there was bonding and there was *bonding*.

Finally able to extricate myself from the grasp of my assailant, I looked into a face that at first I didn't recognize. The cheeks were streaked with tears, but the eyes and smile were beaming.

"Marva?" I asked. She stepped back and twirled in a circle to let me get a better look at her. She wore a yellow sundress with a wildly flowered print—and no glasses.

"Call me Rose," she said. "It's my middle name, and I've always liked it better than Marva." No surprise there.

"It fits," I said, examining her carefully. "And you know what else?"

"What?"

"Marva Rose is a very attractive person." It was true. Not that Marva had suddenly turned into a beauty queen. She was just *attractive*. Someone you'd be drawn to. She made me feel good just being next to her. Like her drawings, she made me want to laugh. Marva Rose came in for another hug, and this time I hugged her back.

"It's a start," she said, releasing me. Her expression turned serious. "I know I've still got a long way to go. It took everything I had to put on this dress and come over here. I started out the door at least fifty times and went back in." She looked down at her dress and blushed. "You don't think it's too much, do you?" She stepped back, letting me get a better look at her outfit. She was wearing lime-green elevator clogs that matched her dress.

"Over the top," I said. "Truly out of this world psychedelic." She began to frown. "But it's completely you," I said. "A perfect fit."

Her smile returned, and she beamed again.

"You know what? Now that you know who you are, I don't think it really matters what you wear. Your light is so bright that the clothes don't have a chance."

"Thank you," Marva Rose said, her voice choking a bit. She looked at Roger. "Both of you. You're my angels. The answer to my prayers. God sent you to tell me to stop whining and get over myself, and that was exactly what I needed to hear."

"But I didn't do . . ." Roger began to say but then was cut off as the woman in yellow moved in and hugged him hard. Then she kissed him on the cheek that didn't already have a red smudge. Using my keen detecting skills I surmised that this was actually the second kiss. That must have been what had caused the terror I had seen in Roger's face when I walked in. She stepped back, and both Roger and Marva Rose turned red, avoiding each other's eyes. This was getting interesting

"I have to go," she said. "Thanks again."

She left, and I looked at Roger, who stood speechless, touching his cheek.

"First Permelia and now Marva Rose," I said. "You're going to need to tell me your secret with women."

Maybe I imagined it, but I thought I saw something flash in his eyes. Something that looked like anger—and not the punch-me-in-the-arm-stop-teasing-me type of anger. Something much darker. Then, just as suddenly, the darkness was gone and the nerdy scientist returned.

"If she calls, I'm not home," Roger said. "I told you I don't do relationships."

"Then you really should stop kissing on the first un-date," I said, reaching up with my shirttail to wipe at his cheek. "It makes you seem easy."

He moved away from me and down the hallway toward his room, mumbling to himself.

* * *

The rest of the week I followed a pretty stringent schedule. My early mornings were spent running with Joseph; late mornings were reserved for catching up on sleep; afternoons I spent time at the library doing research; and evenings, of course, were set apart for the increasingly popular un-dates.

By Friday, I had learned a few things. First, I learned that Joseph was in much better shape than I was and that he probably wasn't going to push me off a cliff despite having plenty of opportunities. I think he actually enjoyed having a running partner, although I was sure he wouldn't admit it.

I also learned a few things about Roger. I reviewed his school records up through high school and noticed that a definite pattern began to emerge— Roger was a bona fide nerd, with a capital *N*. He was captain of the chemistry team, his parents were both physics professors, and he was allergic to anything athletic. All in all, he seemed like a pretty normal geek. No deep, dark secrets anywhere to be found.

I also checked into the background of any person who didn't seem completely forthright in our un-date discussions. There were a few of these, but all of them seemed to check out—except of course, Colt Mangum. His story didn't check out at all. First of all, he was operating under an alias. His first name was not really Colt, and his last name was not really Mangum. Okay, his last name *was* Mangum, as Zack was keen to remind me, but his first name was Eugene, which to me was a blatant misrepresentation.

Eugene's childhood (I liked thinking of him as Eugene) was not a happy one. An alcoholic, abusive father. A mother addicted to pain pills. A history of fighting, bullying, and generally being a teenage nuisance. No animal cruelty that I could find, which for some reason disappointed me. I thought I might find at least an incident of tying firecrackers to a cat's tail. But aside from that, he fit the profile of a seriously troubled youth. He left home at sixteen, worked in shipyards and migrant farms up and down the west coast, and then enrolled in the Marines when he was old enough.

And that's when things seemed to change for Colt. His military file was exceptionally clean, and his record was stellar—right up until the time when he was honorably discharged. His second tour in Afghanistan ended when he was caught in a firefight and took a round in his leg. This explained his limp. The rest of his patrol was killed. Colt escaped—the only survivor. He received a Purple Heart and a plane ride home.

But the role of returning hero didn't seem to sit well with Colt. He applied for reinstatement three times and each time was denied. He began to make visits to a psychiatrist and was arrested twice in bar fights. He left a world of structure and discipline where he seemed to thrive and entered back into one where he didn't seem to fit in at all. I had to admit, I felt a little sorry for Colt Mangum—but I was still going to call him Eugene the first chance I got. I would also continue to watch him carefully. It was possible he might have an ax to grind with a government that used him up and then spit him out.

I wish I could say that I spent all of my time researching suspects. But I had to admit there were times I was distracted. The face of Zelphinus Cork kept appearing before my face at the most inopportune times—usually on my computer screen.

I decided to do a Google search on Delancey Street, the rehab center where he was currently in residence. I did not like what I found, and I liked myself less for what this said about me.

Rehab centers were usually a dime a dozen. To the hard-core cons they were just a part of the revolving-door process. Delancey Street claimed to be different. Its entrance requirements were strict. To get in you had to be a multiple-time offender, a hard-core drug or alcohol abuser, unskilled, illiterate, and have a history of gang membership and violence. This was not a "rehab for the stars" kind of a place. Delancey used no government money, hired no professional staff, and ran a series of businesses, including a moving company and a popular restaurant. But probably the most amazing thing about Delancey Street was that it seemed to be working. Ninety percent of the people who went through the program never went back to the life. This was not just amazing; it was unheard of.

I shut down my computer and walked out of the library. I did not want to think about the monster who killed my mother as someone who could be rehabilitated.

I put Delancey Street out of my mind and focused on the other piece of information I had gained in the library—the address of Zelphinus Cork's daughter. It was the place to which he would likely return when he finished his time in San Francisco.

I walked to my car and began to drive. I knew that my movements were being tracked, so I had to be careful. I wouldn't want Zack to know I was spending my time looking up old friends. Luckily, the address I had for Cork's daughter was on one of the main roads from the university back to my apartment. Even more convenient, it was only a few houses down from the parking lot of a Smith's grocery store. I could stop, go into the store, buy a paper, and read it in my car—parked in the shade at the corner of the parking lot. The same corner that faced Cork's daughter's house. See, I was good at this undercover stuff.

It was an older house—probably built in the 1950s. A screen door hung precariously by one hinge, and most of the paint had long ago peeled away from the wood siding. A few minutes after I arrived, a sandy-haired boy of about eight came barreling out through the door like he was being pursued by Jack Nicholson in *The Shining*. He dove headfirst through a tire swing that hung from one of the two huge oak trees that covered the yard and then swung in wide circles, laughing and shoving something into his mouth. A woman appeared at the door holding a flyswatter. I was too far away to hear, but I imagined her saying something like, "Try that again, young man, and I'll have your hide. That Twinkie was for *after* dinner." She didn't come through the door but instead watched the boy from the doorway as he flew around the yard. A feeling of loss hit me in the chest so hard that I almost couldn't breathe. I saw myself in the swing and my mother in the doorway—finally out of apartments and into our own little house. The one we had been planning for. The one that had been taken away by this woman's father.

I watched for a while and thought that if my father was Zelphinus Cork, I wouldn't want him anywhere near this boy.

Maybe I could help with that.

Just as I turned on my engine to leave, a mail truck pulled up to the house. The mailbox was battered aluminum and sat precariously atop a rotting post in the front yard. The boy immediately stopped his swinging and ran toward the box. The mailman handed him a bright orange envelope, and the boy sprinted back toward the house, opening it and yelling as he ran. I thought I heard him say, "Grandpa." Maybe it was my imagination.

I drove home and entered the apartment. Roger was waiting. Once again I could see panic in his eyes. I quickly scanned left and right, wondering if Marva Rose might have come to visit again. But the apartment was clear.

"What's wrong?" I asked.

"Apartment 23 cancelled for tonight." He stood behind the couch, seemingly paralyzed.

"So?"

"It leaves us alone with apartment 24," Roger said. "Permelia's apartment." He wrung out his fingers like he was milking a hundred-year-old cow.

"So?" I said again.

"So? So that means it's going to be you, me, Permelia, and Hope Winslow. Alone. Together."

"Oh," I said, beginning to understand. "No other men tonight?"

"We've run out of men," he said.

"Can't we just reschedule? Find a time when apartment 23 can come?" I began to pace the room looking for another cow to milk.

"I tried. Permelia wouldn't hear of it. She said this was the only time that she and her roommate were available on the same evening this month. I think she just likes to make me squirm."

He was right about that.

"So what are we going to do?" Roger asked.

I searched my mind for an escape route but could find none. "We're going to go through with it," I said, forcing myself to stop in my tracks. "We are going to carry out this un-date just like all the others. We've got the structure down, we've got some momentum, and we know what to expect with Permelia. How bad could it be?"

* * *

My question was answered convincingly two hours later. Roger and I had just taken our seats when Permelia showed up in what looked to be a prom dress. In her hand she held a plastic container with a pin-on boutonniere inside. We stood, and she opened the box and proceeded to pin the flower onto the pocket of Roger's T-shirt.

"You forgot my corsage, didn't you, honey," she said, patting his shirt. "Well, that's okay. The important thing is that we can spend the evening together."

"Permelia," I said. "You know this is not a real date."

"I'm not senile," she said, her prom dress flowing behind her. "Give me some credit." She turned to Roger and touched his arm. Roger blushed and looked like he might pass out.

"Take it easy, Permelia. We're likely to lose him if we're not careful. I think it's time for you to come clean." I could see the flight response registering in Roger's eyes, and I was afraid he was going to take off.

"Oh, all right," she said. "You can relax, Roger. I've had my fun for the night, and I guess for the year too. You have to admit, though, the boutonniere was a great touch."

"Classic," I said, laughing. "Where did you find a prom dress? I wish I had a camera."

"Borrowed it from one of my friends' grandkids," she said. "Two hundred dollars and she only wore it once."

Roger sat down, looking confused.

"Don't look so sad," said Permelia. "I know it must come as a blow to you to find out I've been faking it. But it was fun while it lasted. One of my favorite years ever." Permelia let out a long breath. "It's going to be difficult to find something else to occupy my time."

Roger blinked. "This was all an act? The whole time?"

Permelia curtseyed. "Did I mention I used to be in theater?"

"Weren't you supposed to bring your roommate?" I asked, looking around.

"She'll be here any minute," Permelia said. "At least I hope she will. She's nearly as averse to dating as Roger is. I had a heck of a time getting her to commit to come."

"You were messing with me," Roger said, talking to himself and shaking his head. "This whole time, you were just messing with me?"

"All good things must come to an end," said Permelia. "Speaking of which, here comes Hope now."

We all turned to see the infamous Hope Winslow enter the cafeteria. She was wearing light-green scrubs and had her ample hair tied back at the nape of her neck. I noticed that she moved like a dancer—an angry dancer who was ready to kick some butt.

She approached the table but did not sit down. She examined Permelia in her prom dress and Roger with his flower sticking out of his T-shirt. I swear the flower wilted under her gaze. Or maybe that was Roger.

"I thought you said this was a group activity," Hope said to Permelia.

"Sit down, dear. It is a group activity. We're just a rather small group."

"It should be pretty painless," I said, pulling out my un-date papers. "And it really won't take very long." She turned her icy gaze on me, and I knew how the flower felt.

"You must be Matthew Knight," she said.

"The *K is* silent, but it's usually pronounced without a hiss," I said. I thought I saw a flash of humor in her eyes when I said this, but it might have been wishful thinking.

"Let's just drop the pretense," she said. "We all know what's really going on here." Her penetrating gaze nearly convinced me that Hope Winslow somehow knew everything. My profession, my mission, the brand of underwear I was wearing. The truth was, although she was not high on my suspect list, she was still a suspect. Her advanced degree in medical chemistry made her one of the few people that might have the expertise to engineer a bioweapon that could pollute a water supply.

I said nothing but I knew I looked guilty. After all, my underwear was a generic Wal-Mart brand.

"C'mon," she said. "Permelia's been trying to line us up ever since you arrived. She knows I don't date, so she and you concocted this whole 'un-date' scenario to get around that inconvenient fact. Well, I don't like games, and I don't have any patience for them." Her nose twitched a little to the side as she talked. It was actually kind of cute.

"It's really not a game," Permelia protested. "And it's not a date."

"Permelia," Hope said. "Look at yourself."

"What?"

"You're wearing a prom dress."

"But really . . ." Roger began then stopped as the icy glare turned his direction.

"And you have a boutonniere."

"Could you take our picture?" Permelia asked, scooting closer to Roger.

Hope groaned. I laughed, trying to break the tension. It didn't work. Hope glared even harder.

"What's your problem?" I asked.

"I told you. I don't like games. If you want to ask me out, then ask me out. Don't hide behind all this pretense."

"You said you don't date."

"I don't. But you should at least give me the courtesy of saying no."

"I'm not sure I'd want to go out with you," I said. "Permelia's a lot more fun."

"Then why the whole charade?" she asked, a tiredness creeping into her voice.

"You tell me."

"What do you mean?"

"What are you trying to hide?" I asked.

"I'm not the one hiding anything."

"You're definitely hiding something," I said. *Why else would you have all that hair?* "I think you're using your righteous indignation about the un-date as a diversion. You don't want to be here, and this is a convenient excuse." Some of the anger passed beyond her eyes, and she bit at her bottom lip.

"What are you so afraid of?" I continued. "We're really not that scary." I glanced over at Roger and Permelia and almost had to take back my words. They looked like a couple of extras from a low-budget horror movie.

Hope Winslow's lower lip began to tremble slightly, and she bit it again to get it to stop. Without another word, she turned on her heels and walked out the door.

After a long silence, Permelia said, "Well, that went well. Do you think you'll ask her out again?"

* * *

Roger and I escorted Permelia home and then began to make our way back to our apartment without saying a word. As we rounded the corner of one of the buildings, I spotted Colt Mangum and two other men standing behind the trunk of a car in the parking lot. Instinctively, I stopped and held Roger back. Not just because I thought Colt Mangum probably wanted to pummel our brains, but also because of the two men who were with him. There was something about the way they held themselves. They were dressed in black T-shirts and baggy cargo pants. They were not muscle-bound like Colt but rather moved in a precise, almost orchestrated way. I'd seen this type of men before. They were either military or ex-military. And they were about a million times more dangerous than Colt Mangum. What had little Eugene gotten himself into?

The trunk of the car slammed, and Colt glanced up in our direction.

"Run," I said to Roger.

Roger ran. So did I. Like a cat with firecrackers tied to its tail.

CHAPTER 12

The Truman Center

WE CIRCLED BACK IN THE dark and approached our building from the rear. I peered around the corner before giving Roger the all clear, and we hurried into our apartment. Joseph was sitting on the sofa, working on his laptop.

"Playing kick-the-can again?" he asked, noticing our rush to get in the door.

"Colt Mangum," Roger said between breaths.

"Typical bully," Joseph said. "Punch him hard in the nose once, and he'll back down." Joseph might have been right about Colt. But he hadn't seen Colt's two friends.

There was a knock at the door, and Roger about jumped out of his skin. "I don't think we should open it," he said.

The knock came again, but it was not the break-down-the-door kind of knock I would have expected from Colt. I pushed Roger aside and looked through the peephole. Roger was right. Opening the door was going to be dangerous. I opened it anyway.

"Peace offering," said Hope Winslow, holding out a single flower. I took it, not knowing what to say. I'd never received flowers from a woman before. She looked past me to Roger.

"The apology applies to you too," she said, looking at his T-shirt. "But you already have a flower."

She turned her eyes back on me. They were an amazingly deep color of blue.

"Permelia told me what happened with the other apartment being sick," she said. "I still didn't believe her, so she made me call Marva." Hope seemed to be a little uncomfortable in her shoes. "I think what you did for her was great."

"I didn't do anything for Marva," I said. "Marva did it all for herself."

"But your un-date helped," she said. "Permelia also told me that my actions were completely inappropriate and that I needed to come and apologize."

I looked down at my flower. "Apology accepted," I said. I pulled my eyes away from her hypnotic gaze, searching behind her for any sign of Colt and his two compadres. Everything was quiet. I looked back at Hope. Her eyes were still blazingly blue, and they were still looking at me.

"What you said about me hiding something . . ." she began.

"I didn't mean to hurt your feelings," I said. "I was just being defensive."

"I want to explain . . ."

"Can you take this love fest outside?" Joseph asked, cutting her off. "I'm studying for an exam." Joseph could be a real jerk at times.

I stepped outside with Hope. Roger didn't follow.

"You don't have to explain anything," I said to her. "You were having a bad night. It happens to all of us."

"I *was* having a bad night. But I still want to make it up to you." The eyes were drawing me in again. So was the hair. I had a sudden urge to reach out and fluff it with my hands. I resisted.

"Can you meet me somewhere tomorrow evening?" she said.

I was taken a little off guard and was temporarily at a loss as to how to respond. Finally, I managed, "I don't really date," and for some reason immediately regretted it.

"It won't be a date," she said, smiling. Did I mention her smile? Her perfect white teeth. Her full, pink lips. Had I really just turned down a date with Hope Winslow?

"It will be an un-date," she continued. "In fact, it will be the continuation of tonight's un-date. I never did get a chance to share my peak experiences, and I would rather show than tell."

"Are Roger and Permelia coming along?" I asked. "We could stop by the costume store and find some appropriate outfits for them. How about the guy from *Psycho* and his mother?" Come to think of it, Roger did bear a striking resemblance to a young Anthony Perkins.

Hope giggled. It was the first time I had heard her laugh, and I immediately wanted to find something clever to say so she would laugh again. My mind went blank. What good was it being a smart aleck if your wit left you in times like these?

"I think Permelia and Roger were scary enough tonight," she said. "Why don't we take this one on our own. Do you have something that I can write on?"

I checked my pockets. No pencil and no paper. I was holding a flower, but that wasn't going to work.

I held out my almost empty hands and shrugged. "Looks like we'll have to go back inside and face the wrath of Joseph."

"He'll get over it," she replied. "Maybe he's just having a bad night. It happens to the best of us."

"Joseph's condition is a little more chronic," I explained before I opened the door and we stepped back into the apartment. Hope met Joseph's glare with a sweet smile, and I thought for a moment he would waver. I found some paper and a pen, gave it to Hope, and looked down to find she had not written down an address but instead the name of a hospital and a floor number.

"Meet me here at seven o'clock tomorrow," she said. "I'll just be getting off my shift."

I tried to think of a witty comeback, but before I could, she smiled, said good-bye and left.

"I hope this isn't going to become a habit," Joseph said after the door closed.

"I should be so lucky," I mumbled under my breath.

* * *

From the outside, the Truman Center for Cancer Research didn't look anything like a hospital. Nestled in the hills near the University of Utah, the buildings were hidden from the road by acres of manicured gardens and trees.

I drove up to what I thought was a security booth, but there was no crossbar blocking my entrance and no guard asking me my business. Just a nice young woman who welcomed me and gave me directions to the correct parking area.

The main building looked like a five-star hotel, both inside and out. The lobby was filled with live trees, hanging plants, and small waterfalls. There was the odor of citrus in the air. The place certainly didn't look or smell like a hospital. I made my way to the fourth floor nurses' station and announced my business. The woman behind the desk looked at me over reading glasses that were perched on the tip of her nose. "You're here to see Hope?" Her tone said that this was about as likely as me announcing I was about to lift an elephant with my pinkie.

"That's right. She asked me to meet her here." I tried not to sound defensive.

"She's never had any man meet her here before." The woman's dark eyes reflected off the lenses of her glasses so it felt like two people were staring at me. "Why would she ask you here?"

"Not to be rude," I said, "but I'm not sure that's any of your business."

"My business is to decide who gets into those doors and who doesn't." She beckoned with her eyes to the large metal doors behind her. "So, if you want to see Hope, you *will* answer the question."

"All right," I said. "Hope and I had a misunderstanding. She told me she could explain things better if I met her here."

"What kind of misunderstanding?"

I considered my options. Madge (that's what her name tag said) was starting to annoy me. She was a little too nosy for her own good. But I could see by the expression on her face that I was not getting past her without telling the story. I decided on an abbreviated version.

"Hope mistakenly thought I was trying to finagle a date with her," I said. "I got defensive and told her I thought she was afraid to open up and let others get to know her."

Madge leaned back in her chair and whistled. "I hope you didn't say she was hiding behind her hair?"

"Of course not," I said. I didn't tell her I had been thinking it.

"You stupid, stupid man." Madge shook her head like I had just committed a felony. "Do you know anything at all about Hope Winslow?"

"Not really. We barely met."

"Are you in the habit of insulting women on the first meeting?"

I looked around for a rock to crawl under. "I wasn't trying to insult her. I was just making an observation." For some reason I felt a need to explain myself further to Madge. "It was a church group doing an exercise to get to know one another better," I said. "We were sharing pivotal events from our lives. Hope didn't want to participate, so I thought she might be hiding something." From the look in Madge's eyes, I thought she might come after me with a hypodermic needle.

"Do you know what we do here at the Truman Center for Cancer Research?"

"Uh . . . You research cancer," I guessed.

"We research and treat cancer *in children*," she said. "Do you know what we do here on the fourth floor?"

I looked at the sign on the desk. "Chemotherapy?" I ventured. See, I wasn't a stupid, stupid man. "And, of course, you make first-time visitors feel really welcome."

Madge didn't even flinch. "So, have you put two and two together yet?" she asked. Obviously, I hadn't. I didn't have a clue as to what she was getting at. Maybe I did deserve the double "stupids." She waited. I shrugged.

"I guess I'd better show you," she said, getting up. "But you're going to feel like a major idiot when you see." At least she hadn't called me stupid this time. And, by the way, I already felt like a major idiot, so I was ahead of the game. Madge handed me a surgeon's mask and a bottle of hand sanitizer. She put on her own mask and swiped a card on the side of the double doors. "Follow me," she commanded, talking through the mask. I thought she sounded a little like Darth Vader.

I followed.

We walked down a long, sterile hallway toward another set of magnetic doors. She swiped her card again, and the doors opened into a commons area that looked more like the garden setting of the lobby than what I had seen so far of the fourth floor. However, there was a difference, and quite a big one. This commons area was filled with people. Little people. Little bald people. Perhaps forty kids. Madge was right. I really was stupid. Hope Winslow worked on the chemotherapy floor. With children. Madge was looking at me over the top of her bifocals, her eyes communicating a smug *I-told-you-so*.

Some of the kids were standing, but most of them sat, coloring or playing quietly with toys or games. The atmosphere was hushed. The kids seemed to move in slow motion. Some of them had tubes taped to their arms and trailed IV carts behind them. I felt like I was witnessing life on an alien planet.

A door opened on the other end of the room, and it was as if a wave of electricity had been channeled inside. Drooping, bald heads perked up, and little bodies began scrambling toward the source of the energy.

Hope Winslow seemed to float into the room. She wore similar scrubs as the night before, but I could swear they were infused with a brilliant light. She also wore a surgical mask, but from the crinkles at the corners of her eyes, I could tell she had a beaming smile underneath. Roger was right—Hope Winslow was an angel. The kids were pulled toward her like a magnet. She met every child, one by one, with a big hug and words that I couldn't hear from where I stood. Each bald, frail-looking creature plunged his or her hands into Hope Winslow's hair, held it there for a moment, and then moved aside for the next child to take a turn. As they pulled away, it seemed as if they carried with them a newfound power that buoyed them up. After this ritual, the children seated themselves on the floor in front of Hope. She opened a book and began reading them a story.

"You still think she's hiding something?" Madge asked.

I felt like I had the morning before, sitting on the edge of a cliff watching the sunrise with Joseph. I was witnessing a miracle. "Madge," I said. "I *am* a stupid, stupid man."

"I told you," she said, but the scolding tone had left her voice. Actually, she was whispering. We both were. At this moment in time, anything louder than a whisper would have sounded like blasphemy. At this moment in time, this room was a temple. A temple of Hope.

"How does she do it?" I asked. "It's got to be more than just the hair."

Madge studied me. "Maybe you're not as stupid as I thought," she said. "Let's just say there's no place these kids can go that Hope hasn't been to already."

I looked at Hope and her flowing curls amidst the stark baldness. I tried to imagine her without hair. "You mean Hope had cancer?"

Madge hesitated and then decided to tell me. "That's part of it. A few years ago, she was as bald and sickly as any of these kids. She was diagnosed with cervical cancer. Terminal. There was nothing anyone could do."

"These kids?" I asked. "They have terminal cancer?"

"Every one of them," Madge's whisper became even softer, and I could see the concern in her eyes.

"But Hope's cancer went into remission?"

"Nope," Madge said. "No remission. Her cancer is gone. It disappeared almost overnight. No sign of it left. She's a modern-day miracle."

I looked back at Hope as the kids erupted in laughter. She must have reached a funny part in the book. Or maybe they just needed to laugh. I felt like crying as I watched them.

"She really is hope for these kids," I said in wonder.

"In more ways than you know," Madge said.

"What do you mean?"

The openness in Madge's eyes started to fade again. "I've said too much." She was still whispering, but the hardness was back in her voice. "I think that both Miss Winslow and I have been way too generous already."

I would have protested, but Madge was right. Allowing me into this room—this inner sanctum—was truly a gift. One I did not deserve. I started to ask Madge to tell Hope that I had never shown up—that she had never seen anyone by the name of Matthew Knight. But it was too late. Hope Winslow had spotted me. She held up her hand, indicating she needed about five more minutes. I pointed back to the doors behind me, telling her I'd wait outside. I took one last look at the surreal scene in front of me and turned around.

CHAPTER 13
Going to See Jesus

I GUESS I FIGURED THAT Hope Winslow would still be wearing her scrubs when she came through the doors, but she had on a dark skirt, a white blouse, and a scarf. How had she changed so fast? She smelled good too—like she was ready to go out on a date. I looked down at my khaki pants and button-up shirt. These were the best clothes I owned. I felt like a slob.

And not only did I feel like a slob, but a schmuck too. I had basically accused Mother Theresa of hiding behind her habit. I found I was having a hard time meeting Hope's eyes. Maybe I was ashamed, or maybe it was because she looked so good. I cleared my throat as she walked up. I looked over at Madge. She looked amused.

"Listen," I said. "About what I said last night."

Hope held up her hand. "No apologies," she said. "We both acted badly, and I'm not really in the mood to get into a pity match to decide who was worse. Let's get something to eat. I don't know about you, but I'm starving."

I realized that I was also quite hungry. "Sounds good," I said. "Where do you want to go?"

"Here will be fine."

I looked around. "Here?"

"Not here on the fourth floor, but *here* at the Truman Center."

"There's a cafeteria?"

Hope looked at Madge, and they shared a smile. "Something like that."

We took the elevator down and went through a back door into a courtyard. We walked through a small park for about five minutes and then came to what looked like a Mediterranean village, complete with cobblestone streets, small shops, and a few restaurants.

"What is this place?" I asked. The streets weren't crowded but neither were they empty. Several couples strolled leisurely, holding hands as if on vacation. I was not holding on to Hope Winslow's hand, but I could feel it swinging precariously near mine. My palms started to sweat.

"It's all a part of the Truman Center," she answered. "The hospital, the park, two hotels, a movie theater, several restaurants, and even a water park. It's an amazing place, and most people don't even know it exists. The owner is a philanthropist who likes to do wonderful things for others but doesn't particularly like publicity."

I scratched my head. "If he doesn't want publicity, why did he name the place after himself?"

"He didn't," Hope said. "The owner is not Mr. Truman. Truman was the name of his son—a son who had cancer. He's the reason this place was built. Even with all of his billions, the founder could not find a place to care for his son that felt more like a home than a hospital. So he decided to create one. He took all of the best ideas from his son's favorite places in the world as well as the latest medical practices and incorporated them into the Truman Center. The kids get the treatment they need, the parents are able to stay onsite in a resortlike setting, and the whole place is infused with a dose of human-ness that you don't typically find in a medical facility."

I looked around again at the smiling people and shopkeepers on the street. "Are you sure they're human? I think I saw a movie like this once and everyone turned out to be robots."

Hope laughed, and I felt the same thrill I had the night before.

"It is a unique place," she said. "But believe me, all of the people here are tragically human. The people you see on the streets are the parents, relatives, and friends of some of the kids you saw with me in the hospital. The village setting helps them deal with the stress of a hopeless situation."

"Do you think the surrounding environment really makes a difference?" I asked.

"I know it does. The empirical studies show that the Truman Center adds an average of six months of life to each terminal child. That's six additional months the family gets to be with their kids. Six more months to read to them, go to movies, go swimming, and tuck them into bed. And those six months at the Truman Center can be a lot more enjoyable than any amount of time in a traditional hospital."

We arrived at a stone building that looked like a restaurant. The letters above the door read *San Giovanni in Fiore*. A man dressed in white opened the door for us to a view of a stone hearth with a fire and candlelit booths arranged along the sides.

"I hope Italian is okay," Hope said as we walked in.

"I love Italian," I said. "I pretty much live on Little Caesar's pizza." I thought the man at the door might faint.

"He's a student," Hope explained to the man apologetically. We were met by another man, this one dressed in a tuxedo, who showed us to our table. It was dark, in a corner, and . . . kind of romantic.

"I hope you don't mind," Hope said. "They've only been open a few months and I've really wanted to eat here. I haven't been able to juggle schedules to get Permelia to meet me, and I really didn't want to eat in a place like this by myself." The waiter brought menus and a big basket of breadsticks with marinara sauce that smelled heavenly.

"Permelia's loss is my gain." I looked across the table and knew that I was falling in love—with the breadsticks, that is. Did I mention that they smelled divine? I picked up the basket and offered it to Hope Winslow.

"Ladies first," I said. *But you'd better move fast.*

She took a breadstick and said, "Thank you."

I took two, splashed some marinara on my plate, and then took a bite. The taste was as good as the aroma—only better.

"Permelia is going to be upset that she missed this," I said.

"It serves her right for constantly trying to line me up." Hope took a bite, and her eyes widened. "These really are good."

"So are you going to tell me?" I asked after a moment.

"Tell you what?"

"Why you're so against dating?"

"Maybe later," she said, opening her menu. "What about you? You don't date either. What are your reasons?"

"I've just changed my mind," I said taking another bite. "If this is what dating is all about, then I'm all for it. Nobody told me I would get breadsticks. And these are even better than Little Caesar's."

Hope laughed again. "Keep it quiet. I thought the doorman was going to have a heart attack."

I looked across the breadsticks and into Hope Winslow's eyes. "You were amazing with those kids today. I never should have said anything about you trying to hide something."

"No need to apologize. I was being rude, and you just reflected back my vibe. It's me who should apologize. I was just frustrated."

"Because of Permelia?"

"She was part of it. But it was mostly because of your little exercise."

"My exercise? What about sharing peak experiences would frustrate you?"

I thought I could see her eyes moistening just a bit. "You were there today," she said. "You've seen what my peak experiences are like."

"That was one of the most amazing things I've ever seen in my life," I said, meaning it. "Why would you not want to share that?"

"That's just it. I want to share it, but I don't know how. Every time I've tried to explain it to someone, I start to bawl and fail miserably. They think I'm crazy, and I feel like I've turned something sacred into a joke. It's one of those things you really can't explain. You just have to experience it. Can you understand that?" She wiped a tear off her cheek.

I nodded. I understood. Kind of like trying to tell Zack about the sunrise at Moose Lake. I suddenly felt like a trespasser. I had been offered a glimpse into a world that I was not entitled to see. I should have just kept my mouth shut and felt lucky I had been given the opportunity. Instead I asked another question.

"Madge said that you gave the kids hope because you had been where they had been. That you had cancer."

She looked at me for a minute as if making a decision and then said, "Yes, I had cancer. It was three years ago. And yes, I lost all of my hair."

"That's a great wig." I gestured toward her flowing locks, which dipped precariously close to the marinara sauce.

She dipped her index finger in her water and flicked it at me, nailing me with a drop square in the eye. "My hair eventually came back, faster and thicker than ever. But there was a time when I thought I would never see it again."

I started to ask another question but then stopped myself, realizing that I might be headed somewhere I ought not go. Hope saw my hesitation.

"I don't mind talking about it," she said.

I cleared my throat. "How do you handle it?" I asked. "Knowing that the kids are going to die? It must be unbelievably sad."

"It is sad," she said. "And I do a lot of crying. But let's just say that death isn't the tragedy that most people think it is."

"Madge said that you were cured by a miracle."

"She did? The most Madge is usually able to muster with strangers is 'assume the position.' She must like you."

"I didn't get that impression," I said. "And you don't need to talk about any of this with me if you don't want to. I think you've already gone above and beyond in sharing your peak experience."

"You're right," she said. "I have. And you owe me a turn. I'm expecting something really profound. But I really don't mind talking about the miracle— that is, if you think you can handle it."

"What do you mean?"

"I've found that people love to hear about miracles in history or in the abstract, but when confronted with one directly they tend to squirm and back away." The light coming through the window illuminated half of her face and a strand of hair that hung out of place against her cheek. I had a sudden urge to reach up and brush it back until I realized with horror that I was suddenly trapped in a scene from a Nicholas Sparks book. I put one hand under the table and sat on it. The other I quickly occupied with another breadstick.

"I never back away from anything," I said, not sure why I said it.

She studied my face for another few moments and thankfully pushed the strand of hair back into place.

"I believe you," she said finally. "But I'm not going to tell you until after we eat. I've waited for a long time to come to this restaurant, and I'm not going to spoil it."

I wondered what about a miracle could spoil a meal, but I accepted her wishes. We ordered from the menu and talked about myriad issues, including the Truman Center, new methods for treating cancer without chemotherapy, and how she had become roommates with Permelia. She asked me about my thesis, and we did all this while devouring a thoroughly fabulous meal.

When the waiter came with the check, I said, "Let me get this. I haven't had a meal this good in years. Whatever it costs, it was worth it." Of course, I said this before I looked at the amount hidden inside the leather portfolio. When I did open it, I was confused more than shocked.

"I think this is a bad sign," I said. "There's no price on this check. Is this the kind of place where if you have to ask, you can't afford it?"

"You probably *couldn't* afford it if they charged market price," Hope said. "Angelo is one of the most famous chefs in the world. Lucky for you, employees at the Truman Center eat for free—guests included. So do patients and their families. The only reason you would ever need money here is for the shops."

"That doesn't sound like a very profitable business model."

"It's not. The center is actually a nonprofit. Most of the people who work here do so for about half of what they could make somewhere else. But I don't think any of them would leave for more money."

"Can I at least leave a tip?"

"Of course."

I looked in my wallet. The smallest bill I had was a twenty. I'd never left a twenty-dollar tip in my life. I placed it on the table and somehow felt like I was being cheap.

"Thank you for a wonderful dinner," Hope said. "Now I guess I owe you my story. Would you like to talk here, or would you rather walk?"

"I'm all for walking," I said. "I think I need to work off about twenty breadsticks." I also thought it might be a good idea to remove myself from a very romantic environment with an extremely pretty woman.

We left the restaurant as the sun was sliding behind the horizon in the west. This really was a beautiful campus. The cobblestone walkways were lit by street lamps, and there were several families and couples out and about enjoying the evening. I tried hard not to dwell on the tragic circumstances that brought them here and instead focused on enjoying the remainder of my time with Hope. She hadn't started her story yet but I decided to let her proceed at her own pace.

A small missile dislodged itself from one of the family groups ahead of us and speeded toward my kneecaps. Just before making contact, it squealed, "Charlie," and launched upward toward my chest. Taken by surprise, I caught little Meggy in my arms and gave her a big squeeze. We'd only shared one plane ride together, but I felt a certain connection.

As she hugged me, a feeling of fear worked its way into my gut and refused to let go. I pulled Megan out in front of me so that I could get a good look at her. I brushed her thick dark hair out of her eyes. There seemed to be a chunk of it missing from one side. I asked as nonchalantly as I could, "Meggy, what are you doing here?"

"I got gum in my hair and Daddy had to cut it out." She put her hand up to the side of her head to show me. As she did so, she spotted Hope and literally leapt from my arms into hers. My knees became weak as I tried not to think about why little Meggy would be acquainted with Hope.

"Hello, Meggy," Hope said, giving her a squeeze. Hope looked at me and asked me the same question I was afraid to ask her. "How do you know Meggy? And why does she call you Charlie?"

"Charlie colors princesses," Megan said.

I shrugged. "We met on my flight out here."

As I explained our chance meeting to Hope, Missy Brentwood and several of her family members realized that Meggy had run into the arms of strangers and made their way toward us.

Before they arrived, I asked Hope the question that I was dreading to hear the answer to. "How do you know Meggy?"

Before Hope could answer, Meggy said, "Benji might get to go see Jesus." Meggy jumped from Hope's arms back into mine. I looked at Hope for translation.

"Benji is her brother," Hope said. "He came to the Truman Center a few weeks ago." I felt a rush of relief that Meggy was okay and wanted to hug her even tighter.

"That's my daughter you're holding, mister. I hope you've got an explanation." I recognized Missy Brentwood's hard-edged voice behind me.

"Don't shoot the babysitter," I replied as Missy walked up. "I think this puts me on the clock." Missy gave both Hope and me a hug and then introduced us to the other family members. I recognized one of the boys from the airplane ride. The other was conspicuously absent.

I pulled Missy to the side. "Megan was telling me that Benji might get to see Jesus?" I said, meeting her eyes. I wanted to tell Missy how sorry I was, but from her warning glance, I could see I was right not to. She obviously wanted to insulate Megan, but I could see the sadness in her eyes.

"That's right," Missy said. "But we won't find out until some more tests have been done. Until then, he gets to live in this really cool place, and we get to come visit. Right, Meggy?" She tickled her underneath the arm, and Megan giggled.

"They have a swimming pool with a dragon slide," Megan said, putting her little hands on my cheeks and pulling my eyes even with hers.

"No way," I said.

She nodded her head up and down emphatically. "Uh-huh, and a merry-go-round with unicorns."

"That is so cool."

"So how is it that Meggy finds two of her favorite people here together?" Missy asked. I thought I caught a hint of the courtroom interrogator in her tone.

"Are you getting married?" Megan asked, pulling my gaze again back to hers. "I think Hope is pretty."

I looked at Hope. Megan was right. She was pretty. Very pretty. "Do you think we should?" I asked Hope. Hope blinked rapidly for a moment and then realized I was messing with her.

"We're just friends," Hope said to Megan.

"Charlie—" Hope said the name as if it were an indictment—"goes to my church. So we're like a brother and sister."

I figured I could say *sayonara* to a good-night kiss.

"Sometimes I fight with my brothers," Megan said.

Hope looked at me as if considering whether to punch me in the chops.

"We sometimes fight too," I replied. "She always wins. But only because I'm not allowed to pull her hair." Megan giggled.

"It's the female advantage," Missy interjected, looking sideways at her husband. "If we sense defeat we can always cry."

"I have a hard time picturing you in the courtroom in tears," I said.

"That's because I've never admitted defeat," Missy said. But she looked like she was ready to cry right now. "We'd better go," she said, holding her arms out to Megan. "It's past your bedtime." Megan gave me another hug and then rapidly shifted her weight to hug Hope. I can't really explain what happened next, but as Megan leaned over, half of her weight in my arms and half in Hope's, something happened.

I felt a wave of energy run through my body from the top of my head to the tip of my little toe. It jolted me and then settled—like the first set of tumblers on a combination lock falling into place. The weird thing is, I was almost certain that Hope felt it too. I blinked my eyes a few times and shook my head, gently pulling Megan back and breaking the connection.

I handed Megan to Missy. "You need to come over sometime and color with Meggy," she said.

"I'll try."

"Bring Hope too," Megan commanded. I didn't say anything to this. I was still trying to figure out what had just happened.

"Bye-bye, Meggy," Hope said. Her voice seemed a little weak.

We waved good-bye and moved in the opposite direction from the Brentwoods. We walked silently on the cobblestone sidewalks for a few hundred yards, and then Hope breathed a big sigh.

"It's tragic," I said in response. "Meggy's brother."

"It is," Hope said. "And it isn't." She spoke slowly, and I wondered what she was getting at.

"If Benji dies, he really will get to see Jesus. And it will be more wonderful than anything he's ever experienced in this life. Do you understand what I'm saying?"

"I think so," I said. "You have faith in an afterlife."

"It's more than faith," Hope said. "A lot more. I *know* that Benji will see Jesus. I've been there. I've taken that path."

I stopped and looked at her, but it was probably abundantly clear from the blank expression on my face that I still wasn't getting it.

"I wasn't cured of my cancer," Hope said. "I died from it. I went to see Jesus."

I didn't know how to respond to this. I really didn't understand what she meant. Finally, I ventured, "You seem pretty well preserved—for a dead person, I mean."

Hope laughed. "I did come back—eventually. But I'm not sure I wanted to. It was so peaceful there. No pain. No strife. No mutant cells waging war with the chemicals injected into my veins. Just comfort. Just glorious light. Just a feeling of love so strong that I felt I was being held in one long and tender embrace." Her eyes had a faraway look, and they seemed to radiate their own form of light. "I felt completely whole for the first time in my existence. I felt that I had finally returned home and that I never wanted to leave again. Do you have any idea what that feels like?" Tears began to well up in her eyes, and she pulled a handkerchief from her purse and attempted to stem the tide.

I shook my head. I had never in my entire life felt whole.

I let the silence settle then said, "So why *did* you come back?"

She half laughed, half cried. "I don't know," she said. "I sometimes wish I hadn't. I was given the choice. He said I could stay if I wanted to but that I had a mission to perform if I stayed. I was shown the faces of children in pain and families without hope and told that I could bring them much comfort. I was told that I could take some of the light and peace I was feeling back with me and pass it on to these kids. I sat there in His presence, and I could literally feel the overwhelming love He felt for these children. In the end I really didn't have any choice at all. I had to come back."

"And your cancer?"

"I was in a coma for three weeks. The doctors wanted to pull the plug, but my parents and seven protective brothers wouldn't let them. When I woke up I was starving for some real food. I pulled the tubes from my body and began wandering the hallways. Madge was one of my nurses. You should have seen the look on her face when she found me in the cafeteria eating strawberries. I was rushed back for tests and X-rays, but the cancer was gone."

We walked for a long time in silence.

Finally, Hope said, "Well, you probably want to take me home now."

"Why do you say that?"

"I don't share this story with many people," she said. "But when I do, things usually get awkward. People don't want to tell me that they don't believe me, so they tend to be very polite but aloof."

"I've never been very good at being polite," I said. "You can ask Marva."

"But you don't believe me."

I thought about it before responding. "I'm kind of caught in a weird spot," I said. "I'm not sure I even believe in God, so when I hear a story like this, my inner skeptic comes out."

Hope's shoulders seemed to sag a bit, and she nodded her head as if she had heard these words before.

"The thing is," I said, "I may not believe in God, but I believe you. I don't doubt what you say at all. Maybe it's because I saw you with the kids. You *were* filled with light. Who am I to let my doubts diminish your miracle?"

She relaxed her stride a bit and turned to look at me. "Can I ask you a question?" she said.

"Sure."

"If you believe me, how can you not believe in God? Either I died and went to heaven, or I didn't. If I did—and you say you believe me—then there is a heaven, and there is a God."

Tough question. One that I really wasn't ready to answer. Too much had happened to me in my life that made me question God's existence. "Let's just say I'm not ready to take that leap of faith yet," I said. "Can it be enough that I believe you?"

I could feel that she wanted to press me further, but she didn't. Instead she smiled. A bright, beaming, wonderful smile. "I'll take that," she said. "Thank you for being honest." She grabbed my hand and squeezed. "It's been a long time since I've had a good talk with a member of the opposite sex. I really miss it."

"What was it like growing up with seven brothers?" I asked, wanting to move the subject away from my personal convictions and on to safer ground.

"It was awful," she said. "And wonderful. I was the youngest and the only girl. They teased me to no end. They were also very protective and seemed to take great pleasure in making my dates nervous. Any boy who came to the house was guaranteed to get the third degree."

"So one of them's going to be waiting with a shotgun when I take you home tonight?"

"Fortunately for you, no," she said. "They're spread out all over the country. But it doesn't matter anyway. This isn't a date, remember?"

"I remember," I said. "But it sounds like you used to date. Why not now? Is it because of how people respond to your . . . uh . . . miracle?"

"It is because of the miracle," she said, "but not because of people's response. Pretty simple, really. When I came back, I had a purpose. I'm here to help these kids. To give them hope and to ease their suffering. To take the light I received and pass it on. That is my entire focus. Everything else is a distraction. I'm not sure how much time I've got left, but I figure that one day my mission will be through and I will be called home again. It wouldn't be fair to a man to bring him into this."

I thought that there would be plenty of men who wouldn't mind the sacrifice.

"We've spent enough time talking about me though," Hope said. "It's your turn. I think I've done a pretty exceptional job sharing my peak experience, and you've barely told me anything."

"I had a dog named Buster," I offered.

She shook her head. "Not good enough."

"I ran a marathon."

"Weak. You owe me."

I did feel a debt to Hope Winslow. By bringing me to the Truman Center and allowing me to see her interacting with the kids, she had truly given me a precious gift. She had also opened herself up in ways that made her completely vulnerable. I did owe her. I owed her big time. But most of my secrets I couldn't talk about. How was I going to balance the scales?

Hopefully I would think of something before we parted ways.

"We can talk as I walk you to your car," I said.

"I rode the bus," she said. "You'll be taking me home."

Dinner, a moonlight walk, and now driving the girl home. This was feeling more and more like a date all the time.

CHAPTER 14
Demetrius and Chico

I COULDN'T READ HOPE'S REACTION when she saw my car, but as far as I could tell she was just able to suppress a gag reflex.

"Let me clear off the front seat for you. I'm not used to having passengers." I picked up an armload of books and moved them to the back.

"Was that a Book of Mormon?" she asked. "I thought you didn't believe in God."

"I said I didn't know if I believed in God, and it's an assignment from Zack. To tell you the truth, I haven't cracked it open yet."

"Why do you call him that?"

"Call who what?"

"You just called Bishop Shepherd 'Zack.'"

Oops. I was going to have to be more careful about that. "Uh . . . what does everyone else call him?"

"Sometimes Bishop Shepherd, sometimes Bishop, and sometimes even Bishop Zack, but I don't think anyone calls him just Zack."

"I have a secret to tell you," I said conspiratorially. "I tend to have issues with authority."

"Really," she said, eyeing me.

"So there you have it. I've known you less than a day, and I've already bared my soul to you." I let out a long breath. "That was tougher than I thought, but I actually feel better now that I've opened up."

She punched me in the arm. I deserved it, and a lot worse. Hope Winslow had shared with me some of the most intimate moments of her life, and here I was cracking wise. She was a saint. I was evil.

"And you accuse *me* of hiding," she said, getting into the car with a sigh. "Just take me home."

Logically, that is exactly what I should have done. I had found out everything I needed to about Hope Winslow, and she was definitely not a terrorist. Therefore, being around her any longer did not serve any purpose, and sharing anything more about myself could only put my cover at risk. This is what I told myself as I got into the car and started the engine. In my heart, I felt like the lowest mud-sucking scum of all the earth.

A few minutes went by, and I looked out the window and realized I had driven toward the city and not toward the Village. The roads began to look familiar. They had changed in many ways, but I knew where I was, and I knew where I was going.

"You're right," I said, breaking the silence. "I have been hiding something. But like the Truman Center, it is a little beyond words. I need to show you." We drove past a train station and a downtown shopping center called the Gateway, which didn't exist the last time I was in town. Beyond, the streets got dirtier and darker. I wasn't sure what I was doing. This wasn't a safe part of town. But for some reason I felt I *needed* to take this journey with Hope. Maybe it was because she deserved it for opening up to me. Maybe it was because I needed to open up to someone else.

"What could you possibly have to show me in this part of town?"

"My childhood," I said. It was getting late. There were people out on the streets, but they were the homeless, the prostitutes, and the drug dealers. Luckily, my car fit right in. Hope was looking a little nervous.

"You grew up here?"

"Here and other neighborhoods like this." I pointed to a run-down apartment building up ahead. "My mother and I lived on the top floor at the back. It's where the missionaries found us."

"The missionaries came into this part of town?" There was a note of admiration in her voice. I had never really thought about it before, but those missionaries must have been pretty brave.

"Not at night," I said. "Never at night." I thought about stopping in front of the apartment and telling her about my mother's conversion story, but I kept driving. If Hope Winslow wanted to know who Matthew Knight really was, then I was going to show her. We went a few blocks more, and I found the alleyway and pulled in. It ended in a cinder-block wall. A dead end. For some reason the distance from the wall to the street seemed a lot shorter than what I remembered. It couldn't have been more than fifty yards. That night it had seemed like a mile.

I put the car in park and began to talk without looking at Hope.

"One night when I was eight, we were walking home from serving meals at the homeless shelter. Several people offered to give us rides, but my mom declined. She wanted to look at the stars. She'd recently emerged from a mostly medicated state, and she wanted to experience every legitimate sensation the world had to offer. For some reason the night sky fascinated her."

Hope looked back toward the alley as a shadow seemed to move behind us. "Wasn't she scared?"

"She wasn't. I was. She felt a connection to everyone around her, no matter how degenerate they were. 'Don't forget there is a brilliant spirit in there,' she used to tell me, pointing to the lowest gutter dweller. 'You just have to see them in the right light.'

"We were passing by the front of this alley when we heard the cries for help. I wanted to keep moving, but she had to stop. She never passed up an opportunity to help someone, even when she was an addict. We saw them by the Dumpster—a tall skinhead standing over a bloodied black man. I think he was resting between blows. I was shaking in my shoes, but my mother stepped right up. 'Get away from him!' she yelled. 'You've got no right.'

"She was fearless. She stepped in to stop the beating. There was a struggle, and she was thrown against the Dumpster. She hit her head, went to the ground, and didn't move."

Hope didn't say anything, but she put her hand on my knee and squeezed. I should have stopped talking, but my lips kept moving.

"I just stood there, wanting to run to her but afraid to get any closer." I paused and took a breath. I didn't look at Hope.

"Everything seemed to be frozen in time. I looked at my mother, looked at the giant skinhead, and then ran. I ran and I ran, and I kept running. Even when it was safe. Even when there were other people around who might have been able to call the police and get an ambulance for my mother, I still ran. I didn't stop running until I couldn't run anymore."

I finally looked at Hope. "I should have gone to her. I should have held her head in my lap. I should have at least found a police officer and gotten back to her quickly. Instead, I ran."

Her face was calmer than I expected. She moved her hand from my leg, wiped her eyes, and then touched my arm. "You were a little boy," she said. "A child. Kids get scared. They don't know how to act in a crisis. I see it every day. Maybe you should give that child a break."

I could almost feel the healing light I had sensed coming from her in the hospital. I shrugged, breaking the connection of her fingers on my arm, and felt the light go out of me. The alley was dark. I should not have brought her here. "I'm pretty sure this is the worst un-date you've ever been on," I said. "I'm sorry."

She touched my arm again, as if the physical connection was an aid to her communication. "I'm glad you shared this with me," she said. "And you may not want to hear this, but there's nothing for you to feel guilty about. Whether you ran or not. You are not responsible for your mother's death because she didn't really die. She just moved on. I'm a bit of an expert on this. I'm sure she's watching you now and that she wants you to let this go."

It happened again—the same feeling I'd had while Hope and I were sharing a hug with Megan. The feeling that something was falling into place. Then headlights shone in through the back window, and the moment was gone.

"Uh-oh," I said.

"The police?" Hope asked.

"I don't think so," I said, squinting my eyes and making out the silhouette of a car that looked like a beat-up Cadillac. The car's nose protruded into the alley, but I knew that there still might be room to drive around it. I thought about making a run for it—until two men stepped out of the car. They walked slowly toward us.

"Stay here," I said to Hope. "Don't get out of the car under any circumstances. Get in the driver's seat. If I point at you, back up as fast as you can and shoot through that gap out of the alley. Don't worry about damaging my car. Force your way through if you need to. Wait for me a few blocks away. If I don't show up within minutes, call the police. But please, wait for my signal."

"Why don't we just call the police now? I have a cell phone."

"Because I'm going to try to talk us out of this. They're probably just looking for drug money, and I've got fifty bucks left in my wallet. With any luck, they'll take the money and let us go."

"Wouldn't it be better to just to drive past them now?"

"I don't run," I said, stepping out of the car. "Not anymore."

I walked quickly toward the two men, putting some distance between us and the car. One was a short Black man with a series of gold chains around his neck, and the other was a large Hispanic-looking guy with a leather vest and no shirt. Either the vest was rather small or his muscles were really large.

"You lost or something, homie? This ain't the part of town to be showing around a fine woman like that. If you like, Chico here could take her off your hands."

I looked at Chico. He smiled but didn't say anything. He was big enough that he could probably take anything he wanted.

"I think the Village People convention is on the other side of town," I said. "Isn't one of you supposed to be wearing a hard hat?" Chico stopped smiling.

"Besides, I know nothing is going to happen to that woman with you guys watching my back."

The Black man looked at me and then at Chico. "The homie made us already. We must be getting sloppy. I told you that vest was a bad idea."

"I actually like the vest," I said. "Very authentic. And the beater Cadillac is good too. Especially in this neighborhood. But you've been on my tail since the Truman Center. Following too close. Anyone with any training would have made you. You know you don't have to follow so close. The GPS will tell you where I am."

"We tried the safe-distance thing in Miami. That didn't work out so well for you or us. Our bosses weren't very happy."

"You were on my protection detail in Miami? What are you doing out here?"

"Penitence," Chico said. "They said they were giving us a second chance. And to not screw it up this time."

"You guys didn't screw anything up. We all thought the mission was over. I gave the okay to release my security detail."

"That's what we keep telling them," the Black man said. "But for some reason they won't listen. They won't be very happy with us if the same thing happens again on our watch."

"They probably wouldn't be very happy if they knew you were talking with me right now either."

"Probably not. But who's going to see us this time of night? Besides, we wanted to offer a little advice that might make both our jobs easier. Like maybe not going for midnight runs in the mountains with guys that look like terrorists. Or not bringing your date to deserted alleyways in the wee hours of the morning when you might run into people who would just as soon slit your throat as look at you. We want to keep you alive, homie, but you really need to help us out." He looked at Chico. "Chico likes dressing casual. We don't want our careers to end in an office somewhere, pushing paper."

"I appreciate the advice," I said. "But I can't help you. The fact is that your careers aren't important and neither is my life. If we don't find and stop these guys, millions of people could die. If I get killed on a midnight run with an Arab, that's a good thing. It means we've identified the terrorist." I didn't say anything about bringing Hope to the alley. That really wasn't very smart.

The Black man sighed and looked at Chico. "Why did we sign up for this work?"

Chico shrugged.

He looked back at me. "By the way, my name's Demetrius, and this is Chico. We'd shake your hand, but your girl might get suspicious."

I wanted to protest and say she wasn't my girl, but I had more important matters on my mind, and we didn't have much time. "I'm actually glad we could talk," I said. "I want you to watch for something. There's a couple of ex-military guys hanging out in the wee hours with one of my neighbors."

"We marked them a couple days ago," Demetrius said. "They remind me of Delta."

"More like ex-Delta," I said. "The kind they let go because they like their jobs a little too much."

"Don't worry," Demetrius said. "Chico eats Delta for breakfast. We won't let them lay a finger on you."

"That's the thing. The guy they're hanging around with is looking for a confrontation, and I'm guessing it won't be long before I have to face him. I want you to back way off. Don't advance unless there is a gun to my head and the bullet is coming out of the barrel. I need these guys to see me as a nonthreat, and I might have to take a few blows to prove it."

"It's not going to look good if we let you get killed."

"They won't kill me," I said. "At least not within the city limits."

"What if they throw you in the trunk of a car?"

"Then follow," I said. "But do a better job of tailing than you did tonight."

"I think the girl is getting restless," Chico said, nodding toward my car. "We need to end this."

"You want to play the hero in front of your girlfriend?" Demetrius asked. "Maybe do some fancy kung fu to disarm us?" He pulled out a large knife and waved it around.

"She's not my girlfriend," I started to say, but my words were drowned out by squealing tires. I looked up to see the back end of my car speeding toward us. Before it reached us, the brakes locked up, and my little car did an almost perfect one-eighty. Demetrius dove left, and I went right. Chico took a small step to the side. The front side panel of the car caught him in the thigh. The car bounced off Chico like a pinball and stopped. Chico didn't move. There was that smile again. The passenger door flew open and Hope said, "Get in." She seemed anxious but not scared. I got in, and Hope accelerated, leaving Chico and his smile behind in the alleyway and clipping the front end of the Cadillac on the way out.

After a few blocks she pulled to a stop and looked at me. "Are you okay?" she asked. Her hands were shaking slightly on the steering wheel.

"I'm fine," I said, although I was shaking a little myself. *Who was this woman?*

"Why did you do that?" I asked. "Somebody could have gotten hurt." I was wondering about Chico's leg.

"He had a knife. I thought he was going to kill you."

"He was just showing off," I said. "I was just getting ready to pay them off."

"You were talking for a long time."

"They were a little chatty."

Hope didn't say anything for several seconds and then took a deep breath. I expected that at any moment she would burst into tears as the adrenaline drained from her limbs. I had seen it dozens of times in both men and women—even some who were trained for this type of work.

Instead she giggled. "That was kind of exciting. This is definitely the best un-date I've ever had. Did you see that guy? He was huge. I thought he was going to lift up the car and throw it."

I stared at her with my mouth open. She was actually enjoying this. "I think you'd better let me drive," I said.

"Not a chance," she said. "This little puppy's not much to look at, but it's got some horses under the hood." To make her point she put the car into drive and took another six months off the life of my already balding tires.

When we got to the Village, I walked Hope to her door. I kept reminding myself that this was not a date and that I should have no expectations of anything happening at the doorstep.

That was about the time that Hope turned around and kissed me. Well, okay, so it was on the cheek. But it was still a kiss, and her lips were very soft. "Thank you for a wonderful evening," she said. She touched my arm again. She was a touchy person. I didn't mind. "Thank you for letting me get to know you."

"You started it," I replied.

Hope stepped back, but I could still feel her lips on my cheek. It was probably some sort of twenty-four-hour lip gloss.

"I told you why I don't date," Hope said before stepping inside. "What about you?"

"Oh," I said, searching my mind. *What was my reason again?* When I remembered what it was, I found I was reluctant to tell her.

"Well?"

"It's just that . . ." I tried to find the words.

"Yes?"

"Well, I'm kind of in love with someone." I watched Hope carefully to see how she would react to this. Was I hoping for disappointment? Maybe devastation?

"When can I meet her?" she asked. She sounded excited for me.

"It's complicated," I said. "She's already taken."

"Oh," Hope said. "I'm sorry."

Was she really sorry or was there a hint of something else in her voice?

"You know what?" Hope said, touching my arm one more time. "You are the perfect boyfriend."

"Excuse me?"

"A friend who happens to be male," she said. "I used to be able to go to my brothers and tell them everything. They made me feel safe. I like talking to guys, but I've always had to worry about them hoping our friendship would turn into something else. But it sounds like I don't have to worry about that with you. You're safe. With you, I don't have to worry about romance."

I wished she would tell that to my cheek.

"I'm adopting you," Hope said. "You are my new big brother. I hope you can deal with the repercussions."

"What repercussions?"

"Oh, just me stopping by on almost a daily basis. Using your shoulder to cry on when I need it. Talking to you about life, the universe, and everything. Besides, you need a study buddy."

"A study buddy?"

"For your Book of Mormon assignment." She yawned. "Now I have to go and get some sleep. It's been a long night."

Before I could argue about the studying thing, she kissed me on the cheek again and went into her apartment. Curse that lip gloss. I was never going to get the feeling off my cheek.

I drove my car around to my building, wondering how I was going to avoid Hope Winslow in the future. It wasn't that I didn't want her as a friend—but I was pretty sure I could rule her out as a terrorist, and I was also pretty sure that being around her might become a distraction. A pleasant distraction, but a distraction nonetheless.

As I thought about these things, I nearly drove right into Colt Mangum and his two friends.

CHAPTER 15

Taking One for the Team

COLT'S FRIENDS WERE PARKED CLOSE to where I had seen them the previous time. And once again, they were gathered around the back of Colt's Dodge Challenger. I pulled around behind them and parked in an empty space about eight cars away. As I passed by, the men squinted and shielded their eyes from the glare of my headlights. Just to be courteous, I turned on the high beams. I could see that they were looking into a large white cooler that sat in the trunk. I wasn't high up enough in my car to see what was inside.

I turned off my engine, got out of my car, turned toward the scowling men, and said, "Don't you guys ever go to bed?"

"You," Colt Mangum said. The other two guys didn't say anything, just looked at me as if sizing me up. One of them closed the cooler. I needed to tread carefully here. This might be an ideal time to glean some information. It also might be an opportunity for me to blow my cover.

"What's with the brights?" Colt asked. "You're just begging for trouble."

"Were my brights on?" I asked. "Sorry about that. I don't want trouble. I just want to go to my apartment and go to bed."

"You think it's gonna be that easy? You think you can just run away again?" I knew that it wasn't going to be easy, but I had no intention of running this time.

I stepped away from my car and out into a grassy area. If I'd been Clint Eastwood, I would have spit out a wad of tobacco and thrown the front of my Indian poncho over my shoulder.

Colt began to move toward me.

"Not here," one of the men said. "Not in the light." He looked down at the cooler. "The last thing we need is police. If you really feel the need to pound this weasel, go someplace else." His eyes were flat and dead, but the second man's gaze showed a gleam that said he would like nothing better than to put me on the pavement and gut me with a knife.

"You don't want to watch?" Colt asked.

"No," the first man said. The second looked disappointed.

"Behind the building," Colt said. "Let's go." He didn't seem too excited about this idea. Maybe he was the type that needed an audience.

"Just go," he said, walking over and pushing me when I didn't move on my own.

"Is this how you treat all your dates?" I looked behind me at the two men, but they were pulling bags out of Colt's Challenger and transferring them into their own car—a dark brown Ford Taurus. I wanted to see if they took the cooler, but Colt kept pushing me, and I lost sight of them behind the corner of a building. I heard an engine start and a car pulling quickly away. These guys really did not like being seen.

Colt pushed again, but this time I didn't move. We were far enough away not to wake anyone, and I was afraid that if we went any further, Demetrius and Chico would start moving in for the rescue.

I really wanted to see if I could get some information out of Colt before I lost this fight. And I *was* going to lose. Not that I didn't think I could take him, but beating Colt in a fight was the worst thing I could do for my cover.

"Out selling ice cream?" I asked. "You know you'd probably do a little better in the daytime."

"Just shut up," he said. "Don't try to be a hero, and you might get out of this without any broken bones."

"You're the hero," I said. "And the last thing in the world I would want to do is be like you."

The color rose in his face. I could see that I had pushed one of his buttons. There was something fake about Colt, besides his name, and I really had to wonder about the whole Purple Heart thing.

He came at me, and I stepped in, slipping into my hand-to-hand training as if it had been yesterday. He threw a roundhouse punch, and I let it land in a glancing fashion, remembering too late that this was the cheek where Hope had landed her kiss. I staggered back as if stunned and touched my cheek.

Colt looked at his knuckles and smiled. "Is that lipstick? I thought I saw you drive by with the Ice Queen. I'll bet she's a tiger when you get her alone. It's the frosty types that always surprise you."

I wasn't sure if it was the desecration of my cheek or the defaming of Hope's reputation that set me off, but suddenly I was in a different place where I was no longer worried about gathering information from Colt. I just wanted to hurt him.

He loomed before me in the night. A dark figure—laughing, taunting, moving in for another blow. He was no longer Colt Mangum, and I was no longer Matthew Knight. He was Zack the Hammer in full body armor, and I was a focused weapon, looking to strike the target points marked in red that would shut down his nervous system. Throat, groin, temple, bladder, and a dozen other places that would render the assailant helpless—or dead.

Like a chess player, I choreographed the successive moves I would make—three, four, five steps ahead. Depending on his reactions, I would improvise. But all movement would lead to the same result—him lying on the ground unable to move.

I started with a kick to the inside of his good knee to open him up and then followed with a harder kick to his supposedly damaged one. I was ready to go to the groin next and then follow with a knee to the head. After that he would likely be on the ground and I would have several options.

"Never stop until the threat is eliminated," Zack had taught us. "Locate the targets and attack." I was in autopilot mode now, not even thinking about what I was doing. Like a well-rehearsed dance. A deadly dance.

The dance was interrupted when I made contact with his damaged knee. He stifled a scream and almost went down. This was not what I expected, and because it was unexpected, it interrupted my flow. The kick hadn't landed that hard, but Colt was in extreme pain. He might be faking a lot of things, but having an injured leg was not one of them. His reaction to the pain left him vulnerable and completely exposed. He was mine if I wanted him. But I didn't want him anymore. I didn't know what I wanted. It was if I had just awoken from a nightmare. My hands began to shake.

Colt, on the other hand, seemed to quickly recover his composure and, with a great yell of rage and pain, launched himself off the ground. I saw the uppercut coming toward me, but it was too late to get out of the way. His fist landed hard under my chin, and I thought my teeth might be driven back through my head. I saw the stars above me and then the ground racing toward me, and then everything went black.

An undetermined amount of time later, I woke up but did not open my eyes. I was lying down, a pillow under my head and apparently on a couch or a bed—not lying on the grass, not riding in the trunk of a car, not cut up into little pieces and sitting in a cooler. I heard movement in front of me. I opened one eye to a slit and watched as Colt Mangum paced back and forth. He limped as he walked and rubbed his leg.

I was in an apartment that looked a lot like my own but with different furnishings. It must have been Colt's. I wasn't tied up, and I didn't notice anyone else in the room. Maybe Colt had brought me here to kill me, but he didn't look menacing—he looked worried.

I decided I was not going to learn anything valuable by pretending to be unconscious, so I decided to wake up. I was tired and sore and didn't want to pretend anymore.

I opened my eyes and pulled myself to a sitting position. There were still a few stars in my eyes and my jaw hurt, but I didn't think I had a concussion. I didn't throw up, at least. That was a good sign.

I thought I saw Colt breathe a sigh of relief, then he seemed to catch himself and forced his face into a scowl. The manic look came back into his eyes.

"You're alive then," he said.

"Why'd you do that?" I tested my jaw with my hand. It still moved back and forth.

"Do what?"

"You were pacing back and forth like you were worried about me, and then when I woke up you became the old Colt again."

He started like he was going to protest then took a deep breath and sat down next to me. "I thought I might have hit you too hard," he said. "I sometimes forget I'm military combat trained. Trained to fight and trained to kill. I shouldn't ever use that training on civilians. I just wanted to rough you up a little bit, not really hurt you."

This just made me feel guilty. If he only knew what I had almost done to him.

"My fault," I said. "I shouldn't have kicked your Purple Heart leg. I really thought that with all your bluster, you might be faking it."

Colt laughed a hard, chopped kind of a laugh. "You really are a smart guy."

"You almost went down," I said. "You weren't faking the pain."

He stood up and moved to the kitchen, wincing as he walked. "Just because the pain is real doesn't mean I'm not faking," he said. "Let me get you some ice for that jaw." He filled a plastic bag with ice and tossed it to me. I put it next to my face and grimaced.

"What do you mean?" I asked.

Colt seemed to consider how much he wanted to tell me then said, "I guess I owe you since I almost took your head off." He sat down again and placed his own bag of ice on his leg.

"The Purple Heart's a joke," he said. "I'm no hero."

I nodded to his leg. "That wound doesn't look like a joke."

"You'd feel differently if you knew how I got it."

"Maybe," I said. "Maybe not."

He touched his leg and winced, seeming to consider whether he should say anything else. "What I tell you stays between us. No one else can know. Not even Bishop Shepherd."

This put me in an awkward position since Bishop Shepherd was my boss and my whole reason for being here was to find out Colt's secrets and pass them on. But I really didn't think he was going to reveal to a stranger anything that was directly related to a terrorist mission. Whatever he gave up, I figured I could pass on the gist of it without giving up any confidences.

Besides, Colt looked like he wanted to talk. Like he had a burden he needed to unload. The last thing I wanted to do was to slow the flow.

"I won't tell anyone," I said.

He settled back in the couch, looked up, and spoke to the ceiling.

"I was on my third tour in Afghanistan," he said. "Mountain duty. Most guys hated it. Most guys wanted desperately to get home. Not me. I never did fit in as a civilian. I was a teenage screwup, constantly in and out of juvenile centers. If I wasn't in court, I was fighting with my stepdad. When I turned eighteen a judge spelled it out for me: I could continue down the path I was on and end up in prison, or I could choose another way. I was an adult now. It was up to me. He suggested the military. My stepfather hated the idea. He told me I'd never make it and forbade me to go. I enrolled the next day.

"It was like being born into a different world. No one there knew I was a screwup. No one cared. All that mattered was surviving, and we all learned real quick that this meant relying on each other. I found my real family there. My brothers. I was part of a whole. And I fit. I mattered. There was no way I wanted to go back home.

"We were scouring the hillsides, cave by cave. Searching for hidden Taliban and Al-Qaeda cells. We'd seen our fair share of action, but we kept waiting for a face-card mission—you know what that is?"

I shook my head, but Colt didn't see it. He was no longer paying any attention to me.

"We had these playing cards with the pictures of Al-Qaeda leaders printed on them. Bin Laden was the king, Zawahiri the queen, and on down the line. My patrol had an unwritten goal that before it was all over, we were going to take down a face card. This was before they found Bin Laden in Pakistan. We thought they were all hiding in caves in the mountains.

"Then one night we got a tip. One of the face cards was supposedly holed up in a neighborhood close by. The informant didn't tell us who it was, just that he was big. We got orders to move out immediately, engage the target, and capture him or take him out before he slipped away. My lieutenant shook me awake. 'Roll out, soldier. We got one.' He didn't need to spell it out for me. We all knew what he meant. It was what we'd been waiting for.

"I rolled out, or attempted to. When I tried to stand up, my leg went out from under me. We'd been playing football earlier that day, and I had hurt my knee. But it was more than a twist. Ligaments were torn, and it was swollen up like a basketball. The lieutenant looked at my leg and said, 'Sorry, soldier. You need to sit this one out.'

"I forced myself to my feet. 'Please, Lieutenant,' I begged. 'I've waited three tours for this.' He just looked at me and nodded. Then he wrapped my knee as tightly as he could and helped me out to the transport. 'You slow us down, we leave you,' he said.

"'I won't, Lieutenant,' I told him. 'I promise.'

"When we reached the target, I was assigned to watch the flank while the rest of the patrol moved in. I was still going to miss the action, but at least I would be a part of it. Then I spotted movement along the rooftops. Dozens of men were moving in behind the patrol from the back. The intelligence said we were clear to move in. The intelligence was wrong. It was a trap. My brothers were being herded like cows into the slaughterhouse.

"I yelled, opened fire, and began to hop and skip as fast as I could toward my patrol. The further they moved into the trap, the harder it was going to be to get them out. When I reached them, they were already pinned down. There was a sniper on one of the rooftops, and they couldn't retreat without running into a bullet. But I had a bead on his lair. I couldn't take him out, but I made him keep his head down long enough for the patrol to make their way to my position.

"'Go!' I told them. If they moved quickly they might be able to get out. The sniper had disappeared, but I knew he must be finding another position. The patrol started to move out, and I tried to follow. But my leg had seized up, and I was dead slow. 'Go!' I told them again. 'Get out of here.' But they didn't go. That's not the way we worked. We didn't leave anyone behind."

Colt was breathing hard as he talked, and a light bead of sweat shone across his forehead. He swallowed and forced himself to go on.

"The time it took for them to come back for me was all the sniper needed to find a better vantage point. We radioed for support, but it was minutes away. Too many minutes. The sniper picked us off like ducks in a pond. There was nothing we could do. One by one my brothers were gone. One by one, I saw the light go out of their eyes. I waited for my turn, but it never came. I heard the sound of the Black Hawk's rotors as it made its way up the street toward me. The sniper pulled out, and I tried to get a shot at him as he left. I heard him laughing as he moved out of sight.

"A captain jumped out of the copter, looked around at the carnage, and swore. He spotted my movement and came to me. 'What happened here, soldier?'

"'A trap,' I said. 'Some idiot in intelligence sent us into a trap.' The captain looked as if I'd slapped him, and I knew that he was probably the idiot I was talking about. I didn't care. My brothers were dead because some overeager college boy wanted to get a promotion. 'It was a complete disaster. We didn't have a chance,' I said.

"I saw panic in his eyes, and then he looked back at me. He looked at my leg. 'Bullet or shrapnel?'

"'Neither,' I said. 'I hurt it playing football.'

"He seemed to consider this for a moment and then shook his head. 'Not good enough. Something good needs to come out of this, and it might as well be a hero.'

"I laughed in his face. I was no hero. If it weren't for my leg, I would have been with them. And if they hadn't come back for me, they could have gotten out."

I thought this might be a good time to remind Colt that if he hadn't been with them, they wouldn't have made it out as far as they did. But I didn't want to interrupt. The more I could learn about Colt Mangum, the better.

"The captain didn't like being laughed at. And he didn't like reality getting in the way of his story.

"'These men are heroes,' he said. 'You are the last remaining symbol of their heroics. They can either be remembered as valiant men dying for a cause or the consequences of another military screwup. It's really up to you, soldier. What's it gonna be?'

"I wanted to take him out right there, but he was right. These men were heroes. It wasn't their fault the mission was messed up. 'I'll go along.' I said.

"He looked at my leg one more time and shook his head. 'That will never do. Time to take one for the team.' Then he took out his sidearm and shot me. Heck of a way to get a Purple Heart."

I was silent. This was some story. Colt was sucking in deep breaths, and his eyes were clouded and red. Either Eugene Colt Mangum was the best actor I'd ever seen, or everything he'd told me was 100 percent true. But he wasn't done yet.

"The wound ended my military career," he said. "They even took that away from me. When I got back, I was welcomed as a hero. I started attending singles wards and received two proposals for marriage within the first month. Everyone loves a hero."

I chewed on this for a minute. "That's when you decided to transform yourself into a jerk?" I said. "To avoid the hero worship?"

"I've been a jerk most of my life," he answered. "Not much acting involved. It's a lot closer to the truth than being a hero."

I disagreed, but I didn't tell him this. Colt Mangum was a complex man—another broken member of Zack's flock.

"Why pick on me?" I asked.

Colt laughed. "That's easy. All the ladies love the new guy. Putting a few marks on your face is guaranteed to keep them away from me." He looked over at me and pulled the bag of ice down from my jaw, inspecting my face. "That might do it. I really didn't mean to hit you so hard."

"What about your friends?" I asked. While I had Colt talking, he might be willing to open up about them as well. "Are they faking being antisocial as well?"

"No," Colt said. "They really are antisocial. But they get me. They were in the country. Some of the few people I know who understand what it was like."

"They don't seem like very nice guys."

"They're not. Buy neither am I, really. Maybe I'm just having a hard time letting go of the military."

"They're soldiers?"

"Ex," Colt said. "Forced out. Just like me."

I was pretty sure the reason these guys were forced out of the military was a far cry from Colt's story. But I didn't say so. My guess was that they enjoyed the violence a little bit too much.

"You work with these guys?"

"Nah. I've tried to get them on with me out at Dugway, but they're not interested. They've got their own security gig going on."

"What's Dugway?" I asked, knowing full well what it was—and knowing that Colt's connection to Dugway could be the key to this whole mess.

"Dugway Proving Ground," Colt said. "You might have heard of it on the news."

"I don't think so," I said. I'd heard of Dugway Proving Ground, all right, but it wasn't on the news. It was in one of my bioterror classes. Dugway was one of three places in the United States that was sanctioned by the U.S. government to experiment with biological weapons—from a defensive standpoint, of course. In order for us to know what was possible for terrorists in constructing bioweapons, our government figured we needed to create these weapons ourselves, along with defensive mechanisms to thwart them. These experiments were performed in labs at USAMRIID in Maryland; by Battelle, a New York-based nonprofit technology group; in Ohio; and at Dugway Proving Ground in the west desert of Utah. The last place just happened to be where Colt Mangum—a guy who hung out with mercenaries in the wee hours of the night and kept a mysterious cooler in the back of his trunk—just happened to work.

"Dugway is a military research installation west of here," Colt said. "They test some scary . . . uh . . . crap out there. Anthrax, Ebola, that kind of thing. Stuff that could wipe us off the map if someone accidentally dropped a petri dish. I'm on the security detail."

"Aren't you afraid of getting infected?"

"Nah, we stay on the perimeter. The geeks in the blue suits are the ones who go into the freezers. Besides," he said, "life is overrated."

Great, a bioweapons security guard with a death wish. Even if he did have the purest of intentions, he was in a position to be used by others. I really needed to talk to Zack.

I started to get up. "I'd probably better go."

"Hey, why don't I cook you some breakfast," Colt said. "I've got bacon, eggs, and pancakes. Not items you're going to find in Section 89." He got up, opened the fridge, pulled out a package of bacon, and began throwing down strips that started to sizzle as the frying pan warmed up.

The smell hit me almost immediately, and my stomach started to growl. I decided that frying bacon in front of a hungry man might be as effective in interrogations as sodium pentothal."

"I guess I could stay for a little while," I replied.

* * *

After breakfast, I left Colt's apartment and began crossing the parking lot from his apartment toward my own. A black SUV pulled up beside me, and a deep voice said, "Get in if you want to live." I got in. I couldn't tell if Zack was just using *Terminator* humor or if he really would have killed me. You could never tell with Zack.

"Where have you been?"

"Oh, just having a light breakfast with Colt."

"I can smell the syrup on you."

"You should have smelled the bacon."

"Demetrius says he saw Colt ring your bell and haul you away like a dead man."

"He apologized," I said. "And he cooked me breakfast to make up for it."

Zack studied my face, probably trying to figure out if I was messing with him.

"You've had an eventful night. Demetrius said he found you in a dark alley with Hope Winslow and that you almost ran over Chico." Zack didn't sound very happy about me being out late with Hope.

"It was actually Hope who almost ran over Chico, and he could have just moved out of the way and not left that dent in my car." I pointed over to the Toyota. There was an obvious indentation in the left front fender.

"Chico doesn't move," Zack said.

"How's his leg?"

"He says he might have a scratch." Zack turned up the heat of his burning gaze. "Tell me what you were doing in a dark alley with Hope Winslow."

"Not what you might think," I said, holding up my hands.

Zack continued his gaze. I guess he was expecting a more detailed explanation. "She showed me the Truman Center, and I showed her where I lived as a child. She's adopted me as an honorary big brother, and I've eliminated her as a suspect. That's it."

"She's a beautiful woman," Zack said.

"Yes, she is," I said. "But I'm not interested."

"I don't want her hurt."

"You have nothing to worry about." Zack didn't seem satisfied, but he let it go.

"Learn anything useful from Colt?"

I thought about telling him about the reason for Colt's bad behavior, but I'd promised Colt that I wouldn't. There was still plenty to share.

"You mean other than that he hangs out with ex-military in the dark of the night and they seem to have a serious preoccupation with something in a cooler? You mean other than the fact that he works security at a bioweapons facility known to do experiments with viruses that could wipe out a city in the matter of a few weeks? Or the small detail that he has admitted that he is an outcast from society, kind of wishes he would have died in Afghanistan, and still might have a death wish? No, I really didn't learn anything useful." I paused and took a breath. It was my turn to ask a question.

"Why was Colt's job at Dugway conveniently left out of the file you gave me?"

"I thought you might do better if you found some things out on your own."

"Wouldn't it be important for me to know about a guy who might be smuggling out a weapons-grade bioagent in a cooler?"

"Colt's not smuggling anything. Dugway is secure."

"Oh, really? I seem to remember an anthrax investigation not too many years ago that pointed to a possible breach at Dugway. I remember their security being questioned and some of their people being suspects. And then a scientist conveniently committing suicide at Fort Detrick and suddenly the blame being thrown on him and the case being considered solved. How can you be so sure Colt isn't smuggling anything out?"

One of the cords in Zack's neck began to twitch. "Because there *were* holes in security and those holes have now been plugged. Getting into

Dugway Proving Ground is fairly easy—getting out is another matter. Every person leaving must pass through a series of detectors, showers, and strip searches. Besides, Colt provides perimeter security and isn't allowed anywhere near the freezers. He doesn't have access, and even if he did, there's no way to get anything out."

"Then what's in the cooler?"

"I don't know. But I'm pretty sure it's not a virus from Dugway Proving Ground."

"I'm going to find out."

"Maybe you should. But maybe you should be a little more discreet. Bruised cheekbones aren't much of a benefit to supposed covert agents."

"You should see the other guy," I said. I got out of the SUV. "You know what would be really helpful?" I was getting tired of this conversation. "If you could put a tail on Colt and his friends and find out where they go in the middle of the night and what they put in the cooler."

"I'm sure Demetrius and Chico would love to do that," Zack said. "They can't get enough of tracking people in the middle of the night. I'll tell them it was your idea."

"Please do," I said. "They owe me for the dent."

I looked at my watch. It was almost seven in the morning. The only sleep I had received last night was from my brief period of unconsciousness, and that had not been very restful. I wanted to go home, throw myself on my bed, and sleep for about a week. I left Zack and headed for my apartment.

When I entered, Roger was sitting on the couch.

"You look like crap," he said. "That must have been some date."

"It wasn't a date," I said. "And I had a little run-in with Colt afterward."

"How did that go?" Roger asked warily.

"I kicked Colt in the leg, Colt hit me in the face, and then we went back to his apartment and he cooked me breakfast. He won't bother us anymore. So I guess, all in all, it went pretty well." I moved toward the hallway. "I'm going to bed. You can wake me up sometime next week."

A knock sounded at the door behind me. I continued on toward the bedroom.

"It's for you," Roger called before I could shut my door.

"Tell whoever it is that I'm sleeping."

"Get out here, you slacker," said the voice. "You've had as much sleep as I've had, and I'm able to function."

The voice belonged to Hope Winslow.

CHAPTER 16
A Motley Crew

I GROANED AND TURNED AROUND. Hope stepped in through the door holding a Book of Mormon. Permelia was right behind her.

"Time for early morning scripture study, big brother."

When I stepped into the light, Hope gasped. "What happened to your face? That cheek wasn't damaged when I left it."

"I had a little un-date with Colt," I said.

Permelia stepped forward, her eyes bright. "I'm going to go take care of that Colt Mangum," she said. "He can't just go around roughing up the eye candy."

I decided Colt was right. Hitting me was sure to drive him further out of the graces of the eligible women in the ward—even Permelia.

"Leave Colt alone," I said. "I deserved to get hit, and we've come to an understanding."

"Well, that would be a first," Permelia said. "Nobody understands that boy."

"Just let him be," I said. "He's a troubled soul."

"With amazing biceps," Permelia mumbled under her breath. "I suppose I could give him another chance."

Permelia and Hope came inside and made themselves at home on the couch. About the same time, Joseph came up the steps, presumably finishing one of his night runs. He had a letter in his hands, and he did not look happy.

"I thought we agreed to no social visits in the apartment," he said, looking back and forth accusingly between Roger and me.

"Good morning, Brother Joseph," Permelia said. "It's so nice to see you too."

"What's this all about?" Joseph asked, settling his focus on me.

Before I could reply, Hope jumped in. "We're here for scripture study," she said. "Matthew has received an assignment from the bishop to complete the Book of Mormon, and we are going to help him. Would you like to join us?"

"I've read the Book of Mormon eighteen times," Joseph said. "I don't think I have anything left to learn."

"Really?" Hope said, returning Joseph's glare with sweetness. "I've read it at least thirty times, and I find something new and inspiring every time I open it up."

Joseph looked over at me. I shrugged. He was way out of his league, and he knew it. I was really starting to like this woman.

"I found something new in my Book of Mormon once," Permelia said. "In the Isaiah chapters. It was a piece of beef jerky that I think I once used as a bookmark. Could have been in there for years. It was still edible but a little tough. Kind of like Isaiah, as a matter of fact."

Joseph rolled his eyes and moved toward the bedroom. One of these women was formidable enough, but two of them together was impossible.

Joseph stopped when he got to his door and hesitated without going in. There was something troubling him, and I didn't think it was just the company in the apartment.

"What's up?" I said, moving toward him. "You've obviously got something on your mind, so you might as well spit it out."

He looked down at the letter in his hands. "Someone dropped out of the Uinta 100," he said. "I've been invited to join."

"In theory, you should be excited," I replied. "Did you forget to tell your face?"

"I have to decline," he said, almost spitting out the words. "I don't meet all of the qualifications."

"Why not?" I asked. "You've definitely put in the miles,"

Joseph hesitated and then offered, "I need a crew. I can't run the race without a crew."

"Oh," I said. "You're right. That is a problem, especially since you've chosen to distance yourself from pretty much every living human who could help you out." Hope elbowed me in the ribs. I guess she thought I was being rude. I was actually just stating a fact, and Joseph knew it.

I turned to Roger. "You in?" I asked.

"Completely," Roger said. "I'll brew up an electrolyte-filled, nano-water concoction that will be light-years ahead of what anyone else has."

"There you have it," I said to Joseph. "You have a crew."

"It's not as simple as that," Joseph said. "The crew needs to have at least four people. Two of them must have previous ultracrewing experience, and one of them needs to be a pacer."

"I crewed on a fifty miler that one of my brothers ran," Hope said. "I got pretty good at treating blisters."

"I'm not blazingly fast," I said. "But I should be able to pace you the last few miles after you're worn out."

"I'm in too," Permelia said. "That makes four."

"I appreciate your willingness, Permelia," Joseph said, trying to be civil, which was not natural behavior for him. "But I need someone with experience."

"Don't talk to me about experience, young man. I've got more experience in my little finger than you have in your whole body."

"I'm sure you do," I said before Permelia jumped on Joseph. "But he needs someone else who has experience on an ultracrew."

"I know what he needs," Permelia snapped back. "Do not patronize me. I've crewed on dozens of ultraraces. I used to have a boyfriend who ran those things, and he insisted I be with him. He said he wanted me there because of my amazing chicken and dumpling stew, but I knew it was me he was after." She sighed. "We probably would have gotten married if he hadn't died climbing Everest."

"You never told me you dated an ultrarunner," Hope said. "Was this when you were living in California?"

"Heavens no. This was only about ten years ago. He was seventy-two, and I was sixty-five. Ah, to be young again."

"I want to play," a musical voice said through the open front window. An instant later, Marva Rose knocked and stepped inside. "I've never really participated in athletics that much, but I'm sure I can help."

"You can help Permelia with the food," I said. "We all know you can cook."

"That sounds great. Where will you be, Roger?"

Roger looked like he wanted to be miles away from Marva Rose. He fumbled for words, so I helped him out.

"We'll decide on the particulars once we know more of the requirements," I said. "Is there somewhere that we can get more information on crewing?" I asked Joseph.

"I'll get you a packet," he said and then looked around the room. "You all know you don't have to do this."

"You're family," Hope said. "Like it or not. This is what families do."

Joseph opened his mouth to speak, and I almost thought he was going to say thank you. Instead, he just nodded. Then he shrugged and went into his room. He didn't seem very happy for a guy who was about to fulfill a lifelong dream. Roger mumbled something about having to check on some experiments in the lab and walked out the door. He didn't seem very happy either. Marva Rose frowned as he left. I hoped I wasn't setting her up for another fall. Roger seemed a bit skittish about reentering the world of relationships.

The only people who seemed pleased in the room were Permelia and Hope, who were settling themselves on my couch, determined to have scripture study. I just wanted to sleep.

My train of thought stayed with crewing the ultra. I probably should have kept my mouth shut. Yes, Joseph was still a suspect. But I didn't think there was much plotting he could be doing during a hundred-mile race. So why *had* I opened my mouth? Hope's words echoed in my mind. *That's what families do.*

I looked over at the couch. The spot next to Hope looked inviting, and she smiled at me. It was a dangerous smile. Not that there was anything in it that hinted to anything more than sisterly concern, but there was a warmth there that called to me like the strongest song of any siren. I felt like I could plant myself on that couch and never get up again.

I decided that for everyone's sake I needed to get this session over as quickly as possible and then avoid Hope Winslow as much as I could. This wasn't going to be an easy task with the race coming up, but surely I could find excuses not to be around for scripture-study sessions. My job here was not to find a family. My job was to save this community from a terrorist attack. Hope Winslow was a distraction.

And in my line of work, distractions could be fatal.

* * *

Over the next several days, no matter how firm my resolve to make real progress on the case, I ended up feeling like I was running on a treadmill. My resolution to stay away from Hope Winslow was, of course, a major fail. I tried to make sure I was at the library or away from the apartment when she wasn't working, but her schedule seemed to be somewhat flexible, and most days she was able to find me. Sometimes she brought Permelia, sometimes not. As she left each day, she refrained from kissing me on the cheek—which was a good thing—but she did something else that made me nearly as uncomfortable.

"I love you, Matthew," she would say, watching my eyes until I began to squirm. Then she would add, "Like a brother."

After several awkward attempts at a reply, she finally trained me to say, "I love you too, sis." That's what her other brothers always said to her.

It was all very innocent, but it reminded me way too much of someone else who forced me to say those uncomfortable words.

When Robbie and I first met Becca, we were both immediately impressed. She was completely unlike any other woman we had ever known.

Becca was actually the one who found us. We were in the middle of training, but Robbie had still managed to get us season tickets in the cheap seats at the Redskins games.

"Can I squeeze in between you guys?" she asked about halfway through the third quarter of an October contest against the rival Dallas Cowboys. "The guy next to me can't keep his hands off my knees, and I really want to watch the game."

Before we had a chance to reply, she was between us. She was wearing a Redskins ball cap, a vintage jersey, and Levis with holes in both knees. They were pretty knees. I understood why the guy next to her was having trouble.

We met there every Sunday, and somehow we just all ended up hanging out together whenever we got the chance. Other than her breathtaking beauty, she was really more like one of the guys than anything else. She talked about sports and cars and burgers, not about dresses and relationships and feelings. Which is why both of us immediately fell in love with her. Not in a roses, romance sort of way. But with a knowledge that neither of us could envision life without Becca in it.

I'm not sure when things moved past the buddy stage, but as our training progressed, our time together began to move from friendship to something else. I'd catch Robbie studying Becca with a faraway look in his eyes, and I'm sure he caught me doing the same. We knew a change was coming, and we knew there were parts of this relationship that we just didn't want to let go. But Robbie and I were both clueless with relationships, so we pretended nothing had changed.

"This can't go on forever," she said one day. "You guys are going to finish your training and get shipped out to who knows where. If I don't marry one of you soon, I'm going to be left with nothing." She was completely matter-of-fact about it. There was no drama and there were no tears. She was wholly logical at all times. We had all been thinking it, but Becca was the one who could always throw away the filter and just say what needed to be said.

"One of you is going to have to propose," she said. "If both of you do, I'll have to choose the one who proposes with the most style."

We both groaned. Neither of us was any good at romance, which was probably why we both fell for Becca. She didn't demand it—until now.

The next day Robbie asked Becca to meet him at lunch while I was testing at the firing range. They met at a Chinese restaurant, and Robbie had one of the fortune cookies stuffed with a "will-you-marry me" fortune. In typical Robbie fashion, he messed it up and gave her the wrong cookie to crack, but she eventually figured it out.

She told me about it that night while Robbie was in the shower. "Pretty lame attempt at romance and surprise," she said.

"Very lame," I agreed. "But pretty good for Robbie. And fast too."

"I've never seen him so nervous," she said. "He was sweating buckets. I'm not so sure he's cut out for undercover work."

"He'll never meet a terrorist as intimidating as you. I think he'll do just fine." I *was* sure Robbie would be fine. They both would be. I wasn't so sure about myself. Even though I could see it coming, I felt like my world had been pulled out from under me and I was left alone in a dark abyss.

"So?" she said.

"Yeah?"

"You're not going to even try, are you?" She knew me pretty well.

"How can I top a proposal in a fortune cookie?" I said. "Besides, we both know Robbie would never make it on his own."

"Yes we do," she said. "But that doesn't mean that you'd fare any better."

"I've been on my own for a long time."

"And you were a mess until you met us."

I started to say something more when a finger was placed on my lips, shushing me. Becca put her head on my chest and hugged me. We had hugged before—best-friend kind of hugs, but this was something different. It was as if she melted into my soul and we were one person. I held her like that for a long time.

"You have to come visit us every spare minute you have," she finally said.

"I want the firstborn to be named after me."

"Matthew would be a funny name for a girl."

"I somehow doubt you and Robbie will have any girls."

Robbie came in wearing a robe and toweling off his hair. He saw Becca in my arms, and the color drained from his face.

"How did he do it?" he asked, sitting down on the arm of the couch and letting the towel slip from his hands.

"Not hard to beat a fortune cookie," I said. "That's the best you've got?" Robbie looked stricken. I thought he might throw up.

"Matt didn't ask me," Becca said, cutting to the chase like she always did. "He was just congratulating us."

"You better get over here and kiss your bride before I change my mind," I said. I didn't want to let her go, but I knew she was better off with Robbie. There were demons inside of me, and letting Becca in would just be exposing her to them.

Robbie started to speak, tried to stand up, and then passed out cold on the floor.

Becca and I laughed until we cried. Then she did something that I wish she hadn't. She pulled my face into her hands and kissed me in a way that was very unsisterly.

"Why did you do that?" I asked, when I could breathe.

"Because once I accept Robbie's engagement, there won't be another chance, and I wanted to make sure I wasn't making a mistake."

The kiss was a good one. I wasn't sure about Becca, but I was fairly certain that I was making one of the biggest mistakes of my life.

"And?" I asked.

"Still a toss-up," she said. "I love you both. But you're not ready. You're holding back. There's something inside that keeps you from connecting completely. I hope you're able to drop that someday—with somebody."

They were married the next week at a small ceremony in the Redskins locker room. I handled the refreshments—hot dogs, cotton candy, and beer. Robbie and I began taking assignments soon afterward, and Becca quickly became the perfect Agency wife. While other spouses fretted, worried, and plastered on the guilt, Becca seemed to take everything in stride.

"How do you handle it so well?" I overheard one of the other wives ask her once at a birthday gathering. "Aren't you worried something might happen?"

"It either will or it won't," Becca replied. "Worrying isn't going to help anything. If nothing happens, then I've worried for nothing. If it does, then I'll have gone through it twice."

"Besides," Robbie said coming up behind her, "if I die, she's got a replacement." He pulled me over and put his arm around me. The woman started to smile as if Robbie were making a joke. Becca came to the other side of me and also put her arm around me. The woman made her excuses and left.

In some ways Hope reminded me a lot of Becca, and in other ways she was very different. Both of them were completely open and honest to a fault. But while Becca never let emotion get in the way of logic, Hope was a river of emotion waiting to overflow.

Many times during our scripture-reading sessions she would be moved to tears.

"Are those things made of onionskin?" I asked her once.

"You'll feel the same about them one day."

"I don't know. Joseph claims to have read them eighteen times, and I don't see him bawling."

"He's only read them with his mind, not with his heart. As long as he holds on to his anger, he'll never really feel them."

"I seem to remember seeing you angry at times," I said.

"Yes, I get angry," Hope said. "But with Joseph it's a permanent state. Or at least that's what he shows the outside world. I'm anxious to see what he's like after a hundred miles of mountain beats him down."

"He's definitely at his best in the mountains," I said. "But you won't see it at the aid station. You have to be with him on the trail."

"That's your job," Hope said. "Twenty-five miles' worth. I hope you're up for it." The packet Joseph had given us outlined the requirements for the pacer, and they were a little more aggressive than I expected. I really hadn't planned on running a near marathon.

"Want to trade?" I asked.

"Nope. I love you but not that much."

I wished she would stop saying that. The problem was, I knew she meant it. Hope Winslow loved me. Even if it was as a surrogate older brother. I could feel it. Her emotions were completely transparent.

I found myself wondering what both Hope and Becca would think if they knew what was in my heart. When we came to the part of the Book of Mormon where Nephi cuts off Laban's head with a sword and is told that the action is justified because it's better that "one man should die, than a nation dwindle in unbelief," I couldn't help but envision myself ending the life of Zelphinus Cork in a similar manner. The world would be a better place without him. Too bad someone couldn't have taken care of that before he met my mother in an alley.

But thoughts of Hope, thoughts of Robbie and Becca, and thoughts of my future plans for ridding the world of Zelphinus Cork needed to be put aside. I had a job to do, and time seemed to be slipping away with no progress. Why hadn't I heard anything from Demetrius and Chico?

I really needed to find out what was in that cooler.

CHAPTER 17
The Cooler

I THINK I WAS DREAMING of cutting off the head of Zelphinus Cork with a sword when something shook my bed. I opened my eyes to see Joseph.

"Time to run," he said.

I groaned, wanting to return to my dream. It was some of the best sleep I had experienced in years.

"The race is coming up," I said. "Shouldn't you already be in shape?"

"I am in shape," he said. "But I'm worried that my pacer won't be able to go any more than five miles."

"That hurts," I said. "I'm confident I can hang with you for at least six."

"I need you to be ready for twenty-five. Let's go."

And so we ran. Which was probably a good thing because it gave me time to think. Believe it or not, in between my scripture studies and preparation for a hundred-miler, I was still expected to track down a terrorist. What's more, as a graduate student, I was expected to make progress on my thesis. It was important for my cover. Between reading with Hope, running with Joseph, and writing thesis sections for the professor, I was not making a lot of headway with the case.

"Maybe you should relieve yourself of some of your commitments," Zack told me when we had a chance to talk.

"Maybe you should get Chico and Demetrius to speed up the cooler inspection."

"You really think that will lead us anywhere?"

"Who knows," I said. "But it's the best current lead we have other than angry young Joseph, and I don't really see how he would have time to plan an attack right now."

"Demetrius and Chico are waiting for the right time," Zach said.

"Let's hope they're not too late."

"What do you mean by that?"

"September 11 is in two days. If I remember anything from my training, it's that terrorists have a thing about anniversaries."

"I'll give them a push."

I thought about how much I would like to see Chico and Zack in a push-off. "Okay," I said. "Let me know when you have something."

"One other thing, Mr. Knight." Why was it that I just knew I was going to be scolded when he addressed me that way? "I thought I told you to steer clear of Hope Winslow."

"Not possible without looking suspicious," I said. "She's made it her personal mission to help me live up to my book-reading commitment to you. And she's also on Joseph's ultracrew."

"I don't want to see her hurt, Mr. Knight." For some reason I got the distinct sense that Zack's concern for injury did not extend to me.

"She's adopted me as a surrogate brother," I said. "She misses home. There's nothing to worry about."

"You'd better be right."

* * *

September 11 came and went without incident—and without any word from Demetrius and Chico. On September 12 I was driving back from the university when a beat-up Cadillac pulled out in front of me. I could see Chico's large silhouette filling up the passenger's seat. I got the impression they wanted me to follow.

I tailed them to a parking lot of a Gold's Gym. They got out of the car and walked inside. I noticed that Demetrius dropped something on the way in. I followed and picked up a key-chain card with a bar code on it and walked inside. At the front desk, I scanned the card as I saw Demetrius and Chico entering the men's locker room. I continued to follow and walked around the corner in time to see Demetrius drop a pair of men's swim trunks and a towel on a bench before he and Chico moved to the other end of the locker area and began to change. I deduced that they wanted me to change into swim trunks as well, and so I did. I stuffed my regular clothes into a locker. I worried a little bit that someone might steal my wallet since I did not have any way to secure the locker but I guessed that losing five dollars would only put me back about a week, and since this was official business, I could expense it.

Having changed, Chico and Demetrius went out the doorway that led to the pool area. *Weren't they supposed to shower first?* I briefly considered reporting them then waited a few minutes, showered off, and went out the same door.

Being early afternoon, there were few people around. A woman was swimming laps in the pool, and there was an old guy boiling himself in the Jacuzzi. I guessed that my fellow conspirators were either holed up in the sauna or the steam room. I checked the sauna first, and I was right.

"What you tryin' to do, Knight? Get Chico killed?" Demetrius was his usual eloquent self.

"He doesn't look dead," I said.

In fact, without his shirt on, Chico looked kind of like a young Arnold Schwarzenegger—but more ripped and more mean. There were the remnants of a bruise on his left thigh.

"First your girlfriend tries to run him over—" Demetrius began.

"Not my girlfriend, and he could have moved," I interrupted.

"I don't move," Chico said.

". . . and then you sent us to tail some Delta rejects in the dark," Demetrius continued. "Do you know how hard it is to get close to those guys? Even with the latest night vision and listening equipment, we had a hard time getting within a thousand yards—which is the requirement for our directional microphones. A couple of times I thought for sure they had made us. Luckily, most animals are nocturnal, and there were a lot of other things moving around in the woods."

"The woods?"

"Sort of woods. Mostly sagebrush—which I'm allergic to, by the way. We decided to follow them and see where they were going. They drove up Parley's Canyon, past Park City and Heber, and pulled into a place called Deer Creek. Do you know what that is?"

"Uh . . . a creek maybe?"

"Wrong. It's a reservoir. Apparently one that supplies a lot of the drinking water to different places south of here. Anyway, they pulled into a little corral-looking area, parked the car, and took a trail down to the lake."

"The lake? I thought you said it was a reservoir?"

"Same thing, Einstein."

A guy opened the door to the sauna, took one look at Chico, and then stepped back out.

"They skirted the lake for about a mile, found a place in a deserted cove, and then started doing their thing."

Finally, Demetrius was getting to the point.

"They pulled out these long tubular instruments and started throwing stuff into the lake."

"Reservoir," I corrected.

"Yeah, whatever. Anyway, every once in a while they would retrieve something from the lake and bend over and examine it. I thought it was pretty suspicious until Chico told me it was this thing called 'fishing.' We don't see that much in the inner city. Congratulations, Knight. You risked our lives to follow these guys on a fishing expedition. Apparently, they do it a couple of times a week."

"Did you check the cooler?"

"As a matter of fact, we did. Know what we found?"

"Fish," Chico said.

"I hope you had the fish tested," I said. "They could be using these trips as a cover."

"We retrieved one of the fish from the cooler and sent it to the lab. I think I still have the smell on my hands. Care to guess on the results?"

"Trout," Chico said, before I could answer. "Rainbow."

"No chemicals or biological agents?"

"Not even any mercury," Demetrius said. "Despite the smell, that fish was clean. These boys might appear murderous and edgy, but they don't seem to be involved in any illegal activity."

"Did you capture any conversation?"

"I already told you, we needed to be within a thousand yards for the mics to pick up anything. It took three nights of surveillance, but finally we got something interesting."

"Let's hear it."

"You think I'd bring a tape recorder into a sauna? Where would I hide it?"

I stared at him until he reached into the back of his shorts and pulled out a small device that looked like an MP3 player.

"I can give you the thirty-second version," Demetrius said.

"Blah, blah, bang," said Chico.

"That's more like a three-second version," I said. "But I'd rather hear the whole thing." I realized that I had seen the two guys who hung out with Colt and drawn some conclusions. But I had never really heard them interact much. I wanted to assess the dynamics of the relationship.

"It kind of starts midstream," Demetrius said. "We had to find a place out of the wind for the microphone. There's long stretches of silence that I had to edit out." He pushed a button on his device. The speakers were actually pretty good for such a small contraption. Our tax dollars secretly at work.

"You can stop trying, Colt. It's not gonna happen."

"I can do it," Colt said. "You've just got to give me some time. It's a paranoid kind of a place." I assumed Colt was talking about Dugway and this conversation sounded anything but "blah, blah."

"You don't understand," another voice said. "We don't want to be security guards. We would never pass the clearances. We're not good little Purple Heart–wearing soldier boys like you, Colt. They'd never consider us."

"You *are* like me," Colt said. He was sounding a little defensive. "You're more like me than anyone I know. You were over there. You know what it was like. You risked your lives serving your country just like I did."

"Yeah, but you came home a hero," one of them said. "Let's just say we won't be getting any medals."

"I'm no hero, either," Colt said. "The only difference between you and me is that I got shot in the leg."

There was a soft chuckle. "That's where you're wrong, Colty-boy. You see, you can live in the light, but guys like us are better off in the dark."

There was a sound like the rustling of bushes on the tape. "That's a family of raccoons," Demetrius said. "About twenty yards away going down to the . . . uh . . . reservoir, to take a drink. A mama and six little ones. Really cute."

There was more rustling and then a sound. *Pfffffft.*

Demetrius pushed the pause button, "And that was a silenced pistol that one of the guys pulled out of his jacket. He shot the mama raccoon and just sat there looking at the babies." Demetrius pushed play.

"What'd you do that for?" Colt asked.

"Because he enjoys it," the other man explained. "I told you. We're not like you, Colt. We like living in the dark."

The tape continued for a time, but not much else was said. Finally, Demetrius turned it off. "These guys are psycho," he said. "But I don't see anything here that links them to the terrorist threat. They almost had to beg Colt not to try to get them into Dugway. Does that sound like a terrorist to you?"

"I don't know," I stood up. "But thanks for the info and the surveillance. Despite what everyone says, you guys do a good job." I turned to go.

"Hey, Knight," Demetrius said.

"Yeah."

"If you do find something that can take these guys down, we want to be there." He paused and then said, "Chico's got a soft spot in his heart for mama raccoons."

And I had a soft spot in mine for motherless kids. Maybe there really was nothing going on here, but my gut told me otherwise. I just needed to figure out what it was. And I wouldn't mind having Chico and Demetrius watching my back when I did.

"See you around," I said.

"Not if we're doing our jobs."

CHAPTER 18
Abandon Hope

FOR THE NEXT WEEK, I didn't have much time to think about Demetrius and Chico (mentally, I had nicknamed them D&C). I didn't have time to think about Colt and his fishing buddies. I didn't even have time to consider my intentions concerning Zelphinus Cork. I was completely consumed with another matter—pain. Joseph was making sure I was ready to be his pacer in the Uinta 100.

"Aren't you supposed to be tapering in the last weeks before the race?" I asked.

"This *is* my taper," Joseph said. "My longest runs are fifties." We had gotten into the habit of driving up to the Uinta Mountains every other day and running different portions of the actual course. Joseph would run twenty-five miles or more while I slept in the car. Then he would wake me up and we would do another ten to fifteen miles together. The altitude was killer, and more than once I lost my dinner over the side of a rocky ledge.

"Most of the mules are pacing their runners for the entire last fifty," Joseph said as I coughed up something from Section 89.

"Most of them are also probably ultrarunners," I said. "You'll be lucky if I make it twenty-five."

"You're supposed to push me."

"That's funny. I thought my job was to keep you from curling up into a fetal position and dying of hypothermia." I had been doing some reading about the job of a pacer during an ultra, and I had ascertained that the main function was to keep Joseph pointed in the right direction and make sure he didn't die.

"I can't win if I have to carry my pacer on my back for the last ten miles."

"You have no chance of winning anyway," I said. "I hope that's not your goal."

"Why else would I run?"

"I don't know, maybe to achieve something that 99.99 percent of the population would never even dream about. C'mon, it takes years for most ultrarunners to even finish their first hundred-miler."

"I'm not like most ultrarunners."

"You're right about that. Most of them have more sense."

"Are you done puking yet?"

"For the moment," I said, turning my headlamp to the trail and easing back into my stumbling gait. "But I reserve the right to revisit later."

Joseph didn't say anything. He settled in behind me and barely made a sound as he glided along the trail like my own shadow in the light of the moon.

* * *

Because of my long nighttime and early morning runs, I had developed a habit of napping in the afternoon. On this particular afternoon, in the middle of this particular nap, I heard raised voices coming from the parking lot through my open window and interrupting my rest. I might have ignored the voices except for one thing—they were arguing in Arabic. I couldn't make out many of the words, but their distinct cadence and rhythm left me no doubt as to what language I was hearing. For a few moments, I thought I was back in Miami.

I popped up out of bed, winced as my aching feet met the floor, and peered out through a corner of the curtain. I saw Joseph exchanging words with a beautiful Middle Eastern young woman. She was literally in his face and waving her hands in broad gestures. Joseph's voice was quieter, and he wasn't waving his hands, but I got the feeling that he wasn't backing down either. I quickly pulled on my shoes.

Roger was in the living room frowning at his fish tank.

"Does Joseph have a girlfriend?" I asked.

"That's his cousin, Siham," Roger said. "She stops by about once a month to give Joseph advice. And as you know, Joseph doesn't take advice very well."

"What kind of advice?"

"Not sure." Roger took a sample of water from the tank in a small bottle and capped it. "It's usually in Arabic. But I think she's trying to get him to go back to church. She seems to be lecturing a lot. Joseph doesn't seem too responsive."

I slung my backpack over my shoulder and headed out the door. "I'm going to the library," I said, although I really had no plans to do so. I wanted to get out into the parking lot before the argument stopped to see if I could hear anything that might be useful. So far Joseph had shown himself to be a loner. Terrorists tended to work in teams or "cells." Maybe Joseph was a part of a larger network.

I headed for my car and got close enough to hear some of the conversation.

"You have changed, my brother, and I do not like what I am seeing."

"No, sister, it is you who has changed. You think that because you have a job, you no longer need to keep your place as a woman. You have thrown away your veil and forgotten your deference and your place." The "brother/sister" language was not unusual for Arabic. Especially among close relatives.

"My deference is to God, and yours should be too," Siham said. She was about to say something more when she saw me.

Her dark eyes locked on mine, and then she walked toward me. "You are Joseph's friend?"

I looked at Joseph, not quite sure how to answer this question. "Er, I'm his roommate," I said. "And we run together."

She came up to me, and her eyes softened. "He is not the same obedient boy he used to be," she said quietly. "Maybe you can convince him to return to his God. He's like a lost sheep who enjoys wandering from the fold."

"This is my cousin, Siham," Joseph said. "She is under the strange illusion that she is my mother."

"I tell you only what your mother would tell you if she were here."

"See what I mean," Joseph said, sighing. "But at least I have the opportunity to practice my Arabic. Siham, this is Matthew Knight."

Siham held out a dark slender arm. "Joseph has told me about you," she said.

I took her hand, sensing that this was a very strong woman who perhaps matched Joseph in her stubbornness. I wasn't sure what to say. I was more than a bit surprised that Joseph would talk about me to anyone. "I am pleased to meet you," I said.

She leaned back against a white van, which I assumed she had been driving. It said "Salt Palace" on the side.

"So you work in a palace?" I asked.

She snorted. "Yes, I'm a princess of food handling. It's a menial job, but Joseph seems to think it's still above my station as a woman. I consider it a blessing. And I do not take lightly the blessings I have been given from the Creator."

"Neither do I," Joseph said. "Which is why I spend as much time as I can in the cathedrals of the mountains."

"You cannot run from God."

"No. But I will allow Him to run with me if He can keep up."

"See what I mean," Siham said, throwing up her hands. "He is impossible."

"He is himself," I said, shrugging.

The sternness in her gaze seemed to relax, and she looked at Joseph again. I could see a fondness in her eyes. "I see that you know him well," she said. "He is most definitely himself. He always has been."

"I think this calls for a group hug," I said, holding out my arms.

"Ha," Siham said. "It's true. You are a smart aleck."

I dropped my arms and shrugged. "I am what I am," I said.

She studied me for a minute and then said, "It is good to remember who you are." She was looking at me, but I got the distinct feeling these words were meant for Joseph.

"Now I think it is time for me to go." She turned to leave and moved like a princess, elegantly sliding into her van and driving away. I thought I caught the whiff of an exotic island on the wind.

"Very pretty," I said to Joseph. "But a little preachy."

"She is a royal pain," Joseph said. But I caught a note of fondness in his voice that I didn't think I'd ever heard before.

I headed off to my car. I'd told Roger that I was going to the library, and I thought I'd better follow through on my story. I still hadn't taken the amount of time needed to fully process what I had learned from Demetrius and Chico in the sauna, and the library was as good a place as any.

I found a dark corner of the university library and opened up my laptop. I stared at the blank screen and thought about Demetrius and Chico's fishing expedition. The recorded voices and the senseless killing of the mother raccoon convinced me that these were very bad men. And not only were they bad men, but they were hanging out in the middle of the night near sources of drinking water with a security guard to a bioweapons facility. But if they were planning to use Colt to get into Dugway, why were they reluctant to accept his help to get them inside?

I thought about this until my head began to hurt and then found myself blindly surfing through different types of records, from nanotechnology terrorist threats to bioweapons used on water sources, to see if my brain would make any connections. I didn't really intend to check in on Zelphinus Cork, but somehow I found myself navigating through the back end of some agency programs into Delancey Street records.

When I found Cork and I clicked on his name, I almost fell out of my chair. His status had changed from "current resident" to "graduate." I searched for a release date and took a deep breath. Zelphinus Cork was coming home in fewer than ten days.

Driving back to the apartment I found myself pounding against the steering wheel. This was very bad timing. For a lot of reasons, I needed to put

Zelphinus Cork onto the back burner. I needed to solve this case, and I had enough distractions already. But no matter how hard I tried, I could not get the monster with the big eyebrows out of my mind.

The man who killed my mother was coming home, and I knew where he lived.

When I walked into the apartment, I almost didn't notice Hope Winslow waiting for me on the couch.

"There you are," she said. Usually when she came over, she wore jeans and a sweatshirt, but today she was wearing a pretty spring-colored dress. It was as if she had dressed up without really dressing up. She looked and smelled wonderful. I swear she almost glowed.

"Why the frown?" she asked.

I rubbed my forehead. "I've been at the library," I said. "My brain can only hold so much information."

"Better make room for more. It's study time, and today we hit one of my favorite scripture stories."

I groaned.

"We'll be quick," she said. "And then I have something important I want to talk to you about." There was a look in her eyes that was a combination of excitement and mischief. It actually made me a little nervous.

"Did you read the chapters I assigned you?" Hope was in the habit of giving me reading assignments and then reviewing them with me during our study. I was in the habit of not following through on my assignments.

"Believe it or not," I said, "this time I did." This particular section talked about a group of bloodthirsty savages who were converted to the gospel and made a covenant with God they would never shed blood again. To seal the covenant they buried their swords in the earth. When they were attacked by those who had not been converted, rather than defending themselves they lay prostrate on the ground—willing to give up their lives before breaking the covenant.

"So what did you think?" she asked. "Wasn't it amazing?"

I was tired, ornery, distracted, and my head hurt. I probably should have just told Hope that I wasn't up for a scripture conversation today. Instead, I said, "I actually think what they did was kind of dumb. They should have promised to not take up their swords *except* to defend themselves. They could have saved a lot of lives."

Hope reacted like I had slapped her in the face.

"They had been a bloodthirsty people," she said. "They were worried about being forgiven at all. Burying their swords was a demonstration of their full commitment."

I could see I was getting under her skin, and I felt a twinge of guilt. But, like I said, I wasn't feeling so hot, and I really wasn't in the mood to talk about turning the other cheek.

"What they demonstrated," I said, "was their inability to save their wives and their children because of holding to a bad promise."

Hope stood up. "Did you even read the whole story?" she asked. "Because if you had, you would know that by laying down their lives to keep a promise, they actually saved more souls that day than were killed."

"Tell that to those who watched their family members die," I said.

Hope moved toward the door and paused. I felt like I was standing on the edge of a cliff and the next few seconds would decide whether I was pulled back from the edge or plunged into the abyss. Hope hesitated and, without turning around, said, "One day you'll figure it out."

"What's that?"

"That saving someone isn't the same thing as keeping them from being killed."

And then she left. I fell back onto the couch. No one there to pull me back. I guess whatever important thing she wanted to talk to me about was going to have to wait. She didn't say, "I love you, Knight," and I wasn't given the chance to respond. I felt like the idiot of the century. Hope Winslow was an angel. She didn't deserve to be fodder to my demons.

The phone rang.

"Yeah," I said, not really in the mood to talk to anyone.

"Is Hope Winslow there?" It was Zack's voice, and he did not sound happy. But then again, he rarely did.

"Not anymore," I answered. "She stormed out of here about ten seconds ago. Why?"

There was a long silence and then Zack said, "We need to talk, Mr. Knight. Right now. My office."

* * *

Despite the range in Zack's moods that I had seen throughout the years, I had never seen him lose his composure. But today he looked a mess.

"What's the matter?" I asked, wondering if the terrorist attack was imminent. I thought I saw sweat on Zack's brow. Zack never sweat.

"I told you I didn't want her hurt," Zack said.

"Who?"

"Hope Winslow, of course."

"She's pretty ticked off at me," I said. "But I don't think she's hurt. She'll realize I was just being an idiot and forgive me in no time. That's the way she is."

"That's the problem," Zack said. "I don't want her to forgive you. You need to push her away."

I blinked. I really didn't understand where this was going.

Zack saw my confusion, and his eyes softened a bit. "You remember I warned you about one of these women falling in love with you and ending up getting hurt?"

Now I understood where this was going, and I didn't like it.

"Wait a minute," I said. "Hope thinks of me as an older brother. We're not talking love here. At least, not that kind of love."

"You may not be talking it, Mr. Knight. But Hope came into my office earlier today and said she had been rethinking her life. I've always encouraged her to find a partner and start her own family, but she has always resisted, saying the kids at the Truman Center were her family and mission on earth. But today she told me that she had been reconsidering."

"She's not talking about me," I protested.

"You are the only man she's been spending time with, Mr. Knight. Unless you count Roger or Joseph, and I seriously doubt it's one of them."

It was my turn to sweat. Hope Winslow—the most beautiful, most amazing person I had ever met—was considering starting a family? Hadn't she just said she wanted to talk to me about something important? I felt a wave rush through me like a thrilling wind on top of a mountain at sunrise, both warm and chillingly invigorating at the same time. And then I was dashed on the rocks below as the implications hit me.

"I don't intend to hurt her," I said to Zack as he studied me. "Really, our relationship is perfectly platonic."

"Maybe," Zack said. "And we need to keep it that way. The question is what to do now? I don't suppose you can scare her away by carrying around a Starbucks cup?"

"No," I said. "She'd just make it her personal mission to save me."

Zack seemed to be moving something around in his mouth that he really didn't want to spit out.

"Understand what I'm asking you, Mr. Knight. I want to see Hope Winslow spared from pain as much as possible. I also want to see you focused on and completing this mission so that millions of others are not hurt. However, if you decide you want to pursue something with Hope after the mission is completed . . ."

"No," I said. It came out louder than I intended, and I found myself standing up. Zack had opened a door that I needed to shut quickly. I was a field agent, and I knew the plight of field agents' wives. Most of them were a complete mess. Becca was the only one I knew who handled things well, and Becca was an extraordinary person. I shook my head. Good grief. I'd managed to develop feelings for not one but two untouchable women. I needed to wrap this mission up and get back to doing what I did best. Saving the world from bad guys. Working alone.

"No," I said again, as much to myself as to Zack. "Hope deserves better than what I could ever offer her." She deserved someone who wasn't an emotional mess. She deserved someone like the men in her scripture stories. Someone willing to bury the sword, not take it up in chasing down monsters from the past. She certainly didn't deserve me.

"I'll find a way to break it off for good," I said. "It might not be until after the race, but I will try to avoid her until then." The race was only two days away. I needed to make sure that Hope and I didn't get the opportunity to have any serious discussions during that time.

Zack just nodded. He seemed a little sad.

I could understand why. There was no way to get out of this situation without causing some pain, and Zack would be the one doing cleanup while I moved on to the next mission.

There were advantages to being a loner.

CHAPTER 19
The Starting Line

THE OFFICIAL NAME OF THE Uinta 100 ultrarace was "The Uinta Pain 100," as in, "Are you into pain?" Kind of a goofy name if you ask me, but so was running a hundred miles at high altitude through unpredictable weather. What was even worse, the race began at four o'clock in the morning. This meant Joseph and I needed to leave the apartment at one-thirty. This also meant we didn't really get any sleep the night before. And since the average finishing time for the Uinta Pain 100 (at least for the fewer than 50 percent who happened to finish) was between twenty and thirty hours, this meant I would be running twenty-five miles alongside Joseph after having not slept for almost two days. Not really my idea of a good time.

Maybe I should have bailed on Joseph and instead started tailing Colt's mercenary friends. This probably would have gotten me closer to my ultimate goal, and it might have even been less dangerous. It also would have kept me from having to face Hope Winslow. But I couldn't bring myself to drop the ball. And before I knew it, I was driving Joseph into the parking area at the Mirror Lake trailhead. I looked at him out of the corner of my eye and swore I caught a brief glimpse of the Hadadi smile. I wasn't sure whether Joseph was a terrorist, but I was certain he was a masochist. This was his hour, and no matter how hard he tried to hide it, he was enjoying every minute of it. Were these the actions of someone who was planning to kill millions of people? I didn't think so. But, then again, I didn't know what to think anymore.

We parked the Toyota and picked up our colored bibs, which identified Joseph as a participant and me as a pacer. His color was blue. Mine was pink. The starting line was lit up with construction lights that could probably be seen from space. Even so, they could not completely obscure the amazing star-filled sky above. I felt I understood why both the poetry and science of the ancient world were dominated by references to the night sky. Having this image stare you in the face every night would certainly make you contemplate eternity.

Silhouetted against the stars, a man wearing mountain-man attire stood on a rickety chair and held up a black-powder rifle. He spit a wad of tobacco on the ground and glared until the rumbles of conversation in the small crowd quieted down.

"My friends," he said in a loud, drawling voice. "Y'all are either stupid, severely brain damaged, or just plain weird."

For some reason this insult elicited a raucous cheer from the crowd.

"People die in the Uinta mountains each year. They wander off the trail a few feet, they find themselves suddenly separated from their group, and they are never seen or heard from again. The Uintas are like the Bermuda Triangle of mountain ranges. Because it's a short drive to civilization, people think they're safe." He spit another wad into the dirt. "But they're not safe. In fact, this might be one of the most dangerous races on the face of the earth." Another cheer arose—this one louder than the first.

"I would tell you to be careful, but if you were of the careful sort, you wouldn't be here. So instead I'll just tell you this—keep your water bottles full and your powder dry. Last one back buys the beer." With that he pointed the rifle at the big dipper and pulled the trigger. There was a loud bang and a blanket of smoke. Somewhere up ahead I heard a bansheelike scream. Legs, arms, and dirt mixed together as the racers bottlenecked at the trail entrance and then began to spread out, their headlamps casting long, eerie shadows against the trees. I looked for Joseph, but he was nowhere to be seen.

I was supposed to drive to the halfway point and meet up with Hope, Roger, and the others. But I wasn't ready for that. I looked up at the stars in the still-dark sky and wished that I could disappear inside their vastness. I wondered if my mother was up there watching from somewhere. I wondered if she was as ashamed of me as I was of myself for what I was planning for her murderer. I shook my head and moved to my car. Stars could really mess with your mind.

I drove up the road a distance and pulled off to the side. If I was going to pace Joseph for the last twenty-five miles of his race, I really needed to get some sleep. Now would be an ideal time. I reclined the seat and closed my eyes, but my mind would not turn off. I switched on the cab light, cranked up the heater, and pulled out a notebook and pen from the glove box. I forced my mind away from Hope, away from Zelphinus Cork, and on to my job. I had been on this case for weeks and still wasn't any closer to understanding who was behind the attack or how he was going to do it.

I couldn't really write any words on the paper—someone might find it and wonder why his name was in my glove box—so I began to doodle. Doodling, in fact, had gotten me into a lot of trouble during my school years. Not as much trouble as my smart mouth but significant trouble all the same. My teachers didn't appreciate it when they found that my diligent note-taking was nothing more than a bunch of lines and squiggles. What they didn't understand was that, in my own way, I actually was taking notes. I found that if I could reduce the concepts down into shapes, it helped me remember them. When my test scores began to come in, my teachers eventually left me alone.

I drew a large circle and some wavy lines like waves in a lake. Someone wanted to attack a water supply with the objective of, as the e-mail had stated, killing "tens of millions of people." I drew a big question mark inside the circle. *If this was his aim, why choose Utah?* There weren't tens of millions of people to contaminate in the entire state.

I began to draw stick figures. The first one in the form of a runner. Like Winston Churchill's view of Russia, Joseph was a riddle wrapped in a mystery tucked inside an enigma with a permanent scowl tied on top. His motivations seemed clear—become an elite ultrarunner and graduate first in his class at medical school. But I didn't get the sense that he really wanted to be a doctor and help people. I realized I didn't even know what kind of doctor he was planning to be. I was getting sloppy. This was information I should know. Was his ultracompetitiveness a mask for other motivations? Could his father's death have damaged him so much that he would actually undermine his father's antiterrorist efforts? I felt a special bond between us from our runs in the mountains, but I didn't pretend to know Joseph at all.

I drew another figure. This one I placed next to the large circle, and I drew some fish within the circle for him to watch. I hadn't spent much time thinking about Roger, yet he was the only one who might have the scientific capability to carry off a large-scale attack on water using the smallest machinery imaginable. Like Permelia had said, Roger was hiding something. But he wasn't trying to hide the fact that he was hiding it. Like Hope, Roger's emotions were close to the surface. I was pretty sure that if I point-blank came out and asked him if he was involved in terrorist activity, his blushing would give him away.

I put an *X* through Roger and drew three more figures. One of these had a crew cut, and the other two carried fishing poles that looked kind of like rifles. I drew a fence representing Dugway Proving Ground and beyond the fence some globs of nasty-looking stuff representing biological agents. I tapped my pen on the two guys with the fishing poles. I knew from their record and from the raccoon incident that they were bad dudes. But if they were planning a bioweapons attack, why didn't they want Colt's help to get them into Dugway? I moved the tip of my pen to crew-cut guy. *Why did these guys want to hang around with Colt?* I didn't believe for a minute that they were building lasting friendships. But like Zack said, if they wanted Colt to smuggle out biomaterial, Dugway security procedures would surely prevent this. And despite all his faults, Colt didn't seem like the kind of guy to give up his country for filthy lucre. The mercenaries were right about one thing—Colt wasn't like them.

As my pen rested on crew-cut stickman's head, I suddenly figured out what Colt was smuggling out of Dugway.

I almost pulled out my phone and called Zack right them. But it was still only four-thirty and I wanted to think this through before I made the call.

Colt wasn't smuggling out biological weapons or materials. It wasn't anything that would show up on the scans or full-body searches as he left the facility. He *was*, however, bringing out a precious commodity and giving it away to mercenaries—but he didn't even realize it. Everything the mercenaries wanted was conveniently stored away in Colt's overly large head. He didn't have knowledge of or access to biological weapons or agents stored at the facility. He probably didn't even know what experiments were being conducted. He was an expert in only one thing, and that one thing was security. I was sure that Colt's friends were using their fishing trips to pump Colt for information about security measures at Dugway, and I could envision Colt inadvertently giving up the goods. Colt was an innocent. He wouldn't realize that these guys were using these casual conversations to case the joint. He definitely wouldn't realize that they were using him to plan an attack.

I looked at the paper again. It all seemed so obvious to me now. All arrows pointed at Colt's head. *Why hadn't I seen it before?*

I pulled out my cell phone and looked at it. No bars. I wondered if I should turn around now, drive back to Salt Lake City, and tell Zack what I suspected. But that would leave Joseph without a pacer, and I didn't think that the Deltas would act in the next twenty-four hours.

Sleep was now out of the question. There were too many loose ends to piece together. *What exactly were these guys after?* Bioweapons, yes. But what kind of bioweapons? And how would they know what to look for and where to find it after they got inside Dugway? I tapped my pen on the fence I had drawn and then drew another figure on the other side. There had to be someone else. Someone on the inside. Someone who had knowledge of and access to the biological agents.

I got out of the car and began pacing back and forth. It was starting to get light, and the predawn cold air hit me like a bucket of ice water. Zack was right. I was slipping at my job. I'd allowed myself to get pulled into the community of the Village and pretended that I belonged. I had begun to feel like I was part of something larger. I should have known better. I should have made these connections days ago. I had always worked best alone. It allowed me to stay objective.

I looked up at the fading stars and knew what I needed to do. I would help Joseph with his race, and then I would begin cutting the ties. I was pretty sure I knew who the terrorists were now and at least a little bit of what they were up to. I needed to give them my full attention.

I got back in my car, turned on the engine, and cranked the heat back up. I set my watch, reclined in my chair, and closed my eyes. I had to run twenty-five miles today, and I needed my strength. But this race wasn't what worried me. Of the people I needed to distance myself from, Hope was first on the list. But I wasn't sure how to do it. I thought about borrowing a beer from one of the other crews and letting her see me with it, but I didn't think this would do the trick any more than the Starbucks.

"Lord, help me," I said out loud. It was more of a statement of frustration than a prayer. Even so, I was startled when my phone chimed with an incoming text message. I looked at my phone, which still showed no bars. *How did the text get through?* Was this a text from God? The modern way of answering prayers?

I almost laughed at the thought—until I read the message on my phone. It wasn't a text from God, but it might as well have been. At first my heart soared at the news I was reading. Then I looked more closely and realized what I held in my hands. If I needed a way to end my relationship with Hope, however platonic it might be, these words would likely do the trick. I closed my phone without deleting the message. I would reply to it later. I had the ammunition I needed. The only question was if I would have the courage to use it when the time came. I closed my eyes again and fell into a dark and troubled sleep.

I awoke to the sound of my watch alarm beeping. It was eleven o'clock, and I needed to get to the halfway point before Joseph arrived, which I estimated would be between two and six in the afternoon. After fifty miles of running at altitude, maybe he would decide to call it a day. Not likely, knowing Joseph, but one could always hope. I turned out of the parking area and entered the long and winding road.

As I pulled into the parking lot I immediately spotted our crew. A green canvas tent was set up in case Joseph wanted to change clothes. There was a small table with medical supplies, a few folding chairs, and a portable Camp Chef stove. Permelia stood over it, stirring a pot. Marva Rose sat next to her.

"My famous chicken and dumplings," Permelia said as I got out of the car. "With Marva Rose's help, they're even better than usual. They'll be ready in about five minutes." Marva Rose waved and smiled as I walked up and then turned her attention back to Roger, who seemed to be fiddling with some bottles of blue liquid on the other side of the campsite. I didn't see Hope. I was glad.

"Isn't this ready a little early?" I asked, nodding my head in the direction of the pot, which I had to admit smelled really good.

"You need to have more faith in your runner," Permelia said.

"But it's not even eleven-thirty." I looked around at the other crews. They did not seem to be preparing meals yet. "The course record is just over eighteen hours. I don't expect we'll be seeing any runners, let alone a first-timer, for an hour or two."

Permelia tasted her soup with a wooden spoon then turned her attention to me. She held the spoon in my face and shook it.

"And just how many ultracrews have you been on?"

"None," I said backing away.

She pulled the spoon out of my face. "Exactly. Some of 'em like to run the first half really fast. It sends a message to the rest of the pack. By my reckoning, we should be seeing the leaders anytime now."

I looked around and didn't see any sign of runners coming in, but I decided not to press the point with Permelia. I still didn't see Hope.

"She's in the tent changing," Permelia said as if reading my mind. "She's been looking for you too."

I felt my ears burning, and I thought about protesting the fact that my mind had been on Hope, but I heard the zip of the tent door and saw her step out.

"Hey, bro," she said, mumbling through the rubber band she held in her lips as she pulled her hair behind her in what would have been a ponytail on an average person. On Hope it was more like the tail of a Clydesdale. She studied the expression on my face while I tried hard not to look at her legs.

"Nervous?" she asked.

"Extremely," I said. I didn't tell her my nerves had nothing to do with the run.

"I thought I might meet you at the finish line and run the last stretch," she said. "So I put on my running shorts."

"I hope you're strong enough to haul in two expired corpses."

"I don't think Joseph will expire," Hope said, fighting a grin. I realized sadly that this might be one of the last times I would see her smile. "Hey," she said. "I wanted to apologize for the other day . . ." She started to say something else when we heard clapping.

"Told ya," Permelia said. "Here comes the leader."

A lanky man with a ponytail sauntered up to one of the tents and sat down in a chair. Immediately his crew took off his shoes and started inspecting his toes. They worked quickly and methodically. A car with a pizza delivery light pulled up, and a young man jumped out with a red warming container holding a large pizza box. He handed it to the sitting man.

"I hope I'm not late," he said

"Just in time," said the man as he pulled the meat-topped pizza out of the box, folded it in half, and began devouring it.

"He's a vegetarian most of the time," Permelia said. "But during a run he likes to have the all-meat special." I had to admit, Permelia knew her ultrarunning.

"Won't that make him sick?" Hope asked.

"Anyone else it would, but that's Emerson Longfellow. He's won every ultrarace known to man and is still going strong at forty-five. At this point in the race you need as many calories as you can get."

"Emerson Longfellow?" I asked. "Sounds more like a poet than a runner."

"He is a poet," Permelia said. "Watch his form as he glides out of here."

Permelia was right. Emerson Longfellow was indeed poetry in motion as he strode out of the halfway point back the way he had come. Of course, this was after he had wiped the pizza sauce from his face with his bare hands, downed a two-liter bottle of Mountain Dew, and let out a huge belch. But I had to admit his legs were impressive. After fifty miles they still moved like loaded springs. Although in the leg department, I still gave Hope the advantage.

I thought the clapping I was now hearing was in honor of his exit, but another runner emerged from the trees about the same time. She looked like a sixteen-year-old girl, and her medium-length hair stuck out in pigtails on both sides of her head. Kind of like a disheveled Princess Leia, unwound and having a bad hair day.

"Ah," said Permelia. *"La Brujita Dos."*

"'The Little Witch Two?'" I translated using my limited Spanish.

"Regina Camp. She's been pushing Longfellow the last several races and has broken several women's records in the process. But the press keeps focusing on her failure to break through and beat Longfellow rather than the fact that she is one of the most successful ultrarunners of all time—male or female. They love to bring up the gender issue, and it just makes her mad."

"She looks young." When I said this, Hope stepped forward into my line of vision as if to remind me that her legs were still superior.

"She's nineteen," said Permelia. "And this is a sport where many don't even start competing until they're a little more mature. So, yeah, she's young. But don't let that fool ya."

"Why the nickname?'" I asked.

"The first ultrarunner referred to as 'the witch' was Ann Trason," Permelia said. "She also dominated the sport. In the Leadville race a slick promoter convinced a group of Tarahumara Mexican Indians to enter the race and drummed up publicity by making a big deal of them not liking to run against inferior women. It was all crap of course—the Tarahumara thought no such thing—but they didn't speak English, and Ann Trason didn't know any better, so she gave them the evil eye. They named her '*la bruja*,' and some of them felt she put a curse on them. Somebody captured a picture of Regina giving the same look to Longfellow and gave her the nickname."

"To me she just looks very determined," Hope said.

"Determined and mean," Permelia said. "We need to warn Joseph to stay out of her way."

As if on cue, we heard another round of cheers, and to my surprise I saw Joseph running toward us. I looked dumbly at my watch. He had been on the trail for fewer than eight hours and was already at the halfway point. I noticed Regina Camp glaring at him as he strode past her. I thought for a moment she was going to trip him. "She is a little witch," I mumbled under my breath.

"Roger, get ready," Hope yelled as she pulled a chair around into the shade and opened up her medical box. Roger appeared from somewhere behind the tent and approached empty-handed, his jaw hanging open. I didn't think we were ready to put our pit crew up against that of Emerson Longfellow.

"Roger, get the water," Hope said again. She and Permelia seemed to be the only ones who were not paralyzed with surprise at Joseph's appearance. Joseph made his way to the chair and plopped down. Hope immediately began taking off his shoes. Joseph tensed at first but then allowed her to do her job. His feet did not look good. They didn't smell very good either. But this did not seem to bother Hope as she washed them off in a soapy bucket and then began applying first aid to the several blisters that had popped up. Permelia placed a bowl of steaming hot chicken and dumplings in his hands.

"What are you doing?" I asked him.

"Eating," he said, not looking at me.

"At this pace you're going to flame out before mile seventy-five," I said, "and I was kind of looking forward to getting a run in today." He finished his bowl and handed it back to Permelia. Roger handed him a bottle of blue liquid, which he quickly downed.

"How many in front of me?" Joseph asked.

"Just two," Permelia said. "Longfellow and Regina. And I think three more runners just arrived."

Joseph looked at Hope. "How much longer on the feet? I need to get going."

"Almost done."

"Wait a minute," I said. "You're not seriously trying to win this thing?"

Joseph ignored my comment and focused on pulling on a clean pair of socks.

"Are you crazy? This is your first ultrarace. You should be thinking about finishing, not winning. If you're not careful, you're going to crash and burn."

Joseph pulled the laces of his shoes tight and stood up. "Where's the weigh-in tent?" he asked. Permelia pointed him in the right direction. Finally he looked at me.

"Why run if not to win?" he said and trotted off.

I turned to Permelia. "He's crazy, isn't he?"

She shook her head. "All ultrarunners are crazy. He fits right in."

* * *

Despite the amazing flavor of Permelia's chicken and dumplings and the breathtaking sight of Hope, the next few hours were some of the most uncomfortable of my life. Hope was in a sprightly mood and continually tried to engage me in conversation. She mistook my standoffishness for nerves, which was completely fine with me except that she apparently felt it her duty to relax me by massaging the tension from my shoulders. I would say that her fingers felt heavenly, and maybe they would have if I didn't feel like the spawn of Satan plotting secretly to clip the wings of an angel. Her touch burned me with shame, and I quickly excused myself to the tent, saying I needed to try to nap. I lay there wondering if I had the courage to do what I knew needed to be done and lamenting what I was about to lose.

After what seemed like days, I groaned and rolled to my feet. I looked at my watch. I needed to get to the trailhead at the seventy-five-mile mark. It was only three o'clock, but Joseph had averaged nearly a four-hour marathon for the first two legs, and I didn't want to miss him. However, I knew that most likely he had worn himself out or at least slowed way down by now. I would probably end up freezing my butt off on a mountain top waiting for him to arrive—if he ever did. Maybe I would die of hypothermia. For some reason, this thought cheered me.

I stepped out of the tent. I saw Hope, reclining in a chaise lounge, sunning her legs and reading a book. She smiled when she saw me and immediately stood up.

"Able to calm the nerves with some Zs, big brother?"

I shook my head. "I might as well get up there."

Roger handed me a glass of the fluorescent blue liquid he had given to Joseph. "Drink some of this. I also filled your CamelBak with it. It's time-released so the nutrients will be there when you need them."

"Why is it glowing?" I said, swirling the liquid at arm's length.

"Actually, all of the important molecules are colorless and tasteless," Roger said. "Making it into a work of art was Rose's idea." He still wouldn't get anywhere near Marva Rose, but at least he said her name without flinching.

I looked at Marva Rose. The color of the liquid matched both her blouse and eye shadow. She smiled broadly at me. What had I done to this poor, reclusive girl?

"Here's to tastelessness," I said and downed the concoction.

CHAPTER 20

The Finish

WHEN I ARRIVED AT THE trailhead for the seventy-five-mile mark, I was ready to run. But I still had a two-mile hike ahead of me before I'd get to where I would meet up with Joseph.

"I'd take it kind of easy on the way up if I were you," said a toothless man with stringy hair and a volunteer vest. "There's a pretty steep descent the first ten miles, and if you run out of gas you won't want to turn back."

"What if I run out of gas before I start?" I said.

Apparently he thought I was kidding, because he laughed. I discovered he wasn't completely toothless. There appeared to be some rotted brown stumps still attached to his gums. An interesting odor filled the air when he opened his mouth.

"I'd better get up the trail," I said, moving away from him. He was right. I did not want to come back this way.

The afternoon was pleasant, and the trail to the meeting place was scenic and mostly flat. I probably would have made good time if I hadn't broken my toe. I was rounding a bend in the trail when I came face-to-face with a bull moose coming down the other way. I knew exactly what to do because I had been told at least three times at the starting line before the race began: "Moose are territorial. If they are on the trail, it is theirs. They won't move. If you meet any moose, get off the trail quickly. If you move out of their way, they probably won't bother you."

I hadn't really been paying much attention to the instructions, but I moved. And I moved quickly. The only problem was that I didn't see the rock beneath the bush that I jumped into. The little toe on my right foot smashed squarely into the stone and sent a stab of pain all the way up into the base of my spine. I swear I heard a crack, but I think it was drowned out by my scream. At the sound, the moose dug his forelegs into the dirt and then leapt off the trail in the other direction, crashing through the brush. It sounded like he was taking down small trees. So much for moose not ceding the trail. Next time I would just scream.

I lay writhing for a while, the sharp edges of the bush gouging into my back. Finally, I got to my knees and crawled over to a large pine tree and leaned my back against it. I pulled off my shoe and inspected the damage. The toe didn't look so good. Blood was oozing out from under the nail, and it was bent in an unnatural position. I touched it gingerly and immediately wished that I hadn't. I bit back another cry of pain. So much for Joseph having a pair of fresh legs to pace him.

I pulled out a small bottle of Advil and swallowed four pills. They were supposed to be for Joseph, but he would have to wait in line. He was only running a hundred miles. I, on the other hand, had stubbed my toe.

Really badly.

I pulled out a roll of white athletic tape and fastened my little toe to the one next to it. Then I put my sock and shoe back on and tested my foot. It hurt, but I could walk. I didn't think I could run twenty-five miles, but the least I could do was get to the meeting place and tell Joseph what had happened. I started to fantasize that maybe he wouldn't show. Maybe he had burned himself out by running too hard in the first half of the race. But in my heart I knew that Joseph would be there and that he would expect me to help him finish the race. He was just going to have to get over it.

A few minutes later I rounded a corner and saw a woman wearing a volunteer vest sitting on a rock by the crossroads of a trail. I nodded to her, found another rock to sit on, and pulled out my water bottle. She nodded back at me. I noticed she held a radio in her hands.

"How long before they get here?" I asked.

"Depends on who you're talking about," she said, smiling. "Longfellow smoked by here about half an hour ago, and Regina was right on his heels." She continued smiling at me. She had pretty teeth, which at first was a relief. But something about her smile and stare was unsettling. She watched me drain my water bottle and then pointed at a yellow cooler with a push-button dispenser.

"If you fill up now, you can probably catch him," she said.

"Why would I want to catch Longfellow?"

"Not talkin' about Longfellow, dude. Talkin' about the Arab-looking guy that just passed a few minutes ago looking for his pacer. He wasn't very happy that you weren't here."

I stood up and winced in pain. "Joseph was already here? He's still in third place?"

"Fifth, actually. There were a couple of other dudes in front of him and behind Regina. But judging by their condition, my guess is he'll catch up before too long. He looks good for a rookie. Between him and the Longfellow/ Regina duel, this race looks to be one of epic proportions." She watched me as I hobbled over to fill my water bottle.

"You don't look so good yourself."

I ignored the comment. "Joseph was here only a few minutes ago?"

She looked at her watch. "About five."

I should have cut my losses and headed back down to my car, but for some reason I didn't. I could feel her eyes on me as I started out walking and then tested my foot with a tentative trot.

"You want some first aid before you go? There's blood coming out of your shoe."

I thought about it. I was sure her first aid would be better than my crude tape job, but I was already behind Joseph and I wasn't sure that if I removed the shoe I could ever get it back on.

"I'm good," I said and started to leave.

"If you go down that hill, you're not going to want to come back up."

"Yeah," I said. "I heard that. I guess I'll see you at the finish." It was a stupid, macho thing to say, but it helped me get moving down the hill. I needed to catch Joseph and at least run with him for a while. He was counting on me being there, and I was letting him down.

I moved as fast as I could and tried not to think of the jarring pain that coursed through me every time my foot hit the ground. It wasn't too long before I saw someone ahead of me. The man had long gray hair. Unless Joseph had aged fifty years in the last seventy-five miles, it wasn't him. His legs were so skinny that I thought his shins would snap every time they hit the ground. He had a pacer moving slightly in front of him, an attractive blonde who looked to be in her early forties. She guided him off to the side, and they let me pass.

"You guys are doing great," I said, slowing.

"This is what Pops asked for at his seventieth birthday party," the woman said. "His daughter as his pacer. Does your dad ask for crazy stuff like that?"

"No," I said, not wanting to get into the fact that I never knew my father. "Just my roommate. You see a darker-skinned guy pass you in the past few minutes?"

"You his pacer?"

"Yup."

"Not far. He just passed us. You should catch him soon."

"Let's stop talking and get moving," the old man said. "I want to catch Longfellow."

The woman shrugged, and I moved out in front of them, wondering what I would be doing at age seventy and if I would ever have a daughter to indulge me in my follies.

The volunteers were right. The trail moved steeply downhill in switchback fashion. This made for fast going. It also drove my toes into the front of my shoe with every stride, and I wondered at times if I was going to pass out. Luckily, the Agency had put me through enough survival courses that I was used to working through hostile situations and pain. I put the toe out of my mind and kept going.

I moved out of some trees and high brush to where I could see a figure in a yellow T-shirt striding in a regular rhythm about two hundred yards ahead of me. I increased my pace and caught him just as we reached the bottom of the hill.

He turned as he heard me coming and slowed to a walk to let me catch up.

"You missed the checkpoint," he said in his typical condescending tone. In his eyes I saw irritation but I also thought I saw a hint of relief. I'd been running less than three miles. He'd done almost eighty. I couldn't imagine the mental fortitude it took to stay focused for so long. I thought of my toe and knew that his body must be feeling the same type of pain in a thousand places at once. My job—the job of the pacer—was to get his mind off of it and get him to the finish.

"I believe the proper protocol is to wait for your pacer before moving on," I said. Joseph looked like he wanted to hit me. Good, I was doing my job.

I took a drink from my water bottle then pulled out a pouch of Roger's blue nanoconcoction and gave it to Joseph. He accepted it and drank.

"You need food?" I asked. He nodded. I handed him a Clif bar, and he ate as we walked. The evening shadows had begun to deepen, and the colors of the mountains around us seemed to reverberate with a richness that had been hidden in the pale light of noonday.

When I saw he was nearly finished, I broke into a trot and said, "Enough loitering. We've got a witch and a poet to catch."

His eyes flashed again. I knew the loitering comment got to him. But I could also see by the twitch of his lips that he knew what I was doing and appreciated it.

I moved out faster, testing my toe. It was unbelievably painful. I took the pain and in my mind wrapped it inside of a thick piece of down bedding and set it off to the side. Today was not about me and my troubles. This was Joseph's day, and I would get him to the finish line.

We ran steadily for a long time, like we had done on many occasions—not speaking but aware of one another all the same. Each deriving strength from the other.

Three more miles and we passed the next runner and his pacer. They had slowed to walking on a moderate uphill stretch. I nodded as we passed and then pushed even harder. I was afraid that if we slowed, we would keep slowing. Joseph kept pace right behind me.

The evening shadows quickly turned to darkness, and I pulled out our headlamps and helped Joseph with his. His eyes seemed to be going in and out of focus, and I wondered if I my pace was too aggressive for this stage of the race.

After getting us into our night gear, I started off again at a slower pace.

"What are you doing?" Joseph yelled, his voice a bit raspy.

"Guaranteeing a finish," I said. "There's fifteen miles left, and it's dark. If we don't do anything stupid, we'll make it in one piece."

Joseph didn't say anything for a few minutes, and I thought he had accepted my answer. Then we saw the two headlamps flashing in the distance across a valley ahead of us. They could have been half a mile away or three; it was impossible to tell. Either way, I knew exactly what Joseph was thinking before he said anything.

"Those are two of the most elite ultrarunners in the world," I said before he spoke. "Finishing third behind them in your first race is unheard of. You'll have plenty of chances in the future to beat them."

I felt him pick up his pace and push so that he was nearly clipping my heels. The lights bobbed in front of us like a beacon calling to a lost ship. I shrugged my shoulders and moved out faster, telling myself once again that this was Joseph's race and I was here for him. It would be impossible for us to catch them but it was also impossible that we were now in third place. So why not go for it?

The next five miles passed like a blur in the night. We lost sight of the headlamps in front of us and had no idea if we were gaining or falling further behind. Then we rounded a corner and something changed. I listened intently trying to figure out what it was. Then I knew. Something was different in Joseph's stride. Whereas his feet had been gliding along the ground, they now seemed to be pounding into the trail like a jackhammer. It was almost as if all the lubrication had drained from his joints and he was running on stilts. I slowed and handed him another pouch of Roger's blue Kool-Aid.

"What are you doing?"

"You need hydration," I said, studying him as he came up to me. "Are you cramping?"

He took a drink but we kept walking. "I don't think so," he said. "Everything just all of a sudden feels stiff and tight."

"Only ten miles to go," I said, trying to sound cheerful. "We can crawl that if we have to."

"How far ahead do you think they are?" Joseph asked, ignoring my comment.

"Hard to say. They might have kicked it into a higher gear and are already approaching the finish." I took a drink myself and handed Joseph a packet of carbohydrate gel to replenish his energy. "Then again, maybe we gained on them and they're around the next corner."

"My mind's all over the place," Joseph said. "I'm starting to see things."

"What kinds of things?"

"All sorts of things. Bears, rattlesnakes, land mines in the trail." He paused and sucked on the gel. I didn't think he was going to say anything more, and then he said, "I saw my father."

I had heard the stories about hallucinations in the last stages of a race. The lack of sleep combined with the physical exertion created the perfect breeding ground for seeing things that weren't there. I caught myself wishing that I would see my mother and then realized I needed to get Joseph's mind back in the present.

"Did he tell you how far ahead Longfellow is?" I asked, trying to snap his séancelike mood.

"No," he said. "He asked me why I was letting the woman take my glory."

I saw his shoulders slump just slightly. I had also heard of this. In marathons, runners speak about hitting the wall. In ultrarunning, it's a series of walls, as emotional as they are physical. Periods of elation followed by utter hopelessness and depression. In the last stages of the race they can cycle back and forth with increased frequency. Joseph was in a low. My job as the pacer was to pull him out of it.

"Funny," I said. "I had the same question." Joseph looked up at me curiously. "Why are you letting Regina Camp steal your glory? Physically you must be stronger than her. The only thing I can think of is that she is tougher mentally."

This comment seemed to hit him like a slap in the face, but his gaze was still cloudy.

"Why are we sitting here analyzing your dreams while a little slip of a girl like Regina is kicking your tail?"

"Regina?"

"Regina Camp—the woman who is ahead of you."

Joseph's eyes cleared, and he seemed to rejoin me. He rubbed at his knees. "We need to do something different," he said. "I don't think I can travel the next five miles like I did the last. My mind is getting fixated on the pain in my legs. I can't seem to think of anything else."

"You could hallucinate," I said.

"Tried that. It made things worse."

I thought for a minute. I was sure experienced pacers had lots of tricks for these types of situations. Unfortunately, I was more of a rookie than Joseph. But I did know a few things about keeping the mind focused under severe duress. I thought about my stint in Miami, locked in a basement waiting to be beheaded.

"What's on your iPod?" I asked.

"I tried that too," Joseph said. "I ran the first half of the race to music. Lines from the songs started to repeat in my head. It made me nauseated."

"I wasn't suggesting you turn the iPod on," I said. "I just asked you what was on it."

He shrugged. "Mostly reggae. Some Dennis Brown, some Chalice, and quite a bit of Bob Marley."

"The *Bob Marley Legend* album?

"Yes, why?"

"Follow my lead," I said. "Don't question it, just trust me. I cleared my throat and started running.

Then I began to sing. My voice was loud and painful even to my own ears. I'd been invited to sing in the choir only once. After they heard my voice, they stopped asking.

"What are you doing?" Joseph said from behind me.

I stopped singing and looked over my shoulder. "Do you want to spend the rest of the race fixated on those knobby knees or do you want to catch these people? Try it for a few miles. Trust me."

I continued singing, despite being 98 percent sure Joseph would not follow my lead. But after a few minutes, I heard something behind me. This time I stopped singing and looked back. Joseph wouldn't meet my eyes, but he kept singing. He was not a prime candidate for the choir either. I turned back around and joined him in the chorus.

For the first few hundred yards, I thought I might have made a mistake. Singing in order to take your mind off of being killed was one thing, but singing while running seemed to expend unnecessary breath that neither of us had. But after a while our voices quieted some and the words blended in with the natural rhythm of our breaths. When I heard Joseph's voice begin to falter, I would sing louder.

After a few miles we rounded a corner and almost ran over Emerson Longfellow. He was sitting in the trail, his legs extended, pulling the tips of his toes back toward him. His eyes were wide as he moved one hand to shield them from the beam of our headlamps.

I slowed to a stop and looked around. Longfellow looked pale, and he was obviously cramping up.

"You chaps real?" he asked. "You scared the dickens out of me. I thought I was being chased by a band of angry Rastafarians."

"Where's your pacer?" I asked.

He reached out a hand, and I helped him to his feet. "I haven't used one for years. The more I won, the more people began accusing me of using performance enhancers. They couldn't believe I could win so consistently without getting help."

"So you dropped your pacer?"

"My pacers were accused of smuggling me the goods. I removed any doubt." He bent at the waist and continued massaging his calves. "Although I could sure use someone to carry me down off this hill right about now. I think this cramp might really be a muscle tear."

"We can send someone back for you." I could sense Joseph getting antsy behind me. With Longfellow out of the race, we were now in second place.

"Don't bother. I can hobble to the end if I have to. I just wish I could be there to see Regina's face at her victory. I remember the first time I beat the reigning champ. It's the best feeling in the world."

"You don't mind her beating you?"

He waved his hand dismissively. "Other races, other places. It'll actually make things more interesting. We're going to have some exceptional battles in the future."

I wanted to stay and ask him more, but it was time to move on. Joseph and I had a witch to catch.

"How far ahead is she?" Joseph asked before we took off.

Longfellow scratched the grizzle of his beard. "Not really sure. My sense of time isn't too great right now. Could be ten minutes; could be a lot more."

"Let's go," said Joseph. This time he began singing as we hit the trail. The tactic must have been working for him.

We passed the four- and three-miles-to-the-finish marks with no sign of Regina. Then, ahead of us and slightly off the trail, I thought I saw a fluorescent light floating through the trees. I shook my head and blinked my eyes, but the image was still out there in front of me. It was not Regina Camp. It looked like a woman in a white dress, illuminated and floating through the trees.

"You see that?" I asked Joseph.

"You mean the ghost woman? I thought I was hallucinating again."

"Not unless we both are." The distance and the trees allowed us only intermittent glimpses of the figure. Then another light appeared in the trail in front of us, and we completely forgot about the ghost.

"It's Regina," I said. "We're gaining." There was only one light, which meant that Regina wasn't using a pacer either. The race rules required one, but I guessed she didn't want Longfellow to find any way to say he had bested her. At this pace, it was clear to me that we were going to catch her.

We had stopped singing when we spotted her, but she heard us when we got to within about thirty yards. She tried to increase her pace, but she was hurting. When we passed, her eyes widened and her jaw hung slack. I think she was maybe expecting Longfellow, not a rookie she'd never heard of. We had less than two miles to go, and Joseph was in the lead.

"I can't believe it," I said. "You're really going to win this thing."

"Told you," Joseph said. "What did you expect?"

I glanced behind me and saw that he was grinning. The Hadadi smile. I think Joseph had surprised even himself.

"Get ready to be famous," I said.

Maybe I shouldn't have said it. Maybe it was my words that jinxed us. Whatever the case, we did not make it to our fifteen minutes of fame. At that moment I heard a grunt behind me and turned in time to see Joseph going down. His ankle rolled underneath him, and I thought I heard a loud pop. Joseph lay writhing on the ground, grasping his ankle. I knelt down beside him.

"Do you think you can put any weight on it?"

Joseph winced, shook his head, and put the back of his hands against his forehead as I took his foot in my hands. Regina Camp came around the corner.

"Looks like it's raining men," she said with a smirk. "First Longfellow and now you."

"It's his ankle," I said. "I can't tell how bad."

"Bad enough," she said as she passed, kicking dust up from her shoes and into my face. I briefly considered lining her up with Joseph. They seemed like the perfect pair.

I gingerly pulled off Joseph's shoe and got out the athletic tape. We weren't going to catch Regina, but if I could tape and stabilize the ankle before it started swelling, we might be able to get Joseph to the finish line. My whole body shook with fatigue as I completed my wrap job. I had put the pain in my toe out of my mind, but Joseph's injury reminded me of it, and each throb threatened to put me on the ground.

I finally completed a haphazard tape job and struggled to my feet. "Let's test it," I said, reaching under Joseph's arms and lifting him. It felt like he weighed three hundred pounds.

I heard a noise on the trail and saw Longfellow come around the corner in a kind of hop step.

"I got a bit of a second wind," he said. "How far ahead is Regina?"

"At least ten minutes."

"Too bad. I wanted to be there for her victory." He turned and loped off into the darkness.

I got Joseph onto the trail with me supporting him. He tried to put some weight on his foot. He was breathing hard and winced noticeably with each step.

"What do you want to do?" I said. "We're only two miles from the finish. I can have them bring a stretcher if you want."

Joseph scowled. "Just help me finish."

We moved out onto the trail, my arm around Joseph, both of us hobbling slowly like a couple of hundred-year-old men. The first mile took us forty-five minutes. Four more runners passed us. The second mile took us more than an hour, since Joseph insisted on walking without my support. This was probably a good thing. Supporting his weight was grinding my toe into the fires of hell.

I could hear cheers ahead of us as the runners reached the finish line. I didn't care anymore what place we came in, and I didn't think Joseph did either. I just wanted it to end.

An illuminated figure moved through the trees ahead of us. It was the ghost woman. She had white hair and was wearing a white dress. She was literally glowing. She came within about twenty-five yards of us and then beckoned us to follow.

"Come, weary travelers. The end is near and your reward awaits you."

Now I could see the reason she was shining. There were numerous glow sticks hanging from her dress, and her face was painted with white makeup.

"Permelia?" I asked.

She squinted. "Is that you, boys? I wondered when you'd show up. You're in seventh place if no one else passes you. But after Regina beat Longfellow, no one's paying much attention to the rest of the pack."

"What are you doing?" I asked her.

"Just having a little fun. Every runner deserves at least one good hallucination. Otherwise the runners have no stories to tell."

"Didn't I see you off the trail a few miles back?"

"I've been all over this last five-mile stretch. Got tired of sitting around and decided I needed some exercise. Why are you boys walking?"

"Ankle," I said, nodding to Joseph. "Happened a few miles back."

"Only about a thousand yards left. At this pace you'll get there in about fifteen minutes. You need any help?" The thought of a seventy-five-year-old woman helping two young men in their prime might have seemed ludicrous at one time, but I had no doubt that at this moment Permelia was stronger than both of us put together.

Joseph cleared his throat. "I want to run. I don't want to finish walking."

"You sure that's possible?" I asked him.

His lip twitched. It wasn't quite the famous Hadadi smile, but it was a smile all the same. "I might need a song," he said. "You want to start?"

I drained the last bit of Roger's blue liquid from my water bottle and prepared myself for the pain that was to come. I decided to start with the chorus from "Three Little Birds"—the part about how everything was supposed to be all right. My voice sounded shaky at first but then rose to an annoying crescendo.

I heard Joseph's voice join me and then Permelia's as we eased into a sort of loping run. Others heard our singing as we neared the finish line. They must have even been able to recognize the song because they began to sing along. Ultrarunners really were strange people.

By the time we crossed the line, it sounded like a hundred people had joined in. Hope, Roger, and Marva Rose came running out to meet us on the trail, and we all crossed the finish line together. I felt tears come to my eyes. If I hadn't been dehydrated, they might have even made it to my cheek.

If I didn't know what I was about to do, this might have been the happiest moment of my life. I had just helped a friend complete an impossible task, and now we were surrounded by our friends. By our family. I breathed in the cool night air and tried to capture the moment in my memory. The pain, the utter weariness, the smell of sweat, pine, and dirt. The feel of Hope's arm around my shoulder and her hair brushing gently against my cheek in the night. I didn't ever want to forget it. We looked like a dirtier version of Dorothy and her friends as they sang and danced together down the yellow brick road.

Regina Camp came over and stood in front of Joseph. A small wooden boot was attached to a leather thong around her neck.

"That all they give you?" Joseph said, gesturing to the totem.

Regina shrugged. "It's better than a belt buckle I don't need." A few news trucks were illuminated in the parking lot, and a reporter was beckoning to her. She nodded to Joseph's ankle. "If it wasn't for that," she said, "you'd be getting all the attention."

"Other races, other places," Joseph said. "Don't get comfortable."

Regina half scowled, half smiled. The target had been moved from Longfellow and was now squarely on her back.

"Besides," Joseph said. "It wasn't a fair race—I had a pacer."

With that, Regina nodded to me and took off to meet the press.

CHAPTER 21
A Punch in the Face

JOSEPH AND I HOBBLED OVER to a couple of chairs. Hope pulled off Joseph's shoe, looked at the ankle, and said, "I think we should leave it taped and get you over to the medical tent to let them have a look at you. Roger, can you help me here?" Roger and Marva Rose came over and assisted Joseph to his feet.

Permelia handed me a bowl of her chicken and dumplings. "You'd better eat this. Joseph, when you get back, you need to eat too. I'm going to go in the tent and get out of this white dress before someone proposes." Permelia stepped toward the tent and then turned back to Joseph. "Never seen a first-timer do as well," she said. "I always knew you were an ornery son, but tonight it served you well. Just don't forget who your friends are." Joseph met her eyes, and Permelia went inside the tent.

Roger and Marva Rose helped Joseph move in the direction of the medical tent. Hope and I were left alone. Suddenly, I felt drained. This was good. If I'd had an ounce of emotion left in me, I didn't think I could do what needed to be done.

I pulled my phone out of my pack, struggled to my feet, and motioned to Hope. "I need to talk to you," I said. We moved over to the parking lot near my car, which Roger and Hope had shuttled from the seventy-five-mile trailhead.

Hope put her hand on my back. "I thought you were going to crash and burn, bro, but you did great. I'm proud of you."

"Please don't touch me," I said, shrugging her off.

"Are you hurt?" she asked, pulling her hand quickly away.

Even now she didn't realize that I was the one dishing out the pain.

"This has to end," I said. "Hope, I can't be your friend anymore."

She stared at me in confusion. She frowned, started to smile, and then frowned again.

"This is some kind of joke, right?"

"No joke," I said. "Just the way it has to be." My words came out flat and empty. Exactly the way I envisioned the rest of my life.

I saw the tears come in a rising flood as Hope tried to register what I was telling her.

"If I've done something . . ." Hope began. She reached out to touch me again, and I stepped back. As devoid of emotion as I was, I still didn't think I could handle her touch.

"You haven't done anything," I said. "I have. I've been lying to you all along." Of course, this was accurate. I had been lying to Hope about my occupation and my purpose in Utah. But I had also been more open with Hope than I had ever been with anyone in my life—even Robbie and Becca. Working undercover, I'd had to tell many lies, but the one I was about to tell Hope Winslow made me feel sleazy in a way I never had. I handed her my cell phone.

Hope took it and read through the words on the screen. She looked up at me and then read the words again. I could see her lips moving as she seemed to memorize the message.

"Who's Becca?" she asked, her words perched on the edge between anger and tears.

"My best friend Robbie's wife."

I saw the blood rise in her cheeks, and I braced myself for the inevitable slap on the cheek.

It didn't come.

Instead, Hope pulled back her fist and punched me in the face as hard as she could. I was expecting a strong reaction but not this strong. I barely had time to register what was happening and turn my jaw enough so that she didn't break her hand. Still, the blow landed solid. It hurt. I wanted it to hurt. This contact would likely be the last that Hope Winslow and I would have.

When I didn't go down, I think she considered hitting me again. I wished she had. Then the tears came back. She tossed the phone at my feet and stomped away, her arms wrapped tightly around her body.

I bent down, picked up the phone, and rubbed my jaw, wondering at the intensity of Hope's reaction. I looked again at the words on the screen. It was indeed a text from Becca. The words said, "*Greetings, hotshot. Pull out the cigars because congratulations are in order. It's a boy. You're going to make a great daddy. P.S. Robbie doesn't know I'm texting you. He'd be furious.*"

Becca and Robbie had always said that when they had their first child, I would be the godfather. Becca's words were an innocent statement of this sentiment. Robbie would be furious because making contact with an agent in the field was strictly forbidden. But taken out of context these words provided the only way I could think of to sever my ties with Hope. It's what Zack had ordered me to do, and it made sense for me to get rid of distractions and focus on the mission. But I still felt lower than the lowest life form on earth. I told myself that Hope Winslow was better off without me in her life. I was sure I was right.

I moved to my car and leaned against it, finding I could barely stand. I just wanted to go back to the apartment, get some sleep, get up tomorrow, catch the bad guys, and pay a visit to Zelphinus Cork. Then I wanted to leave this place and never come back. I looked up at the night sky. The darkness crept into my lungs, and I had to choke it back.

I saw Roger and Marva Rose helping Joseph back toward the tent, and I waved for them to bring him over to me. Once Hope told them what I had done, they wouldn't be speaking to me any longer either. I just wanted to get Joseph and get away.

"I'll drive," Roger said, helping Joseph into the passenger seat. "Your legs are going to stiffen up, and you might go off a cliff somewhere."

"Already did," I said, getting into the driver's seat. "See you at the bottom." Before Roger could argue, I turned the key and pulled out of the parking lot.

As I drove off, I saw Hope in the rearview mirror, sitting in a chair by the tent, her head in her hands, covered by a mountain of flowing hair.

* * *

My legs did stiffen on the way back, and driving proved to be difficult. Unfortunately, I did not go off a cliff. It would have made things so much easier. I got Joseph to his room, took a shower, and fell into my bed. Dead to the world.

It felt like only minutes had passed when a progressive pounding began in my head. I waited for it to go away, but it only got louder. I looked at my watch: 7:00 A.M.

"Go away," I mumbled.

"Mr. Knight, I suggest you open this door right now before I break it down." It was Zack. He must have heard the news.

I stumbled out of bed and briefly went to my knees as I was reminded of my hurt toe. I unlocked my door, and there stood Zack, fuming in a black suit and a black tie.

"Going to a funeral?" I asked.

"You might say that," he said. "Let's go out to my car. I want to talk to you." I could tell that he really wanted to yell more than talk. But I figured I might as well face it now so I could go back to sleep.

He looked down and winced. "What happened to your foot?" I purpose-fully did not look. If the condition of my toe made Zack cringe, then I knew it must be bad.

"Not much. Severe trauma followed by twenty-five miles of pounding on rocks. I'm sure it'll be fine once they amputate."

Zack grunted and moved toward the outside door. We passed Roger in the living room. He did not look at me.

We got inside Zack's SUV, and he turned to me. "Mr. Knight. What in the Sam Hill do you think you are doing?"

I thought of half a dozen snappy comebacks, but I could tell Zack wasn't in the mood, so I gave it to him straight. "You told me to break it off with Hope," I said. The sound of her name on my lips for some reason made my cheek hurt. "I was following orders."

Zack winced as if he had been hit.

"Heck of a time for you to actually become an obedient agent."

I wasn't sure what Zack was trying to say. *Did he regret giving me the order to break things off with Hope?* For a moment, I almost entertained the thought.

Then I caught myself. The truth was that at some point in time I would have gotten to the same place with the same choices. I had admitted to myself that I was falling in love with Hope Winslow, and I couldn't bear to let the situation continue any longer.

"Did you have to use a sledgehammer when a precision tool would have done just fine?" Zack asked when I didn't say anything.

"You know how determined Hope is," I said. "I wasn't going to keep her away with a Starbucks cup."

"So you told her that you were fathering a child with the wife of your best friend? I admire your subtlety, Mr. Knight."

"Becca sent me a text. She and Robbie are pregnant. She told me I would make a great father. It seemed like a way out."

"But you're not the father." It was a statement, but there was still a hint of question in it.

"Not possible on many counts, including conflicting geographies and lack of intimate relations."

Zack took a deep breath and let it out slowly. "I'm not sure you understand how effective your methods were."

I shrugged. "She was under the impression that I was a decent guy, and now she thinks I'm a creep, a backstabber, and an adulterer."

A weariness crept into Zack's voice. "Do you remember when I told you that everyone in my flock was broken?"

I nodded.

"It was a true statement. True for everyone in my ward *except* Hope Winslow. Because of what Hope has experienced and because of who she is, I never considered her as broken. But she wasn't *complete* either. I've encouraged her not to rule out marriage just because of her mission with the children. I've felt strongly that she could experience even greater joy if she found the right man and opened herself up to the possibility of a family."

"You and I both know that I'm not the right man," I said.

Zack just stared through me, seeming not to hear my words. "Hope came to me last night in tears. She was shaking and she could barely speak. I thought someone in her family might have passed away. She doubted herself—doubted her ability to judge people. She wondered how she could have been so wrong about you. By morning she had come to a conclusion: You were a test. A trial placed in her path to convince her to not abandon her single-minded focus on serving the children. A warning of what could happen if she opened herself up to a man. When she left this morning, she had regained her composure and her resolve. I don't think Hope will be open to a relationship ever again.

"You know what the worst part was, Mr. Knight? As her bishop, I couldn't refute her conclusions. I couldn't tell her that you were stupid and impetuous but not someone who would betray a close friend. Because I am your boss and because I needed to protect your cover, I could only watch her eternally erase a family from her future—at least in this life."

I dropped my head. "I'm sorry," I said. "I really didn't mean to . . ."

"It's not your fault Mr. Knight," Zack interrupted. His voice was almost gentle. "It's mine. I was so busy playing the protective father that I forgot to let agency have its due. Who knows? You might have made a great couple."

Zack put his head in his hands and rubbed at his eyes. I was astonished that he would even consider a future for Hope that included me in it. But no matter what he thought, I knew the truth. No, I was not an adulterer who betrayed my best friend but there was an evil in my heart that was just as dark, and there was no way that I would let my darkness invade Hope's light.

I decided to change the direction of the conversation. If we talked any more about Hope, I thought we might both start bawling. "I think I know who the terrorists are," I said, "and I think I know what they want."

Zack pulled his head from his hands and arched his eyebrows at me. He knew I was trying to change the subject, but for now it seemed that he was okay with that. "Colt's mercenary friends?" he asked. "I thought we determined there were only fish in the cooler."

"We did, and there were. But I think the fishing trips served a different purpose. I think they were designed to get Colt talking about his work at

Dugway Proving Ground. To get him discussing his role in security—and giving out details about the facility."

"For what purpose?"

"I think the Deltas want to gain entrance, obtain a bioweapon, and either use it themselves or, more likely, sell it to someone else who has already agreed to pay them."

"And you think Colt could give them enough information to accomplish this?"

"No. They'd need to have someone else working on the inside. But Colt's information could get them past the perimeter and past security. Look, these are bad dudes. Why else would they be out fishing with a Purple Heart recipient?"

"But these guys don't seem to have any ties to Islamic terrorists."

"They don't have ties to anyone. They're mercenaries. They'll hook themselves to any wagon filled with dollars."

Zack chewed on his lip. I could tell that what I said was making sense to him. And I think we were both happy not to be talking about Hope Winslow.

"But if all these guys wanted from Colt was information, why are they still hanging around him? My guess is that Colt gave up everything he knew about Dugway on the first fishing trip."

"I don't know," I said. "Maybe there's a critical piece of information they still need from him. Maybe it has something to do with timing. Maybe they're just staying in touch in case something changes in the security procedures. But out of all our leads, this is the one that makes the most sense. These guys aren't hanging around Colt because they are his friends, and they've made it clear they don't want him to help them get a job inside. It has to be information."

Zack put his hands on the steering wheel and then began tapping one of his fingers.

"Maybe we should just bring these yahoos in for questioning. I don't care how tough they think they are. I guarantee they will talk. We could prevent an attack before it gets started." Zack's voice sounded tough but tired.

"Maybe," I said. "But pulling them out of the game at this point is going to flag whoever is behind all this, and they might go deep underground. We might never find them. They'll just start plotting a different attack."

"All right," he said. "I'll have Demetrius and Chico put a tracking device on the mercenaries' car while they're on one of their fishing trips. You stay close to Colt. I'd rather no one else get hurt in all this. Hopefully, the terrorists decide to make a move soon. I'm ready for this to be over."

I was ready for this to be over too. I thought of Hope Winslow. Maybe if she heard the whole story, she would reconsider her resolve to never start a family. Not with me—I couldn't let my demons destroy her—but maybe she could find happiness with someone else. "When this is done," I said, "maybe I can give Hope a call and try to explain."

Zack pushed the unlock button on his car door, indicating it was time for me to get out. He spoke without looking at me. "I think it might be better if you left that part up to me, Mr. Knight."

CHAPTER 22

Hostage

OVER THE NEXT WEEK, I had no trouble finding time to spend with Colt. Nobody else would talk to me. School was starting, which took Joseph and Roger out of the apartment for long stretches of time, and I spent a lot of time in the university library acting like I was working on my thesis.

Colt wasn't attending school, so he was open for breakfast after my early morning runs. I preferred his apartment over Section 89 for my meals these days. Colt was still fishing with his psycho friends, and I wanted to make sure they got used to seeing me in the parking lot as they pulled in from the all-night expeditions. I found out from the doctor that my toe wasn't badly broken, just bruised. But bruised badly enough that my runs were now of the two- to three-mile variety rather than the ten to twelve. Joseph's ankle was badly sprained, and he was out of commission for at least a few weeks, so my runs these days were solo.

On my way home from the university each day I made a small detour to the Smith's grocery parking lot. I watched the house of Zelphinus Cork's daughter while I ate a stale prewrapped sandwich bought from the store's deli. The redheaded boy had been cleaning up the yard, and it didn't look as though he needed a lot of coaxing from his mother. He moved with an excitement and purpose that transcended mundane chores. I knew what the occasion would be. Zelphinus Cork was coming home. I wondered how he would react when he found me there to meet him.

Once in a while I touched my cheek and thought of Hope Winslow. I hadn't seen her since the night of the race. Permelia had tried to call once, but I hadn't answered. The best thing now was for me to wrap up this case and move on so Hope could find someone who could make her happy. I didn't go to church the next Sunday, and I had stopped reading my scriptures. Maybe I was going to hell. Maybe I was already there.

The days were beginning to feel like weeks, and I was anxious for something to happen.

Sometimes you should be careful what you wish for.

I usually returned from my run about the same time Colt and his fishing buddies were pulling into the parking lot. On this occasion, I was running a little late. I had decided to extend my mileage a bit and see how my toe and other extremities would handle it. Normally, I would come into the parking lot about five, go shower and shave, and then meet Colt for breakfast at his place at six.

The mercenaries weren't expecting to see me as I rolled in at five-thirty. My guess was they weren't expecting to see anyone. Otherwise they probably wouldn't have been pushing Colt up against his car and shoving a 9mm Sig Sauer pistol into his face. I ducked in behind some cars and moved closer to hear what they were saying.

"I should have guessed," Colt said through clenched teeth. "You were never real soldiers."

"Oh, we're soldiers all right," said the large one with the hairy arms. "Pino and I just happen to have our own army."

"You're nothin' but killers," Colt hissed. "Dirty guns for hire."

"You got that part right," said the skinny one who seemed to be in charge, "and Reg here would just as soon pop you as continue this little dance. But I think it would easier if you came along. Not necessary, mind you, just easier. So why don't you drop the patriot act and get into the car."

Colt continued to resist, bracing his legs down into the ground as the men tried to force him through the door and into the seat. Colt was strong, but there wasn't a lot he could do with a gun to his head unless he wanted to get himself shot. And I was getting the feeling that this was exactly what he was trying to do.

"I'm not afraid to die for my country."

The man named Pino laughed. "You hear that, Reg? He's not afraid to die for his country. The same country that let him take a bullet and then forgot about him. The same country that helped him get a night-security job making ten dollars an hour. Me, I'd rather die trying to make a half million. What about you, Reg?"

"Can I just kill him now?" Reg said, pushing the gun harder into Colt's skull. "It'll be light soon and someone might see us."

Pino looked down at his watch and sighed. "One last chance, Colt. I really hate to waste a fellow outcast."

Colt spat in Reg's face. I could see Reg's fingers begin to whiten on the trigger as he looked to Pino to give him the nod. If I didn't do something soon, Colt Mangum would be dead. If I did do something, we would probably both be dead.

I came out from behind the car and said in a light voice, "Hey, guys, what's going on?"

Reg jumped and almost pulled the trigger. Pino pulled out his own pistol and leveled it at me. "Move out into the light," he said.

I moved slowly, limping slightly and breathing hard. I acted surprised. "Is this some kind of military training exercise?"

"Get over here," Pino said. Colt struggled more violently, and Reg hit him with the pistol barrel across the face.

"Hey," I said, wincing at the violence. "What's this about?"

As I came within reach, Pino grabbed me and pushed me up against the car. "This is convenient," he said, grinning.

"Don't hurt him," Colt said. "He's not involved in this." I was beginning to really like Colt Mangum.

"He's involved now," Pino said. "Let me put it to you simply, Colt. Either you come with us or we pop your breakfast buddy."

Colt hesitated. The logical choice would be to let them kill us both. Whatever they wanted at Dugway was probably going to do a lot more damage than ridding the world of two relative acquaintances. I thought I could see Colt weighing the scales in the balance. Luckily Colt was more loyal than logical. He looked at me and nodded.

"Okay," he said. "Let him go. I'll do what you say."

Colt relaxed and let Reg push him down into the driver's seat. Pino opened the back door and beckoned me in.

"Hey," Colt said. "I thought you were letting him go."

"Did I say that?" Pino raised his eyebrows at Reg. "I thought I said we wouldn't pop him. And we didn't. We need this guy for insurance. Wouldn't want you deciding to try to drive us into a telephone pole. Reg is going to keep his finger on the trigger. You so much as drive us over a bump wrong, and your friend takes one. Understand?"

Colt hung his head. "Sorry to get you into this," he mumbled in my direction.

We pulled out of the parking lot and turned west, toward Dugway. I looked for Demetrius and Chico's Caddy, but I didn't see it. Maybe they were getting better at trailing people. Or maybe they were off enjoying a breakfast muffin somewhere. The tracking device had been placed under the car of the mercenaries, but we were in Colt's car. I was wearing my GPS watch, which was also being tracked. But D&C were used to me taking off to places all over the county and might not sense anything alarming.

"This a drug deal or something?" I asked.

"These guys aren't that honorable," Colt mumbled.

"Shut up," said Pino. "Say anything else and Reg puts a bullet in your friend's foot."

I looked down at my feet, thinking they had already been through enough.

"We're not drug dealers," Reg said, a note of defiance in his voice, like this was completely beneath him.

"Reg," Pino cautioned.

"What's it matter?" Reg said. A look passed between them, and Pino shrugged. He didn't care what Reg told me. This was not a good sign.

"We're mercenaries," Reg said. "Not drug dealers."

"It seems like drugs would pay better," I said.

"Not if you find the right job," Reg replied. He looked at Pino again, and his grin widened.

"This is what you call a seven-figure deal."

I tried to sound impressed as I said, "Wow, more than a hundred thousand dollars."

I saw a look of doubt cross Reg's face, and I could see the wheels turning as he counted up zeros in his head.

Pino finally answered, "No, you idiot. Seven figures. Millions, not thousands."

I whistled. "You guys get your hands on a nuclear bomb or something?"

"Or something," Pino said. His tone suggested that this was the end of the conversation, and I had unwittingly shut Reg up by introducing math into the equation.

I sat silent for a while until we turned out into the west desert. "Wait a minute," I said. "We're going to the Dugway Proving Ground. That's why you need Colt. You're going to score a bioweapon."

Pino looked at Colt and shook his head. "Your friend's a real Einstein. I can see why you two get along."

"So what is it," I asked, still playing the dumb but curious college student. "Ebola? Maybe smallpox?"

"We don't know and we don't care," Reg said, apparently getting his faculties back. "We just pick it up, pass it on, and collect the money."

"You're kidding, right?" I asked. "You're taking possession of a bioweapon and you don't even know what it is? You guys could be bio-mules and not even know it."

Reg squirmed a little in his seat. "What do you mean? What's a bio-mule?"

"Don't worry about it," Pino said. "It's probably something he read in a comic book somewhere."

"Actually I saw a special on the Discovery Channel a couple of weeks ago," I said. "Some of the Islamic extremists are starting to question the suicide-bomber tactic—it only works once, right? So they got an idea from the drug runners. Why smuggle drugs across the border and risk being caught when you can have someone else do it for you? They started placing the drugs in the bags of unsuspecting travelers, letting them take the goods across the border and then stealing their bags on the other side. They call the travelers drug mules." Reg pressed his gun harder against my neck, but he didn't stop me from talking.

"What's this have to do with terrorists?" Pino asked.

"Same idea," I said. "Letting someone else shoulder the risk. Rather than the terrorists driving a truck full of explosives into a target and committing suicide, they let some unsuspecting person do the driving while the terrorists live to kill another day. With bioweapons it's even more slick, but you've probably figured that out by now." I saw Reg's eyes go back into thinking mode. It looked painful.

"Spell it out," Pino said.

"With a bioweapon, the mule actually becomes the bomb. They think they are getting paid to pick up a package and deliver it to a buyer. But after they get the package in their hands, the buyer doesn't show. They don't even get paid. What they don't realize is that by handling the package, they've been exposed to a virus. They walk around exposing thousands of others and don't even know it until they start to crash and bleed out. The courier becomes the weapon." Reg's face was as vacant and slack as that of a dead raccoon. Pino's jaw was tensed and twitching like a stretched rubber band, ready to break. I could smell the fish on their hands and the stale sweat in their clothes. But I wasn't sure if they were more bothered by the prospect of becoming infected with a deadly virus or not getting their money.

Pino turned his face back to me. "Shut up," he said. "That's not what is happening here."

"Besides," Reg said, "we already got ten percent up front."

All was quiet for several moments. Then Colt said, "I wonder if you'll get a chance to spend it."

Pino dug his Sig Sauer deeper into Colt's face. "Just drive," he said. "No more talk."

We drove for several minutes, then I cleared my throat and said, "So you guys really don't know what kind of virus you're picking up. But you probably brought biohazard suits and respirators, right?"

"Hit him," Pino said.

Reg smashed the butt of his pistol into my forehead. I put my head in my hands and groaned. My head hurt desperately but I was smiling. The good news was that I was getting under their skin. Any hesitation on their part might give me an edge later on. The bad news was that if I got too far under their skin, there might not be a later on.

CHAPTER 23
Dugway

"PULL OVER," PINO SAID TO Colt. "Back down that dirt road and turn off the lights."

We were probably about half a mile from Dugway, and I wondered if Colt's and my time was up.

Colt did what he was told. "What now?" he asked.

"We need to make sure we aren't being followed."

This was not good news. Being followed was exactly what I was counting on. Hopefully, Demetrius and Chico would be watching the movements of my GPS and notice that we had stopped. Hopefully, they wouldn't just see that we were headed to Dugway and follow blindly, trying to catch up. I caught myself praying again. I didn't want Demetrius and Chico to be taken out by a couple of losers like Pino and Reg.

We waited for about a half an hour. I rubbed my head and moaned once in a while like I was in pain. It was easy to make my act convincing. I *was* in pain.

No cars. No lights. No Cadillac driven by my two compadres. Maybe they were being smart and were waiting for my GPS signal to start moving again. Or maybe the cavalry wasn't coming.

"Reg, get him out of the car," Pino said. Reg motioned for me to get out.

"Wait," Colt said. "If he gets out, then I don't drive."

"Relax, hotshot. We're putting him in the trunk. Reg is going to get in there with him until we get through the gates. You try anything, your friend takes one in the heart."

"Hey," Reg said. "It smells like fish in there." They were starting to argue. Maybe they would shoot each other. One could only hope.

"It'll only be for a few minutes."

"Where are you going to be?"

"In the backseat, under the tarp, which, by the way, also smells like fish. I'll have my gun on Colt. You keep yours on his little buddy. Any false moves and we pop them both and then pop the guard."

Reg pushed me out of the car, and Pino had Colt pop the trunk. There seemed to be a lot of talk about popping going on this morning. Reg threw the cooler out on the ground along with several fishing poles. He pulled out an olive canvas tarp and handed it to Pino, who was now also outside the car. Pino put the tarp in the backseat and came back to help Reg. Reg motioned me to the trunk with his gun, and I climbed in. Luckily the trunk in Colt's Challenger was roomier than it looked. Still, there wasn't a lot of wiggle space when Reg wedged himself in next to me. The gun was jammed into my chest. I hoped that Colt didn't hit any bumps.

Reg glared up at Pino.

"Five minutes," Pino said and slammed us into blackness. I heard the engine start up again, and we began to move.

Now would have been an ideal time to use my hand-to-hand training, wrest the gun from my assailant, and use it on Pino when the trunk opened again. There was only one problem: I couldn't move. And any struggle on my part was likely going to result in a bullet going through me—intentionally or by accident. I decided to wait for a better time. I hoped there would be one.

I could feel Reg's breath on the side of my cheek. It had a stale, cheesy smell to it. I felt the car slowing and saw some light trickle in through the edges of the seat backs, as if we had driven under a spotlight. The voices were slightly muffled, but I could hear them.

"Hey, big guy. You're not scheduled today."

"I need to get into my locker," Colt said. He sounded guilty. "I left my driver's license."

"Engaged in illegal activities, huh?"

"What?" Colt said.

"Driving without a license," the guard explained and then laughed. "What's under the tarp?" I tensed. If the guard decided to look, not only would he take a bullet, but it would likely mean the end for Colt and me.

"Just some crap I take fishing," Colt replied. I couldn't help but smile.

"Smells rotten," the guard said. He must have been standing close to the window.

"Rotten to the core," Colt replied.

"You're killing me, you know," the guard said. "I'm going to have to search through that on your way out."

"I know," Colt said. "I'm sorry."

We drove slowly from that point on, making several short turns.

"Is this building C?" I heard Pino say. Then, "There he is. Stop here."

I jumped as Reg pounded on the inside of the trunk. "Get me outta here."

I also wanted out. But I wondered how long Colt and I would last now that we were inside. I would need to make some kind of move soon, but I wanted to glean as much information as I could about what these guys were picking up and from whom.

The trunk lid opened, and Reg almost smothered me in his attempt to get out. I pulled myself from the enclosed space and looked around. We were parked in a small parking lot near a cinder-block building with a steel door and no windows. Waiting outside in the shadows stood a man in a white lab coat. He was holding something in his hands.

He started to walk toward us and Pino said, "Hold it right there."

The man in the lab coat stopped in his tracks. Now in the light, I could see that he held what looked like a gallon paint can in his hands.

"What's in the can?" Reg asked.

"That wasn't part of the deal," the man said. His voice was high and cracked when he talked. He was either going through puberty, or he was a very nervous man. "I'm just supposed to hand it off. No talking. No questions."

"Do we look stupid to you?" Pino asked. "You think we're going to pick up a biological weapon without knowing what it is?"

"That wasn't part of the deal," the man said again. His voice was like the whine of a two-year-old.

"What's in the can?" Reg asked again, taking his gun off me and pointing it at the man.

"You don't want to do that," the man said. "You might hit the package."

"I guarantee you he won't hit the can," Pino said. "But he will take out a kneecap unless you tell us what we need to know." Reg angled the gun to point toward the man's knees. The man started to shake.

"It's anthrax," the man said weakly. "Weapons grade."

"Why's it in a paint can?" Pino asked. "Shouldn't you be in a biohazard suit or something?"

"This is transport protocol," the man said. "There's a sealed inner container packed in wet gauze. It's not dangerous unless you open it. Do you think I would be holding this if it were hazardous?"

Pino seemed to relax a bit. This wasn't good. At some point in time his focus would return to his plans for Colt and me.

"He's been vaccinated," I whispered to Pino. "That's why he's not wearing a suit. Ask him."

Pino glared at me but still asked the question. "Are you sure you don't feel safe because you've been vaccinated? How do we know we won't be infected?"

The man seemed to be clearing something from his throat, and his Adam's apple bobbed up and down. "Vaccinations are required," he said weakly. "But this is still perfectly safe. It's the way we transport anthrax from facility to facility."

Pino pursed his lips and then spat on the ground. "Reg, go get the can."

Reg looked at Pino with raised eyebrows but didn't move.

"You should send Colt," I suggested. "He's probably been vaccinated too. He can wrap it in the tarp and put it in the trunk."

Colt looked confused. I met his eyes, and in that glance I thought we understood each other. We needed to make a move soon before these guys shot us and blasted their way out of the facility. If I could get Colt out of the line of fire and in possession of the bioweapon, maybe he could secure it while I made a move on Reg and Pino. Maybe someone would hear the gunshots and put the facility in lockdown.

"Did anyone ask you to speak?" Pino said, raising his pistol and pointing it at my head.

I held up my palms. Pino spat again. "You go," he said.

I blinked repeatedly. "But I haven't been vaccinated." This, of course was a lie. But they didn't know that. Also, I really didn't think there was any danger from the anthrax. The scientist was telling the truth. He was using standard transport protocol. Unless we broke into both containers, no virus was getting out.

"I don't care," Pino said. "Reg, why don't you take care of our little problem."

Reg moved to the car, pulled a silencer out of the backseat, and twisted it onto the muzzle of his gun. He raised his pistol and nonchalantly shot the scientist in the head. The scientist slumped to the ground, still holding the paint can. Reg grinned broadly, like this was something he had been waiting to do since he set eyes on the man. The killing had begun. We were out of options. Reg turned his gun on me.

Pino held up his hand to Reg then turned to me. "Go get the can."

I nodded and moved toward the dead man. I looked at Colt again. All of the boastful bravado was gone from his eyes. But the cold determination that remained chilled me. Colt was not going to let these guys leave this facility with a biological weapon. As soon as I was out of the way, he would make his move. It was now my job to secure the bioweapon.

I stumbled, feigning wobbly knees. As I pulled myself up, I tested my stiff muscles. I needed to be ready to move fast.

When I got close to the scientist, I bent down and pried his fingers from the handle of the paint can. I grasped the can firmly in my hands and then darted left and ran for my life.

"Hey," Reg said, and I heard a spitting sound as pockets of dust exploded from the cement wall behind me. From the corner of my eye I saw a blur of bodies as Colt dove at Pino's legs. I was around the corner before I could see what happened, but I heard a nonsilenced pistol bark twice in the breaking dawn.

"Get him!" Pino yelled.

Reg's combat boots echoed loudly on the asphalt as he rushed toward me. I crossed the street and moved quickly into a maze of small storage buildings. I could either run, hide, or fight. I wanted to fight. I wanted to turn back and make Pino pay for shooting Colt. But I had the anthrax in my hands, and I knew that my job was to keep it away from the bad guys. I figured my best chance at doing this was to put as much distance between Reg and me as I could. If I could shake him, I was pretty sure he wouldn't be able to stick with me for long.

I guessed right. I could tell by the sound of Reg's steps that he was falling behind. I heard the security sirens go off, telling me that Dugway was now in lockdown. All I had to do was stay away from Reg until help arrived.

Then I turned a corner and ran straight into a dead end. The street looked like it had once gone through but someone had decided to tack a garage onto one end. The metal door was secured with a heavy chain and padlock. I didn't have time to retrace my steps, and I looked frantically for another way out. There was none.

"Like a rat in a trap," Reg said between heavy breaths. He moved slowly toward me, steadying his gun.

"You'll never make it out of here with this," I said, nodding down at the can. "And if you take it from me, it will probably kill you."

"I'm not going to touch it," Reg said. "I'm gonna use you to get me outta here."

"I'm not going with you," I said.

"Suit yourself. I can blast my way out of here if I have to. Ten percent ain't so bad." He leveled the gun at me, and I held up the can.

"You hit this, and you'll be infected."

"I'm a good shot," he said, grinning.

I looked to the left and the right, but I had no place to go. My only comfort was that I didn't think the anthrax would leave the alley either.

A shadow rose up behind Reg like a mountain covering the sun. Reg's gun hand was pushed up into the air, and I heard the sickening crunch of cartilage as his elbow bent back at the joint. A huge hand grabbed him by the neck and lifted him effortlessly against a wall.

"Who are you?" Reg asked through clenched teeth as he looked vacantly at his dangling right arm.

"The protector of baby raccoons," Chico said. Reg was a big man, but in Chico's grasp he looked like a child. The adrenaline began to drain from my limbs, and they shook as I began to walk toward Chico.

Then another voice called out. "Drop him." It was Pino. He was pointing his gun at Chico's back.

Chico turned quickly and held Reg up in front of him with one arm, blocking any shot Pino might have. "I don't think so," he said.

Pino shrugged. "Okay, if you want to play it that way. Drop him or I shoot the civilian." Pino's gun shifted to point toward me. You'd think these guys would be more original.

"Not so fast, cracker," another voiced drawled. "I think you're outnumbered." Demetrius ambled out into the light. His eyes were sleepy, and he looked like he was annoyed to be up this time of the morning.

Pino glanced around him, assessing the situation, but didn't lower his gun.

More sirens sounded in the distance.

"Might as well put it down," Demetrius said, his voice conversational. "About a hundred federal agents are on the way."

The gun stayed pointed at my head. Pino didn't look like he had any intention of putting it down.

"It was always going to come down to this someday," Pino said, a note of resignation in his voice. "Guys like us, we're soldiers, right? We were meant to go out in a blaze of glory. Even Colt understood that. My guess is that I can put down the jogger and maybe get one into you or the big guy before you're able to take me out. But if not," he shrugged, "at least it will be quick."

Pino was ready to die, and I was okay with that. But he was ready to take me with him, and this I wasn't so keen on.

"You're nothing like Colt," I said. "The last thing you deserve is a soldier's death." I swung the can of anthrax in a circle and launched it at him in my best fast-pitch softball throw. He tried to shoot me and dodge the can at the same time. He was successful at neither. The paint can hit his shooting arm, and the shot went wide. Demetrius's shot also seemed to be a bit off. Pino was wearing body armor. Agency protocol dictated that the shot should go to the head. Demetrius somehow missed the head and put a round into each of Pino's kneecaps. Chico planted his forehead into Reg's temple and dropped his limp body to the ground.

I rushed up and kicked the fallen gun out of Pino's reach. Not that he could have gone for it anyway. He was writhing on the ground hugging himself, trying to plug the holes in his knees.

I checked the can. It was still intact.

"Are you crazy?" Demetrius asked, abandoning all precept of calm. "He could have blasted a hole in that can."

I shrugged. "It's anthrax. We've been vaccinated, and so has everyone in this facility."

"When you say 'we,' who do you mean exactly?" I thought Demetrius might pass out.

"Demetrius doesn't like needles," Chico said.

I picked up the can and Demetrius backed away. "Don't worry," I said. "It's double packed and undamaged. This is how they send it through the mail."

"Just the same, why don't you stay over there."

A black SUV pulled up to the end of the alley, and Zachary Shepherd got out.

"Is the weapon secure?" he asked. His voice sounded hollow.

"Looks to be," I said. "We should probably bring in hazmat just in case."

"They're on their way." He looked down at Pino and Reg. "An ambulance is on its way as well. I hope these guys are fit for questioning."

"They'll live," Chico said. "We were just getting them prepped."

"Right." Zack's voice still held an edge, but there was a weariness in it. I thought I might know the reason.

"Colt?" I asked.

"He'll live," Zack said. "Two rounds in the leg but missed the artery. Life Flight is en route."

I breathed a sigh of relief. "He deserves a medal," I said. "Without Colt those guys might have gotten away with it."

"He'll get his medal," Zack said. "I'll make sure of it. I'm downright proud of that boy."

Zack looked around him at the situation in the alley. "Put that down," he said, pointing to the can. "Demetrius, Chico, wait here for the hazmat team and accompany these two yahoos to the hospital. Don't leave them until they are in final custody in a holding cell. Agent Knight, come with me. We need to get you on a chopper."

I walked with Zack to his SUV and got in. He started the engine. I assumed we were going to the FBI offices for a debrief—my least favorite time of any mission. I just wanted to go back to my apartment, shower, and sleep. And then, no matter what Zack said, I wanted to find Hope Winslow and tell her I was sorry.

Zack nodded to the backseat. "I had Roger pack up some of your things."

In the backseat was a suitcase. My suitcase.

"Why are my bags packed?" I asked uneasily.

"The chopper will take you to the airport. You're flying back to Washington in an hour."

I blinked at him dumbly and looked back at the suitcase again. "If this is about Hope . . ."

Zack cut me off. His voice was raw, like he had just drunk a mug full of glass.

"It's Robbie," he said. "He's been killed."

CHAPTER 24

Funeral for a Friend

I GOT OUT OF THE taxi, opened my umbrella, and paid the driver. When the cab drove off, I stood at the intersection but did not cross the road. The rain poured down from a dark, uncaring sky. I looked across the street at the church. The door opened periodically as people went in, and a cold, artificial light was swallowed by the darkness. I watched a small sparrow's nest float down the gutter in the gray water, struggle against the drain, and then finally get sucked down into the dark abyss.

My mind entered a whirlpool and spun there.

I tried to make sense of the past several hours. I'd had my life threatened by terrorists, saved by Colt Mangum, and then thrown completely into chaos by hearing the news about my best friend.

My eyes remained locked on the sewer grate, and my feet refused to move.

"You gonna cross, or are you going down with the twigs?" I knew the voice.

"Do I have a choice?" I kept my focus on the brackish water.

The rain continued to pound. The debris continued to flow down into the dark drain. "There's always a choice. You know that," the voice said. "But I don't think you're going to fit through the grates."

I turned to face the voice. Like me, he was dressed in a dark suit. It seemed out of place.

"Hey Super Geek," I said. "Where's your lab coat?"

"Back at the lab." His name was Jennings Frye, and he had been part of our graduating class. He was by far the smartest guy in our section, with expertise in chemistry, forensics, and every other obscure science that most of us had no clue about.

"Still shooting it out with microbes?"

"Better than shooting it out with the terrorists," he said. "That's a nasty bump on your head. I think I'll take my chances in the lab." Jennings didn't look like a geek. He was six foot four and solid muscle. His physical strength had always given him the advantage in combat training. But unlike most of us, he'd never aspired to be a field agent.

"Sorry about Robbie," he said. "That really sucks."

"Big time," I agreed.

"I heard about your collar this morning. Bagged, tagged, and the weapon secured. Looks like another victory for the golden boy."

"It doesn't feel much like victory," I said.

We both stood there for a moment, the rain pounding hard against our umbrellas. He gestured toward the church. "We should probably go in." He started to step across the storm drain and I stopped him. "Can I ask you a question?"

"Sure."

"You've been monitoring my efforts from this end, right?"

"It's one of the dozen cases I'm assigned to."

I looked down at the water washing down the dark hole. "What would happen if I poured a bottle full of weapons-grade anthrax down there?"

He studied me through the rain dripping off his umbrella. "Having a hard time letting go?"

"Humor me," I said. "Things wrapped up kind of quickly."

He followed my gaze to the drain. "That stuff is manufactured to go airborne," he said. "As soon as you opened the jar, the spores would be jumping out, looking for someone's lungs to find a home in. But if it was raining hard enough, it's possible that no one would be harmed."

"What if someone got it into the water though?" I pressed. "What would be the impact on the city?"

He shrugged. "Hard to know. Probably minimal. A few people might get sick, but the water would disperse the anthrax pretty quickly."

"But don't I remember something from one of our classes about anthrax spores surviving in water?"

"Oh, they survive all right. But that doesn't mean they're dangerous. I mean, getting people to inhale the spores is pretty much a sure kill, and there are cases of people eating infected meat and dying. But we just don't have a lot of documented cases of anthrax-infected water—with good reason. Like I said, water is a great diluter. You'd need lots of anthrax in a little bit of water. Lakes, streams, and city water cisterns are just too big. If you wanted to poison someone with water using anthrax, you wouldn't want to use anything bigger than a drinking glass."

A large stick got swept against the storm drain and refused to go down. I rubbed my forehead with my free hand. "But our intelligence was entirely based on a water attack," I said. "How does that jive with the anthrax at Dugway?"

"It doesn't," Jennings said. "But the water threat always seemed a little weird to me. They've already started testing the anthrax you recovered, and it's got the same properties as the NBC strain—it almost jumps into the air. It's definitely built for inhalation. If you took some of that stuff to Vegas and dropped it in a few air vents along the strip, you could do some major damage. But mixing it in liquid would just be watering down a sure thing."

"So the water intelligence was all just a smokescreen?"

"That's my best guess. Unless these guys are dumber than we think—which is always a distinct possibility. It would be like using a submachine gun as a club."

I squatted down to remove the struggling branch from the storm drain and tossed it up onto some grass.

"Huh," I said, sitting on my haunches.

"Let it go. You've done your part. Figuring out terrorists is like figuring out women—the more you try to make sense of their actions, the more your head hurts."

I stood up and looked at the church. "I don't really want to go in there," I said. "I have no clue as to how to act or what to say."

"Nobody does," he said. "But with Robbie gone, you know she's going to need you."

"I know," I said, and we walked across the street.

Inside the church, a line wound around the outside of the pews and led up to a casket near the pulpit. I recognized a few of the people but not many. I was a little surprised at the numbers. It was tough to make friends in our business and tougher to lie to your friends day in and day out about your occupation.

Becca stood at the front of the line. She was dressed in black and strikingly beautiful, even at this distance. Her stomach protruded in only a slight curve that anyone who didn't already know she was pregnant would miss. She stood alone, no family on her right or her left. It struck me that all three of us had been orphans of a sort. Both Robbie's and Becca's parents had passed before we entered the academy. And none of us had any brothers or sisters. Maybe that's why we had gravitated toward each other. I felt a sudden hollowness. With Robbie gone—with my mission completed— Becca and I were all that was left.

As the line moved forward, I could see Becca better. In true Becca fashion, she looked strong and perfectly composed. Other than her place at the front of the line, she did not look the part of the grieving widow. Others were crying; others were breaking down; Becca was comforting them, telling them it would be all right. She reminded me of Hope among the cancer patients, lifting everyone around her. I touched my cheek. I wondered if Becca had ever punched anyone.

Her concentration was so focused on each individual that came to pay their respects that she didn't see me until I was about ten yards away. She looked at me for a moment, blinked her eyes, and then all semblance of composure fled. Her lips began to quiver, and her eyes welled with tears. In that moment I felt her loss, her pain, and the empty, ever-enlarging hole that sat in the place where her heart had been. In that moment we were one, and my own tears flowed as they had not done since I was a child.

When I finally got to her she fell onto my shoulder and sobbed.

"You came," she said. "I thought I was going to have to do this alone."

"I'm here," I said quietly.

I held her like that for a long time. Two orphans holding on to the only thing they had left in the world.

"I think we're causing a pileup," I said finally.

"I don't care. All that matters is you came. Can you stay?"

I thought about it and realized that I really had nowhere to go. No case to solve. No roommates waiting for me in my apartment. No Hope knocking on my door for scripture study. "I can stay," I said. "For as long as you need."

"That might be a long time," Becca said, looking up into my eyes.

"I'm here."

She looked at the line of people waiting to pay their respects.

"Still have your key?" she asked.

I nodded.

"Go," she said. "I'll meet you when this is over."

"You don't want me to wait for you?"

She shook her head and wiped at her eyes. "I think I'll do much better if you're gone."

I released her and nodded at the casket. "I'll say good-bye to Robbie, and I'll meet you later."

She grimaced as she followed my gaze. "I wish they would take that thing away. It's not him, you know. It doesn't even look like him. It might be his body, but Robbie is gone."

I looked into the air. "Maybe he's here somewhere. Watching to see who'll show up."

"I don't think so," Becca said. Her tone was as dark as I'd ever heard. "Now I know why you avoided churches. You were right all along. I didn't see it when my parents died. But they were old. Robbie was young, like your mom. All that's left is a hole. He's gone, and he's never coming back."

Her words worried me, and I wanted to say more, but the line was pressing in behind us.

"We'll talk later," I said, letting go of her hands.

I moved to the casket and looked down. The thing that lay before me was a pale imitation of Robbie—like something you would find in a bad wax museum. I thought about kissing his forehead in farewell but decided against it. It was his body, but he wasn't in there. Becca was right. Robbie wasn't here. He was gone. But I realized that I knew something that Becca didn't know. Something I had learned recently from a woman named Hope Winslow and a little girl named Meggy.

I knew where Robbie was. He had gone to see Jesus.

* * *

I drove to Robbie and Becca's apartment complex. It was in a wooded area, with dense trees throughout the grounds. On the outside, it reminded me a little bit of the Village, but I realized that in all of the times I had stayed with Robbie and Becca, I had never met any of their neighbors. I used to consider this place my home. I didn't even have an apartment of my own. When I was between jobs, which was usually for only a few weeks, I stayed here. For some reason it didn't feel like home anymore.

My thoughts flew back to the Village, to Section 89, to the mountain trails on which I loved to run. My thoughts flew to Joseph and Roger, my roommates, and finally to Hope Winslow. I looked out at the woods and thought I could smell her hair.

The woods are lovely, dark, and deep, I said to myself, remembering the words of a poem by Robert Frost. *But I have promises to keep.*

I thought of Robbie's insistence that if anything ever happened to him, I would take care of Becca. "You need to do more than take care of her," he said. "You need to marry her. I can't bear to think of her with anyone else."

"Nothing's going to happen to you," I told him. That kind of talk always made me uncomfortable.

"I've already discussed it with Becca," Robbie said. "You know she could just as easily have married you. I mean, you're not nearly as handsome or smart, but she loves you too. You have to promise me," he said.

"Okay," I said finally. "But only on the condition that you never bring this up again."

The rain had stopped, and the smell of rich earth kissed by water filled the air. I had often found myself imagining what life would be like married to Becca. These thoughts always made me feel guilty, as if I were betraying a trust. The guilt coursed through me once again as I realized that Robbie's promise was in front of me. If I broke the promise, I would be betraying him. If I followed through with it, I might be betraying my own heart.

"The woods are lovely, dark, and deep," I said again to myself as I walked up the steps, pulled out the key to the apartment, shook off my umbrella, and went through the door. I closed it behind me and did not look back.

Becca came through the door a few hours later.

"I'm glad that's over," she said, shaking off her raincoat and placing it on a peg. "I don't think I have another ounce of emotion left to drain."

I remembered how I felt after the ultrarun. I remembered the numbness after my own mother's funeral. There are times when lying in the corner in a fetal position seemed to be the only legitimate option.

"I'm getting out of this dress and putting on some sweats," she said. "Then I can make us some coffee if you like."

"Water's good for me," I said. "But I could make you coffee if you want."

She studied me with curiosity. "Maybe not," she said. "I'm having a hard time sleeping anyway. Why don't you change too. I just want to sit on the couch for a while and veg."

I took my bag into the spare room and changed into my own pair of sweats. I could hear the water running in the bathroom as Becca took off her makeup. I'd been with her in this apartment many times before, even alone at times. But I was starting to feel a little weird about this.

I went out to the couch and Becca joined me.

"I'm so glad you're here," she said, snuggling her head into my shoulder. "I really just needed someone I could talk to without putting up a front."

"Go ahead," I said. "Yell and scream and cry. Whatever you feel like."

"That's the problem," she said, nestling herself closer into me. "I don't feel anything. It scares me. It's like there's a big hole that has sucked in everything I ever thought I felt or believed."

I didn't say anything.

"I owe you an apology," Becca said. "I always thought you had taken the loss of your mom too hard. I'd lost both of my parents and it hurt, but I got over it. But it's different losing someone who has lived a long life. You know they'll die someday. You anticipate it. But having someone you expect to spend the rest of your life with suddenly yanked away, that's a different thing altogether. Even with the dangers of Robbie's job, even with his love of everything risky, I always expected him to come home. I don't think it's ever going to be okay. I don't even think I believe in God anymore."

These words jolted me more than I thought they would. Of the three of us, Becca had always been the religious one. Robbie believed in God but had an allergic reaction to organized religion, and I had always been the doubter, mainly choosing not to say anything so as not to offend Becca.

"Tell me what happened," I said because I didn't know what else to say.

Becca took in a deep breath. "He was going to pick up a pizza. He was taking longer than he should have, and I thought he might have stopped to get some drinks. Then I got the phone call from the hospital." I felt Becca's tears dripping onto my arm.

"They said the truck ran a stop sign, hit Robbie on the driver's side, and didn't even slow down. Dead on the point of impact. Probably didn't feel a thing. They found the truck abandoned later. It had been reported stolen. The police think it might have been some kids joyriding."

"I'm sorry," I said and pulled her even closer. "Robbie would have made a great dad."

"Yes, he would have," she said. "And he was starting to turn into a pretty good husband too." She wiped at her eyes. "He was even starting to learn responsibility. Did he tell you he was going to quit the Agency?"

I straightened my back and looked down at her. "I thought you were both always okay with it."

"That was his story," Becca said. "The perfect service wife. Always supportive. No complaining. And I tried to be that wife, I really did. But with the baby coming, I didn't want him in the field anymore, and I told him so."

"What did he say?" I had a hard time envisioning Robbie doing anything but field work. He gravitated toward the risk.

"He told me he'd already put in a request to become an instructor at the academy."

I pushed Becca away far enough so I could see her face. "Robbie? An instructor?"

"A bit ironic, isn't it, considering all of the hell he gave them. I told you, Robbie had changed. It was a good thing too because there was no way I was going to be a mom *and* be married to an agent in the field." She looked at me when she said this last sentence as if it were meant for me.

I let the thought sit in my mind. Robbie had intended to leave the field. "You're right," I said. "Robbie had changed. Big time."

"He was turning into such a great man," Becca said. "I was so looking forward to seeing him as a father." Her voice was full of longing and then turned hard. "You were right all along. A loving God wouldn't take Robbie away from his unborn son, and He wouldn't take a single mom away from an eight-year-old boy."

I let the silence settle in the bitter darkness and then said, "I don't think I believe that anymore. I think there is a God." I was surprised to hear the conviction in my own voice.

Becca pulled away and studied me. "Don't you try to comfort me," she said. "I won't have it."

"It's true," I said. "It's real."

"How could you even know that?" she said. "It's all just words because nobody wants to look into the emptiness."

I thought about her question. *How did I know?*

"I have a friend," I said. "Someone who I trust and believe. Someone who would not lie to me."

"So," Becca said.

"She died and came back." I thought of Hope among the cancer kids. "She touched the light and brought some back with her."

Becca didn't say anything.

"It's real," I said again. "Robbie's spirit is alive, and you will see him again. We both will. I'm sure of it." Once again I felt a conviction that I previously had not known was there.

Becca began to shake her head, but then a feeling entered the room that stopped her. A sense of peace descended like a warm blanket and wrapped itself around both of us. I'm not sure quite how to describe it except that all darkness and emptiness fled the room, and in its place was an unspeakable feeling of hope and light. I looked into Becca's eyes, and they widened with wonder. She put her head back onto my shoulder, and it felt as if we were both encircled in the arms of an everlasting love.

We sat there for a long time, not speaking, just taking it all in. I felt Becca's breathing slow and deepen and her head became heavy on my shoulder as she melted into sleep.

"Thank you," I said silently, not really knowing why. But all I felt was an overwhelming sense of gratitude.

In the silence, I thought I heard an answer. The answer was not, "You're welcome," but rather, "I forgive you." I wept.

I wept for Becca. I wept for Robbie. I wept for my mother. And I wept for myself. But most of all, I wept for joy at the gift of peace and comfort we had both just been given.

After a while I realized Becca was snoring. I smiled. Robbie always said she snored. I wasn't going to wake her. She needed the rest. So I settled my back into the couch and tried to find a semicomfortable position. Here I was, alone in an apartment with a beautiful, dark-haired woman sleeping on my chest. I thought of little Megan and the plane ride that had taken me to Utah; I thought of Bishop Zack and wondered if he would approve of me being alone on a couch with a now-single woman; I thought of Hope Winslow and how she had changed my life and my view of the world both above and below.

I thought of the promise I had made to Robbie and Becca's insistence that she would not be married to a field agent. I thought about the hard decisions I would need to make. Robbie was right. It was time to grow up. I had promises to keep.

I looked down at Becca again and stroked her dark hair.

In the midst of all the truth that had flowed into me this evening, one more thing was perfectly clear.

I loved this woman who lay sleeping against me.

I loved her like a sister.

CHAPTER 25
Promises

I AWOKE TO A PLEASANT, familiar smell—brewing coffee. I realized I hadn't smelled that aroma in a long while. It reminded me of my mother. It reminded me of more pleasant times with Robbie and Becca. It reminded me of Zack's lecture on forbidden substances.

I opened my eyes. Becca entered from the kitchen wearing one of Robbie's oversized T-shirts as a nightshirt. The shirt was as long as a sundress, but I squirmed a bit as she came and sat next to me. She leaned across and kissed me on the cheek.

"I made coffee," she said.

I took inventory of myself. My white shirt was rumpled, but I noticed that I now had a blanket over me and had somehow managed to end up on a pillow on the couch in a prone position.

I sat up, and Becca placed the coffee on top of a coaster on an end table. A few short weeks ago I would have already had it in my hands. Now I was hesitant to pick it up.

"We need to talk about last night," Becca said. Her voice was serious.

I began to run through my memories of last night, trying to pick out which part we needed to talk about. The last thing I remembered was holding her in my arms before we fell asleep. But I knew that wasn't what she wanted to talk about.

"Where did that come from?" she asked.

"Where did *what* come from?" Answer a question with a question. It was the safest path to take. I was afraid that what had seemed so real last night might wither in the light of day.

"Don't play dumb. I know you felt it too."

I sighed. "Yes," I said. "I felt it."

"What happened to you?" she said. "You left as the doubting Thomas among us, and you came back full of conviction and faith. I've never felt such peace before."

"You can't blame me for that," I said. "I'm pretty sure the feeling came from somewhere else."

"Yes, I'm sure it did," she said. "But don't pretend you didn't play a part. Your words—your certainty about Robbie's spirit being alive—opened the door. You can't tell me that was a coincidence."

I didn't answer. She knew I didn't believe in coincidences. I thought of Zack's words telling me that I had been sent on this job for a reason. Maybe he was right. Maybe all of it—from running with Joseph to seeing Hope Winslow with the cancer patients—had been to get me to a point where I could help open a window of peace and be an instrument of comfort for Becca when she needed it most.

"You know, I still feel an emptiness," she said.

"I know," I said. "And that part won't go away."

"But it's different than it was—more about separation rather than loss. For some reason, separation allows for hope. Does that make any sense?"

"It makes perfect sense," I said. Placing the words *separation* and *Hope* in the same sentence regarding a feeling of emptiness fit better than anything else I could think of.

"Anyway," she said, "I wanted to thank you again. I don't know what I would have done without you." She gripped my hand hard. "I was in a dark place. But after last night I think I'll be okay—eventually." She pulled my hand toward her and put it over her pregnant belly. "And I really need to be okay."

I thought I felt something move inside her. I started to pull my hand away and she caught it.

"Promise me you'll be here for us," she said, gripping my hand tightly. "We're really going to need you to get through this."

I looked at her dark, intent eyes. Her hand locked around mine, on top of her stomach. I had promises to keep.

"I'm not going anywhere," I said.

She released my hand and smiled. "The graveside service is at one," she said. "Robbie wanted it small. Just family."

I raised my eyebrows.

"That means you, me, and the minister," she said. "I've got to go to the grocery store. There's nothing in this house to eat. Want to come?"

I thought about it. "I've got some paperwork to take care of," I said.

"Your coffee is getting cold."

I thought about telling her I didn't drink coffee anymore. That my bishop didn't allow it and that he might tear off my ear if I drank it. But in reality I had no bishop. I had no roommates other than Becca, and I had no Church brothers and sisters. All I had were my promises to Robbie.

I reached for the cup and took a sip.

"How is it?" Becca asked. She had never been very good at making coffee.

"Just fine," I lied. In truth it was the bitterest cup I had ever tasted in my life.

I had promises to keep.

But first I needed to go in to the office.

* * *

Jennings Frye didn't seem particularly surprised to see me. "I thought you might show up," he said. "You never did like loose ends."

"Or split ends," I said. "But with my new conditioner, they're a thing of the past."

"You seem in a better mood than last night."

"Last night was not a good time," I agreed.

"How's Becca?"

"She's getting through it." Jennings seemed like he wanted to ask me another question about her, like had I stayed in her apartment last night and was I going to fulfill my promise to Robbie and marry her—but to his credit, he didn't. Robbie had made sure every eligible bachelor in the Agency knew about the promise so they wouldn't descend on Becca like vultures if he ever kicked the bucket.

Instead, Jennings said, "What can I help you with?"

"You've got access to all of the research on the Utah case?"

"Every spec."

"Have you read it all?"

Jennings laughed. "Nobody's read it all, at least no one person. That's not how it works." He rolled his eyes. "Field agents."

"Why don't you enlighten me, lab geek? How does it work?"

"On a case like this, we've got intelligence flying at us from all sides. It would take years for one person to go through it all. So we hire scores of junior analysts to sift through the sands and float anything to the top that might be significant."

"Do you have detailed files on the people in the Village?"

"We've got a whole hard drive dedicated to the Stepford Estates. What do you want to know?"

"Stepford Estates?" I had no reason to be offended by the name, and I tried not to sound defensive. But something must have come through in my voice.

"Just a nickname," Jennings said. "You know how the guys are with nicknames."

He was on his heels a bit, and I should have let it go. Instead, I said, "I'll make sure to pass that on to Zack. Zack loves a good nickname." Jennings had spent some time in a Zack headlock when he had inadvertently slipped and called Zack "the Hammer," so he knew what I was talking about.

The color drained from Jennings's face. I decided to let him loose.

"Just kidding," I said. "Pull up the information on my roommate Roger."

Jennings's fingers began clicking on his keyboard. "Why him?"

"Remember what you said about the water supply being a poor choice for a terrorist attack?"

"Yeah."

"What if you used nanotechnology to transport the poison? Would that make any difference?"

"Sure, but you'd have to be a nanogenius to make something like that work."

"Roger *is* a nanogenius," I said. "Specifically, he claims to be studying how to purify large bodies of water that have been contaminated."

"So you think maybe he could reverse the process?"

"Would that be possible?"

"I guess so," Jennings said. "But your guy would have to be really good, and I mean exceptional."

I thought about Roger and his intellect. "This guy might be exceptional," I said.

"Okay, I've got his profile up. What do you want to know?"

I thought about something that had been tugging at the back of my mind for a long time. Something that just didn't add up with Roger.

"Tell me about his ex-wife," I said.

Jennings's fingers went back to work. He stared at the screen and said, "Hmm."

"What?"

"Roger Livingston doesn't have an ex-wife."

I came around behind Jennings so I could see what was on his screen. "You mean he was never married?"

"No, he was married all right. But there was no divorce. His wife died in a plane crash. Along with his two-year-old daughter."

The obituary was on the screen in front of me. Roger's wife was named Amy. His daughter was Lilith. The small plane had been owned by Amy's father, and she had been on her way back from visiting her family in Idaho when the plane went down. Roger was not on the plane. Another picture showed Roger, his wife, and his daughter in a family photo. The happiness on all their faces was evident. A perfect little family. No wonder Roger was hesitant to enter into relationships.

"You think it put him over the edge?" Jennings asked.

"I don't know," I said. "He tells everyone that his wife left him."

"That's a pretty big lie," Jennings said.

"Yes it is."

"Makes you wonder what else he might be lying about."

I thought about Roger. About his lies. About his pretending to avoid relationships because he'd had a bad marriage. I thought of the darkness in his eyes and the way it began to dissipate whenever he was around Marva Rose. I was still having a hard time seeing him as a terrorist. He seemed too much like a damaged brother.

"Pull up my other roommate," I said.

"Joseph Hadadi?"

"Yes."

"But you already know everything there is to know about Joseph Hadadi. It's part of the public record."

"Find me something I don't know," I said. "Something that might have caused a bright, optimistic young man to turn cynical."

"What, like his father being beheaded by terrorists live over the Internet?"

"Let's look before then," I said.

Jennings's beefy fingers began clicking again. The keyboard looked like it was too small for him. He shook his head a few times then paused and said, "Huh."

"What did you find?"

"Might be nothing," he said. "Do you remember the orphanage in Jordan that got bombed, the one where Ahmad Hussein was killed?"

"The man they called 'the Shepherd'? Of course I remember. More than a hundred innocent orphans were killed in a country friendly to ours. Sure, we took out the man who was supposed to be Bin Laden's personal mentor, but we also gave those who hate the West something to pin their rhetoric on. But what does that have to do with Joseph?"

"Nothing," Jennings said. "Except he was there at the time."

"What?"

"He was with his father on a humanitarian visit. He had a cousin in Jordan with four children. This man and his wife had been killed when a car bomb exploded in a public market. His four children were left as orphans. Three boys and a girl. Joseph was accompanying his father to retrieve his cousins and bring them back to the United States. It was supposed to be a triumphant story. Hadadi adopting the orphans. A camera crew followed him to document the reunion." Jennings took a sip of water from an aluminum water bottle next to his computer. "But the story of his visit got buried."

"The kids he was there to pick up were in the orphanage that was bombed?"

"Some of them."

"Did we know we were bombing an orphanage?"

"Apparently we received intel that the orphans were moved to another location and that Hussein took over the facility with his guards and followers."

"Bad intel?"

"You tell me." Jennings pointed at his monitor. On it was an aerial surveillance photo of what looked like a compound full of soldiers armed with guns. At the center of the picture was a man. His face was turned to the sky, and he was clearly recognizable as Ahmad Hussein—the Shepherd, the man some said was Bin Laden's inspiration for an attack on American soil.

"The women and younger boys had been moved, but orphan boys over the age of fourteen remained in the facility," Jennings explained. Hussein passed out AK-47s and was having his men teach the boys how to shoot. When the drones flew over, all they saw was a group of highly armed soldiers taking target practice. They didn't know that two of these boys were going to be adopted by the Hadadi family the next day."

"Wait a minute," I said. "I thought you said there were three boys and one girl?"

"There were. The girl and the youngest boy were among those who had been moved. In fact, they were taken back to the United States by Joseph and his father and adopted into the family. But because of the circumstances it was kept pretty quiet."

"Was the Hadadi girl named Siham?" I asked.

"How did you know?"

"I've met her," I said.

"What about the surviving boy?" Jennings asked. "Did you meet him?"

"No," I said. "Joseph never mentioned him. What was his name?"

"Mohammed," Jennings answered. "Like the prophet. And here's another interesting thing. Apparently, one of the orphans who had been moved made a call that afternoon to our command facility, tipping us off that there might be an attack on Abraham Hadadi. So we acted on the intelligence."

"Between the surveillance photos and the phone call, there seemed to be ample justification. Of course, the world didn't see it that way the next day when the news reported that Americans had bombed an orphanage."

I tapped my fingers on the desk.

"What are you thinking?" Jennings asked.

"I'm thinking I don't know my two roommates nearly as well as I thought I did," I said.

"Do you think they have anything to do with the threats?"

"I don't know, but I'm starting to believe that there might be a smoke screen in this after all."

"So you agree with me? The water attack intel was a diversion?"

"Maybe," I said. "Or maybe the intel was good and the smoke is coming from somewhere else."

"The anthrax?" he asked. Jennings Frye was a smart guy. "But if that's the case, then the danger is still out there."

"Maybe," I said.

"Then who's the target?"

"Are there any big conventions or meetings coming up in Salt Lake City? Maybe ex-Air Force generals or drone operators?"

Jennings punched keys on his keyboard. "No government or military groups," he said. "The only convention of any size is a religious one this Saturday—the Other Sheep conference. A cross-denominational meeting of about five thousand leaders from several Christian groups, including Catholics, Protestants, and even Mormons."

"Will the pope be there?"

"No pope. No prophet. Not even an archbishop. These are strictly the frontline pastors, priests, and ministers—not a celebrity in the bunch. But it is getting a lot of press. I guess these guys don't get together too often."

"I think Zack mentioned that he is going in his role as bishop."

"Those other ministers don't stand a chance," Jennings said. "If it comes to a fight, I put my money on Zack."

"It's supposed to be a friendly convention," I reminded him. "You did say it was five thousand and not ten million, correct? Doesn't sound like it fits our profile for a target."

"Nothing in Utah really does. It never has."

I tapped a pencil on Jennings's desk and thought more about my roommates. "Can you print me a copy of that picture of Ahmad Hussein?" I asked.

"Sure. Why?"

"I don't know," I said. "There's just something about it that bothers me."

CHAPTER 26
Redemption Song

I TOOK A CAB BACK to the apartment and found that Becca had already changed into her funeral dress—the same black gown she had worn the night before at the viewing.

"I guess I'd better get some use out of it," she said, wiping at imperceptible wrinkles along her hips.

"You look great," I said. "As always."

"Where'd you go?" she asked.

"I ran to the office for a few minutes." I moved past her into the guest room, closed the door, and began to change into my suit.

"You're a field agent, you don't have an office," she said through the door.

"Not *my* office. *The* office. I just needed to check on some things."

"I thought you said your case was solved."

"I thought it was," I said, more to myself than to Becca. I quickly put on my slacks and shirt and opened the door.

"Sorry," she said. "I know better. I'm not supposed to ask you about the specifics of a case."

"Did that work?" I asked. "With you and Robbie. I think it would be hard not to share some of the details with your wife."

"He was good about following the rules," Becca said. "But that doesn't mean it was easy. We were open and honest about everything. We didn't talk about his work, but his emotions were never hidden from me. I could tell when he was perplexed. I could tell when he was bothered by something he had done. And I could tell when he was worried." She was applying eyeliner in a mirror on the wall, and I saw her hand stop.

"The worst was when you were in Miami. He was home on leave before he was called in to help. He couldn't tell me about it. It was killing him."

"It was nearly killing me too."

"I know," Becca said. "I heard about it later."

"So Robbie did break the rules."

Becca smiled. "No," she said. "That was you. Don't you remember? You came back and told us both about the whole experience."

"I probably wasn't supposed to do that." I said. "For some reason I didn't think about you as an outsider."

"Thank you," she said, studying me. "So what's bothering you about this case?"

"I can't tell you," I replied.

Becca smiled again. "It was worth a try."

* * *

We drove in Becca's car to the funeral home, and I helped load the casket into the hearse for the trip to Arlington National Cemetery. Robbie would lie among the graves of thousands of other heroes who had served their country, and everything would be paid for on the government's dime. It was one of the few perks of being in the civil service. You couldn't talk to your wife about your job, but when it came to the funeral, everything was first class.

Becca and I both rode in the backseat of the hearse—not the very back, that seat was reserved for Robbie, but one seat back from the driver. The same soft organ music played through the speakers in the hearse as was playing in the funeral home. Becca tapped on the driver's shoulder and handed him a CD.

"Last request of the deceased," she told him. "He said to crank it up."

"We always honor last requests," the driver said in a very professional tone. What he was probably thinking was, *Finally, I get to listen to some decent tunes.*

After a few seconds of silence, the organ music was replaced by Bob Marley. *Legend*—Robbie's favorite album. Mine too. The music should have reminded me of all the good times the three of us had experienced together. It didn't. Instead I thought of a night run several days ago and how Joseph and I had used this music to almost win a race.

Both of my roommates had experienced significant emotional events in their lives. Events that, according to my training, could turn someone from a normal, everyday person into someone who had the potential to do nasty things.

I couldn't help but wonder if one—or both—of them had taken that step. Could Roger or Joseph really use their emotional hurt to justify taking the lives of innocents? My mind said it was possible, but all I could get from my heart was that I loved both of them—like they were my brothers. Like I had loved Robbie.

I could hear Becca gently humming to the music as we rode through traffic for what must have been about forty minutes.

And then the track changed from "Waiting in Vain," to "Redemption Song."

At first I began to smile. I could not think of this song without envisioning Joseph on the trail behind me shouting out the words at the top of his lungs. I could hear his voice as clearly as if he were in the car with us. He sang about prophets being killed while bystanders watched—doing nothing. And then rockets seemed to go off in my head. I thought of the Islamic cleric with the nickname of "the Shepherd" and Joseph being in Jordan at the time he was taken out by a U.S. military missile, along with dozens of innocent orphans. How many people had stood by and watched while it happened? Did Joseph feel he was one of them?

My mind jumped to what Jennings Frye had said about poison and water and any method of poisoning that required more than a glassful being pointless. I thought about smoke screens and anthrax and the original threat that had sent me to Utah. *The time will soon be at hand when they shall drink to find refreshment and taste only death. Millions shall mourn, even tens of millions.* I thought of the surveillance picture in my pocket and knew what bothered me.

By the end of the song I thought I had most of it figured out. With all respect to Robbie, I wasn't thinking about him anymore. Becca must have seen it on my face.

She took my hand. "What's up?" she asked. "You look like you just got jammed with a taser."

"Sorry," I said. "It's nothing."

"It's something to do with the case, isn't it? Your wheels have been spinning all morning long."

I squeezed her hand. "I'm sorry," I said again. "Today should be about honoring Robbie. Whatever is going on can wait until tomorrow." But as I thought about it, I didn't know if it could wait until tomorrow. I really wanted to look at my watch, but Becca held my left hand.

"It was the same with Robbie," Becca said. "I could always tell when he'd figured something out, and I about had to bite my tongue not to force it out of him. You've got that same look—cuffs ready and perp in your crosshairs. And I won't ask you any more about it."

If Hope Winslow was an angel, then Becca was surely a saint. Neither Robbie nor I deserved her. I thought about our line of work and the wedges it forced between families. I thought about my promises to Robbie and Becca's insistence that she would not go through another relationship where complete honesty was impossible. I thought about how the tension between these two opposing ideas might mean my days at the Agency were numbered—or over.

"Tell you what," I said. "If you do one thing for me, after this service is over I will break every rule that Robbie and I ever signed up for and tell you all I know or think I know about this case."

"You don't have to do that," she said and then smiled conspiratorially. "What do you want me to do?"

"Tell me what day it is," I said. "I seem to have lost track."

"It's Friday," Becca said.

I felt like I'd just downed a cup of wet cement. If I was right in my thinking, I definitely didn't have a day to spare. Tomorrow was Saturday. If I didn't do something today, millions would mourn. Even tens of millions.

* * *

I believe Robbie would have greatly enjoyed his graveside service. Not only was he in the company of his best friends in the world, but the minister had replete instructions to keep his comments to fewer than five minutes. Short and sweet. Emphasis on the short. With the final words, the lowering of the coffin, and Becca tossing in a handful of dirt in good-bye, the sweet feeling of peace from the night before arrived once again and enveloped both Becca and me. I think the minister felt it as well. Tears flowed freely from all of us. Tears of gratitude.

And though this moment was supposed to be about Robbie and comforting Becca in her loss, again I thought I heard the words whispered into my ear: "I forgive you."

Maybe I imagined it or maybe it was the hearse driver forgiving us for the overly loud reggae on the ride to the grave site. But I didn't think so. In fact, I knew the words were meant for me. I knew it as much as I had known any fact in my life. Someone understood the enormity of the guilt I had been carrying around since I was a child. Someone understood everything about me. With such a strong impression, I could do nothing but accept the gift.

"Thank you," I whispered back. "Thank you again."

After the service we asked the driver if he could wait a few minutes while we sat by the grave alone. The minister left, and the driver moved off to the hearse. It was just me, Becca, and Robbie.

I started at the beginning and spilled my guts. I told Becca about the case from the time I entered the Village to the anthrax incident at Dugway. I left out no details except those concerning Hope Winslow and my feelings toward her. I was determined to fulfill my promises to Robbie, and I didn't think bringing up information about Hope would help. I brought Becca up to the time of my visit earlier that day with Jennings Frye, the things I had learned about Joseph and Roger, and the epiphany brought to me by Bob Marley and the ride in the hearse. And then I told her about my suspicions of what was still to come.

"So," I said when I had finished, "tell me that I'm crazy and that grief and sleep deprivation have caused me to hallucinate."

"You *are* crazy," Becca said. "But I also think you're right. However, you don't have any solid proof and you don't have any time. Do you think Zack will believe you?"

"Before I talk to Zack, I need to confirm some things for myself."

"How?"

I stood up. "Let's go," I said. "I need to place a phone call and then make a visit. If everything goes as planned, I just might have enough evidence to convince Zack or at least enough to get him to take precautions." Becca took my hand and I helped her up.

"This is exciting," she said and then glanced down at the coffin. Her voice cracked when she spoke again. "I wished I could have shared more moments like this with Robbie."

With those words we turned away and dashed off toward our ride.

* * *

When we got into the back of the hearse, I pulled out my cell phone and began to dial. Becca nodded in the direction of the driver.

"Are you sure that's a good idea?" she said. Now that Becca was on the inside she was playing this covert agent thing to the hilt.

"I don't think he's a danger," I said, putting the phone to my ear. "And besides, I'm about out of time, and I'm probably already going to get fired."

On the third ring, a voice picked up and said hello. Lucky for me, it was the voice I was hoping for.

"Roger," I said. "It's Matt."

"Matt?" Roger said. "Are you okay? It's like you were here one minute and then gone the next. The bishop came and packed up your things. He said you had a friend who died."

"I did," I said. "A very good friend. I'm coming from the funeral now." Roger started to offer his apologies, but I cut him off.

"Roger," I said. "Why did you lie to me about your wife?" This was probably another instance of me chucking the rule book. If you suspect someone is a terrorist, you should never tip them off—at least not until you have them in handcuffs. But although Roger's lies definitely made him a suspect, in my gut I didn't believe he was a bad person, and I was learning to listen to my gut. Still, Roger's reaction in this conversation would tell me what I needed to know.

There was silence on the other end of the phone for a long time. "Roger?" I said.

"How did you find out?" He sounded resigned and a little relieved.

"I saw an old newspaper article about the crash," I said. "You were a beautiful family." I didn't tell him that the newspaper article was a part of a file created on him in case he was a terrorist.

"Why did you lie to everyone?" I asked again.

Roger took a minute to answer. Either he was a terrorist and thinking up an elaborate story, or he was just a broken and damaged man.

"I guess it was just easier," he said finally. "I could either be the nerd who was terrible at relationships or a tragic figure who'd had it all and then lost it." He breathed hard through the phone. "I didn't want sympathy. I didn't want to try to recapture what could never be put back together. I didn't even want the pain to heal, if that makes any sense. I didn't want to forget them. So I made up a story and buried myself in my work."

"Then you're not really a nerd?" I asked.

Roger choked. I couldn't tell if it was a laugh or a cry. "The nerd part is true," he said. "The rest is a lie."

Roger's explanation sounded genuine, but I had to be sure. "Roger," I asked, speaking very slowly. "Are you planning to use nanotechnology to pollute the water supply and kill millions of people?"

I thought the hearse driver was going to drive off the road. Maybe it wasn't a good idea to conduct business in the backseat. Becca's eyes widened in alarm. But it was Roger's reaction that I was waiting for.

"What?" he asked, and he didn't say anything else. He didn't try to justify; he didn't try to explain; he just seemed completely dumbfounded that anyone would ask such a question.

"Never mind," I said. "You know that moving on doesn't mean you will forget your family. Marva Rose is a pretty great person."

"I know," Roger said. "But I've been playing this game for a long time, and I'm not sure I know how to change."

"Simple," I said. "When the experiment doesn't work, you change the variables."

"Are you coming back?" Roger asked. "I could use your help."

"I can't come back," I said, glancing sideways at Becca. "But that doesn't mean that I won't help you with Marva Rose. However, right now, I need you to do something for me."

"Anything."

"This is going to sound weird," I said. "But it's important."

"Everything you do is weird," Roger said. This guy was definitely not a terrorist. He was too perceptive.

"Do you have the ability to test for poison in the apartment?"

"What?"

"If I were to give you a capsule to test, could you test it in the apartment?"

More silence, and then his inner scientist must have kicked in. "I'd really need to take it into the lab if you wanted a breakdown of the ingredients," he said. "What do you want me to test?"

"I don't need a breakdown," I said. "I just need to know if something is poison or not. Do you have a way to do that?"

"Not without killing my fish," Roger said, "but even that wouldn't give us a very good reading. A lot of foreign substances would kill them." I remembered the aquarium in our living room and the two perch swimming around inside.

"Listen, Roger, this is important. I need to find out if Joseph's vitamins contain poison, and I need to know it as soon as humanly possible. I don't want you to kill your fish, but I need to know."

"He's due to return from a run any minute now," Roger said. "If I grab a few pills and take a bus to the lab, I can call you from there."

I thought for a minute about Roger waiting for a bus.

"Is my car still in the parking lot?" I asked.

"Yeah," Roger said. "The keys are hanging in the kitchen."

"Take it," I said. "Call my cell as soon as you find out."

Roger didn't say anything for a few seconds, and then he spoke. "Does this have anything to do with the terrorist attack you mentioned earlier?"

"It might," I said.

Roger was silent. I was sure he didn't like pondering the idea that Joseph could be a terrorist. I didn't like it either.

"There's not enough pills in that bottle to contaminate a large body of water," Roger said. "Not without some major chemical engineering."

"Forget the large bodies of water," I said. "I need to know if one of those pills could kill someone if it were slipped into a glass."

"You're not just a student, are you?" Roger asked.

"No, I'm not," I said, looking at the hearse driver, who seemed to be a little too interested in my conversation. "But I can't tell you any more right now."

"I think Joseph is coming," Roger said. "I'll call you from the lab." He hung up.

"So?" Becca asked me when I finished the conversation.

"At least one of my roommates is not a terrorist." I said. I thought I saw the driver breathe a sigh of relief.

"Is he going to be able to do what you asked him?" Becca asked. She kept her words careful and generic. I think she was probably better at being a covert agent than I was. But the driver had already heard everything that she had.

"I don't know," I said. "Joseph was coming, and he had to hang up."

"So what if Roger can't do it? How are you going to be sure about Joseph?"

I wanted to call Zack with my suspicions, but I wanted to do one more thing first. Neither Zack nor the Agency would come out looking very good if he acted on my information prematurely.

"I think Joseph's mother lives near D.C. I need to go see her."

"I'm coming with you," Becca said. I thought about arguing but then remembered all of the years that she had faithfully remained in the dark.

"You got an address?" a deep voice said from the front seat. "I'm off the clock. I can take you there if you like." So much for being undercover. I might as well rent a billboard.

"Give me a minute," I said. "I'll make a few calls." I probably shouldn't have involved either Becca or the hearse driver in company business, but the hours in the day were passing quickly, and we were running out of time. As I called Jennings Frye, I wondered if I would still get a pension if I got fired.

CHAPTER 27

The Mother

MRS. HADADI LIVED IN A nice suburb with lots of mature trees, landscaped lawns, and flower beds—and several curious neighbors who I was sure were wondering why a hearse had pulled up in front of her house.

Mrs. Hadadi herself didn't seem fazed at all by our last-minute visit. When I told her on the phone that I had been Joseph's roommate, she insisted that we stop by immediately to chat with her. That was fine with me since I was wondering how to tell her that we were currently pulling into her cul-de-sac.

She met us at the door, and I introduced her to Becca.

"Come in, come in," she said. "I've been squeezing fresh lemonade, and I was just wondering who I was going to share it with." She looked behind us at the hearse and studied our black clothing.

"Please come and sit down. I can see that you've experienced a loss in your lives, and I know from experience that these times are never easy."

She moved with the fluidity of someone who was used to entertaining. While Joseph greatly resembled the pictures of his father, he retained none of his mother's grace except when he was running. She seated us, went into the kitchen, and then reappeared with a glass pitcher filled with ice and lemons and a silver platter holding about a dozen small cookies dusted with powdered sugar. I hadn't eaten since breakfast. When my stomach growled, Becca gave me a look that suggested one did not allow one's stomach to protest in the presence of proper company. I knew only one way to stop it, so I accepted the offered cookie and was glad when Mrs. Hadadi placed the remainder on a coffee table well within my reach.

I let the two women talk for a few moments. It didn't dawn on me until they began speaking that Mrs. Hadadi's condolences might hold more weight with Becca than others she had received. Some people might say they knew what she was going through, but Mrs. Hadadi spoke from experience. Her husband had also been taken in the prime of his life.

Light seemed to emanate from Mrs. Hadadi's countenance. She looked nothing like a grieving widow beaten down by the unfairness of life. I think Becca might have seen in her something that she could become, despite her trials.

After what seemed the exact appropriate amount of time, Mrs. Hadadi turned her attentions to me.

"You say you are a roommate of my son Joseph," she said. "To what do I owe this visit?"

Since Mrs. Hadadi was being up front with me, I responded in kind.

"I'm worried about Joseph," I said.

"That makes two of us," she replied. "He rarely calls anymore, and when he does, I can find no light in his voice. So different from who he was as a child. Different from what he was even a year ago."

"Do you mind if I ask," I said, "what *was* Joseph like as a child?"

Her eyes brightened, and she reached for a large photo album on the coffee table. "I'll show you," she said. "Although the pictures will not do him justice. Joseph is one of the brightest people who has ever walked the earth."

"He's at the top of his class in medical school," I said.

"I've heard," Mrs. Hadadi replied, offering me another cookie. I took it quickly and avoided Becca's eyes. I probably had powdered sugar on my lips. "But that is not the kind of brightness I am talking about," she continued. "Ever since he was a child, when Joseph entered a room, the place literally lit up. The biggest compliment that anyone ever gave me was when they said that he had his father's looks but my personality. They were wrong of course—at least partially. His sunny disposition was similar to mine, but Joseph's was magnified a hundred times. I sorely miss having him in this house."

I thought about the Joseph I knew and for some reason had a hard time seeing it.

Mrs. Hadadi opened the book. I got to see Joseph naked in the bathtub, Joseph running naked through the sprinklers, and Joseph naked at the top of a tree house. I was beginning to wonder if Joseph was a nudist when Mrs. Hadadi turned from his pictures at two years old to three. Even in the pictures, I could see what she meant. Whether clothed or not, the boy was always smiling—the Hadadi smile. Blessed with his mother's personality and his father's smile, this boy had the world at his fingertips. But something had gone terribly wrong.

"When did you notice a change in Joseph?" I asked as she reached for a second volume of photos, beginning at age four. I was wondering if it coincided with his trip to Jordan.

"Joseph didn't change. Not until he left for graduate school. He hasn't been back to visit since, and he won't let me come and visit him. I've threatened to just show up on his apartment steps, but he has made me promise that I will not do so. There is something so desperate in his voice. I don't understand what has happened to him."

"It must have been hard on him when his father died," I said.

"It was devastating. But he did not lose his light. He was determined to carry on his father's legacy. But now . . . I hear nothing of this in his voice. I've even talked about it with Bishop Shepherd, and he has encouraged me to give it some time. I believe Bishop Shepherd is a wise man."

I knew that Joseph's mother was a Mormon, but for some reason I had not thought about it until she mentioned Zack. For some reason this realization made her seem less like a stranger I had just met and more like family. I used this familiarity to justify taking another cookie. I could feel Becca's glare, but she didn't understand. She wasn't part of the clan.

"What about Joseph's trip to Jordan when he was a young man?" I asked. "Could that have contributed to his change?"

"It was a hard time," she admitted. "He and his father had gone expecting to bring home seven adopted siblings. And although Siham and Mo are dear children, they never quite recovered from the tragedy. Despite our best efforts, they never fully accepted us as their family. This made Joseph's childhood more difficult, but he never lost his light. He tried to involve them in the social activities of his youth, but the two mostly kept to themselves. They seemed anxious to leave our family as soon as they were old enough. Especially after my husband died."

"I've met Siham," I said. "But where is Mohammed now?"

"Mo was a difficult one," she said. "I love him as my own son, but he has never made it easy. He always felt like he should have died with his brothers and not have been been saved with the women. As such, I don't think he fancies being around the female gender very much. It's as if it reminds him of his shame. Who knows where he is now. Siham says she has talked to him and that he is well. I pray for him every day, but I doubt I will ever see him again."

She was now showing me pictures of Joseph when he was five. He was beginning to wear pants now, which was a relief.

"You have asked me about my son," she said. "Now it is my turn. What can *you* tell me about Joseph?"

I thought for a moment. I didn't want to talk about his surly tone and the way he drained light from the room when he entered. She already seemed to know about his success in medical school. "Has he told you about his ultrarace?" I asked.

"His what?"

"Joseph recently completed a hundred-mile run through the mountains," I said. "And he very nearly won."

I didn't know what I expected to see in Mrs. Hadadi's eyes. Maybe pride, maybe surprise. But what I saw was an unmistakable look of alarm.

"A hundred miles of running?" she said.

"You didn't know."

"If what you say is true, then Joseph has changed even more than I thought. He always hated running. Joseph was a swimmer."

"I bet he received a ton of medals," I said, thinking about Joseph's competitive drive.

"A few," Mrs. Hadadi said, looking more confused than ever. "But I think he mostly swam to be part of the team. For Joseph, everything was social."

It was my turn to be confused. The Joseph that Mrs. Hadadi described and the Joseph I was seeing in the pictures seemed to have nothing in common with the Joseph I knew—nothing other than the Hadadi smile.

"What about Mohammed?" Becca asked. "Did he like to run?" As soon as she asked the question, I knew what she was thinking, and I knew I should have seen it earlier. I held my breath waiting for Mrs. Hadadi's answer.

"Mohammed ran all the time," she said. "Day and night. Mainly, I think, to get out of the house."

"Do you have a recent picture of Joseph?" I asked. "Something within the past two years?"

"Of course," Mrs. Hadadi said and reached for an album high on the shelf. "This is the picture of him when he graduated with his second undergraduate degree from Georgetown. He always loved school. He never wanted to leave."

I looked at the picture. The man who looked back at me looked exactly like the Joseph I knew. Except the smile. And the eyes.

"Did Mohammed look a lot like Joseph?" I asked.

"They could have been twins," Mrs. Hadadi said. "But there were never two more different people in all the world."

With her words the final piece of the puzzle fell into place. Joseph Hadadi was not a terrorist, but neither was he my roommate. My roommate's name was Mohammed, and I not only knew who he was, but I knew exactly what he was going to do. I needed to call Zack right away.

I looked at my watch. "I'm very sorry, Mrs. Hadadi. But we need to leave."

"There's something going on with Joseph, isn't there? Something you've learned from our conversation."

I should have made something up, but I looked into her eyes and could not lie to her.

"When is the last time you spoke to Joseph on the phone?" I asked.

"I believe it was a week ago today," she said. "He didn't sound good."

"Mrs. Hadadi," I said. "I am an agent for the United States government. I believe the man in Utah claiming to be Joseph Hadadi is not your son. I believe your son has been kidnapped and is being held against his will. Since you have spoken with him, it means he is still alive. I will have someone contact you as soon as possible, but if we are going to save your son, time is of the essence."

I could see my words register, and Mrs. Hadadi nodded. "It's Mohammed, isn't it?" she said. "The man impersonating my son. He is involved in something terrible."

"Not yet," I said. "Not if I can stop him."

CHAPTER 28
Canceled Debts

We hurried from the house and jumped into the backseat of the hearse. Both of us had our cell phones out, ready to dial.

"Who are you calling?" Becca asked.

"Zack," I said. "We don't have all the evidence we need, but it's time to pick up the man who calls himself Joseph Hadadi and stop this thing." I looked at the phone in her hands. "What about you?"

"The airport," she said. "We need to find you a flight back to Utah."

I started to tell her that there was no need—I wasn't going back to Utah—when my cell phone buzzed. I looked at the screen. It was Roger.

"It's cyanide," he said without saying hello. "Commercial grade."

"Enough to kill someone?"

"Enough to kill several. One of these capsules in a pitcher of water could kill twenty people within hours, maybe minutes."

I could feel Roger's silence reaching through to me over the phone line. Finally, he said, "Does this mean Joseph is one of the bad guys?"

I thought about this question. I thought about a young man whose parents had been killed, waiting in an orphanage to be adopted by a cousin from the West and then experiencing a second tragedy as his brothers were annihilated by those who were supposed to be the good guys. I thought about running with this young man through the mountains, about watching his drive and determination and his willingness to share with me a view from a mountain top. I did not pretend to know what went on in the heart of Mohammed Hadadi, but I didn't want to believe he was a bad guy. I loved him like a brother.

I didn't answer Roger's question directly. "He's not Joseph Hadadi," I said. "The man posing as our roommate is Joseph's cousin and foster brother. His name is Mohammed, and he could pass for Joseph's twin. He's working with a group of terrorists."

"Sounds like a bad guy to me," Roger said.

"Not *bad*," I said. "*Broken*." For some reason I could not bring myself to label Mohammed Hadadi, even though I was pretty sure he was preparing to commit a terrorist act with the potential to harm so many.

"Where are you?" I asked.

"Just leaving the lab. On my way home."

"Don't go to the apartment," I said. "Go back into the lab, pull out your cot, and spend the night there. I know you've done it before."

"I want to help," he said. "Maybe I can destroy the capsules before Joseph can use them." I understood his need to stop Mohammed. It was the need of a brother pushing a sibling out of the way of a moving train.

"Don't even think about it," I said. "I'm calling Zack right now. We'll let him take care of it."

"The bishop's involved in this too?"

"Up to his elbows," I said.

"I don't think you'll to find him tonight," Roger said. "He's at a wedding."

"He can step out."

"He may not be able to. He's performing the ceremony. It's Jenny from the ward."

I looked at my watch. It was now eight o'clock Washington time, which meant it was six o'clock in Utah.

"There's plenty of time," I said. "As long as I talk to him before tomorrow morning."

"Why don't you just call the police?"

I'd thought about that. But it would take too long to explain. If I couldn't catch Zack, then I would call Missy Brentwood, but I wanted to try Zack first. Joseph or Mohammed—or whatever his name was—was one of Zack's flock. Zack deserved to hear the information first.

"I'll get hold of him," I said. "I really don't think anything will happen before tomorrow. But it is important that you stay away from the apartment. Do you understand?"

"Yeah," Roger said. "I got it." He paused and then said, "I'm going to tell Rose." At first I thought he meant about Joseph, but then he continued. "About my wife and daughter. She deserves to know. She's a wonderful person."

"She's the best," I said. "And so are you. You may have just saved someone's life." I cut off the call and dialed Zack.

The call went immediately to voice mail.

"Zack," I said. "This is Matt. The anthrax was a smoke screen. I think the attack will happen tomorrow, and I believe I know when and where. I need to talk to you as soon as you get this. Call me." I hung up.

"There's a red-eye leaving at midnight," Becca said, putting her phone into her purse. "It will get you to Utah at about five in the morning."

I sighed and looked directly into Becca's eyes. They were lovely, dark, and deep. "I don't need to leave," I said. "Zack can take care of this."

"You don't want to be there?" she asked. I wondered if she was testing me. Would I keep my word to Robbie? Would I give up everything to fulfill a promise? "They don't need me," I said. "You do. You and the baby."

"You're not thinking about that stupid promise are you?" Becca asked. *Was this another test?*

"I promised that I would be here for you and for the baby," I said, nodding toward her belly.

"And you have been," she said. "I was on the verge of hopelessness, and you brought me back from the edge. And then there was this afternoon—"

I felt the shame wash over me. "I'm so sorry," I said. "I don't know what I'm doing. It's the afternoon of your husband's burial, and I'm dragging you all over town in his hearse. I'm sure Robbie is rolling over in his grave."

Becca laughed. "Don't you dare apologize. This has been the most enjoyable evening I've had since Robbie died. It's almost as if Robbie were here, allowing me to share the work that he loved. He's not rolling over in his grave. He's smiling."

"You're a natural," I said. "You spotted the imposter before I did."

"I *was* good, wasn't I," she said. "Admit it. I make a good partner." She took my hand and squeezed.

I squeezed back. "You make a great partner," I said. I let the words hang there between us, and she let go of my hand.

"Now about that promise," she said, "the one Robbie forced you to make. Are you prepared to fulfill it?"

"I told you that I will always be here for you," I said.

"And I will hold you to that. But that doesn't mean you have to marry me. Robbie didn't have you make that promise for my sake—it was for yours. We both knew that if he ever died, I wouldn't have any problem finding someone new if I chose to. But we agreed that I might be the closest thing to love that you would ever find. He made me promise that I would take you in."

I must have been blinking dumbly because Becca laughed. "So I tell you what—if you release me from the promise, I will release you."

I didn't know what to say. In my mind I had burned my bridges and prepared myself to give my life to Becca and the child. I was afraid to even entertain the thought of what might be possible now.

"You don't like me?" I asked.

She grabbed my hand again and looked deeply into my eyes. "I love you," she said. "More than any man alive. With Robbie gone, you are my best friend in the world. And I expect you to be a part of my life forever. But that doesn't mean I want to marry you." A smile played at the edges of her lips. "The truth is, you don't need me anymore. You've changed, Matthew. More than you realize. And my bet is that a woman has had something to do with it. I'd like to know her name."

I must have looked dumbfounded because Becca giggled.

"Why would you think there's a woman involved?" I asked weakly.

"Last night, you mentioned a friend who had died and come back. You said 'her' when you described this friend. And then when you told me everything that had happened to you in Utah, there were places where it seemed like you had to work around a key part of the story."

"Her name is Permelia," I said. "She is seventy-five and lovely."

"Seriously?" For the first time in this conversation, Becca was the uncertain one.

"Seriously. Permelia is lovely." I let Becca sweat for a moment then continued. "But there's also someone else. Someone named Hope Winslow. She's Permelia's roommate."

"And is this Hope Winslow also in her seventies?"

"Not so much," I said.

So I filled in the blanks and told Becca about my interactions with Hope Winslow, from the first time I saw her in church, to our un-date at the Truman Center, to our study sessions, to the point where I showed her Becca's text and Hope punched me in the face.

"She thinks you are the father of my baby?" Becca said, sounding mortified. "You idiot." She reached for her phone. "What's her number? I'm going to call her right now and explain."

I put my hand on hers and gently forced the phone back down.

"It's okay," I said. "You can explain to her later. But I'd like to take a stab at it first—in person." I could see the driver looking at us in the mirror. He seemed to approve.

"What time did you say that flight was?" I asked.

CHAPTER 29
Bishop Zack

BECCA ARRANGED MY FLIGHT OVER the phone while I repacked the few things I had taken out of my bag. I continued to try Zack's number and then finally gave up and called Missy Brentwood. She didn't answer either. I left a message with her as well. It was Friday night. *Where was everybody?* I thought about calling the police or other members of the Agency, but they really didn't understand the situation and pulling in the wrong people at this point in the game could work against us. We didn't need a bureaucratic chain of command slowing things down. Zack was one of the few people I thought had both the ability and the inclination to act on this quickly.

The flight was nearly empty, and I rested my head against the window, closed my eyes, and tried to sleep. But there were too many ideas floating through my head. My mind flitted from the roommate I knew as Joseph to Zelphinus Cork to Hope Winslow. I had unfinished business with each of them, and I wasn't certain any of the situations would play out the way I wanted them to.

As we approached Salt Lake International Airport, the pilot announced that we were not yet cleared for landing because of storms moving through the area. We would be put in a holding pattern, and he would let us know when it was our turn to land. This was the good news. The bad news was that this particular plane was not equipped with the phones in the back of the headrest, so I had no way to find out if Zack or Missy had gotten my messages. I looked at my watch. I only had a few hours to stop what I needed to stop. If my flight circled for too long, I might have to hijack the plane.

Just when I thought we were never going to pull out of our holding pattern, the pilot came on the intercom and said that we had been cleared for landing. By the time we got on the ground and I turned on my phone, it was after seven. I looked at my screen. Four messages. Zack had been trying to call me. Good. As soon as I left the plane, I found a deserted gate and punched in

Zack's number. I didn't want anyone hearing this conversation. What I had to say might cause a bit of a panic in Salt Lake City.

"Where have you been?" Zack answered without saying hello.

"Stuck on a red-eye," I said. "I'm in the Salt Lake airport."

"I'll send someone for you."

"There isn't time," I said. "Once you hear what I have to say, you're going to need to act. By the way, where have you been? I tried to call you most of the night."

"I had a wedding," he said, his voice sounding tired. "And then I was at the Truman Center."

His words were measured and solemn, and I thought I might know why.

"Missy Brentwood?" I asked.

"I was with her most of the night. Benji had a seizure and went into a coma. He never came out of it."

"He went to see Jesus," I whispered quietly.

"What?"

"That's what Meggy told me. She said her brother was going to see Jesus. How are they coping?"

"It was a rough night, but they're doing okay." Zack paused. "She was asking about you, you know."

"Meggy?"

"Her too. But I was speaking of Hope."

"Hope asked about me?"

My heart found a trampoline and began doing backflips. I couldn't help it. But Zack seemed a little tentative to elaborate on Hope's interest in me.

"What did you tell her?"

"The truth. That you had a good friend pass away, and I didn't know if you would be back."

"I want to see her," I said.

Zack seemed to think about it and then asked, "How's Becca?"

"She was in a dark place," I said. "But she's coming out of it."

"Did you have anything to do with that?"

Why did I feel like I was being interviewed again for worthiness? "I was there for her," I said. "As a friend."

"Anything to confess to your bishop?"

I thought about telling him he was no longer my bishop, but I wasn't really sure if that was the case. "I took a sip of Becca's coffee," I said.

"What about the promise?"

"What promise?"

"The one Robbie made you make in the event that he ever died."

"You know about that?"

"Everyone knows. Robbie made sure of it."

"I've been released," I said. "Becca said it was idiotic."

"She was right." I could hear Zack breathing on the other end of the line. I wasn't so sure that he was happy I wouldn't be fulfilling Robbie's promise. He'd made it clear that Hope Winslow was like a daughter to him, and I had done nothing so far but bring her pain.

I decided it was time to change the subject. "The anthrax was a smoke screen."

"I figured that," he said. "But a smoke screen for what?"

"For a terrorist attack that I'm pretty sure is going to happen this morning in Salt Lake around ten o'clock. An attack that you will be able to stop."

For the next few minutes, I filled Zack in on what I'd found out about Joseph and my suspicions about what he was going to do. I held my breath as I finished. The info on Joseph's real identity was solid, but the rest of my theory was pure speculation. If Zack believed me, he would be putting his reputation on the line in a number of different ways.

"You'd better be right about this, Mr. Knight."

"I am," I said.

"Do you want in on the bust? This is your show."

I thought about it. I did have a desire to see the end of this road, but Zack was much better suited to handle things from here on out.

"I just want to talk to Joseph before they ship him out," I said.

"He's not Joseph."

"He is to me."

"All right. I'll see what I can do. I'd better get going. I've got some heavy convincing to do with people in high places."

"You're a bishop," I said. "They can't help but believe you."

I hung up the phone and went out to rent a car. There were other reasons why I didn't want to accompany Zack in his efforts to stop the attack. I wanted to go and see Hope Winslow. But that would come later, hopefully after I'd had a chance to get a shower and pop in a breath mint.

Right now I had another mission, and I wanted to get it accomplished without delay.

Zelphinus Cork had been released from Delancey Street.

It was time to slay my monster.

CHAPTER 30
The Monster

On the way to the house, there were several times I almost turned around. This confrontation was something I had sought for, planned for, and fantasized about for most of my life. Now that the time was here, though, I really didn't want to go through with it. But the problem was, if I didn't take care of this now, I didn't think I ever would.

The welcome-home banner hung on the eaves above the front door—a little slack, a little faded. It was only 7:30 a.m.—too early for me to be knocking. I knocked anyway. The door frame was splintered, and I brushed small slivers from my knuckles after my hand came away. I heard footsteps in the hallway, and the door opened to reveal the half-awake eyes of Zelphinus Cork's daughter. The eyes studied me for several moments without speaking.

"It's early," she said.

"I know. I need to speak with your father."

"You a cop?" Her eyes were guarded. I wondered how many times throughout her life the police had come to her door during inconvenient hours asking to be let in.

"No."

"What then?"

"I knew him," I said. "From before."

She studied me again, this time longer. Probably wondering if I had been Aryan Brotherhood, looking for the tattoos on my knuckles and arms. A large shadow filled the space behind her.

"Who's there?" The booming voice was one I could never forget.

"He says he knows you."

The shadow eclipsed the woman as she stepped back and Zelphinus Cork came to the door. His beard was gone, his head was no longer shaved, and I swear he had trimmed his eyebrows. But he was the same man. The same muscled shoulders. The same pitch-black eyes.

As he came around to where he could see me, his eyes widened, and I thought his ruddy cheeks lost a little of their color. He looked like he'd seen a ghost.

"You all right, Zelph?" his daughter asked. Not, "You all right, Pops," or "You all right, Dad," but calling him by his first name.

He steadied himself and was back to looking like a solid piece of granite.

"What do you want?" His voice was icy with challenge.

"Let's walk," I said. "I need to talk to you." I turned to go, wondering if he would follow. He did. What I was about to do was going to be hard enough. I didn't need any spectators. I heard the voice of a boy call from the hallway.

"Where you goin', Grandpa?"

"Back soon, son," Zelph answered, his voice gentle and a bit unsure.

I led him around behind the Smith's grocery store, out of sight of the house. Out of sight of anyone. There was a green metal Dumpster shoved up against a wall. The place reminded me a lot of a certain alleyway many years ago.

"Far enough," Zelph said. "What do you want, boy?" He was older than when I had seen him last, but his voice had lost none of its power. The muscles in his neck and shoulders testified to years of pumping iron. The tattoos that once circled his forearms were now faded scars.

I thought about his question. Thought about the menace in his voice that at one time would have caused my knees to go weak.

"All my life I thought what I wanted was to kill you," I said. My words sounded calm and flat, without passion or fire. They were merely a statement of fact. "Right now, I'm not so sure."

He didn't look surprised. He didn't look alarmed. "You're the kid," he said. Not a question. "I knew that night would catch up to me someday." He seemed to settle into his legs, as if preparing for a fight. He looked back longingly toward his daughter's house, and then the commanding voice came back.

"You bring a gun?"

"No," I said, wondering if I should have.

His lips twitched in a slight smile. "Your mistake."

He came at me then, the way big men do. Fast and hard, like Mike Tyson in his prime, intent on using his power to take me out before the fight even began. His shoulder took me in the chest and I went down. I guess I should have been expecting his attack, but I'd been too focused on what I was going to do. However, as soon as I hit the ground, my reflexes kicked in.

I let the momentum of his weight carry us down, and I pushed my feet against him and sent him flying over the top of me. He was quick for a big man with years on him, and as I rose from the ground he was already on his feet, ready to meet me.

"You don't think a little Judo training is going to make a difference, do you?" he said and spat into the dirt. "I've cut my teeth on men who thought they were experts at martial arts. They don't understand that when you get into a street fight there are no rules."

"I'm not here to fight you," I said.

"Too late, son. I've paid my debt to society. The man they put me away for—the man they said I killed—was somebody else's doing. I paid my time for a life, fair and square. I'm not going back."

He moved toward me again and I circled him. I knew that if I got within reach of those massive arms they would crush me like a grape.

He lunged again, and this time I sidestepped and sent the palm of my hand up under his nose. I heard the crunch of bone as it broke, but I felt no satisfaction in it. Blood began to run down his face, and he blinked his eyes quickly to clear his sight.

A broken nose would stop most assailants, and it was one of the most basic moves that Zack had taught me. But I had broken Zack's nose at least three times, and it had never stopped him. I didn't think it would stop Zelphinus Cork either.

There was blood in his eyes now. Blood and rage. Before, he had not seen me as a serious opponent. Now he would be more careful—and more dangerous.

He jabbed at my head, and I caught the blow with my shoulder. It felt like my rotator cuff had been driven out the other side of my body. Only one person I had ever known had that kind of power. Luckily that person had trained me.

He jabbed again, and I let his arm slide past me. I threw one arm above his elbow and one beneath and wrenched them in opposite directions. The joint should have separated. But his elbow did not break. His huge tendons were like steel. Even so, I could see that I'd hurt him. But I knew better than to think that hurting Zelphinus Cork was such a good thing. All sense of focus left his eyes, and he came at me wearing a mask of rage.

He stopped being careful and came in swinging with both arms. An uppercut caught me in the side and lifted me off the ground. He followed it with a straight right that sent me through the air and into the side of the Dumpster. My body slumped to the ground and I groaned with pain.

"I've never lost a street fight," he said. "You should have brought a weapon." He looked back toward his daughter's house and sounded almost apologetic.

"Not exactly true," I said, pushing my back against the Dumpster and raising myself up. "I seem to remember you wrestling for a cane with a woman less than half your size—and she won."

He had been moving toward me, moving in for the kill, but these words seem to temporarily stop him. I did not wait. I launched myself from my position and wrapped my arms around his neck.

"All you need is four seconds," Zack had coached me countless times. "If you can get behind the man and get your forearm positioned in a headlock on the vagus nerve, four seconds and he is out." Zelph tried to stop me. He flailed frantically, but his iron grip could not take hold. I'd seen all the moves before. I'd trained for them day and night with one of the best teachers in the business. I pulled myself up behind his head and anchored my position. Unlike Zelph, I'd lost plenty of fights. It's how I'd learned.

Zelph thrashed wildly and stumbled to his knees. I released my grip and spun around in front of him, my hand pushing back on his forehead, exposing his throat. I looked into his eyes. They were no longer glazed over with rage. They were not fearful either. More than anything, they seemed resigned.

"Go ahead," he said. "Lord knows I deserve it."

"No you don't," I said. "None of us do. But I'm going to give it to you anyway." What I needed to do, I needed to do now. Before my resolve was completely gone. From the time I had felt the peaceful voice after Robbie's funeral, I knew this was what I needed to do.

I bent down even closer and whispered in his ear, "I forgive you, Zelphinus Cork. I forgive you for the death of my mother."

I released my hold on him and pushed away. He stared at me in shock. And then he slumped down and buried his head in his arms.

I sat down too, in the gravel a few yards away. After a while, I asked, "How well do you remember that night?"

He grunted. "Like yesterday. The nightmares won't let me forget."

"Me either," I said.

Zelph rubbed at his neck. "I've always been confused about one thing. You had your chances. Why didn't you give me up to the police?"

"I've wondered that too," I said. "For a long time I believed that I was so afraid of you that I had blocked your face from my mind. And I *had* blocked the memory, but you weren't the monster I was running from."

"What d'you mean?"

"Did you mean to kill her?" I asked.

He shook his head. "I just wanted to get her off me," he said. "I just wanted to send a message. But I'm a strong man. I should have eased up."

I thought back to that night. It was amazing to me how the memories flowed. For most of my adult life many of the details had been a blur. Now they were clear as crystal. My mother and I had been doing volunteer work at the homeless shelter and were on our way home when we encountered Zelphinus Cork assaulting a Black man. What I didn't tell anyone, what I had even hidden from myself until recently, was the fact that I knew who the man was. The kids in the neighborhood called him "Old Patrick," and I hated him with all my heart.

Anytime he would see me alone, he would yell, "Hey, white boy, what you doin' in my neighborhood? Tryin' to pass for a brother?"

I didn't answer. I never answered. Just kept my head down and walked faster. Old Patrick carried a cane that had the brass figure of a panther on top. He shook it at me when he spoke. The cane scared me. But not as much as his words.

"I think I figured it out," he said one day. "I think that maybe you do belong on this street after all. Your mama seems to be friendly with our people over at the shelter." He rested on his cane, grinned at me, and winked. "Mighty friendly. I think you might secretly be one of us." He spat into the street. "Tell me, boy, who's your daddy?"

This time I did not walk away. I ran. His high, wheezing laugh echoed after me. It also echoed to others on the street who had heard him, and it was not uncommon for one of the local youths to approach me in the street after that, bump me as they walked by, and whisper, "Who's your daddy, white boy?"

I had no answer for them. This was the one subject my mother would never talk about. My father could have been a Black man. He could have been Asian, Russian, or Indian. I knew nothing about him other than he was a drug addict and had died of an overdose. Old Patrick's words revealed my shame. Other boys on the street might have had fathers who were deadbeats, drug dealers, or convicts, but they still had the advantage over me. They had fathers.

When I saw Zelphinus Cork standing over Old Patrick, beating him in the street, I'd been happy. Finally, someone was giving him what he deserved.

"Well, if it isn't Saint Jenny," Cork had said to my mother when he saw her. "It's been a long time since California. I heard you was in these parts." He was upright and strong. With his height and broad shoulders he looked to be invincible. I remember thinking that I wouldn't mind it if he were my father.

"Leave the old guy alone, Zelph," my mother had said. "He's done nothing to you."

Zelph laughed. "Now how would you know what he's done or hasn't done? I have good reports from my people that he's been terrorizing the white folks in this neighborhood." He looked directly at me and winked. "Isn't that right, little Timmy?"

"His name's Matthew," my mother said. "And you've already beaten the man senseless. Leave him be." Old Patrick groaned, mumbled an obscenity, and spit blood on Zelphinus Cork's shoes.

Zelph laughed again. "Doesn't look like he's completely senseless yet," he said. "It's getting late, Jenny. Shouldn't you be making tracks about now?" He wasn't talking about her leaving, and she knew it.

"I'm clean, Zelph," my mother said quietly. "I kicked it—months ago."

"Nobody kicks it, Jenny. Once you get on that train, you are on it for life. There's only one way off. You should know that better than anybody."

"You're wrong," she said. "It's not easy, but with the help of God and good friends it is possible. You just need a purpose bigger than the need."

Zelphinus Cork stiffened at this remark. He turned his attention from my mother back to me. "Your mother thinks I should help this fine gentleman up," he said. Old Patrick was cursing again, trying his best to spit his blood out at Zelph. "Such a fine gentleman," he said again. "Boy, why don't you hand me his cane so I can assist him."

I looked down by my feet and saw the thick, knobby cane with the bronze panther head on top. I was only a boy but I wasn't stupid. I knew what would happen if I handed the cane to Zelphinus Cork. I knew that he would use it on the cursing, spitting, mean old man who taunted me when I walked down the street minding my own business.

My mother shook her head. "No, Matthew," she said. I looked at Zelphinus Cork. His eyes held mine, and I was powerless to look away. Without really thinking about what I was doing I reached down quickly, picked up the cane, and tossed it to him. My mother stared at me in disappointment and shock.

Zelphinus Cork gave me a nod then lifted the weapon above his head. Before he could drive the blow home, my mother stepped in and grabbed the end of the cane. She was a small woman, and not very powerful, but she wasn't going to let go. Zelph bellowed in rage and tried to shake her off. When she didn't release her grip, he set his legs and swung the cane like a baseball bat. The momentum picked my mother up off the ground, and she flew into the side of a green Dumpster. She still gripped the cane. She had taken it from Zelph.

The blow to her body probably would have only knocked the wind out of her and maybe caused some major bruising, but the side of her temple connected squarely with one of the large metal grommets that protruded from the Dumpster's corner. She went down in a heap, and blood began to seep from her head. Her eyes were open and lifeless—the look of shock and disappointment frozen on them forever. Disappointment in me.

I felt my life slip away with the life of my mother. I looked at Zelphinus Cork, who no longer seemed so powerful. His eyes were wild and confused.

For several seconds I froze. Then I ran. I ran and did not look back.

I shook the memories from my head and brought my mind back to the present.

"I should never have given you the cane," I said to him. "My mother died as much because of my actions as yours. I wanted you to hurt Old Patrick. If there's a monster in all of this, it was me."

"You were a kid," he said. "You should give yourself a break."

I sat silent on my haunches for a moment and then stood up. "I think I finally can," I said. Then I turned to walk away.

"You know, when I saw you at the doorstep, I thought for a minute you were your father," he said.

I stopped dead in my tracks and turned back toward him. "You knew my father?"

"Jenny didn't tell you about him?"

"She wouldn't talk about him."

Zelph nodded. "Was she really clean that night, like she said?"

"For six months," I told him. "She'd been free from the heroin for six months."

"How'd she do it?"

I considered this question. My mother had struggled with her addictions for years. But when the missionaries showed up, something changed. "She stopped relying on her own strength and turned the reins over to someone else," I said.

Zelph nodded again. "Jenny was always destined for sainthood."

This statement bothered me for some reason. "Then how did she get involved with heroin in the first place?" I asked.

He stared hard at me. "You really don't know?"

I shook my head.

"Your father's name was Timothy Blackburn," Zelphinus said. "A nice kid with a good heart. I guess that's what Jenny saw in him—why she married him."

"They were married?" I tried to get my head around the thought that not only did I have a father, but I was also the product of a legitimate marriage.

"That's what Jenny said, and I don't believe she would lie about it. I told you he was a nice kid, but he was also an addict. An addict of the first order. Some can play around with it and get out. But for others it only takes one time—one seemingly harmless dance with the beast—and they're slaves for life. Tim was a slave. But Jenny wouldn't see it."

"She was an addict too," I said.

"Not at first. Not then. Her whole purpose in life was to get Tim out of the life. Him and everyone else. She was determined to rescue us all, whether we wanted to be rescued or not. I think she thought you would be the final piece that would pull Timmy from the dark side. She believed that he wouldn't be able to bear the thought of raising a kid while he was a junkie." Zelph stopped for a moment and tenderly touched his neck where I had choked him. "In a way she was right. Tim didn't want his kid to grow up with a junkie father. But he didn't see a way out of the situation either. On the night you were born, he put a gun to his head and found another way. I'm sure in his mind he thought he was doing it for Jenny. But thinking straight isn't really a strong point for a junkie."

I wanted to get up and run from Zelphinus Cork. Run like I had run before. But I couldn't. I now knew the reason why my mother had never talked about my father. In a way, I was responsible for the death of both of my parents.

I forgive you. I felt more than heard the voice deep within me. For a moment, I felt like I was floating above the earth. I thought I saw both my infant self and myself as a little boy. I looked down on the two broken spirits and whispered the words, "I forgive you." A weight seemed to lift off my shoulders.

"Tell me the rest," I said.

"Your mother was sick with grief. Her whole world was pulled out from under her. The heroin had won. I think she turned to the drugs as an act of defiance, to show Tim, to show us all that it could be done. That she could overcome it. But when you dance with the devil, sometimes he won't let you go." His voice became quieter. "But in the end she beat it. In the end she found a way."

We were both quiet for what must have been several minutes. I went to Zelph and reached out a hand. He took it, and I helped him up. We both groaned as I lifted his weight. For a moment he seemed less like a professional wrestler and more like an old man.

"What now?" he said.

I shrugged. "You still owe a debt to society."

He looked again at the direction of his daughter's house, and I saw lost years and lost opportunities flicker in his eyes.

"I'd like a few weeks."

"I'm sorry," I said. "I can't let you do that."

His shoulders sagged, but he nodded.

"That boy needs a father figure in his life," I continued. "Someone that's not going to leave. Someone permanent."

His head snapped up. "You're letting me go?"

"No," I said. "I'm handing you a life sentence. Prison is easy. Family is hard."

CHAPTER 31
Moose Lake Trailhead

AFTER LEAVING ZELPHINUS CORK, I got into my rental car and drove home. At least it felt like home. Actually I was driving to the Village. I needed a few hours' sleep and then a shower. Luckily, I still had my key.

My phone buzzed in my pocket. I thought it might be Zack giving me an update, but the caller ID said that it was Roger.

"Hey, Roger," I said. "I'm on my way to the apartment now."

There was silence on the phone, and then a voice said, "I think you need to make a detour." The voice did not belong to Roger.

"Joseph?"

"I understand that you now know that is not my real name."

A feeling of dread crept over me. Joseph should have been picked up by the authorities hours ago. Why was he calling me from Roger's cell phone?

"Where's Roger?" I asked, trying to keep the panic out of my voice. I'd told Roger not to return to the apartment.

"Roger's not important. You've got bigger worries."

"What do you mean?"

"I've got someone with me who wants to talk to you."

I heard the phone change hands, and then a voice said, "Matt, I'm sorry. Don't come. Call the police. He's got a gun and . . ."

"That should be enough," Mohammed said, coming back on the line.

I felt like a hole had opened up and the world had fallen out from under me. "Why do you have Hope?" I asked, trying not to let my voice shake. "She has nothing to do with this."

"Because I want you to meet me. Moose Lake trailhead, forty-five minutes." He paused. "Please come alone, and don't call the police. I would hate to see anything happen to Hope."

The line went dead. So did my heart. Mohammed Hadadi—a confirmed terrorist—was holding Hope Winslow at gunpoint. What had gone wrong? And why did he have Roger's cell phone?

Roger.

I pushed the gas pedal down as far as it would go. I would do as Mohammed instructed and drive to Moose Lake, but first I needed to find out about Roger.

I pulled into the parking lot of the Village, flew up the steps of the apartment, and threw open the door, which was unlocked.

Roger's body lay on the couch. I looked for blood but didn't see any.

I ran to him. Roger opened his eyes and sat up.

"Are you all right?" I asked.

He shook his head. "I had to lie to the FBI. I told them Joseph—or whatever his real name is—had packed his bags and left yesterday afternoon, that he looked like he was going away for a long time. I couldn't tell them the truth." He groaned as he spoke. "I'm sorry. He has Hope."

"I know," I said. "I thought I told you to stay away from the apartment."

Roger hung his head. "I couldn't help it. This guy was my roommate. My friend. I thought I could stop him from doing something terrible." He rubbed his palms on his forehead. "I thought I could remove the cyanide before he had a chance to use it. But when I came back, the bottle was almost empty. He caught me looking at it. I told him that I knew he wasn't Joseph but that he was still my friend and that he didn't have to hurt anyone. We were arguing when Hope came to the door. She wanted to know if we'd heard anything from you. I didn't tell Joseph that you were the one who told me about the pills, but he seemed to know. He pulled out a gun and told me that if I wanted to see Hope alive again, I would do as he said. He packed some things and took Hope with him." Roger stopped. He seemed to be having trouble catching his breath.

"I'm sorry, Matt. It's my fault. He told me that if I said anything to anyone before you got here, he would kill Hope. I don't even know where he took her."

"I do," I said. "C'mon, we're going to get her back."

We turned to go out the door and very nearly ran over Permelia and Marva Rose. Permelia was in sweats and looked like she hadn't slept. Marva Rose was dressed in a white and pink spring dress, with matching shoes and earrings. She held scriptures in her hands.

They both jerked back when they saw me.

"I should've known you were back," Permelia said. "Hope didn't come home last night. I thought she was working, but I called and they hadn't seen her."

I looked down at my watch. I was supposed to meet Mohammed in half an hour, and any satisfactory explanation to Permelia would take at least that much time. I thought about rushing past her to the car and facing the consequences later. But I saw the concern and determination in her eyes. I had no doubt she would chase me down and tackle me if she had to.

"Permelia," I said. "I don't have time to explain what's going on, but Hope has been taken hostage by a terrorist, and I need to get to her now."

As I heard the words leave my lips I recognized how preposterous they sounded, but Permelia didn't appear to doubt them for an instant.

"Not without me," she said.

"I have to go alone."

"You're taking Roger with you," she pointed out.

Good point. *Why was I taking Roger with me?* Agency protocol said that it was time to call in reinforcements. They would dispatch a hostage rescue team trained in dealing with these kinds of situations. But I didn't want an HRT involved. I was afraid that one of their snipers would get a clear shot on Mohammed and take it. I wanted Hope safe, but I also wanted to save Mohammed if I could. It was a delicate situation.

"She's right," I said to Roger. "You need to stay here too."

Voices of protest arose—from Permelia, from Roger, even from Marva Rose.

"It's not safe," I said, trying to get a word in. "I can't be worrying about Hope *and* all of you."

I was almost past them when I heard it. *Take them.* It wasn't a voice exactly—more of a feeling—but the message was distinct and clear. *Take them.* This made no sense. Taking civilians into a hostage situation was a recipe for disaster. *Take them.* The feeling came a third time. I decided not to ignore it.

"Okay," I said, abandoning everything I had learned in my training. "Get in the car. I'll fill you in on the way."

Without another question, Permelia went to the car and jumped in the backseat. Marva Rose was right behind her.

"No," Roger said as Marva Rose got in. He walked to her door and opened it. "I want you to stay here."

"Why?" Marva asked.

Roger seemed to fumble for the right words. "Because I care about you, Rose," he sputtered. "I don't want you to get hurt."

The light in her face shown as bright as one of her paintings, but the set of her jaw did not relax.

"I care about you too, Roger. That's why I'm coming."

Roger looked almost panicked, but we didn't have time to waste. I jumped in the driver's side, and Roger just made it in before I took off.

I filled Permelia and Marva Rose in on the salient pieces of the story as we drove up the canyon. I didn't tell them what Mohammed was planning with the pills. I was afraid of what Permelia might do to him.

"That explains a lot," Permelia said. "But that doesn't excuse you from acting like pond scum."

"I know," I said. "I aim to apologize when I get the chance."

"Hope deserves a lot more than an apology."

I nodded. I knew that too.

"So what's the plan?" Permelia asked. "Do you want to drop a few of us off before the meeting place so we can circle back behind him?"

I had come to know Permelia well enough not to question that she could accomplish any task she put her mind to, but I didn't really want her sneaking up on Mohammed while he held a gun to Hope's head. I looked from Permelia to Roger to Marva Rose and assessed the resources I had available. A scientist, an artist, and a senior citizen. Not exactly Delta Force.

"We find them and then we talk," I said. "That's all."

"I don't think that's what Jack Bauer would do," Permelia said. "You don't act much like an antiterrorist agent."

"Jack Bauer wouldn't have brought you along," I said. She was right. I wasn't acting like an agent. I hoped with all my heart that I was doing the right thing.

We pulled into the trailhead parking area, and I saw my Toyota, off the road and next to a grove of yellow-leafed quaking aspens. I drove into a parking spot and got out of the rental car.

"It's probably safer if you all stay in the car," I said.

Everyone got out. Together we walked toward the grove of trees.

Mohammed sat on a fallen tree next to a fire pit. He did not look happy. Next to him sat Hope Winslow, a pistol pointed at her head.

"I warned you to come alone," he said.

"I've been alone almost my whole life," I replied. "I'm getting kind of tired of it."

"We're not the police," Roger said. "Why don't you give it a break."

"I'd like to break something," Permelia mumbled under her breath.

I looked at Hope. She didn't look like a hostage who'd been kidnapped the night before. She smiled at me, and I thought she looked like the most beautiful creature ever to set foot on God's green earth. In that moment I forgot about everything else—Mohammed, the gun, and the people behind me. My mind was filled only with Hope.

"I'm so sorry, Matt," she said. "I heard that a friend of yours was killed." She didn't sound scared in the least.

"My best friend, Robbie," I acknowledged.

"The husband of the woman you told me about?" Her voice held only concern. There was no sign of the anger that had caused her to punch me.

"Yes."

"Do you love her?"

"We don't have time for this," Mohammed said, looking down at his watch. He grabbed Hope by the arm and pulled her to her feet. Hope winced, and I really wanted to punch Mohammed in the face, both for causing Hope pain and for interrupting our conversation. We were just getting to the critical part.

"Everyone move to the car," Mohammed said. "There's something you need to hear." He grimaced as if the words pained him.

Mohammed threw me my keys as we walked. "Get in and turn on the radio. Find a news channel."

I did as instructed and then looked at my own watch. It was ten forty-five. I hoped that I had guessed right about the target and that Zack had been able to stop things in time. If he had, there would be nothing to report.

I found a news channel, and my heart froze as the words blasted out of the speakers: . . . *attack at the Salt Palace. I repeat, there has been an apparent terrorist attack at the Salt Palace Convention Center, where thousands of Christian religious leaders have been meeting to—*

"The poison," Roger said, drowning out the radio. "Siham works for Salt Palace catering. She put cyanide in the water pitchers. That's what you've been planning."

"It's the Other Sheep conference," Marva added.

"The one the bishop is attending," Permelia growled.

All icy eyes turned toward Mohammed.

He shrugged. "A shepherd for a shepherd," he said. "It seems only fair."

"Why, you little—" Permelia said.

I put my hand up. "Quiet," I said. "We need to hear this." I didn't like the sound of the words *terrorist attack*. Where was Zack?

. . . *Medical and police personnel are flooding the scene, and we have received confirmation that at least one person is dead. A young woman was arrested and then apparently ingested poison, taking her own life.*

I looked at Mohammed's face. I saw no surprise. Only sadness and resignation. The plan had never been for Siham to escape. This was a suicide mission.

"It should have been me, sister," Mohammed said quietly to himself. "I told you all along. It should have been me."

. . . *We are trying to get someone from the FBI on who can give us a statement.*

A voice came on the radio. A familiar voice.

"That's the bishop," Marva Rose said.

Mohammed's head snapped up.

Is it true that this was a planned terrorist attack? the reporter asked.

There was a plan, and there was a threat. Zack's voice boomed through the radio. *But let me make it clear. There was no attack. At no time were members of this conference in any danger.*

Mohammed turned his eyes toward me. His gun hand began to shake slightly, and he pulled his other arm across his stomach.

What about the woman who was killed? the reporter asked.

She was under surveillance from the moment she entered the building and arrested as soon as she engaged in illegal activity. Unfortunately, we did not know she had a poison capsule concealed in her cheek.

Were any others apprehended?

That is something I cannot comment on other than to say the woman was acting alone at the conference and we are in the process of investigating others who may have been involved in the planning. We are currently sweeping the building to be absolutely certain there is no further danger, and then the conference will resume.

Why was the woman under surveillance?

We received a tip a few months ago about a potential attack in Salt Lake City. The prevention of this attack was the result of some excellent undercover work by an agent who must remain unnamed but—

"Turn it off," Mohammed said.

"It's just getting to the good part," I said. He pointed his gun at me. I turned the radio off. It was probably a good thing. I think I was starting to blush.

Mohammed glanced around the parking area. "Is this when your backup agents come charging out to arrest me?"

I stared directly into his eyes. "I told you before. I didn't bring any backup. I brought your crew. It's over. You can put down the gun."

"I don't think so," he said. "Get out of the car and move over by the others." He still held Hope's arm, and I saw a distant look in his eyes that scared me. I carefully moved out of the car. He was about ten yards away, and his gun was again pointed at Hope's head.

"How long have you known?" he asked.

I figured it out yesterday," I said, "when I read about two surviving Hadadi orphans and the killing of a man referred to as 'the Shepherd,' in Jordan. I kept wondering what tragedy in the waters could cause tens of millions of people to mourn. The answer was right in front of me all along. What better way to strike at the West than to attack Western religion? What better way to exact revenge on the beloved religious leader of your people than to take out the beloved religious leaders of America? Millions would surely mourn, even tens of millions. When I visited with your mother, my suspicions were confirmed."

"She is not my mother." Mohammed's eyes flashed.

"She would be," I said softly. "If you would let her. I know she cares about you."

Mohammed hugged his stomach more tightly.

"I'm sorry about your mother and father—" I said. "About your brothers. It was a terrible tragedy."

"It was no tragedy," he said softly. "It was a massacre." His voice was low, almost a whisper, and he leaned against the car and hung his head.

"No," I said. "Not a massacre. Suicide. As intentional and senseless as that of your sister."

Mohammed's eyes were bright with hatred. "My sister's death was not senseless. She will receive her glory in the world to come. The glory that should have been mine."

"There's no glory in being used and deceived," I said. "You've been lied to from the beginning."

"What are you talking about?" Mohammed's face was a mask of rage and pain. The gun was pointed at me now, and I thought he might use it.

"I need to show you something," I said. I carefully removed the picture from my pocket and handed it to him. He kept his eyes and the gun on me as he unfolded it with his mouth and his other hand. Then he glanced down.

"It's a picture taken a few hours before the drone attack on the orphanage," I said. "The man in the picture is—"

"I know who he is," Mohammed snapped.

I kept my voice calm and took a few steps back. "When I first saw this picture, there was something about it that bothered me. Something about the look on the Shepherd's face. I didn't understand it at first. How could we be so lucky? I mean, the man was a master of disguise. He'd slipped through the hands of U.S. intelligence for years. There were rumors among his people that he had the power to make himself invisible. But here he was, looking up at the sky at the exact time a surveillance plane is flying over. Looking up and *smiling*. That bothered me most of all. Why was the Shepherd smiling? And then it hit me: he knew he was being photographed. He *wanted* to be attacked. The orphanage was the perfect suicide bomb."

"No," Mohammed said. "He would not . . ."

"Why not?" I asked. "Suicide missions are common practice among your people. And this one worked particularly well. The shame and outrage that came against the West created a resurgence in a terrorist effort that had been dying for years. What better way to attack the enemy than to turn public opinion against them?"

Mohammed was breathing hard. "But *I* made the phone call. *I* was responsible for—"

"No, you were not responsible for the deaths of your brothers. The people you work for just let you *think* you were. If you look at the picture again you will see a time stamp at the bottom. That was the other thing that bothered me about the photo—the time it was taken. Supposedly, the attack was ordered because of a telephone tip from a young boy. A tip that came in the afternoon. But the photo was taken in the morning. The attack had already been ordered before you ever made the call. You were not responsible for the drone attack. But that didn't stop them from letting you think you were. These people are not your friends, Mohammed. They've let you live with the guilt for years because they wanted to use you as a weapon in their cause."

I let the weight of my words sink in and watched as Mohammed struggled against himself.

"We are your crew," I said softly. "We are your friends. We always have been."

There were tears running down his cheeks now. Hope reached over and touched him lightly on the arm. He brushed her hand violently away and took a step back.

"No," he said, talking directly to me. "You would not be so quick to forgive if you really knew me. If you knew everything I have done."

"I think I know you pretty well," I said. "Time together on the trail will do that. How long did it take you to figure out I was an undercover agent?"

Mohammed grunted a laugh. "We knew from the moment you arrived," he said. "Your photo was taken in Miami when you were unconscious. The picture was distributed out to the cells."

"So you made the call that first night that almost got me killed?"

"I called them, but I did not ask for your death. They were idiots. A dead agent would have brought too much scrutiny. We already had a smoke screen set up with the mercenaries and the anthrax."

"But the mercenaries were slow to act and I was slow to discover their plans. You needed something else to distract me. Something to keep me occupied. That something was you. You and the race. You thought if you kept me running down false trails, there was no way I would see the truth."

"I wanted your attention diverted, but I did not want the job. I wanted to be with Siham." A sad smile crossed his face. "Instead, I became the distraction, and Siham received the glory. May her soul rest in peace." Mohammed Hadadi raised his head and looked up at the sky. "I never really needed a crew, you know. To enter the Uinta 100."

"Yes you did," Permelia said, her voice softening. "Everyone needs a crew."

"You took the fall on purpose," I said. "You could have won that race—

you should have won it. Instead, you let Regina Camp beat you. And all because of vengeance directed at the wrong people."

He smiled again. "It seems I am destined to let women steal my victories." There was regret in his eyes.

I knew that he had wanted to win that race. Maybe more than anything else in his life. "It's a shame," I said. "They took even that away from you."

I looked out at the mountains, remembering our runs. Remembering the pain, the joy, the connection. I didn't want to ask the next question. I was afraid of what the answer would be.

"Was it your idea to have Robbie killed?"

Mohammed's eyes arched in surprise, and then he slowly shook his head. "No," he said. "It was not my idea. But I knew they were considering it."

Hope gasped. "That wasn't an accident?"

Mohammed didn't answer.

"I was getting too close," I said. "They wanted me out of town at the time of the attack. The irony is that without my trip to Washington, I probably would not have pieced things together." I stared at Mohammed and felt only pity.

"What about your stepbrother, Joseph? Is he still alive?"

"As far as I know. They needed him for the weekly calls to his mother. But now . . ."

"Tell me where he is," I pleaded. "We could still save him."

Mohammed shook his head. "I don't know. It's too late."

"That's the thing," I said. "It isn't. You can still be that boy who was trying to do the right thing—trying to save your family. You can still help me try to save Joseph."

Mohammed stared at me with dead eyes. "I don't think I was ever that boy."

Marva Rose stepped forward. "It doesn't matter who you've been in the past," she said. "We get to decide who we are. We decide every day."

"Besides," Roger said. "I'd really like to meet my real roommate."

Mohammed's face grimaced with pain. "I think you are all overlooking something very important," he said through clenched teeth. I thought at any moment he might double over and collapse.

I was looking at the gun, and he caught the direction of my gaze. He shook his head and lowered it.

"What are we overlooking?" I asked.

He smiled grimly. "My need to win."

"What do you mean?" The hair on the back of my neck began to prickle.

"After Regina, I decided I was never going to throw another race. I decided to win, no matter what. Even if Siham was unsuccesful. Even if you figured things out and returned. I was not going to lose this race. And because of this, you will never forgive me. Because of this, forgiveness is impossible."

I stared at him without comprehending. "I don't understand. What are you talking about?"

"Matt," Hope said softly, "Mohammed took one of the pills. He made me take one too."

I looked from Mohammed to Hope. I could see it now. They were both in pain—and not just anguish of the soul. They had ingested cyanide—a dose Roger had said would kill a person in less than an hour. A dose that made a trip to a hospital useless. The most brilliant, shining being in all the world was dying, and there was nothing I could do. All because Mohammed Hadadi had decided he wasn't going to lose.

Not to me.

His words rang in my ears, "Forgiveness is impossible." A small flame rose from the cold ashes of my heart. A flame I thought had been extinguished when I had forgiven myself and Zelphinus Cork for the death of my mother. A flame that grew as I considered the utter senselessness of what Mohammed Hadadi had just done. I could forgive him for a lot of things. I could forgive him for wanting to avenge the death of his brothers. I could forgive him for joining with terrorists because of the guilt he felt. I could even forgive him for not telling me Robbie was in danger. But I could not forgive him for this. Hope had nothing to do with this. Her death served no purpose.

My hands began shaking, and I took a step toward him.

Forgiveness is impossible.

Suddenly, it was clear to me. My master's thesis was no longer a theory. I knew why good men committed violent acts. I knew why families were torn apart, why villagers attacked their neighbors, and why countries warred with each other for centuries over barren patches of desert. They did it because they felt they had been undeservedly wronged. They did it because someone they loved had been hurt. They did it because they were *justified*.

Forgiveness is impossible.

I took another step. Mohammed Hadadi was already dying, but I could still cause him pain. Pain beyond his wildest dreams. It didn't matter that he held a gun. It didn't matter that he was going to shoot me. Bullets couldn't stop my fury. I held the sword of justice in my hands, and I would not be denied.

I could hear voices as if through a fog, urging me to stop. The voices of Roger, Permelia, and Marva Rose. The voice of Hope. But I was beyond hearing. My rage consumed me. Mohammed Hadadi might win, but he would not celebrate his victory.

I took another step, and a different voice penetrated through the others and pierced into my heart. The voice was not loud. It barely registered above the whisper of the breeze. But it stopped me in my tracks.

It was the voice of my mother. "Forgiveness *is* impossible," she said. "But not in the way you think."

I felt the peace again, attempting to break through the barrier of my rage. But I would not let it in. This sin was too great. The fires of my righteous anger were too strong. Nothing in this world could stop me now. I moved toward Mohammed.

Forgiveness is impossible.

He was almost within reach now. Barely five yards away. I began to mark the places on his body that would cause him the most pain. A thumb to the eye, an elbow to the throat. Broken joints in the elbows and wrists. Just a few more steps and . . .

Suddenly, I found myself on my knees. I tried to get up, but I couldn't move. It was as if a great force was pressing me down. At first, I thought I'd been shot, but Mohammed had not fired his gun. I looked around to locate the source of my paralysis, and for an instant, it was as if I saw the world through another's eyes.

I saw people. Thousands of them, maybe millions. Rich people and poor. Old people and young. I saw their faces, and I saw their hearts. I saw the compassion that drove them to acts of kindness and the hate that drove them to unspeakable cruelty. I saw their goodness and their shame. I saw their hope and their fear. There was no strength or weakness that was hidden from my view, and weakness was abundant. There was pain, hurt, avarice, and greed. There was loathing and lust. There was the desire for blood and vengeance.

Forgiveness is impossible.

And then I felt love. It began as a small trickle and then grew to a wave so large that it seemed to fill the immensity of space. In the face of this wave of unbounded compassion, the human weakness that I had just seen suddenly appeared very small. Like a flickering candle in the midst of a great ocean. The love was unfathomably big. Like the love a parent has for a child—only bigger. Much bigger. It was the love of an infinite Being, an eternal Parent. It was so large, so all-encompassing, that I felt myself drowning in its overwhelming vastness. I gasped for breath. Another instant and I would surely be consumed.

"Stop," I said. "Please."

I found myself facedown in the dirt, staring at a particle of dust that clung to a blade of grass. I felt an affinity to the dust that I had never felt before. So small, so insignificant. I wondered if I could crawl under it and hide in its shade.

I lay there in awe. I was nothing. *Man* was nothing. And yet man was everything. I was having problems wrapping my mind around it.

Forgiveness is impossible.

Because forgiveness is a miracle.

I felt arms around me, picking me up. No more than a few seconds could have passed, but it felt like an eternity. I looked around me in wonder. The leaves on the trees seemed to reveal shades of color I'd never noticed before. Each petal of each flower emitted fragrances that were both distinct and harmonic as they blended to form a symphony of aroma within the meadow.

Several voices spoke to me at once, urging me to listen.

I chose to focus on Hope.

"Matt, it's going to be okay. It really is. I hold no fear for death. I've already been there, remember? It's okay."

I smiled at her, and she beamed. Even the flowers couldn't compare with her beauty. I wanted to bury my face in her hair and breathe in her delicate scent.

I forced myself to look at Mohammed.

There was pain in his eyes and in his soul. Pain I didn't think even I could comprehend.

But I knew Someone could.

I considered trying to tell him of my experience, trying to explain the boundlessness of God's love. But I didn't think I could. It would be like trying to explain sunrise at Moose Lake to someone who hadn't experienced it. The words would just sound trite. For some things, you really had to be there.

"Don't tell me that you can forgive me," he said.

I shook my head. "I won't. I'm not sure I ever could. Lucky for you, it's not my role to be your judge."

Mohammed would meet his Judge soon enough. As for me, I felt suddenly lighter.

Mohammed leaned over and retched into the bushes. I turned my attention back to Hope.

"Matt," Roger said tugging at my elbow.

"Just a second," I said. My earlier conversation with Hope had been interrupted, and I wasn't going to let it happen again.

"But Matt—"

I held up my hand. "Whatever it is, it can wait for a minute."

"You were asking me about Becca," I said to Hope.

Her eyes locked with mine. "I asked you if you loved her," she said.

"The answer is yes," I replied. I thought I caught a hint of disappointment in Hope's eyes, and I was glad.

"I do love Becca," I said. "I love her like a sister."

"And you are not the father of her baby?"

"Just a godfather."

Hope's smile was mischievous as if she didn't have a care in the world. As if her body wasn't being consumed by poison. "What about me, Matthew Knight? Do you love me?"

"Yes," I said. "I love you with all my heart."

"Like a sister?"

I shook my head. "Not so much."

Hope leapt up, ran to me, and threw herself into my arms. Immediately, I was buried in a mountain of hair. She clung to me so tightly that it seemed as if we were one person.

"I wish we had more time," I said into her ear. "I was hoping to ask you to marry me."

She pulled her head back so she could see my eyes. "We'll have eternity for that. He can't take that away from us. No one can."

We kissed, long and slow. I wanted it to go on forever. I wanted us to go on forever.

Once again, I thought I felt the peace that goes beyond words.

"It's going to be okay," Roger said. I felt his hand shaking my shoulder.

"I know," I said grudgingly, although I did not want to admit it. I couldn't deny what I had experienced.

"No," he said, shaking harder. "You don't know. It really is going to be okay. I switched the pills. No one here is going to die today. At least not from poisoning."

The hugging stopped, and we all looked at Roger.

"I wanted to prevent Mohammed from hurting anyone," he said. "I thought if I could find a pill that looked similar, I could go back to the apartment and make a switch. I was too late. When I got there, there were only two pills left in the bottle. But I did replace those two."

"But I can feel the poison inside of me," Hope said, her hand going to her stomach.

"Sorry about that," Roger said. "I've been working on a nanovitamin remedy for colds. It contains a megadose of vitamin C that is absorbed almost instantaneously but is a bit of a shock to the system. I haven't perfected the side effects yet. You're going to have severe cramping, nausea, and maybe diarrhea."

"Roger," Hope said, moving to embrace him. "I love you."

After our recent kiss, I was sure she meant "like a brother."

"Me too," Marva Rose told Roger. "You are a genius." She placed herself between Roger and Hope and then planted a wet one directly onto his lips.

He struggled a bit at first and then seemed to surrender to the inevitable. With women, sometimes you just have to learn to stop resisting. I wanted to kiss Roger as well, but it looked like I was going to have to wait in line.

"Did I hear a marriage proposal earlier?" Permelia asked.

"People say all sorts of things under duress," I replied. "I'm not so sure you can hold me to that." I was kidding of course. The one thing I knew for certain in my life was that I wanted to marry Hope Winslow.

Hope began to glare at me, and then her look turned thoughtful. She hesitated before she spoke. "Maybe you *should* reconsider," she said carefully. "You've got your job to think about, and after the cancer, I don't know how many years I've got left." She looked at the ground and lowered her voice. "I can't give you any children."

I laughed out loud. "You're not getting away as easy as that. With my picture being circulated, I don't think I'll be doing much more undercover work. And as for children, I want to adopt as many as we can feasibly afford." I took a breath. "As for that other thing," I didn't even want to put a name to the idea that Hope's cancer might return, "you may be special, but you are not unique. None of us knows how many days we have left. All we can do is make the most out of each moment, and I want all of my moments to be spent with you. So, I'm asking you, Hope Winslow, and this time under no duress. Will you marry me?"

She didn't officially accept, but by the way she again launched herself into my arms, I was pretty sure that the answer was a yes. As I twirled her around and tried not to suffocate in her hair, I thought I felt the final tumbler of a lock falling into place somewhere in the universe, and for the first time in my life, I was completely whole. I felt my mother watching me. She was smiling.

"That's a relief," Permelia said. "I thought I was going to have to grab Mohammed's gun and perform a shotgun wedding with a pistol."

At the mention of the pistol, I stopped twirling Hope and looked in Mohammed's direction. His retching had stopped. He was standing upright, no longer holding his stomach. He was pointing the gun at me.

"Don't you ever give up?" I asked.

"You know I don't." His face held a resigned trace of the Hadadi smile.

Roger stepped in front of me. "So what now? You're going to kill the best friends you've ever had in your life?" Marva Rose moved in unison with Roger.

"God's given you a second chance," Hope said, moving in front of all of us. "Please, Mohammed, don't let His gifts go to waste. You haven't hurt anybody yet."

"I don't think he can take down all of us if we rush him," Permelia whispered.

I stepped out from behind the crowd and held out my hand. "Why don't you give me the gun," I said.

"Shooting you would be a lot easier." Mohammed's hand was steady and pointed directly at my forehead.

"And shooting yourself even easier still," I said. "After all, you've already resigned yourself to death."

"Matt," Hope hissed and tugged at my shirt.

Mohammed seemed to consider what I said, and he started shifting the barrel of the gun from me toward his own head.

Hoped tugged more fervently at my shirt. "*Do something.*"

Before Mohammed had time to act, I said, "Of course, there is a another option. But it wouldn't be easy."

Mohammed hesitated and looked into my eyes.

"It's probably not even worth thinking about," I said. "You'd have to be stupid, severely brain damaged, or just plain weird to even consider it."

There was a flash in his eyes, and for a moment, I saw my old roommate return. Fearless, resolute, determined. Then the light seemed to flicker and burn out.

"I know what you're trying to do," he said. "It won't work."

"You know what the beautiful thing is about these mountains," I said. "If you don't like the trail you're on, you can always choose another one. Switching is as easy as making a choice and changing direction. You can run off a cliff, or you can watch a sunrise over a lake. It's all about the trail you choose."

"I've been on this trail a long time," he said. "I don't think I could change."

"You're probably right," I said. "It'd be too difficult."

I saw the light flicker in his eyes again. I didn't want it to go out.

"It's just a shame that the only ultra you ever entered was one where you had to let a pigtailed Punky Brewster kick dust in your face because you weren't allowed to run your own race."

Mohammed gave just a hint of a smile. "I don't think they will let me enter Badwater after this."

"Other races, other places," I said.

He glanced at the mountains behind him and then back at me. "You would send people after me."

"That's my job. And with choppers and the latest surveillance equipment, you probably wouldn't last more than a few hours. Heck, your ankle isn't even fully healed. Like I said, it's a crazy idea."

"Why suggest it, then?"

"Why? Because I don't want you to shoot us. Because, even after all you've almost done, I don't want you to shoot yourself. Why? Because you may be the only chance we have of finding the real Joseph alive and I feel an obligation to an elegant lady in Virginia who invited me into her home and fed me cookies and lemonade. She was concerned about both of her sons."

This time Mohammed did not react when I referred to him as her son.

Roger stepped up next to me and joined his arm in mine. Hope, Marva Rose, and Permelia followed his example. We stood together, linked and unified—his crew.

Mohammed dropped the gun to his side and began to turn away.

"Wait," I said, pulling out a cell phone from my pocket and tossing it to him. He caught it and looked down. "In case you do find something out about Joseph."

"You could use this to track me," he said.

"Only when you turn it on."

"Unless it has been doctored by your scientists."

"Hey," Roger said. "That's *my* phone."

At this, Mohammed smiled. It was the full Hadadi smile. He checked to see that the phone was turned off and then dropped it into his pocket.

"You could also text me the names of those who hired you," I said. "If you happen to get into a mood."

Mohammed didn't answer. He was no longer paying attention to me. He wasn't paying attention to any of us. His focus was on the trail—on the impossible task ahead of him. I could almost hear the words of Bob Marley running through his head as his feet hit the ground and he began to move away in a rhythmic, poetic motion. Maybe everything really was going to be all right.

We all watched as Mohammed Hadadi—roommate, terrorist, and friend—disappeared into the shadows of the everlasting hills. The feeling of peace seemed to settle like a warm blanket over the entire range of mountains.

The sound of tires on gravel interrupted the peace of the morning. A car was pulling into the trailhead parking lot. A beat-up Cadillac containing two passengers. They got out of the car.

"It's the men from the alley," Hope said, grabbing my arm.

"I thought you guys would be reassigned by now," I said to Demetrius and Chico as they walked up.

"Zack asked us to hang around for a few days," Demetrius said. "We picked up your signal and thought we'd better check things out."

Hope gasped. "They're with you? I could have killed him." She was looking at Chico. Chico just smiled and nodded.

"Chico isn't real easy to kill," Demetrius said. His eyes met mine. "What's with being up here in the mountains again? You planning on going for another run?"

"I'm through with that," I said, liking the feel of Hope against my side. "In fact, I don't think I'll ever run again." I grasped her hand and held it tightly.

"Any sign of your roomie?" Demetrius said, looking over my shoulder. "Zack asked for us to keep an eye out."

"You just missed him," I said.

"Where? Here?" Demetrius reached for his gun.

"That won't be necessary," I said, turning around and staring at the hills. "My guess is that he's long gone by now."

CHAPTER 32
After

HOPE WANTED TO GET MARRIED in the temple, for time and all eternity. I wanted that too. But getting me ready for the temple was going to take some time, and we didn't want to wait. We both understood the fleeting nature of mortality.

We decided on a small civil ceremony in the chapel of the church building at the Village, with the temple wedding to come later. *Small*, however, was a relative term. With all of Hope's family and friends, this meant that the chapel, the overflow area, and half of the basketball court were filled. The attendees representing my side were a lot less numerous, but just as important—at least to me.

I was able to convince my superiors that with my picture being circulated, my life could still be in danger. This allowed me to lobby for Demetrius and Chico to come to the wedding. I really wasn't too worried about my life being in jeopardy. I just wanted to see both of them in tuxes.

Permelia was Hope's maid of honor, and her bridesmaids were Marva Rose, little Meggy Brentwood, and a very beautiful and very pregnant Becca. I was a little worried about Becca and Hope at first, but they hit it off famously, and in the time since Becca arrived a few days earlier, I hadn't seen much of either of them. Meggy had been coached by her mother on where to sit and how to act during the wedding, but she still spent most of her time nestled in between Hope and me, which was fine with both of us.

Hope also had her parents and brothers in attendance, and I was pleased that her father and brothers at least seemed to tolerate me. Her mother even laughed at my jokes. Maybe she was just being nice.

When the children at the Truman Center learned that Hope was getting married, all of them asked to attend the wedding. Because of the risk of infection, this was not possible. However, I had a few connections with some electronics people at the CIA, and they were able to rig up a videoconferencing screen so the kids could participate in our wedding real time, and Hope could see their faces reflected during the ceremony.

I had two best men: Roger, of course, and Colt Mangum. He had recovered nicely from his wounds and looked handsome in his newly pressed uniform, which sported several medals—including a Purple Heart. He may not have earned it on his first tour, but he had certainly earned it later. Since the Dugway incident, Colt had toned down his boisterousness considerably. I guess he had nothing left to prove. I was pretty sure that Permelia was developing a crush on him. From the swooning looks of women in the audience, she was not alone.

Despite a nationwide manhunt, there had been no sign of Mohammed Hadadi. He had seemingly gone for a run in the mountains and never come back. Despite having access to a cell phone, he did not send any text messages, and he did not return my calls. Maybe he just wasn't very chatty. Maybe he was dead in a ravine somewhere.

Hope looked breathtaking in her gown. With her flowing hair and her tiny waist, I imagined that anyone seeing the wedding photos might accuse them of being retouched. But there was no fakery here. Hope Winslow, soon to be Hope Winslow-Knight, was the most beautiful woman in the world. I was convinced that every man in the audience was extremely jealous of me at this moment, but they were just going to have to learn to deal with it. This angel was officially off the market.

Zack stood in front of us, and I swear that beams of light shone out from his face. He was as proud as any father could be, and despite all of our confrontations throughout the years, there was no one on this earth who had been more of a father to me. He cleared his throat, indicating that the ceremony was to begin.

"Before performing this marriage of two of my favorite adopted children," he began, "I'd like to say a few words."

I wanted to point out that we didn't have time for long speeches—there was a honeymoon to get to—but I didn't get the chance. Before Zack had said a word, the chapel doors imploded inward, and a man in a mask rolled into the aisle and landed on his knees. Tires squealed in the parking lot.

Demetrius and Chico immediately went into action. Chico ran to the man in the mask, and Demetrius pulled his weapon and went through the door. Instinctively, I also moved toward the man, making sure I kept myself in between Hope and whatever he might hold in his hands.

"Stay down," I said to her and then moved cautiously down the aisle.

Chico and I reached the man about the same time as he began to stand up.

"Back on your knees," Chico said, covering the man with his weapon. "And don't move."

The man had a dark hood tied over his head. In his hand he held a cell phone. I thought I also saw something on his back, which worried me just as much as the cell phone in his hands. If the man was rigged with explosives, my dream wedding had the potential of becoming a nightmare.

I put my hand on his shoulder and turned him so that I could see his back. At first, I thought it might be a joke, but then I remembered that terrorists don't have a sense of humor. I frisked him to make sure there weren't any wires connecting the item with the cell phone and then pulled a large red bow off his back. Attached was a silver greeting card.

I pulled the cell phone from his hands. On the screen was a short text.

It said, "Open the card."

Demetrius came through the side door. "Whoever it was is long gone," he said.

I turned to let Hope know it was okay to approach and found she was right behind me.

"I thought I asked you to stay down," I said.

"I haven't made the promise to obey yet," she said.

Zack was also there, looking thoughtful. "What is this?"

"I believe this is a wedding present," I said.

I opened the card. The words inside were short and to the point. "Best wishes. You were a good pacer. Check the phone's directory." The signature simply said, "Your brother."

"Take off the hood," I said to Demetrius. He untied the knots. The man under the hood blinked rapidly as the light met his eyes and he took in his surroundings. He looked at Hope, looked at the people sitting in the church pews, and then looked up at the video screen that showed dozens of bald, concerned children, wondering what was going on. "Am I in heaven?" he asked.

"Better," I replied. "You are home, Joseph Hadadi. Welcome to your ward." He hesitated for a moment as if not believing what he was seeing and hearing. Then the smile came.

The Hadadi smile.

"Are you Matthew?" he asked.

I nodded.

"I was told to give the phone to a man named Matthew. I thought he would be my executioner."

"You didn't recognize the voice of the man who brought you here?"

"He spoke very few words, and only in a whisper."

"It was your cousin, Mohammed. He rescued you from the terrorists."
Joseph looked confused. "But they told me he was helping them."

"He was," I said. "He had a change of heart."

I scrolled through the phone and pulled up the directory. There were dozens of Middle Eastern names with addresses and aliases. I didn't think they were Roger's friends. I passed the phone to Zack.

"Joseph," Zack said, pocketing the phone and holding out his hand. "I'm Zachary Shepherd, your bishop. I spoke to your mother this morning, and she desperately wants to hear from you. If you will come with me, I will take you to my office where you can call her. Then, if you will excuse me for just a few minutes, I have a wedding to perform."

This made Joseph smile even more broadly. His mother was right. The two cousins could have been twins. But this Joseph seemed to smile a lot more.

"That would be amazing," he said.

And I'm sure it was, being able to speak to his mother after wondering if he would ever see her again. But I'm not so sure that Joseph's amazing moment was any better than mine. For in the next ten minutes I exchanged vows with the most wonderful woman on the face of the earth. Meggy was a little unnerved by all of the excitement, and I ended up holding her against my neck for the entire ceremony. Missy Brentwood pleaded with her to come sit on a bench, but she wouldn't budge. I didn't mind.

It had only been about a month since her older brother had gone to see Jesus. She needed someone to hold on to. The world can be a dark and dangerous place. The only way any of us make it through is by holding on to each other. A wise man once told me that we are all broken. I believe he was right. But I also believe there is a Healer watching over us. Someone who can kiss our hurts and make it all better. Someone who acts as our Pacer to help us finish the race.

I looked out at the wedding attendees and thought of those who were not here. I thought of Meggy's brother Benji; I thought of Robbie; I thought of my mother.

I hadn't been able to save any of them.

But they were saved just the same. And somehow I knew as surely as I know anything that they were there, watching us.

The world is a dangerous place. Full of darkness and despair. But if you knew what I knew, you would also know that it can be a place of beauty and of wonder. A place full of hope. It all depends on which race you choose to run and who you've got on your crew.

I leaned forward and kissed my bride.

Author Bio

Frank Holdaway has been a fan of action thrillers from the time his father handed him an Alistair McLean novel at the age of ten. Since then, he has delighted in finding a tale that can take him from airport departure gate to destination hotel and back to long-term parking in such a state of engrossed concentration that he is in danger of missing his shuttle stop. When he's not lost at the airport, he enjoys creating stories that he hopes will cause others to miss their buses. He currently lives with his wife and two kids in the foothills of Pleasant Grove, Utah.